My Dark Vanessa

My Dark Vanessa

a novel

Kate Elizabeth Russell

wm
WILLIAM MORROW
An Imprint of HarperCollins*Publishers*

This is a work of fiction. Names, characters, places, and incidents are products of the author's imagination or are used fictitiously and are not to be construed as real. Any resemblance to actual events, locales, organizations, or persons, living or dead, is entirely coincidental.

MY DARK VANESSA. Copyright © 2020 by Kate Elizabeth Russell. All rights reserved. Printed in the United States of America. No part of this book may be used or reproduced in any manner whatsoever without written permission except in the case of brief quotations embodied in critical articles and reviews. For information, address HarperCollins Publishers, 195 Broadway, New York, NY 10007.

HarperCollins books may be purchased for educational, business, or sales promotional use. For information, please email the Special Markets Department at SPsales@harpercollins.com.

FIRST EDITION

Library of Congress Cataloging-in-Publication Data has been applied for.

ISBN 978-0-06-294150-3

20 21 22 23 24 LSC 10 9 8 7 6 5 4 3 2 1

I grew up in Maine and was educated there—first at a private (day) school in ninth and tenth grades, until I withdrew for personal reasons, and later at college. Because of the similarities between those broad facts and certain fictional elements of My Dark Vanessa, *I am aware that readers who are loosely familiar with my background may jump to the erroneous conclusion that I am telling the secret history of those events. I am not; this is a work of fiction, and the characters and settings are entirely imaginary.*

Anyone who has been following the news over the past few years has seen stories that suggest the narrative of this novel, recast by my imagination. Into that I have worked other influences such as critical trauma theory, the pop culture and postfeminism of the early aughts, and my own complicated feelings toward Lolita. *All of that is the normal process of fiction writing. But in a surfeit of caution it bears repeating that nothing in the novel is intended as recounting any actual events. Apart from the broad parallels noted above, this is not my personal story nor that of my teachers or of anyone I know.*

For the real-life Dolores Hazes and Vanessa Wyes whose stories have not yet been heard, believed, or understood

My Dark Vanessa

2017

I get ready for work and the post has been up for eight hours. While curling my hair, I refresh the page. So far, 224 shares and 875 likes. I put on my black wool suit, refresh again. I dig under the couch for my black flats, refresh. Fasten the gold name tag to my lapel, refresh. Each time, the numbers climb and the comments multiply.

You're so strong.
You're so brave.
What kind of monster could do that to a child?

I bring up my last text, sent to Strane four hours ago: So, are you ok . . . ? He still hasn't responded, hasn't even read it. I type out another—I'm here if you want to talk—then think better and delete it, send instead a wordless line of question marks. I wait a few minutes, try calling him, but when the voicemail kicks in, I shove my phone in my pocket and leave my apartment, yanking the door closed behind me. There's no need to try so hard. He created this mess. It's his problem, not mine.

At work, I sit at the concierge desk in the corner of the hotel lobby and give guests recommendations on where to go and what to eat. It's the tail end of the busy season, the last few tourists passing through to see the foliage before Maine closes up for the winter. With an unwavering smile that doesn't quite reach my eyes, I make a dinner reservation for a couple celebrating their first anniversary and arrange for a bottle of champagne to be waiting in their room upon return, a gesture that goes above and beyond, the kind of thing that will earn me a good tip. I call the town car to drive a family to the jetport. A man who stays at the hotel every other Monday night on business brings me three soiled shirts, asks if they can be dry-cleaned overnight.

"I'll take care of it," I say.

The man grins, gives me a wink. "You're the best, Vanessa."

On my break, I sit in an empty cubicle in the back office, staring at my phone as I eat a day-old sandwich left over from a catered event. Checking the Facebook post is compulsive now; I can't stop my fingers from moving or my eyes from darting across the screen, taking in the rising likes and shares, the dozens of you're fearless, keep telling your truth, I believe you. Even as I read, three dots flash—someone is typing a comment right this second. Then, like magic, another appears, another message of strength and support that makes me slide my phone across the desk and toss the rest of the stale sandwich in the trash.

I'm about to head back out into the lobby when my phone begins to vibrate: INCOMING CALL JACOB STRANE. I laugh as I answer, relieved he's alive, that he's calling. "Are you ok?"

For a moment, there's only dead air and I freeze, my eyes fixed on the window that looks out on Monument Square, the autumn farmers' market and food trucks. It's the beginning of October, full-blown fall, the time when everything in Portland appears straight out of an L.L.Bean catalog—pumpkins and gourds, jugs of apple cider. A woman in plaid flannel and duck boots crosses the square, smiling down at the baby strapped to her chest.

"Strane?"

He exhales a heavy sigh. "I guess you saw."

"Yeah," I say. "I saw."

I don't ask questions, but he launches into an explanation anyway. He says the school is opening an investigation and he's bracing himself for the worst. He assumes they'll force him to resign. He doubts he'll make it through the school year, maybe not even to

Christmas break. Hearing his voice is such a shock that I struggle to keep up with what he says. It's been months since we last spoke, when I was gripped with panic after my dad died of a heart attack and I told Strane I couldn't do it anymore; the same sudden onset of morals I've had through years of screwups—lost jobs, breakups, and breakdowns—as though being good could retroactively fix all the things I've broken.

"But they already investigated back when she was your student," I say.

"They're revisiting it. Everyone's getting interviewed all over again."

"If they decided you didn't do anything wrong back then, why would they change their minds now?"

"Paid any attention to the news lately?" he asks. "We're living in a different time."

I want to tell him he's being overdramatic, that it'll be ok so long as he's innocent, but I know he's right. For the past month, something's been gaining momentum, a wave of women outing men as harassers, assaulters. It's mostly celebrities who have been targeted—musicians, politicians, movie stars—but less famous men have been named, too. No matter their background, the accused go through the same steps. First, they deny everything. Then, as it becomes clear the din of accusations isn't going away, they resign from their jobs in disgrace and issue a statement of vague apology that stops short of admitting wrongdoing. Then the final step: they go silent and disappear. It's been surreal to watch it play out day after day, these men falling so easily.

"It should be ok," I say. "Everything she wrote is a lie."

On the phone, Strane sucks in a breath, air whistling through his teeth. "I don't know if she is lying, at least not technically."

"But you barely touched her. In that post, she says you assaulted her."

"Assault," he scoffs. "Assault can be anything, like how battery can mean you grabbed someone by the wrist or shoved their shoulder. It's a meaningless legal term."

I stare out the window at the farmers' market: the milling crowd, the swarming seagulls. A woman selling food opens a metal tub, releasing a cloud of steam as she pulls out two tamales. "You know, she messaged me last week."

A beat of silence. "Did she."

"She wanted to see if I'd come forward, too. Probably figured she'd be more believable if she roped me into it."

Strane says nothing.

"I didn't respond. Obviously."

"Right," he says. "Of course."

"I thought she was bluffing. Didn't think she'd have the nerve." I lean forward, press my forehead against the window. "It'll be ok. You know where I stand."

And with that, he breathes out. I can imagine the smile of relief on his face, the creases in the corners of his eyes. "That's all I need to hear," he says.

Back at the concierge desk, I bring up Facebook, type "Taylor Birch" in the search bar, and her profile fills the screen. I scroll through the sparse public content I've scrutinized for years, the photos and life updates, and now, at the top, the post about Strane. The numbers still climb—438 shares now, 1.8k likes, plus new comments, more of the same.

This is so inspiring.
I'm in awe of your strength.
Keep speaking your truth, Taylor.

❧

When Strane and I met, I was fifteen and he was forty-two, a near perfect thirty years between us. That's how I described the difference back then—perfect. I loved the math of it, three times my age, how easy it was to imagine three of me fitting inside him: one of me curled around his brain, another around his heart, the third turned to liquid and sliding through his veins.

At Browick, he said, teacher-student romances were known to happen from time to time, but he'd never had one because, before me, he'd never had the desire. I was the first student who put the thought in his head. There was something about me that made it worth the risk. I had an allure that drew him in.

It wasn't about how young I was, not for him. Above everything else, he loved my mind. He said I had genius-level emotional intelligence and that I wrote like a prodigy, that he could talk to me, confide in me. Lurking deep within me, he said, was a dark romanticism, the same kind he saw within himself. No one had ever understood that dark part of him until I came along.

"It's just my luck," he said, "that when I finally find my soul mate, she's fifteen years old."

"If you want to talk about luck," I countered, "try being fifteen and having your soul mate be some old guy."

He checked my face after I said this to make sure I was joking—of course I was. I wanted nothing to do with boys my own age, their dandruff and acne, how cruel they could be, cutting girls up into features, rating our body parts on a scale of one to ten. I wasn't made for them. I loved Strane's middle-aged caution, his slow courtship. He compared my hair to the color of maple leaves, slipped poetry into my hands—Emily, Edna, Sylvia. He made me see myself as he did, a girl with the power to rise with red hair and eat him like air. He loved me so much that sometimes after I left his classroom, he lowered himself into my chair and rested his head against the seminar table, trying to breathe in what was left of me. All of that happened before we even kissed. He was careful with me. He tried so hard to be good.

It's easy to pinpoint when it all started, that moment of walking into his sun-soaked classroom and feeling his eyes drink me in for the first time, but it's harder to know when it ended, if it really ended at all. I think it stopped when I was twenty-two, when he said he needed to get himself together and couldn't live a decent life while I was within reach, but for the past decade there have been late-night calls, him and me reliving the past, worrying the wound we both refuse to let heal.

I assume I'll be the one he turns to in ten or fifteen years, whenever his body begins to break down. That seems the likely ending to this love story: me dropping everything and doing anything, devoted as a dog, as he takes and takes and takes.

I get out of work at eleven and move through the empty downtown streets, counting each block I walk without checking Taylor's post as a personal victory. In my apartment, I still don't look at my phone. I hang up my work suit, take off my makeup, smoke a bowl in bed, and turn off the light. Self-control.

But in the dark, something shifts within me as I feel the bedsheets slide across my legs. Suddenly, I'm full of need—to be reassured, to hear him say, plainly, that of course he didn't do what that girl says he did. I need him to say again that she's lying, that she was a liar ten years ago and is a liar still, taken in now by the siren song of victimhood.

He answers halfway through the first ring, as though expecting me to call. "Vanessa."

"I'm sorry. I know it's late." I balk then, unsure how to ask for what I want. It's been so long since we last did this. My eyes travel the dark room, taking in the outline of the open closet door, the streetlight shadow across the ceiling. Out in the kitchen, the refrigerator hums and the faucet drips. He owes me this, for my silence, my loyalty.

"I'll be quick," I say. "Just a few minutes."

There's the rustle of blankets as he sits up in bed and moves the phone from one ear to the other, and for a moment I think he's about to say no. But then, in the half whisper that turns my bones to milk, he begins to tell me what I used to be: *Vanessa, you were young and dripping with beauty. You were teenage and erotic and so alive, it scared the hell out of me.*

I turn onto my stomach and shove a pillow between my legs. I tell him to give me a memory, something I can slip into. He's quiet as he flips through the scenes.

"In the office behind the classroom," he says. "It was the dead of winter. You, laid out on the sofa, your skin all goose bumps."

I close my eyes and I'm in the office—white walls and gleaming wood floors, the table with a pile of ungraded papers, a scratchy couch, a hissing radiator, and a single window, octagonal with glass the color of seafoam. I'd fix my eyes on it while he worked at me, feeling underwater, my body weightless and rolling, not caring which way was up.

"I was kissing you, going down on you. Making you boil." He lets out a soft laugh. "That's what you used to call it. 'Make me boil.' Those funny phrases you'd come up with. You were so bashful, hated talking about any of it, just wanted me to get on with it. Do you remember?"

I don't remember, not exactly. So many of my memories from back then are shadowy, incomplete. I need him to fill in the gaps, though sometimes the girl he describes sounds like a stranger.

"It was hard for you to keep quiet," he says. "You used to bite your mouth shut. I remember once you bit down on your bottom lip so hard, you started to bleed, but you wouldn't let me stop."

I press my face into the mattress, grind myself against the pillow as his words flood my brain and transport me out of my bed and into the past where I'm fifteen and naked from the waist down, sprawled on the couch in his office, shivering, burning, as he kneels between my legs, his eyes on my face.

My god, Vanessa, your lip, he says. *You're bleeding.*

I shake my head and dig my fingers into the cushions. It's fine, keep going. Just get it over with.

"You were so insatiable," Strane says. "That firm little body."

I breathe hard through my nose as I come, as he asks me if I remember how it felt. Yes, yes, yes. I remember that. The feelings are what I've been able to hold on to—the things he did to me, how he always made my body writhe and beg for more.

I've been seeing Ruby for eight months, ever since my dad died. At first it was grief therapy, but it's turned into talking about my mom, my ex-boyfriend, how stuck I feel in my job, how stuck I feel about everything. It's an indulgence, even with Ruby's sliding scale—fifty bucks a week just to get someone to listen to me.

Her office is a couple blocks from the hotel, a softly lit room with two armchairs, a sofa, and end tables holding boxes of tissues. The windows look out at Casco Bay: gulls swarming above the fishing piers, slow-moving oil tankers, and amphibious duck tours that quack as they ease into the water and transform from bus to boat. Ruby is older than me, big-sister older rather than mom older, with dishwater blond hair and granola clothes. I love her wooden-heeled clogs, the *clack-clack-clack* they make as she walks across her office.

"Vanessa!"

I love, too, the way she says my name as she opens the door, like she's relieved to see me standing there and not anyone else.

That week we talk about the prospect of me going home for the upcoming holidays, the first without Dad. I'm worried my mother is depressed and don't know how to broach the subject. Together,

Ruby and I come up with a plan. We go through scenarios, the likely ways Mom will respond if I suggest she might need help.

"As long as you approach it with empathy," Ruby says, "I think you'll be ok. You two are close. You can handle talking about hard stuff."

Close with my mother? I don't argue but don't agree. Sometimes I marvel at how easily I deceive people, doing it without even trying.

I manage to hold off checking the Facebook post until the end of the session, when Ruby takes out her phone to enter our next appointment into her calendar. Glancing up, she catches my furious scroll and asks if there's any breaking news.

"Let me guess," she says, "another abuser exposed."

I look up from my phone, my limbs cold.

"It's just so endless, isn't it?" She gives a sad smile. "There's no escape."

She starts talking about the latest high-profile exposé, a director who built a career out of films about women being brutalized. Behind the scenes of those films, he apparently enjoyed exposing himself to young actresses and cajoling them into giving him blow jobs.

"Who would have guessed that guy was abusive?" Ruby asks, sarcastic. "His movies are all the evidence we need. These men hide in plain sight."

"Only because we let them," I say. "We all turn a blind eye."

She nods. "You're so right."

It's thrilling to talk like this, to creep so close to the edge.

"I don't know what to think of all the women who worked with him over and over," I say. "Did they have no self-respect?"

"Well, you can't blame the women," Ruby says. I don't argue, just hand her my check.

At home I get stoned and fall asleep on the couch with all the lights on. At seven in the morning, my phone buzzes against the hardwood floor with a text and I stumble across the room for it. Mom. Hi honey. Just thinking of you.

Staring at the screen, I try to gauge what she knows. Taylor's Facebook post has been up for three days now, and though Mom isn't connected with anyone from Browick, the post has been shared so widely. Besides, she's online all the time these days, endlessly liking, sharing, and getting into fights with conservative trolls. She easily could have seen it.

I minimize the text and bring up Facebook: 2.3k shares, 7.9k likes. Last night, Taylor posted a public status update:

BELIEVE WOMEN.

2000

Turning onto the two-lane highway that takes us to Norumbega, Mom says, "I really want you to get out there this year."

It's the start of my sophomore year of high school, dorm move-in day, and this drive is Mom's last chance to hold me to promises before Browick swallows me whole and her access to me is limited to phone calls and school breaks. Last year, she worried boarding school might make me wild, so she made me promise not to drink or have sex. This year, she wants me to promise I'll make new friends, which feels exponentially more insulting, maybe even cruel. My falling-out with Jenny was five months ago, but it's still raw. The mere phrase "new friends" twists my stomach; the idea feels like betrayal.

"I just don't want you sitting alone in your room day and night," she says. "Is that so bad?"

"If I were home, all I'd do is sit in my room."

"But you're not at home. Isn't that the point? I remember you saying something about a 'social fabric' when you convinced us to let you come here."

I press myself into the passenger seat, wishing my body could sink into it entirely so I wouldn't have to listen to her use my own words against me. A year and a half ago, when a Browick representative came to my eighth grade class and played a recruitment video featuring a manicured campus bathed in golden light and I started the process of convincing my parents to let me apply, I made a twenty-point list entitled "Reasons Why Browick Is Better Than Public School." One of the points was the "social fabric" of the school, along with the college acceptance rate among graduates, the number of AP course offerings, things I'd picked up from the brochure. In the end, I needed only two points to convince my parents: I earned a scholarship so it wouldn't cost them money, and the Columbine shooting happened. We spent days watching CNN, the looped clips of kids running for their lives. When I said, "Something like Columbine would never happen at Browick," my parents exchanged a look, like I'd vocalized what they'd already been thinking.

"You moped all summer," Mom says. "Now it's time to shake it off, move on with your life."

I mumble, "That isn't true," but it is. If I wasn't spaced out in front of the television, I was sprawled in the hammock with my headphones on, listening to songs guaranteed to make me cry. Mom says dwelling in your feelings is no way to live, that there will always be something to be upset about and the secret to a happy life is not to let yourself be dragged down into negativity. She doesn't understand how satisfying sadness can be; hours spent rocking in the hammock with Fiona Apple in my ears make me feel better than happy.

In the car, I shut my eyes. "I wish Dad had come so you wouldn't talk to me like this."

"He'd tell you the same thing."

"Yeah, but he'd be nicer about it."

Even with my eyes closed, I can see everything that passes by the windows. It's only my second year at Browick, but we've made this drive at least a dozen times. There are the dairy farms and rolling foothills of western Maine, general stores advertising cold beer and live bait, farmhouses with sagging roofs, collections of rusted car scraps in yards of waist-high grass and goldenrod. Once you enter Norumbega, it becomes beautiful—the perfect downtown, the bakery, the bookstore, the Italian restaurant, the head shop, the public library, and the hilltop Browick campus, gleaming white clapboard and brick.

Mom turns the car into the main entrance. The big BROWICK

SCHOOL sign is decorated with maroon and white balloons for move-in day, and the narrow campus roads are crammed with cars, overstuffed SUVs parked haphazardly, parents and new students wandering around, gazing up at the buildings. Mom sits forward, hunched over the steering wheel, and the air between us tightens as the car lurches forward, then halts, lurches again.

"You're a smart, interesting kid," she says. "You should have a big group of friends. Don't get sucked into spending all your time with just one person."

Her words are harsher than she probably means them to be, but I snap at her anyway. "Jenny wasn't just some person. She was my *roommate*." I say the word as though the significance of the relationship should be obvious—its disorienting closeness, how it could sometimes turn the world beyond the shared room muted and pale—but Mom doesn't get it. She never lived in a dorm, never went to college, let alone boarding school.

"Roommate or not," she says, "you could've had other friends. Focusing on a single person isn't the healthiest, that's all I'm saying."

In front of us, the line of cars splits as we approach the campus green. Mom flips on the left blinker, then the right. "Which way am I going here?"

Sighing, I point to the left.

Gould is a small dorm, really just a house, with eight rooms and one dorm parent apartment. Last year I drew a low number in the housing lottery, so I was able to get a single, rare for a sophomore. It takes Mom and me four trips to move in all my stuff: two suitcases of clothes, a box of books, extra pillows and bedsheets and a quilt she made of old T-shirts I'd outgrown, a pedestal fan we set up to oscillate in the center of the room.

While we unpack, people pass by the open door—parents, students, someone's younger brother who sprints up and down the hallway until he trips and starts to wail. At one point, Mom goes to the bathroom and I hear her say hello in her fake-polite voice, then another mother's voice says hello back. I stop stacking books on the shelf above my desk to listen. Squinting, I try to place the voice—Mrs. Murphy, Jenny's mom.

Mom comes back into the room, pulls the door shut. "Getting kind of noisy out there," she says.

Sliding books onto the shelf, I ask, "Was that Jenny's mom?"

"Mm-hmm."

"Did you see Jenny?"

Mom nods but doesn't elaborate. For a while, we unpack in silence. As we make the bed, pulling the fitted sheet over the pinstriped mattress, I say, "Honestly, I feel sorry for her."

I like how it sounds, but of course it's a lie. Just last night, I spent an hour scrutinizing myself in my bedroom mirror, trying to see myself as Jenny would, wondering if she'd notice my hair lightened from Sun In, the new hoops in my ears.

Mom says nothing as she lifts the quilt out of a plastic tote. I know she's worried I'll backtrack, end up heartbroken again.

"Even if she tried to be friends with me now," I say, "I wouldn't waste my time."

Mom smiles thinly, smoothing the quilt over the bed. "Is she still dating that boy?" She means Tom Hudson, Jenny's boyfriend, the catalyst for the falling-out. I shrug like I don't know, but I do. Of course I do. All summer I checked Jenny's AOL profile and her relationship status never changed from "Taken." They're still together.

Before she leaves, Mom gives me four twenties and makes me promise to call home every Sunday. "No forgetting," she instructs. "And you're coming home for Dad's birthday." She hugs me so hard it hurts my bones.

"I can't breathe."

"Sorry, sorry." She puts on her sunglasses to hide her teary eyes. On her way out of the dorm room, she points a finger at me. "Be good to yourself. And be social."

I wave her off. "Yeah, yeah, yeah." From my doorway, I watch her walk down the hallway, disappear into the stairwell, and then she's gone. Standing there, I hear two approaching voices, the bright echoing laughter of mother and daughter. I duck into the safety of my room as they appear, Jenny and her mother. I catch only a glimpse, just long enough to see that her hair is shorter and she's wearing a dress I remember hanging in her closet all last year but never saw her wear.

Lying back on my bed, I let my eyes wander the room and listen to the goodbyes in the hallway, the sniffles and quiet cries. I think back to a year ago, moving into the freshman dorm, the first night of staying up late with Jenny while the Smiths and Bikini Kill played from her boom box, bands I'd never heard of but pretended to know because I was scared to out myself as a loser, a bumpkin. I worried if I did, she wouldn't like me anymore. During those first few days at Browick, I wrote in my journal, *The thing I love most about being here is that I get to meet people like Jenny. She is so freaking COOL and just being around her is teaching me how to be cool, too!* I'd since torn out that entry, thrown it away. The sight of it made my face burn with shame.

The dorm parent in Gould is Ms. Thompson, the new Spanish teacher, fresh out of college. During the first night meeting in the common room, she brings colored markers and paper plates for us to make name tags for our doors. The other girls in the dorm are upperclassmen, Jenny and I the only sophomores. We give each other plenty of space, sitting on opposite ends of the table. Jenny hunches over as she makes her name tag, her brown bobbed hair falling against her cheeks. When she comes up for air and to switch markers, her eyes skim over me as though I don't even register.

"Before you go back to your rooms, go ahead and take one of these," Ms. Thompson says. She holds open a plastic bag. At first, I think it is candy, then see it's a pile of silver whistles.

"Chances are you won't ever need to use these," she says, "but it's good to have one, just in case."

"Why would we need a whistle?" Jenny asks.

"Oh, you know, just a campus safety measure." Ms. Thompson smiles so wide I can tell she's uncomfortable.

"But we didn't get these last year."

"It's in case someone tries to rape you," Deanna Perkins says. "You blow the whistle to make him stop." She brings a whistle to her lips and blows hard. The sound rings through the hallway, so satisfyingly loud we all have to try.

Ms. Thompson attempts to talk over the din. "Ok, ok." She laughs. "I guess it's good to make sure they work."

"Would this seriously stop someone if he wanted to rape you?" Jenny asks.

"Nothing can stop a rapist," Lucy Summers says.

"That's not true," Ms. Thompson says. "And these aren't 'rape' whistles. They're a general safety tool. If you're ever feeling uncomfortable on campus, you just blow."

"Do the boys get whistles?" I ask.

Lucy and Deanna roll their eyes. "Why would boys need a whistle?" Deanna asks. "Use your brain."

At that Jenny laughs loud, as though Lucy and Deanna weren't just rolling their eyes at her.

It's the first day of classes and the campus is bustling, clapboard buildings with their windows thrown open, the staff parking lots full. At breakfast I drink black tea while perched at the end of a long Shaker-style table, my stomach too knotted to eat. My eyes dart around the cathedral-ceilinged dining hall, taking in new faces and the changes in familiar ones. I notice everything about everyone—that Margo Atherton parts her hair on the left to hide her lazy right eye, that Jeremy Rice steals a banana from the dining hall every single morning. Even before Tom Hudson started going out with Jenny, before there was a reason to care about anything he did, I'd noticed the exact rotation of band T-shirts he wore under his button-downs. It's both creepy and out of my control, this ability I have to notice so much about other people when I'm positive no one notices anything at all about me.

The convocation speech is held after breakfast and before first period, basically a pep talk meant to propel us into the new school year. As we file in, the auditorium is all warm wood and red velvet curtains, sunlight streaming in and setting the curved rows of chairs aglow. For the first few minutes of the assembly, while the headmaster, Mrs. Giles, goes over school codes and policies, her salt-and-pepper bob tucked behind her ears and chronically shaky voice warbling out across the room, everyone looks fresh-faced and brand new. But by the time she steps offstage, the room is stuffy and foreheads have begun to jewel with sweat. A couple rows back somebody groans, "How long is this going to take?" Mrs. Antonova throws a glare over her shoulder. Beside me, Anna Shapiro fans her face with her hands. A breeze drifts in through the open windows and stirs the bottom hem of the drawn velvet curtains.

Then across the stage strides Mr. Strane, head of the English department, a teacher I recognize but have never had, never spoken to. He has wavy black hair and a black beard, glasses that reflect a glare so you can't see his eyes, but the first thing I notice about him—the first thing anyone must notice—is his size. He's not fat but big, broad, and so tall that his shoulders hunch as though his body wants to apologize for taking up so much space.

Standing at the podium, he has to tip the mic up as far as it will go. As he starts to speak, the sun glinting off his glasses, I reach into my backpack and check my schedule. There, my last class of the day: Honors American Lit with Mr. Strane.

"This morning I see young people on the cusp of great things." His words boom from the speakers, everything pronounced so clearly it's almost uncomfortable to hear: long vowels, hard consonants, like being lulled to sleep only to be jerked awake. What he says boils down to the same clichéd stuff—*reach for the stars, who cares if you fall short, maybe you'll land on the moon*—but he's a good speaker and somehow makes it seem profound.

"This academic year, resolve never to stop striving to be your best possible selves," he says. "Challenge yourselves to make Browick a better place. Leave your mark." He reaches then into his back pocket, pulls out a red bandanna, and uses it to wipe his forehead, revealing a dark sweat stain seeping out from his armpit.

"I've been a teacher at Browick for thirteen years," he says, "and in those thirteen years, I've witnessed countless acts of courage from students at this school."

I shift in my seat, aware of my own sweat on the backs of my knees and in the crooks of my elbows, and try to imagine what he means by acts of courage.

My fall semester schedule is Honors French, Honors Biology, AP World History, Geometry (the non-math-genius kind; even Mrs. Antonova calls it "geometry for dummies"), an elective called U.S. Politics and Media where we watch CNN and talk about the upcoming presidential election, and Honors American Literature. On the first day, I crisscross campus from class to class, weighed down with books, the workload increase from freshman to sophomore year immediately apparent. As the day wears on and each teacher warns of the challenges that lie ahead, the homework and exams and accelerated, sometimes breakneck pace—because this isn't an ordinary school and we aren't ordinary young people; as exceptional young people, we should embrace difficulties, should thrive on them—an exhaustion sets in. By the middle of the day, I'm struggling to keep my head up, so rather than eating during lunch, I sneak back to Gould, curl up in my bed, and cry. If it's going to be this hard, I wonder, why even bother? That's a bad attitude to have, especially on the first day, and it makes me wonder what I'm doing at Browick in the first place, why they gave me a scholarship, why they thought I was smart enough to be here. It's a spiral I've traveled before, and every time I arrive at the same conclusion: that there's probably something wrong with me, an inherent weakness that manifests as laziness, a fear of hard work. Besides, hardly anyone else at Browick seems to struggle like I do. They move from class to class knowing every answer, always prepared. They make it look easy.

When I get to American lit, the last class of the day, the first thing I notice is that Mr. Strane has changed his shirt since the convocation speech. He stands at the front of the room leaning against a chalkboard, arms folded over his chest, looking even bigger than he appeared onstage. There are ten of us in the class, including Jenny and Tom, and as we enter the room Mr. Strane's eyes follow us, like he's sizing us up. When Jenny comes in, I'm already sitting at the seminar table a couple seats away from Tom. His face lights up at the sight of her, and he motions for her to sit in the empty chair between us—he's oblivious, doesn't understand why that is absolutely out of the question. Gripping her backpack straps, Jenny gives him a terse smile.

"Let's sit on this side instead," she says, meaning the opposite side, meaning away from me. "It's better over here."

Her eyes skim past me the way they did at the dorm meeting. In a way it seems silly, putting all this effort into pretending an entire friendship never existed.

When the bell rings to signal the start of class, Mr. Strane doesn't move. He waits for us to fall into silence before speaking. "I assume you all know each other," he says, "but I don't think I know all of you."

He moves to the head of the seminar table and calls on us at random, asking our names and where we're from. Some of us he asks other questions—do we have any siblings; where's the farthest we've ever traveled; if we could choose a new name for ourselves, what would it be? He asks Jenny at what age she first fell in love and a blush takes over her whole face. Beside her, Tom turns red, too.

When it's my turn to introduce myself, I say, "My name's Vanessa Wye and I'm not really from anywhere."

Mr. Strane sits back in his chair. "Vanessa Wye, not really from anywhere."

I laugh out of nerves, from hearing how stupid my words sound when repeated back to me. "I mean, it's a place but not really a town. It doesn't have a name. They just call it Township Twenty-Nine."

"Here in Maine? Out on that down east highway?" he asks. "I know exactly where that is. There's a lake out that way that has a lovely name, Whale-something."

I blink in surprise. "Whalesback Lake. We live right on it. We're the only year-round house." As I speak, an odd pang hits my heart. I hardly ever feel homesick at Browick, but maybe that's because no one ever knows where I'm from.

"No kidding." Mr. Strane thinks for a moment. "Do you get lonely out there?"

For a moment, I'm dumbstruck. The question slices a painless cut, shockingly clean. Even though *lonely* isn't a word I'd ever used to describe how it feels living out there deep in the woods, hearing Mr. Strane say it now makes me think it must be true, probably has always been true, and suddenly I'm embarrassed, imagining that loneliness plastered all over my face, obvious enough that a teacher needs only one look to know I'm a lonely person. I manage to say, "I guess sometimes," but Mr. Strane has already moved on, asking Greg Akers what it was like to move from Chicago to the foothills of western Maine.

Once we all introduce ourselves, Mr. Strane says his class will be the hardest we take this year. "Most students tell me I'm the toughest teacher at Browick," he says. "I've had some say I'm tougher than their college professors." He drums his fingers against the table and lets the gravity of this information settle onto us. Then he walks to the chalkboard, grabs a piece of chalk, and begins to write. Over his shoulder, he says, "You should already be taking notes."

We scramble for our notebooks as he launches into a lecture about Henry Wadsworth Longfellow and the poem "The Song of Hiawatha," which I've never heard of, and I can't be the only one, but when he asks the class if we're familiar with it, we all nod. No one wants to look stupid.

While he lectures, I sneak glances around the room. The bones of it are the same as all the others in the humanities building—hardwood floors, a wall of built-in bookcases, green chalkboards, a seminar table—but his classroom feels lived-in and comfortable. There's a rug with a worn path down its center, a big oak desk lit by a green banker's lamp, a coffeemaker and a mug with the Harvard seal sitting atop a filing cabinet. The smell of cut grass and the sound of a car engine starting drift in through the open window, and at the chalkboard Mr. Strane writes a line from Longfellow with such intensity the chalk crumbles in his hand. At one point, he stops, turns to us, and says, "If there's one thing you take away from this class, it should be that the world is made of endlessly intersecting stories, each one valid and true." I do my best to copy down everything he says word for word.

With five minutes left of class, the lecture suddenly stops. Mr. Strane's hands drop to his sides, his shoulders slump. Abandoning the chalkboard, he sits at the seminar table, rubs his face, and heaves a sigh. Then in a weary voice he says, "The first day is always so long."

Around the table, we wait, unsure what to do, our pens hovering above our notebooks.

He drops his hands from his face. "I'll be honest with you all," he says. "I'm fucking tired."

Across the table, Jenny laughs in surprise. Sometimes teachers joke around in class, but I've never heard one say "fuck." It never occurred to me that a teacher could.

"Do you mind if I use four-letter words?" he asks. "I guess I should have gotten your permission first." He clasps his hands together, sarcastically sincere. "If my use of colorful language truly offends anyone here, speak now or forever hold your peace."

No one, of course, says anything.

❧

The first few weeks of the year pass quickly, a succession of classes, breakfasts of black tea and lunches of peanut butter sandwiches, study hours in the library, evenings of WB shows in the Gould common room. I get detention for skipping a dorm meeting, but convince Ms. Thompson to let me walk her dog rather than sit with her in the dorm study for an hour, something neither of us wants to do. I spend most mornings before class finishing last-minute homework, because no matter how hard I try, I'm always scrambling, always on the brink of falling behind. Teachers insist this is something I should be able to fix; they say I'm smart but unfocused and unmotivated, slightly nicer ways of saying I'm lazy.

Within a matter of days after moving in, my room turns into a mess of clothes, loose papers, and half-drunk mugs of tea. I lose the day planner that was supposed to help me stay on top of things, but that's to be expected because I lose everything. At least once a week, I open my door to find my keys hanging from the knob, left by whoever found them in a bathroom or classroom or dining hall. I can't keep track of anything—textbooks end up wedged between my bed and the wall, homework smashed at the bottom of my backpack. Teachers are forever exasperated at my crumpled assignments, reminding me of the points they'll take off for messiness.

"You need an organization system!" my AP history teacher cries as I flip frantically through my textbook for the notes I'd taken the day before. "It's only the second week. How can you be so muddled already?" That I eventually find the notes doesn't negate his point: I am sloppy, which is a sign of weakness, a serious character flaw.

At Browick teachers and their advisees have dinner together once a month, traditionally at the teacher's house, but my advisor, Mrs. Antonova, never invites us over. "I must have boundaries," she says. "Not all teachers agree with me, that's ok. They have students all over their lives, that's ok. But not me. We go somewhere, we eat, talk a little bit, then we all go home. Boundaries."

On our first meeting of the year, she takes us to the Italian restaurant downtown. As I'm concentrating on winding linguine around my fork, Mrs. Antonova notes that lack of organization is my most urgent faculty feedback topic. I try not to sound too dismissive when I say I'll work on it. She goes around the table telling all her advisees their feedback points. No one else has organization issues, but mine isn't the worst; Kyle Guinn hasn't turned in assignments in two of his classes, a serious offense. When Mrs. Antonova reads his feedback, the rest of us stare down at our pasta, relieved we aren't as bad off as him. At the end of dinner, our plates cleared, she passes around a tin of homemade doughnut holes with cherry filling.

"These are *pampushky*," she says. "Ukrainian, like my mother."

As we leave the restaurant and head back up the hill to campus, Mrs. Antonova falls into step beside me. "I forgot to say, Vanessa, you should do an extracurricular this year. Maybe more than one. You must think about college applications. Right now, you look flimsy." She starts making suggestions and I nod along.

I know I need to get involved more and I have tried—last week I went to join the French club but promptly left when I realized its members wore little black berets during every meeting.

"What about the creative writing club?" she says. "It would fit you, with your poetry."

I've thought about that, too. The creative writing club puts out a literary journal, and last year, I read it cover to cover, compared my poems with the published ones, and tried to be objective as I decided whose were better. "Yeah, maybe," I say.

She touches her hand to my shoulder. "Think about it," she says. "Mr. Strane is the faculty advisor this year. He's smart on the subject."

Looking over her shoulder, she claps and calls out something in Russian to the stragglers lagging behind, which, for whatever reason, is more effective than English at getting us to hurry up.

The creative writing club has one other member, Jesse Ly—a junior, Browick's closest thing to a goth, rumored to be gay. When I walk into the classroom, he sits at the seminar table in front of a stack of papers, his combat boots propped up on a chair, a pen tucked behind his ear. He glances at me but says nothing. I doubt he even knows my name.

Mr. Strane, though, jumps up from behind his desk and strides across the room to me. "Here for the club?" he asks.

I open my mouth, unsure what to say. If I'd known there would be only one other person I probably wouldn't have come. I want to back out right then, but Mr. Strane is too delighted, shaking my hand and saying, "You're going to increase our membership by one hundred percent," so it feels like I can't change my mind.

He leads me to the seminar table, sits beside me, explains that the stack of papers contains submissions for the lit journal. "It's all student work," he says. "Do your best to ignore the names. Read each one carefully, all the way through, before you make a decision." He says I should write my comments in the margins, then assign each submission a number from one to five, one being a definite no and five a definite yes.

Without looking up, Jesse says, "I've been doing checks. It's what we used last year." He gestures to the papers he's already gone through; on the upper right corner of each there's a tiny check, check-minus, or check-plus. Mr. Strane raises his eyebrows, obviously annoyed, but Jesse doesn't notice. His eyes are fixed on the poem he's reading.

"Whatever method you two decide on is fine," Mr. Strane says. He smiles at me, winks. As he gets up, he pats my shoulder.

With Mr. Strane across the classroom, back behind his desk, I pull a submission from the stack, a short story titled "The Worst Day of Her Life," by Zoe Green. Zoe was in my algebra class last year. She sat behind me and laughed whenever Seth McLeod called me Big Red as though it were the funniest thing she'd ever heard. I shake my head and try to push the bias out of my mind. This is why Mr. Strane said not to look at the names.

Her story is about a girl in a hospital waiting room whose grandmother dies, and I'm bored by the end of the first paragraph. Jesse catches me flipping to check how many pages there are and in a low voice says, "You really don't have to read the whole thing if it's bad. I edited the lit journal last year when Mrs. Bloom was the faculty advisor and she didn't care."

My eyes dart to Mr. Strane sitting behind his desk, bent over his own stack of papers. Shrugging, I say, "I'll keep reading. It's ok."

Jesse squints at the page in my hands. "Zoe Green? Isn't that the girl who lost it during the debate tournament last year?" It was—Zoe, assigned to argue for the death penalty, broke down in tears during the final round when her opponent, Jackson Kelly, called her position racist and immoral, which probably wouldn't have rattled her so badly if Jackson weren't black. After Jackson was declared the tournament winner, Zoe said she'd felt personally attacked by his rebuttal, which was against the debate rules, so they ended up sharing first place, which was bullshit and everyone knew it.

Jesse leans forward and pulls Zoe's story out of my hands, marks a check-minus on the right-hand corner, and tosses it in the "no" pile. "Voilà," he says.

For the rest of the hour while Jesse and I read, Mr. Strane grades papers at his desk at the back of the room, occasionally leaving to make photocopies or get water for the coffeemaker. At one point, he peels an orange and its scent fills the room. At the end of the hour, as I stand to leave, Mr. Strane asks if I'll come to the next meeting.

"I'm not sure," I say. "I'm still trying out different things."

He smiles and waits until Jesse leaves the room before saying, "I guess this doesn't offer much for you socially."

"Oh, that doesn't bother me," I say. "I'm not exactly a super social person anyway."

"Why's that?"

"I don't know. I guess I just don't have a ton of friends."

He nods thoughtfully. "I understand what you mean. I like to be by myself, too."

My first impulse is to say no, I don't like being by myself at all, but maybe he's right. Maybe I'm actually a loner by choice, preferring my own company.

"Well, I used to be best friends with Jenny Murphy," I say. "From English class." The words tumble out, catch me off guard. It's more than I've ever told a teacher, especially a man, but the way he watches me—soft-eyed smile, chin resting on his hand—makes me want to talk, to show myself off.

"Ah," he says. "The little Queen of the Nile." When I frown, confused, he explains that he means her bobbed haircut, that it makes her look like Cleopatra, and as he says this, I feel a prick of something in my stomach, like jealousy but meaner.

"I don't think her hair looks *that* good," I say.

Mr. Strane smirks. "So you used to be friends. What changed?"

"She started going out with Tom Hudson."

He thinks for a moment. "The boy with the sideburns."

I nod, thinking of how teachers must recognize and categorize us in their minds. I wonder what he might associate with me if someone mentioned Vanessa Wye. The girl with the red hair. That girl who is always alone.

"So you suffered a betrayal," he says, meaning by Jenny.

It's something I haven't considered before and warmth fills my chest at the idea. I suffered. It wasn't that I drove her away by feeling too much or getting too attached. No, I was wronged.

He gets up and walks to the chalkboard, starts erasing the notes left over from class. "What made you want to try out the club? Weak spot on your résumé?"

I nod; it seems ok to be honest with him. "Mrs. Antonova said I should. I do like to write, though."

"What do you write?"

"Poems, mostly. They're not good or anything."

Mr. Strane smiles over his shoulder in a way that is somehow both kind and condescending. "I'd like to read some of your work."

My brain catches on the way he says "your work," as though the things I write are worth taking seriously. "Sure," I say. "If you really want to."

"I do want to," he says. "I wouldn't ask if I didn't."

At that, I feel my face flush. My worst habit, according to my mother, is how I deflect compliments with self-deprecation. I need to learn how to accept praise. It boils down to confidence, she says, or lack thereof.

Mr. Strane sets the eraser on the chalk rail and contemplates me from across the room. He slips his hands into his pockets, looks me up and down.

"That's a nice dress," he says. "I like your style."

I mumble thank you, manners instilled so deep they're reflexive, and look down at my dress. It's hunter-green jersey, vaguely

A-line but mostly shapeless, and ends above the knee. It's not stylish; I only wear it because I like the contrast in color against my hair. It seems strange for a middle-aged man to notice girl clothes. My dad barely knows the difference between a dress and a skirt.

Mr. Strane turns back to the chalkboard and starts erasing again even though it's already clean. It almost seems like he's embarrassed, and part of me wants to thank him again, sincerely this time. *Thank you very much,* I could say. *No one has ever said that to me before.* I wait for him to turn back around, but he keeps swiping the eraser back and forth, cloudy streaks across a green expanse.

Then, as I edge toward the doorway, he says, "I hope I see you again on Thursday."

"Oh, sure," I say. "You will."

So I go again on Thursday, and the next Tuesday, and the next Thursday. I become an official member of the club. It takes Jesse and me longer than expected to finish choosing pieces for the lit journal, mostly because I'm so indecisive, going back and changing my vote multiple times. Meanwhile Jesse's judgment is swift and ruthless, his pen slicing across the page. When I ask him how he can decide so quickly, he says it should be obvious from the first line if something is good or not. One Thursday, Mr. Strane disappears into the office behind his classroom and comes out with a stack of back issues so we can understand what the journal is supposed to look like, even though Jesse was the editor last year so of course he already knows. Thumbing through an issue, I see Jesse's name listed in the table of contents under "Fiction."

"Hey, there's you," I say.

At the sight of it, he groans. "Don't read it in front of me, please."

"Why not?" I skim the first page.

"Because I don't want you to."

I slip the issue into my backpack and forget about it until after dinner, when I'm drowning in incomprehensible geometry homework, eager for a distraction. I take the journal and turn to his story, read it twice. It's good, really good, better than anything I've ever written, better than any of the submissions we read for the journal. When I try to tell him this at the next club meeting, he cuts me off. "Writing isn't really my thing anymore," he says.

Another afternoon, Mr. Strane shows us how to use the new publishing software to format the issue. Jesse and I sit side by side at the computer while Mr. Strane stands behind us, watching and correcting. At one point when I make a mistake, he reaches down and guides the mouse for me, his hand so big it covers mine completely. His touch makes my whole body go hot. When I make another mistake, he does it again, this time squeezing my hand a little, as though to reassure me that I'll get the hang of it, but he doesn't do the same to Jesse, not even when he accidentally x-es out without saving and Mr. Strane has to explain the steps all over again.

Late September arrives and for a week the weather is perfect, sunny and cool. Each morning the leaves are brighter, turning the rolling mountains around Norumbega into a mess of color. Campus looks like it did in the brochure I obsessed over as I filled out my Browick application—students in sweaters, the lawns a brilliant green, golden hour setting white clapboard aglow. I should enjoy it, but instead the weather makes me restless, panicked. After classes I'm unable to settle down, moving from the library to the Gould common area to my dorm room and back to the library. Everywhere makes me antsy to be someplace else.

One afternoon I loop through campus three times, unsatisfied with all the places I try—the library too dark, my messy dorm room too depressing, everywhere else crowded with people studying in groups that only highlight me being alone, always alone—before I force myself to stop at the grassy slope behind the humanities building. *Calm down, breathe.*

I lean against the solitary maple tree that my eyes drift to during English class and touch the back of my hand to my hot cheeks. I'm so worked up I'm sweating, and it's only fifty degrees.

This is fine, I think. *Just work here and* calm down.

I sit with my back against the tree and reach into my backpack, feeling past my geometry textbook to my spiral notebook, thinking I'll feel better if I work on a poem first, but when I open to my latest one, a couple of stanzas about a girl trapped on an island who calls sailors to shore, I read over the lines and realize they're bad—clumsy, disjointed, practically incoherent. And I thought these lines were good. How did I think they were good? They're blatantly bad. Probably all my poems are bad. I curl into myself and grind the heels of my hands against my eyelids until I hear footsteps approach, crunching leaves and cracking twigs. I look up and a towering silhouette blocks out the sun.

"Hello there," it says.

I shield my eyes—Mr. Strane. His expression changes when he notices my face, my red-rimmed eyes. "You're upset," he says.

Gazing up at him, I nod. There doesn't seem to be any use in lying.

"Would you rather be left alone?" he asks.

I hesitate, then shake my head no.

He lowers himself to the ground beside me, leaving a few feet between us. His long legs are stretched out, the outline of his knees visible beneath his trousers. He keeps his eyes on me, watches as I wipe my eyes.

"I didn't mean to impose. I spied you from the window there, thought I'd say hello." He points behind us, to the humanities building. "Can I ask what's upsetting you?"

I take a breath, try to work out the words, but after a moment I shake my head. "It's too big to explain," I say. Because it's about more than my poem being bad, or that I can't pick a study spot without exhausting myself. It's a darker feeling, a fear of there being something wrong with me that I won't ever be able to fix.

I expect Mr. Strane to let it go at that. Instead, he waits the same way he'd wait in class for a response to a tough question. *Of course it seems too big to explain, Vanessa. That's how hard questions are meant to make you feel.*

Taking a breath, I say, "This time of year just makes me feel nuts. Like I'm running out of time or something. Like I'm wasting my life."

Mr. Strane blinks. I can tell this isn't what he expected me to say. "Wasting your life," he echoes.

"I know that doesn't make sense."

"No, it does. It makes perfect sense." He leans back on his hands, tilts his head. "You know, if you were my age, I'd say it sounds like you're in the beginning of a midlife crisis."

He smiles and, without meaning to, my face mirrors him. He grins, I grin.

"It looked like you were writing," he says. "Were you getting good work done?"

I lift my shoulders, unsure if I want to call my writing good. It seems boastful, not for me to say.

"Would you show me what you've written?"

"No way." I clutch my notebook in my hands, hold it closer to my chest, and in his eyes I see a flash of alarm, like my sudden movement has scared him. I steady myself and add, "It's just not finished."

"Is writing ever really finished?"

That feels like a trick question. I think for a moment, then say, "Some writing can be more finished than other writing."

He smiles; he likes that. "Do you have something more finished you can show me?"

I loosen my grip and open the notebook's front cover. It's full of mostly half-finished poems, lines scrawled out and rewritten. I thumb through recent pages to find the one I've been working on for a couple weeks. It isn't finished, but it isn't terrible. I hand him the notebook, hoping he won't notice the doodles in the margins, the flowering vine crawling along the spine.

He holds the notebook carefully in both hands, and just seeing that, my notebook in his hands, sends a jolt through me. No one else has ever touched my notebook before, let alone read anything in it. At the end of the poem, he says, "Huh." I wait for a clearer reaction, for him to let me know if he thinks it's good or not, but he only says, "I'm going to read it again."

When he finally looks up and says, "Vanessa, this is lovely," I exhale so loudly, I laugh. "How long did you work on this?" he asks.

Thinking it's more impressive to come across as an instantaneous genius, I shrug out a lie. "Not long."

"You said you write often." He hands the notebook back to me.

"Every day, usually."

"It shows. You're very good. I say that as a reader, not a teacher."

I'm so delighted, I laugh again, and Mr. Strane smiles his tender-condescending smile. "Is that funny?" he asks.

"No, that's the nicest thing anyone has ever said about my writing."

"You're kidding. That's nothing. I could say much nicer things."

"It's just I never really let anyone read my . . ." I almost say *stuff* but instead try out the word he used. "My work."

A silence settles between us. He leans back on his hands and studies the view: the picturesque downtown, distant river, and rolling hills. I look back to my notebook, eyes turned down at its pages but seeing nothing. I'm too aware of his body next to mine, his sloping torso and stomach straining against his shirt, long legs crossed at the ankle, how one of his pant legs has bunched up, revealing a half inch of skin above his hiking boot. Worried he might get up and leave, I try to think of something to say to keep him here, but before I can, he plucks a fallen red maple leaf off the ground, spins it by its stem, considers it for a moment, and then holds it up to my face.

"Look at that," he says. "It matches your hair perfectly."

I freeze, feel my mouth fall open. He holds the maple leaf there a beat longer, its points brushing against my hair. Then, shaking his head a little, he drops his hand and the leaf falls to the ground. He stands—again blocking out the sun—wipes his hands on his thighs, and walks back to the humanities building without saying goodbye.

When he disappears, a mania seizes me, a need to flee. I snap my notebook shut, grab my backpack, and start off toward the dorm, but then think better and double back to scan the ground for the exact leaf he held up to my hair. Once it's safe, tucked between the pages of my notebook, I move across campus as though airborne, barely making contact with the earth between strides. It isn't until I'm back in my room that I remember he said he saw me from his window, and I squeeze my eyes shut against the thought of him back in the classroom, watching me search for the leaf.

I go home the next weekend for Dad's birthday. Mom's gift to him is a yellow Labrador puppy from the shelter, the reason for owner surrender listed as "pigment too pale." Dad names the puppy Babe, after the pig movie, because she looks like a piglet with her fat belly and pink nose. Our last dog died over the summer, a twelve-year-old shepherd Dad found as a stray in town, so we've never had a puppy before, and I fall in love so hard I carry her around all weekend like a baby, rubbing her jelly-bean paw pads and smelling her sweet breath.

At night after my parents go to bed, I stand in front of my bedroom mirror, study my face and hair and try to see myself as Mr. Strane sees me, a girl with maple-red hair who wears nice dresses and has good style, but I can't get past the sight of myself as a pale, freckled child.

When Mom and I drive back to Browick, Dad stays home with Babe, and in the closed-off space of the car, my chest burns from wanting to tell. But what is there to tell? He touched my hand a couple times, said something about my hair?

As we drive across the bridge into town, I ask in my most casual voice, "Have you ever noticed my hair is the color of maple leaves?"

Mom looks over at me, surprised. "Well, there are different kinds of maple," she says, "and they all turn different colors in the fall. There's sugar, there's striped, there's red. And depending how north you are, there's mountain maple—"

"Never mind. Forget it."

"Since when are you interested in trees?"

"I was talking about my hair, not trees."

She asks who told me my hair looked like maple leaves, but she doesn't sound suspicious. Her voice is soft, like she thinks it's sweet.

"No one," I say.

"Someone must have said it to you."

"I can't notice something like that about myself?"

We stop at a red light. On the radio, a voice reads the top-of-the-hour news headlines.

"If I tell you," I say, "you have to promise not to overreact."

"I would never."

I give her a long look. "Promise."

"All right," she says. "I promise."

I take a breath. "A teacher said it to me. That my hair is the color of red maple leaves." There's a giddy relief as I say the words; I nearly let out a laugh.

Mom narrows her eyes. "A teacher?" she asks.

"Mom, watch the road."

"Was it a man?"

"What does it matter?"

"A teacher shouldn't be saying that to you. Who was it?"

"Mom."

"I want to know."

"You promised you wouldn't overreact."

She presses her lips together, as though to calm herself. "It's a strange thing to tell a fifteen-year-old girl, that's all I'm saying."

We drive through town: blocks of Victorian mansions fallen into disrepair and broken up into apartments, the empty downtown, the sprawling hospital, the grinning Paul Bunyan statue who, with his black hair and beard, looks a little like Mr. Strane.

"It was a man," I say. "You really think it's weird?"

"Yes," Mom says. "I really do. Do you want me to talk to someone? I'll go in there and cause a scene."

I picture her storming into the administration building, demanding to talk to the headmaster. I shake my head. No, I don't want that. "It was just a random thing he said," I say. "It really wasn't a big deal."

With that, Mom relaxes a little. "Who was it?" she asks again. "I won't do anything. I just want to know."

"My politics teacher." I don't even hesitate in the lie. "Mr. Sheldon."

"Mr. *Sheldon*." She spits it out like it's the stupidest name she's ever heard. "You shouldn't be hanging out with teachers anyway. Focus on making friends."

I watch the road pass by. We could take the interstate to Browick, but Mom refuses, says it's a racetrack full of angry people. She drives a two-lane highway instead that takes twice as long.

"There's nothing wrong with me, you know."

She glances over, her brow furrowed.

"I prefer to be by myself. It's normal. You shouldn't give me such a hard time about it."

"I'm not giving you a hard time," she says, but we both know that's not true. After a moment, she adds, "I'm sorry. I just worry about you."

We hardly talk for the rest of the drive, and as I stare out the window, I can't help but feel like I've won.

I'm sitting at a study carrel in the library, geometry homework spread out before me. I'm trying to concentrate, but my brain feels like a rock skipping over water. Or, no—like a rock rattling around in a tin can. I take out my notebook to jot down the line and get distracted by the island girl poem I'm still working on. When I next look up, an hour has passed, and my geometry homework is still untouched.

I rub my face, pick up my pencil, and try to work, but within minutes I'm gazing out the window. It's the golden hour, light setting the fiery trees ablaze. Boys in soccer jerseys with cleats slung over their shoulders head back from the fields. Two girls carry violin cases like backpacks, their twin ponytails swinging with each step.

Then I see Ms. Thompson and Mr. Strane walking together toward the humanities building. They move slowly, taking their time, Mr. Strane with his hands clasped behind his back and Ms. Thompson smiling, touching her face. I try to remember if I've seen them together before, try to decide if Ms. Thompson is pretty. She has blue eyes and black hair, a combination my mother always calls striking, but she's chubby and her butt sticks out like a shelf. It's the sort of body I'm afraid I'll grow up to have if I'm not careful.

I squint across the distance to gather more details. They're close but not touching. At one point, Ms. Thompson tips her head back and laughs. Is Mr. Strane funny? He hasn't ever made me laugh. Pressing my face against the window, I try to keep them in my sight, but they round a corner and disappear behind the orange leaves of an oak tree.

We take PSATs and I do ok but not as well as most other sophomores, who start receiving Ivy League brochures in their mailboxes. I buy another day planner to help with my organization, which gets noticed by my teachers and passed on to Mrs. Antonova, who gives me a tin of hazelnut candies for a job well done.

In English we read Walt Whitman and Mr. Strane talks about the idea that people contain multitudes and contradictions. I begin to pay attention to the ways he seems to contradict himself, how he went to Harvard but tells stories about growing up poor, the way he sprinkles eloquent speech with obscenities and pairs tailored blazers and ironed shirts with scuffed hiking boots. His teaching style is contradictory, too. Speaking up in class always feels risky, because if he likes what you say, he'll clap and bound over to the chalkboard to elaborate on the brilliant comment you made, but if he doesn't like it, he won't even let you finish—he cuts you off with an "Ok, that's enough" that slices to the bone. It makes me scared to talk even though sometimes after he asks the class an open-ended question, he'll stare straight at me, like he wants to know specifically what I have to say.

In the margins of my class notes, I keep track of the details he lets slip about himself: he grew up in Butte, Montana, pronounced like *cute*; before going to Harvard at eighteen, he'd never seen the ocean; he lives in downtown Norumbega, across from the public library; he doesn't like dogs, was mauled by one as a boy. One Tuesday after creative writing club, when Jesse is already out the door and halfway down the hall, Mr. Strane says he has something for me. He opens the bottom drawer of his desk and takes out a book.

"Is this for class?" I ask.

"No," he says. "It's for you." He walks around the desk, puts the book in my hands: *Ariel*, by Sylvia Plath. "Have you read her?"

I shake my head, turn the book over. It's worn, with a blue cloth cover. A scrap of paper sticks out between the pages as a makeshift bookmark.

"She's a bit overdone," Mr. Strane says. "But young women love her."

I don't know what he means by "overdone" but don't want to

ask. I flip through the book—flashes of poems—and stop at the bookmarked page; the title "Lady Lazarus" is capitalized in bold. "Why is this one marked?" I ask.

"Let me show you."

Mr. Strane comes up beside me, turns the page. Standing so close to him feels like being swallowed; my head doesn't reach his shoulder.

"Here." He points to the lines:

Out of the ash
I rise with my red hair
And I eat men like air.

He says, "That reminded me of you." Then he reaches behind me and tugs on my ponytail.

I stare at the book as though I'm studying the poem, but the stanzas blur to black smears on a yellow page. I don't know what I'm supposed to do in response. It feels like I should laugh. I wonder if this is flirting, but it can't be. Flirting is supposed to be fun and this is too heavy for fun.

In a quiet voice, Mr. Strane asks, "Is it ok that it reminded me of you?"

I lick my lips, lift my shoulders. "Sure."

"Because the last thing I want is to overstep."

Overstep. I'm not sure what he means by that, either, but the way he gazes down at me stops me from asking any questions. He suddenly seems both embarrassed and hopeful, like if I told him this wasn't ok, he might start to cry.

So I smile, shake my head. "You're not."

He exhales. "Good," he says, moving away from me, back to his desk. "Give it a read and let me know what you think. Maybe you'll be inspired to write a poem or two."

I leave the classroom and go straight to Gould, where I get into bed and read *Ariel* all the way through. I like the poems, but I'm more interested in figuring out why they reminded him of me and when this reminding might've happened—the afternoon with the leaf, maybe? Maple-red hair. I wonder how long he had this book in his desk drawer, if he waited awhile to decide whether to give it to me. Maybe he had to work up the courage.

I take the scrap of paper he used to mark "Lady Lazarus" and write in neat cursive, *I rise with my red hair*, then pin it to the corkboard above my desk. Adults are the only ones who ever say anything nice about my hair, but this is more than him being nice. He thinks about me. He thinks about me so much, certain things remind him of me. That means something.

I wait a few days before I return *Ariel*, dawdling at the end of class until everyone else leaves and then sliding the book onto his desk.

"Well?" He leans forward on his elbows, eager to hear what I have to say.

I hesitate, scrunch my nose. "She's kind of self-absorbed."

He laughs at that—a real laugh. "That's fair. And I appreciate your honesty."

"But I liked it," I say. "Especially the one you marked."

"I thought you would." He steps over to the built-in bookcases, scans the shelves. "Here," he says, handing me another book—Emily Dickinson. "Let's see what you think of this."

I don't wait to give him back the Dickinson. The next day after class, I drop the book onto his desk and say, "Not a fan."

"You're kidding."

"It was kind of boring."

"Boring!" He presses his palm over his chest. "Vanessa, you're breaking my heart."

"You said you appreciated my honesty," I say with a laugh.

"I do," he says. "I just appreciate it more when I'm in agreement with it."

The next book he gives me is by Edna St. Vincent Millay, who is, according to Mr. Strane, the furthest thing from boring. "And she was a red-haired girl from Maine," he says, "just like you."

I carry his books with me, reading them whenever I can, every spare few minutes and through every meal. I start to realize the point isn't really whether I like the books; it's more about him giving me different lenses to see myself through. The poems are clues to help me understand why he's so interested, what it is exactly that he sees in me.

His attention makes me brave enough to show him drafts of my poems when he asks to read more of my work, and he returns them with critiques—not just praise but real suggestions for making the writing better. He circles words I'm already unsure about and writes, *Best choice?* Other words he crosses out altogether and writes, *You could do better.* On a poem I wrote in the middle of the night, after waking from a dream set in a place that seemed a mix of his classroom and my bedroom back home, he writes, *Vanessa, this one scares me a little.*

I start spending faculty service hour in his classroom, studying at the seminar table while he works at his desk and the windows drape October light over us both. Sometimes other students come in for help on assignments, but most of the time it's only us. He asks me questions about myself, about growing up on Whalesback Lake, what I think of Browick, and what I want to do once I'm older. He says that for me the sky is the limit, that I possess a rare kind of intelligence, something that can't be measured in grades or test scores.

"I worry sometimes about students like you," he says. "Ones who come from tiny towns with run-down schools. It's easy to get overwhelmed and lost at a place like this. But you're doing ok, aren't you?"

I nod yes but wonder what he's imagining when he says "rundown." My old middle school wasn't that bad.

"Just remember," he says, "you're special. You have something these dime-a-dozen overachievers can only dream of." When he says "dime-a-dozen overachievers," he gestures at the empty seats around the seminar table and I think of Jenny—her obsession with grades, how I once walked into our room to find her sobbing in bed with her boots still on, rock salt on her sheets, her precalculus midterm crumpled on the floor. She'd gotten an 88. *Jenny, that's still a B,* I'd said, but it did nothing to console her. She just rolled toward the wall, hiding her face with her hands as she cried.

Another afternoon while he's typing up lesson plans, Mr. Strane says out of nowhere, "I wonder what they think about you spending so much time with me." I don't know who he means by "they"—other students or teachers, or maybe he means everyone, reducing the entire world down to a collective other.

"I wouldn't worry about it," I say.

"Why's that?"

"Because no one ever notices anything I do."

"That isn't true," he says. "I notice you all the time."

I look up from my notebook. He's stopped typing, his fingers resting on top of the keys as he gazes at me, his face so tender it turns my body cold.

After that I imagine him watching me when I'm bleary-eyed at breakfast, when I'm walking downtown, when I'm alone in my room, pulling the elastic from my ponytail and crawling into bed with the latest book he chose for me. In my mind he watches me turn the pages, transfixed by every little thing I do.

Parents' weekend arrives, three days of Browick putting its best foot forward. Friday is a parents-only cocktail hour followed by a school-wide formal dinner in the dining hall with food that never otherwise appears on the menu: roast beef, fingerling potatoes, warm blueberry pie. Parent-teacher conferences are Saturday before lunch, then home games are in the afternoon, and parents who stay until Sunday go downtown in the morning, either to church or out to brunch. Last year mine came to everything, even to Mass on Sunday, but this year Mom tells me, "Vanessa, if we sit through all that stuff again, Dad and I are going to lose our will to live," so they come only Saturday for the conferences. It's fine; Browick is my world, not theirs. They'd probably vote Republican before they'd put one of those I'M A BROWICK PARENT bumper stickers on their car.

After the conferences, they come see my room, Dad in his Red Sox hat and buffalo check flannel and Mom trying to counterbalance him with her sweater set. He wanders around the room, inspecting the bookshelves, while she reclines next to me on the bed and tries to hold my hand.

"Don't," I say as I wrench my hand away.

"Then let me smell your neck," she says. "I've missed your scent."

I lift my shoulder to my ear to ward her off. "That's so weird, Mom," I say. "That's not normal." Last winter break, she asked if she could have my favorite scarf so she could store it in a box and take it out to smell when she missed me. It's the sort of thought I have to push out of my head immediately because otherwise I feel so guilty I can't breathe.

Mom starts describing the conferences, and all I want to know is what Mr. Strane said, but I wait until she works her way through the list of teachers because I don't want to raise suspicion by showing too much interest.

Finally, she says, "Now, your English teacher seems like an interesting man."

"Was that the big bearded guy?" Dad asks.

"Yes, the one who went to Harvard," she says, drawing out the word. *Hah-vahd.* I wonder how it came up, if Mr. Strane somehow dropped into the conversation the fact that he'd gone there or if my parents noticed the diploma hanging on the wall behind his desk.

Mom says again, "A very interesting man."

"What do you mean?" I ask. "What did he say?"

"He said you wrote a good essay last week."

"That's all?"

"Should he have said more?"

I bite down on the inside of my cheek, mortified at the thought of him talking about me as though I were just another student. *She wrote a good essay last week.* Maybe that's all I am to him.

Mom says, "You know who I was not impressed by? That politics teacher, Mr. *Sheldon*." Shooting me a pointed look, she adds, "He seemed like a real asshole."

"Jan, come on," Dad says. He hates it when she swears in front of me.

I push myself off the bed and throw open my closet door, fuss around with my clothes so I won't have to look at them while they debate whether they should stay on campus for dinner or head back home before dark.

"Would you mind awful if we don't stay for dinner?" they ask. I stare at my hanging clothes and mumble that it doesn't matter. When I give them my usual brusque goodbye, I try not to get annoyed when Mom's eyes tear up.

On the Friday before our big Whitman paper is due, Mr. Strane goes around the seminar table and calls on us at random to share our thesis statements. He gives us immediate feedback, deeming our theses either "good but needs work" or "scrap it and start over," and in the process anxiety dissolves us all. Tom Hudson gets "scrap it and start over," and for a second I think he might cry, but when Jenny gets "good but needs work," she really does blink back tears and part of me wants to run around the table, throw my arms around her, and tell Mr. Strane to leave her alone. When we get to my thesis, he says it's perfect.

There's still fifteen minutes left of class after everyone is evaluated, so Mr. Strane tells us to use the rest of the period to fix our theses. I sit, unsure what to do since he called mine perfect as is, and from behind his desk he calls my name. He holds up the poem I gave him at the beginning of class and gestures for me to come to his desk. "Let's have a conference on this," he says. I stand and my chair scrapes against the floor just as Jenny drops her pencil to shake a cramp out of her hand. For a moment our eyes lock, and I feel her watch me walk to his desk.

I sit in the chair next to Mr. Strane and see my poem doesn't have any marks in the margins. "Come a little closer so we can talk quietly," he says, and before I can move, he hooks his fingers around the backrest of my chair and wheels me right beside him so we're less than a foot apart.

If anyone wonders what he and I are doing, they don't show it. Around the seminar table, everyone's head is ducked in concentration. It's as though they're in one world, and Mr. Strane and I are in another. With the heel of his hand, he presses the crease out of my poem from where I folded it and begins to read. He's so close I can smell him—coffee and chalk dust—and as he reads I watch his hands, his flat bitten-down nails, dark hair on his wrists. I wonder why he offered to have a conference if he hadn't yet read the poem. I wonder what he thought of my parents, if he thought they were hicks, Dad in his flannel and Mom clutching her purse to her chest. *Oh, you went to Harvard*, they must have said, their accents opening up in awe.

Pointing his pen at the page, Mr. Strane whispers, "Nessa, I have to ask, did you mean to sound sexy here?"

My eyes dart to the lines he's pointing at:

Violet-bellied & mild, she stirs in her sleep,
kicking back blankets with chipped polish toes,
yawning wide to let him peer inside her.

The question makes me split off from myself, like my body stays beside his while my brain retreats to the seminar table. No one has ever called me sexy before, and only my parents call me Nessa. I wonder if they called me that during the conference. Maybe Mr. Strane noted the nickname and tucked it away for himself.

Did I mean to sound sexy? "I don't know."

He backs away from me, a tiny movement but one I feel, and he says, "I don't mean to embarrass you."

This, I realize, is a test. He wants to see my reaction to being called sexy, and embarrassment means I failed. So I shake my head. "I'm not embarrassed."

He reads on, writes an exclamation point next to another line and whispers, more to himself than to me, "Oh, that is lovely."

Somewhere down the hallway, a door slams. At the seminar table, Gregg Akers cracks his knuckles one at a time and Jenny drags her eraser back and forth over the thesis statement she just can't get right. My eyes drift to the windows and spot something red. Squinting, I see a balloon, its string caught on a bare branch of the maple tree. It floats in the breeze, knocking against leaves and bark. Where would a balloon even come from? I stare at it for what feels like a long time, so focused I don't even blink.

Then Mr. Strane's knee touches my bare thigh, right below the hemline of my skirt. With his eyes still on the poem and the tip of his pen following the lines, his knee nestles against me. I freeze, possum-dead. At the seminar table, nine heads bow in concentration. Out the window, a red balloon hangs limp from a tree limb.

At first I assume he doesn't realize, that he thinks my leg is the desk or the side of the chair. I wait for him to recognize what he's done, to see where his knee drifted and whisper a quick "sorry" and shift away, but his knee stays pressed into me. When I try to be polite and inch away, he moves with me.

"I think we're very similar, Nessa," he whispers. "I can tell from the way you write that you're a dark romantic like me. You like dark things."

Shielded by the desk, he reaches down and pats my knee gently, gingerly, the way you might pet a dog before you're sure it won't turn mean and bite you. I don't bite him. I don't move. I don't even breathe. He keeps writing notes on the poem while his other hand strokes my knee and my mind slips out of me. It brushes up against the ceiling so I can see myself from above—hunched shoulders, thousand-yard stare, bright red hair.

Then class is over. He moves away from me, the spot on my knee cold where his hand has left it, and the room is all motion and sound, zippers zipping and textbooks slamming shut and laughter and words and no one knowing what took place right in front of them.

"Looking forward to the next one," Mr. Strane says. He hands me the marked-up poem as though everything's normal, like what he did never happened.

The nine other students pack up their things and leave the classroom to carry on with their lives, to practices and rehearsals and club meetings. I leave the room, too, but I'm not part of them. They're the same, but I'm changed. I'm unhuman now. Untethered. While they walk across campus, earthbound and ordinary, I soar, trailing a maple-red comet tail. I'm no longer myself; I am no one. I'm a red balloon caught in the boughs of a tree. I'm nothing at all.

2017

I'm at work, staring out across the hotel lobby, when I receive a text from Ira. My body goes rigid as I watch the push alerts pile up on my phone screen, his contact still labeled DON'T DO IT from our last breakup.

> How are you doing?
> I've been thinking about you.
> Would you be up for a drink?

I don't touch the phone; I don't want him to know I've seen the texts, but as I give restaurant recommendations and call in reservations, telling every guest it's my pleasure to serve them, my absolute pleasure, a little fire kindles in my belly. Three months have passed since Ira said we needed to end it once and for all, and I've been good this time. No walking by his apartment building hoping to catch him outside, no calls, no texts—not even drunken ones. This, I think, is my reward for all that self-control.

After two hours, I respond, I'm ok. A drink might be nice. He replies right away: Are you working? I'm with friends eating dinner now. Could stay out and meet you after your shift. My hands tremble while I send a single thumbs-up emoji, as though I can't be bothered to type out "sounds good."

When I leave the hotel at eleven thirty, he's outside leaning against the valet podium, shoulders hunched as he stares down at his phone. Immediately, I notice the changes in him, his shorter hair and trendy clothes, skinny black pants and a denim jacket with holes in the elbows. He jumps when he sees me, slips his phone into his back pocket.

"Sorry it took so long to leave," I say. "Busy night." I stand holding my bag in both hands, not knowing how to greet him, what's allowed.

"It's fine, only been here a few minutes. You look good."

"I look the same," I say.

"Well, you've always looked good." He holds out an arm, offering a hug, but I shake my head. He's being too nice. If he wanted to get back together, he'd be guarded and skittish like me.

"You look very . . ." I search for the right word. "Hip." I mean it as a jab, but Ira just laughs and thanks me, his voice sincere.

We go to a new bar with distressed wood tables and metal chairs, a five-page beer menu organized by style, then country of origin, then alcohol volume. As we step inside, I scan the room, checking each head of long blond hair for Taylor Birch, though I'm not sure I'd recognize her even if she appeared right in front of me. The past couple weeks, I'll see women on the street I'm certain are her, but every time it's only a stranger with a face that isn't even close.

"Vanessa?" Ira touches my shoulder, startles me as though I've forgotten he's there. "You ok?"

I nod and give a thin smile, grab an empty chair.

When the server comes around and starts to rattle off recommendations, I interrupt. "This is too overwhelming. Just bring me whatever and I'll like it." I mean it as a joke, but it comes out harsh; Ira gives the server a look, like *I'm sorry for her.*

"We could have gone somewhere else," he says to me.

"This is fine."

"It seems like you hate it here."

"I hate everywhere."

The server brings the beers—some dark, wine-smelling thing in a goblet for Ira and, for me, a can of Miller Lite.

"Do you want a glass," the server asks, "or can you manage?"

"Oh, I *can* manage." I smile and point to the can, my best attempt at charming. The server just turns to the next table.

Ira gives me a long look. "Are you doing ok? Tell me the truth."

I shrug, take a drink. "Sure."

"I saw the Facebook post."

With my fingernail, I flick the pull tab on the beer. *Click-click-click.* "What Facebook post?"

He frowns. "The one about Strane. Have you really not seen it? Last I checked, it's been shared something like two thousand times."

"Oh, right. That." It's actually up to almost three thousand shares, though the activity has died down. I take another swallow, flip through the beer menu.

Softly, Ira says, "I've been worrying about you."

"You shouldn't. I'm fine."

"Have you talked to him since it came out?"

I smack the menu shut. "Nope."

Ira studies me. "Really?"

"Really."

He asks if I think Strane will be fired and I lift my shoulders between swallows. How should I know? He asks if I've thought about reaching out to Taylor and I don't answer, just flick the pull tab, the *click-click-click* now a *boing-boing-boing* echo through the half-empty can.

"I know how hard this must be for you," he says, "but it could be an opportunity, right? To make peace with it and move on."

I force myself to breathe through the thought. "Make peace and move on" sounds like jumping off a cliff, sounds like dying.

"Can we talk about something else?" I ask.

"Sure," he says. "Of course."

He asks me about work, if I'm still looking for a new job. He tells me he found an apartment up on Munjoy Hill and my heart jumps, a delusional moment of thinking he's going to ask me to move in with him. It's a great place, he says, really big. The kitchen can fit a table; the bedroom has an ocean view. I wait, expecting him to invite me over at least, but he only lifts his glass.

"Must be expensive if it's that nice," I say. "How are you managing that?"

Ira presses his lips together as he swallows. "I lucked out."

I assume we'll keep drinking—that's what he and I usually do, drink and drink until one of us gets brave enough to ask, "Are you coming home with me or what?"—but before I can order another beer, Ira gives the server his credit card, signaling the end of the night. It feels like a slap.

As we step out of the bar and into the cold, he asks if I'm still seeing Ruby and I'm grateful that, at least for this question, I don't have to lie to give him the answer he wants.

"I'm so glad to hear that," Ira says. "That really is the best thing for you."

I try to smile, but I don't like how he says "the best thing for you." It brings up too much—memories of him saying the way I romanticized abuse was troubling, almost as troubling as the fact that I still kept in touch with the man who abused me. From the very beginning Ira said I needed help. After six months together, he gave me a list of therapists he'd researched himself, begged me to try. When I refused, he said if I loved him, I would try, and I said if he loved me, he would leave it alone. After a year, he tried to turn it into an ultimatum, either I go to therapy or we break up. Not even that moved me; he was the one who caved. So when I started seeing Ruby, even if I was going only because of my dad, Ira still acted triumphant. *Whatever it takes to get you in there, Vanessa,* he'd said.

"So what does Ruby think of everything?" he asks.

"What do you mean?"

"The Facebook post, what he did to that girl . . ."

"Oh. We don't really talk about that stuff." My eyes follow the brick pattern in the sidewalk under the streetlights, the fog rolling in off the water.

For two blocks, Ira doesn't say anything. When we reach Congress Street, where I turn left and he turns right, my chest aches from wanting to ask him to come home with me even though I'm nowhere near drunk enough, even though spending a half hour with him has already made me hate myself. I just need to be touched.

Ira says, "You haven't told her."

"I've told her."

He tilts his head, squints. "Really. You've told your therapist that the man who abused you when you were a kid was publicly accused of abuse by someone else and that's not something you two talk about? Come on."

I lift my shoulders. "It's not that important to me."

"Right."

"And he didn't abuse me."

Ira's nostrils flare and his eyes harden, a familiar flash of frustration. He turns like he's going to leave—better to walk away than lose his temper with me—but then he turns back. "Does she even know about him?"

"I don't go to therapy to talk about that stuff, ok? I go because of my dad."

It's midnight. Far-off bells chime from the cathedral, the traffic light switches from red-yellow-green to flashing yellow, and Ira shakes his head. He's disgusted at me. I know what he thinks, what anyone would think—that I'm an apologist, an enabler—but I'm defending myself just as much as I am Strane. Because even if I sometimes use the word *abuse* to describe certain things that were done to me, in someone else's mouth the word turns ugly and absolute. It swallows up everything that happened. It swallows me and all the times I wanted it, begged for it. Like the laws that flatten all the sex I had with Strane before I turned eighteen into legal rape—are we supposed to believe that birthday is magic? It's as arbitrary a marker as any. Doesn't it make sense that some girls are ready sooner?

"You know," Ira says, "these past few weeks while this has been in the news, all I've been thinking about is you. I've worried about you."

Headlights approach, brighter and brighter, and sweep over us as the car turns the corner.

"I thought you'd be a mess over what that girl wrote, but you hardly seem to care."

"Why should I?"

"Because he did the same thing to you!" he yells, his voice bouncing against the buildings. He sucks in a breath and stares at the ground, embarrassed at losing his temper. No one has ever frustrated him as much as I do. He used to say that all the time.

"You shouldn't care so much, Ira," I say.

He scoffs, laughs. "Believe me, I know I shouldn't."

"I don't want your help with this. You don't understand it. You never have."

He tips his head back. "Well, this was my last attempt. I won't try again."

As he starts to walk away, I call, "She's lying."

He stops, turns.

"The girl who wrote the post, I mean. It's a bunch of lies."

I wait, but Ira doesn't speak, doesn't move. Another set of headlights approach and then pass over us.

"Do you believe me?" I ask.

Ira shakes his head, but not in an angry way. He feels sorry for me, which is worse than worrying about me, worse than anything.

"What's it going to take, Vanessa?" he asks.

He starts up Congress Street toward the hill and then calls over his shoulder, "By the way, the new apartment? I can afford it because I'm seeing someone. We moved in together."

Walking backward, he watches my expression, but I don't reveal a thing. I swallow against my burning throat and blink so fast he blurs into a shadow, into fog.

I'm still sleeping at noon when I hear the special ringtone I've assigned to Strane's number in my phone. It inserts itself in my dream, a tinkling jewelry box melody that pulls me out of sleep so gently I'm still half dreaming when I answer.

"They're meeting today," he says. "They're deciding what to do with me."

I blink awake; my groggy mind fumbles with who he means by "they." "The school?"

"I know what's coming," he says. "I've taught there for thirty years and they're tossing me out with the trash. Just wish they'd get it over with."

"Well, they're monsters," I say.

"I wouldn't go that far. Their hands are tied," he says. "If there's a monster here it's the story what's-her-name came up with. She managed to accuse me of something just vague enough to be terrifying. It's like a goddamn horror movie."

"Sounds more like Kafka to me," I say.

I hear him smile. "I guess you're right."

"So you're not teaching today?"

"No, they barred me from campus until they decide. Feel like a criminal." He exhales a long breath. "Look, I'm in Portland. I wondered if I could see you."

"You're here?" I scramble out of bed and down the hallway to the bathroom. My stomach twists at the sight of myself in the mirror, the fine lines around my mouth and under my eyes that seemed to appear as soon as I turned thirty.

"Are you still at the same apartment?" he asks.

"No, I moved. Five years ago."

A beat of silence. "Can you give me some directions?"

I think of the dishes in the kitchen sink caked with food, the overflowing trash can, the lived-in filth. I imagine him stepping into my bedroom and seeing the piles of dirty laundry, the empty bottles lined up alongside the mattress, my perpetual mess.

You need to get over this, he'd say. *Vanessa, you're thirty-two years old.*

"What about a coffee shop instead?" I ask.

He sits at a corner table, at first barely recognizable, a heavyset old man cupping his hands around a coffee mug, but as I move toward him, cutting through the line at the counter, weaving through chairs, he sees me and stands. Then he's unmistakable—the six-foot-four mountain, solid and safe and so familiar my body takes over, throwing my arms around him and grabbing fistfuls of his coat, trying to get as close as it can. Sinking into him feels the same way it did when I was fifteen—that coffee and chalk dust smell, the top of my head barely reaching his shoulder.

When he lets go of me, there are tears in his eyes. Embarrassed, he shoves his glasses up on his forehead and wipes his cheeks.

"I'm sorry," he says. "I know the last thing you want to deal with is a blubbering old man. The sight of you just . . ." Trailing off, he takes in my face.

"It's fine," I say. "You're fine." My eyes are teary, too.

We sit across from each other as though we're ordinary, like people who once knew each other catching up after time apart. He looks alarmingly older, gray all over, and not only his hair, even his skin and eyes. His beard's gone, the first time I've ever seen him without it, replaced with jowls I can't look at without wanting to gag. They hang like jellyfish, pull his whole face downward. It's a shocking change. Five years have passed since I saw him last, long enough for age to ravage a face, but I imagine this happening since Taylor's post, like the myth about people being so overcome with grief they go gray overnight. A sudden thought turns me cold—maybe this could wreck him. It could kill him.

I shake my head to ward off the thought and say, more to myself than to him, "This could all end up ok."

"It could," he agrees. "But it won't."

"Even if they force you out, would that be so bad? It would be like retiring. You could sell the house and leave Norumbega. What about going back to Montana?"

"I don't want that," he says. "My life is here."

"You could travel, have a real vacation."

"Vacation," he scoffs. "Give me a break. No matter what comes of this, my name is ruined, reputation destroyed."

"It'll blow over eventually."

"It won't." His eyes flash hard enough to stop me from pointing out that I know what I'm talking about, that I was once driven out of there, too.

"Vanessa . . ." He leans forward on the table. "You said the girl wrote to you a few weeks ago. You're sure you didn't respond?"

I give him a long look. "Yes, I'm sure."

"And I don't know if you're still seeing that psychiatrist." He bites his bottom lip, leaves the question unsaid.

I start to correct him—she's a therapist, not a psychiatrist—but I know it doesn't matter; that's not the point. "She has no idea. I don't talk to her about you."

"Ok," he says. "That's good. Now also about that old blog of yours, I tried looking it up—"

"It's gone. I took it down years ago. Why are you grilling me like this?"

"Has anyone other than that girl contacted you?"

"Who else would? The school?"

"I don't know," he says. "I'm just making sure—"

"You think they'll try to get me involved?"

"I have no idea. They're not telling me anything."

"But do you think they'll—"

"Vanessa." My mouth snaps shut. He hangs his head, takes a

breath, and then continues slowly. "I don't know what they're going to do. I just want to make sure there aren't any stray fires that need putting out. And I want to make sure you're feeling . . ." He searches for the right word. "Steady."

"Steady," I echo.

He nods, his eyes fixed on me, asking the question he doesn't dare speak out loud—if I'm strong enough to handle whatever might come.

"You can trust me," I say.

He smiles, gratitude softening his face. There's relief in him now, a looseness to his shoulders, his eyes roaming the coffee shop. "So how are you?" he asks. "How's your mom holding up?"

I shrug; talking about her with him always feels like a betrayal.

"Are you still seeing that boy?" He means Ira. I shake my head and, unsurprised, Strane nods, pats my hand. "He wasn't right for you."

We sit in silence through the clatter of dishes, the hiss and whirr of the espresso machine, my thumping heart. For years, I've imagined this—being in front of him again, within reach—but now that I'm here, I just feel outside myself, like I'm watching from a table across the room. It doesn't seem right that we can speak to each other like normal people, or that he can bear to look at me without falling to his knees.

"Are you hungry?" he asks. "We could get a bite."

I hesitate, check my phone for the time, and he notices my black suit and gold name tag.

"Ah, working girl," he says. "Still at that hotel, I take it."

"I could call in."

"No, don't do that." He sits back in his chair, his mood instantly darkened. I know what's wrong; I should have jumped at his offer, said yes right away. Hesitating was a mistake, and with him, one mistake is enough to ruin the whole thing.

"I can try to get out early," I say. "We could go to dinner."

He waves his hand. "It's all right."

"You could spend the night." At that, he stops, his eyes traveling over my face as he contemplates the idea. I wonder if he's thinking of me at fifteen, or if he's thinking of the last time we tried, five years ago, at his house, in his bed with the flannel sheets. We tried to re-create the first time, me in flimsy pajamas, the lights low. It didn't work. He kept going soft; I was too old. Afterward, I cried in the bathroom, the tap running and my hand clamped over my mouth. When I came out, he was dressed and sitting in the living room. We never spoke of it again, and since then stuck to the phone.

"No," he says softly. "No, I should get back home."

"Fine." I push out of my chair so hard it squeaks against the floor, like nails across a chalkboard. My nails on his chalkboard.

He watches as I slide my arms into my coat and heft my purse to my shoulder. "How long have you been at that job?"

I lift my shoulders, my brain snagged on a memory of his fingers in my mouth, chalk dust on my tongue. "I don't know," I say faintly. "Awhile."

"It's been too long," he says. "You should love what you do. Don't settle for less."

"It's fine. It's a job."

"But you were made for more than that," he says. "You were so bright. You were brilliant. I thought you were going to publish a novel at twenty, take over the world. Have you tried writing lately?"

I shake my head.

"God, what a waste. I wish you would."

I press my lips together. "Sorry I'm a disappointment."

"Come on, don't do that." He stands, cups my face in his hands and lowers his voice to a murmur as he tries to settle me down. "I'll come stay with you soon," he says. "I promise."

We exchange a close-lipped kiss goodbye, and the barista at the counter keeps counting the tip jar, the old man by the window continues his crossword puzzle. Him kissing me used to be fodder for rumors that spread like wildfire. Now when we touch each other, the world doesn't even notice. I know there should be freedom in that, but to me it only feels like loss.

At home after work, I lie in bed with my phone, reading over the message Taylor Birch sent me before posting the accusations against Strane. Hi Vanessa, I'm not sure if you know anything about me, but you and I are in the strange position of sharing an experience, something that, for me, was traumatic and I'm guessing it was the same for you. X-ing out of the window, I bring up her profile but nothing new is posted, so I scroll through the old content: photos of her on vacation in San Francisco, eating Mission burritos, a selfie with the Golden Gate Bridge in the background, photos of her at home in her apartment, crushed velvet couch, gleaming hardwood floors, and leafy houseplants. I scroll further back to photos of her in a pink pussy hat from the Women's March, eating a doughnut as big as her head, and posing with friends at a bar downtown in a photo captioned Browick reunion!

I move to my own profile, try to see myself through her eyes. I know she checks on me; a year ago, she liked one of my photos, an accidental double tap she immediately undid, but I still saw the notification. I took a screenshot and sent it to Strane, along with I guess she can't let go, but he didn't respond, uninterested in the nuances of social media, the smug sense of triumph that comes when a lurker shows her hand. Or maybe he didn't even understand what I meant. I forget sometimes exactly how old he is; I used to think the gap between us would shrink as I grew older, but it's still as wide as it's ever been.

Hours pass while I dig deeper on my phone, logging into my old photo hosting accounts and scrolling back in time, 2017 to 2010 to 2007 to 2002—the year I first bought a digital camera, the year I turned seventeen. My breath catches as the photo set I'm looking for finally loads: me with my hair in braids, wearing a sundress and knee socks, standing before a grove of birch trees. In one photo, I'm lifting the skirt of my dress, flashing pale thighs. In another, I'm turned away from the camera, looking over my shoulder. The quality of the photos is low, but they're still lovely, the birches a monochrome backdrop against the pinks and blues of the dress, my copper hair.

I open my last texts with Strane, copy and paste the photos into a new message. Not sure if I ever showed these to you. I think I'm 17 here.

I know he would've gone to bed hours ago but I hit "send" anyway, watch the text deliver. I stay awake till dawn, swiping through photos of my teenage face and body. Every once in a while I check if the text to Strane has changed from "delivered" to "read." There's a chance he could wake in the night and, half asleep, check his phone only to find my teenage self, a digital ghost. Don't forget her.

Sometimes it feels like that's all I'm doing every time I reach out—trying to haunt, to drag him back in time, asking him to tell me again what happened. Make me understand it once and for all. Because I'm still stuck here. I can't move on.

2000

One Friday night per month, a dance is held in the dining hall. With the tables cleared away and the lights dimmed, it's a scene that could be set in any other high school. There's the hired DJ, a cluster of people dancing in the middle of the floor, and the shy kids huddled around the perimeter, divided by gender. Some teachers are there, too. As chaperones, they mill about, maintaining their distance, paying less attention to us than to each other.

This is the Halloween dance, so people are wearing costumes and two giant buckets of candy sit by the double doors. Most costumes are lazy—boys in jeans and white T-shirts calling themselves James Dean, girls in pleated miniskirts and pigtails calling themselves Britney Spears—but a few have gone to elaborate lengths with supplies bought downtown. One girl moves through the dining hall as a dragon with spiny wings and a train of blue-green scales, trailed by her boyfriend, a knight in cardboard armor stinking of spray paint. A boy in a suit waves a fake cigar in girls' faces, laughing behind a rubber Bill Clinton mask. Meanwhile, I'm a half-hearted cat, black dress and black tights, drawn-on whiskers and cardboard ears thrown together in ten minutes. I came only to see Mr. Strane. He's working as a chaperone.

Usually, I never go to the dances. Everything about them makes me cringe—the bad music, the embarrassing DJ with his goatee and frosted tips, the kids pretending not to stare at the couples grinding against each other. I'm forcing myself to suffer through this one because it's been a week. A whole week since Mr. Strane touched me, since he put his hand on my leg and told me he could tell we were similar, two people who like dark things. Since then? Nothing. When I spoke in class, his eyes darted to the table like he couldn't bear to look at me. During creative writing club he gathered his things and left Jesse and me alone ("Department meeting," he explained, but if it was a department meeting, why did he need his coat and everything in his briefcase?), and later when I sought him out during faculty service hour, his door was closed, the classroom dark behind textured glass.

So I'm impatient, maybe even desperate. I want something to happen and that seems more likely at an event like this where boundaries are temporarily blurred, students and teachers thrust together in a dimly lit room. I don't really care what the something else might be—another touch, a compliment. It doesn't matter so long as it tells me what he wants, what this is, if it's anything at all.

I eat a fun-size candy bar in tiny bites and watch the couples dance to a slow song, swaying around the floor like bottles in a pool of water. At one point, Jenny strides across the room wearing a satin dress that vaguely resembles a kimono, chopsticks shoved through her nubby ponytail. For a moment she seems to be headed straight for me and I freeze, chocolate melting on my tongue, but then Tom emerges from behind her wearing his normal clothes, jeans and a Beck T-shirt, not even attempting a costume. He touches her shoulder; Jenny jerks away. The music is too loud to eavesdrop, but it's obvious they're fighting and that it's bad. Jenny's chin wobbles, her eyes screw shut. When Tom touches his fingers to her arm, she plants a hand flat on his chest and shoves him so strongly he stumbles backward. It's the first time I've ever seen them fight.

I'm so fixated that I almost don't notice Mr. Strane duck out the double doors. I almost let him get away.

When I step outside, the night is pitch black, no moon and close to freezing. The sounds from the dance muffle to a heartbeat bass line and faraway vocals as the door clicks shut behind me. I look around; my arms break into goose bumps as my eyes search for him but find only the shadows of trees, the empty campus green. I'm about to admit defeat and go back inside when a figure steps out from under the shadow cast by a spruce tree: Mr. Strane in a down vest, a flannel shirt, and jeans, an unlit cigarette between his fingers.

I don't move, unsure what to do. I sense he's embarrassed to be seen with the cigarette and my mind takes over—I imagine him smoking in secret, like how my dad does in the evenings down by the lakeshore; I imagine he wants to quit and sees his inability to do so as a weakness. He's ashamed of it.

But even if he's ashamed, I think, *he could have stayed hidden. He could have let me leave.*

He twirls the cigarette between his thumb and forefinger. "You caught me."

"I thought you were leaving," I say. "I wanted to say goodbye."

He pulls a lighter from his pocket and turns it over in his palm a few times. His eyes stay on me. With a sudden clarity, I think, *Something's going to happen,* and as the certainty of this settles over me, my heart slows, my shoulders drop.

He lights the cigarette and gestures for me to follow him back under the tree. It's enormous, probably the biggest on campus, its lowest limbs still far above our heads. At first, it's so dark all I can see is the red ember from the cigarette as it moves up to his mouth. My eyes adjust and he appears, as do the boughs overhead, the orange-dead needle carpet beneath our feet.

"Don't smoke," Mr. Strane says. "It's a nasty habit." He exhales and the cigarette smell fills my head. We're standing about five feet apart. It feels so dangerous it's strange to think we've been closer plenty of times before.

"But it must feel good," I say. "Otherwise why do it?"

He laughs, takes another drag. "I guess you're right." Looking me over, he notices my costume for the first time. "Well, look at you. Little pussy cat."

I laugh from the shock of hearing him say that word, even if he isn't using it in the sex way. But he doesn't laugh. He only stares at me, the cigarette smoking in his hand.

"You know what I'd like to do right now?" he asks. His words flow together more than usual and he sways as he points the cigarette at me. "I'd like to find you a big bed, tuck you in, and kiss you good night."

For a second, my brain short-circuits entirely and I'm as good as dead. Moments of nothing pass, a static screen, a wall of noise. Then I come roaring back to life with a harsh, choked sound—not quite a laugh, not quite a cry.

A door opens from inside the dining hall and music spills out from the dance. Over that, a woman's voice calls, "Jake?"

The moment sputters. Mr. Strane turns and hurries toward the voice, throwing down his cigarette without stamping it out. I watch the smoke rise from the fallen needles as he strides back to the doors, to Ms. Thompson.

"Just taking a bit of a breather," he says to her. Together, they slip back inside. I'm hidden by the tree, like he was when I first came outside. She didn't see me.

I stare down at the smoking cigarette, consider picking it up and bringing it to my lips, but instead grind it out with my heel. I return to the dance, find Deanna Perkins and Lucy Summers swigging from a Nalgene bottle as they hold a running commentary on everyone's costumes. Strane stands only a few feet away beside Ms. Thompson, his eyes locked on her. Jenny and Tom stand close together on the periphery of the dance floor, their fight resolved. She winds her arm around his shoulders, nuzzles her face into his neck. It's a gesture so intimate and adult, I instinctively look away.

Whatever they have in the Nalgene bottle sloshes around as Deanna and Lucy pass it back and forth. Deanna, taking a swallow, notices my stare. "What?"

"Let me have some," I say.

Lucy reaches for the bottle. "Sorry, limited supplies."

"I'll tell if you don't let me."

"Shut up."

Deanna waves her hand. "Let her have a drink."

Lucy sighs, holds out the bottle. "You can have a *sip*."

The alcohol burns my throat worse than I expected and I start to cough, like a cliché. Deanna and Lucy don't even try to hide their laughs. Thrusting the bottle back at them, I march out of the dining hall, willing Mr. Strane to notice, to understand why I'm angry and what I want. I wait outside to see if he'll come after me but he doesn't—of course he doesn't.

Back in Gould, the dorm is quiet, empty. Every door is closed, everyone still at the dance.

I stare down Ms. Thompson's apartment door at the far end of the hall. If she hadn't called to him, something would have happened. He said he wanted to kiss me; maybe he would have done it. Still in my costume, I walk toward Ms. Thompson's door. Mr. Strane is probably making her laugh right this moment. At the end of the night, they'll probably go to his house and have sex. Maybe he'll even tell her about me, how I followed him outside and he said that stuff just to be nice. *She has a crush on you,* Ms. Thompson will say, teasing. As though it's all in my head, a narrative sprung without a source.

I grab the marker attached to her dry erase board. Notes from the previous week are still scribbled there: the date and time of a dorm meeting, an open invitation to a spaghetti dinner in her apartment. With one swipe of my hand, I erase the notes and write *BITCH* in big bold letters that take up the whole board.

The first snow comes that night after the dance and covers campus in a heavy four inches. On Saturday morning Ms. Thompson calls us all into the common room and tries to find out who wrote *bitch* on her door. "I'm not mad," she assures us. "Just confused."

My heart thumps in my ears and I sit with my hands clasped in my lap, willing my cheeks not to burn.

After a few minutes of sitting in silence, she gives up. "We can let it go," she says. "But not if it happens again. Ok?"

She nods, prompting us to say ok. On my way back upstairs I look over my shoulder and see her standing in the middle of the empty room, rubbing her face with both hands.

Sunday afternoon I approach her door, my eyes lingering on the whiteboard, *bitch* still faintly visible. I feel guilty—not enough to admit what I did, but enough to want to do something nice. When Ms. Thompson opens the door, she's in sweatpants and a hooded Browick sweatshirt, her hair pulled back, no makeup on her face, acne scars on her cheeks. I wonder if Mr. Strane has ever seen her this way.

"What's up?" she asks.

"Can I take Mya for a walk?"

"Oh god, she'd love that." She calls over her shoulder, but the husky is already barreling toward me, ears pricked and blue eyes dilated, propelled by the sound of the word *walk*.

Ms. Thompson reminds me that it will be dark soon as I slide Mya's harness over her head and clip the leash. "We won't go far," I say.

"And don't let her run."

"I know, I know." Last time I took Mya for a walk, I let her off-leash to play and she ran straight into the garden behind the arts building and rolled in fertilizer.

The temperature rose overnight to fifty degrees and the snow is already gone, leaving the ground spongy and slick. We walk the trail that winds around the sports fields, and I let the leash out long so Mya can sniff and romp around, darting from side to side. I love Mya; she's the most beautiful dog I've ever seen, her fur so thick my fingers disappear to the second knuckle when I give her back a good scritch. Mostly, though, I love her because she's difficult.

Bossy. If she doesn't want to do something, she'll talk back at you in a grumbly howl. Ms. Thompson says I must have a special gift with dogs because Mya doesn't really like anyone except me. Dogs are easy to win over, though, way easier than people. For a dog to love you, all you have to do is keep some treats in your pocket and scratch behind their ears or at the base of their tail. When they want to be left alone, they don't play games; they let you know.

At the soccer field, the trail forks into three smaller paths. One leads back to campus, the other into the woods, and the third downtown. Even though I promised Ms. Thompson I'd stay close, I take the third path.

The storefronts downtown are decorated for the season with fake foliage and cornucopias, and the bakery has already hung Christmas lights. As Mya pulls me along, I check my reflection in every window, a two-second glimpse of my hair fanning out from my face, possibly beautiful, though it seems equally possible I might be ugly. When we get to the public library, I stop. Impatient, Mya looks back at me, flashing the whites of her blue eyes as I stand staring at the house across the street. His house—that has to be it. It's smaller than I imagined it to be, with grayed cedar shingles and a dark blue door. Mya sidles up beside me, bumps her head against my legs. *Let's go.*

This is, of course, the whole reason I came this way, why I wanted to go for a walk in the first place and asked Ms. Thompson if I could borrow the dog. I'd imagined myself passing by as he happened to be outside. He would see me and call me over, ask why I was walking Ms. Thompson's dog. We would talk a bit, standing on the strip of front lawn, and then he'd invite me inside. There the fantasy fizzles out, because what we do after that depends on what he wants, and I have no idea what he wants.

But he isn't outside and it doesn't look like he's inside, either. The windows are dark, no car in the driveway. He's somewhere else, living a life that I know infuriatingly little about.

I lead Mya to the top of the library steps. We're hidden there but still have a view of the street. I sit feeding her bacon bits I stole from the dining hall salad bar until the sun blazes orange and starts to set. Maybe he wouldn't even want me to come inside because of the dog. I forgot he said he doesn't like them. But he'd have to at least pretend to like Mya if he's doing whatever with Ms. Thompson, otherwise how could she live with herself? It would be a real betrayal to date someone who hated your dog.

It's nearly dark when a boxy blue station wagon turns into the driveway. The engine cuts, the driver's door opens, and Mr. Strane emerges in jeans and the same flannel shirt he wore at the Halloween dance on Friday. Holding my breath, I watch him haul grocery bags from the back of the car up the front steps. At the door, he fumbles with his keys, and Mya lets out an indignant whine for more treats. I give her a whole handful and she eats them as fast as she can, her tongue lapping my palm while I watch the windows of the little saltbox house light up as Mr. Strane moves through the rooms.

After class on Monday, I take my time leaving. Once everyone else is gone, I swing my backpack onto one shoulder and say in my most nonchalant voice, "You live across from the public library, right?"

From behind his desk, Mr. Strane looks at me in surprise. "How do you know that?" he asks.

"You mentioned it once."

He studies me, and the longer he does, the harder it is to keep up the nonchalant act. I purse my lips together, try to hold my frown.

"I don't remember that," he says.

"Well, you did. How else would I know?" My voice sounds harsh, angry, and I can tell he's a little taken aback. Mostly, though, he looks amused, like he thinks my frustration is cute. "I might've gone there," I add. "You know, to scope it out."

"I see."

"Are you mad?"

"Not at all. I'm flattered."

"I saw you unloading groceries from your car."

"You did? When?"

"Yesterday."

"You were watching me."

I nod.

"You should have made yourself known and said hello."

My eyes narrow. That isn't what I expected him to say. "What if someone saw me?"

He smiles, cocks his head. "Why would it matter if someone saw you saying hello to me?"

I clench my jaw and breathe hard through my nose. His innocence feels put on, like he's playing with me by playing dumb.

Still smiling, he leans back in his chair, and him doing that—leaning back, crossing his arms, looking me up and down as though I'm entertaining, just something to look at—makes anger flare up inside me, so sudden and strong I ball my hands into fists to stop from screaming, lunging forward, grabbing the Harvard mug off his desk and hurling it at his face.

I turn on my heel, stomp out of the room and down the hallway. I'm furious the whole way back to Gould, but once I'm in my room, the anger disappears and all that's left is the dull-ache desire for meaning I've had for weeks now. He said he wanted to kiss me. He *touched* me. Every interaction between us is tinged now with something potentially ruinous, and it isn't fair for him to pretend otherwise.

My midsemester geometry grade is a D-plus. All eyes turn on me when Mrs. Antonova announces this during our monthly advisee meeting at the Italian restaurant. At first I don't realize she's talking to me; my mind drifts as I methodically tear apart a piece of bread and roll it back into dough between my fingers.

"*Vanessa*," she says, rapping her knuckles against the table. "D-plus."

I look up and notice the stares, Mrs. Antonova holding a piece of paper, her own faculty feedback. "Then I guess there's nowhere for me to go but up," I say.

Mrs. Antonova stares at me over the top of her glasses. "You could still go down," she says. "You could fail."

"I won't fail."

"You need a plan of action, a tutor. We'll get you one."

I glower down at the table as she moves on to the next advisee, my stomach tight at the thought of a tutor, because tutor sessions meet during faculty service hour, which would mean less time with Mr. Strane. Kyle Guinn flashes me a sympathetic smile after he's given similar news about his Spanish grade, and I sink so low in my chair my chin practically rests on the table.

When I get back to campus, the Gould common room is crowded, the TV playing election results. I squeeze onto one of the couches and watch the states get sorted into two columns as the polls close. "Vermont for Gore," the news anchor says. "Kentucky for Bush." At one point, when Ralph Nader flashes on-screen, Deanna and Lucy start to clap, and when Bush comes on, everybody boos. It looks like a sure thing for Gore until right before ten, when they announce they're putting Florida back in the "too close to call" column, and I get so fed up with the entire thing I give up and go to bed.

At first everyone jokes about the election never ending, but it stops being funny when the Florida recount goes into full swing. Mr. Sheldon spends most days with his feet propped up on his desk, but now he springs to life, drawing sprawling webs on the chalkboard meant to illustrate the many ways democracy can fail. During one class he lectures us on all the different kinds of chads—hanging, fat, pregnant—while we try not to laugh and shoot looks at Chad Gagnon.

Meanwhile in American lit, we read *A River Runs Through It* and Mr. Strane tells us his own stories of growing up in Montana—ranches and real-life cowboys, dogs eaten by grizzlies, mountains so big they block out the sun. I try to imagine him as a boy, but I can't even picture what he'd look like without a beard. After *A River Runs Through It*, we start on Robert Frost and Mr. Strane recites "The Road Not Taken" from memory. He says we shouldn't feel uplifted by the poem, that Frost's message is widely misunderstood. The poem isn't meant to be a celebration of going against the grain but rather an ironic performance about the futility of choice. He says that by believing our lives have endless possibilities, we stave off the horrifying truth that to live is merely to move forward through time while an internal clock counts down to a final, fatal moment.

"We're born, we live, we die," he says, "and the choices we make in the middle, all those things we agonize over day after day, none of those matter in the end."

No one says anything to counter his argument, not even Hannah Levesque, who is super Catholic and presumably believes that the choices we make actually matter quite a bit in the end. She only stares at him with her lips slightly parted, dumbstruck.

Mr. Strane passes out copies of another Frost poem, "Putting in the Seed," and tells us to read this one silently to ourselves, and after we finish doing that, he tells us to do it again. "But this time, as you read it," he says, "I want you to think about sex."

It takes a second to sink in, for furrowed brows to give way to flushed cheeks, but once it does Mr. Strane surveys the palpable embarrassment with a smile.

Only I'm not embarrassed. The mention of sex smacks me across the face and makes my body run hot. Maybe this is about me. Maybe this is his next move.

"Are you saying this poem is about sex?" Jenny asks.

"I'm saying that it deserves to be read closely and with an open mind," Mr. Strane says. "And let's be honest here, I'm not asking any of you to think about something you don't already spend a significant amount of time contemplating. Now get to it." He claps his hands to signal we should start.

On the second read through the poem, with sex at the forefront of my mind, I do notice things I didn't before: the details of white soft petals, smooth bean and wrinkled pea, the final image of an arched body. Even the phrase "putting in the seed" is obviously suggestive.

"What do you think of it now?" Mr. Strane stands with his back to the chalkboard, one foot crossed over the other. We say nothing, but our silence only proves him right, that the poem is about sex after all.

He waits and his eyes travel the room, seem to look at every student except for me. Tom takes a breath, about to speak, but the bell rings and Mr. Strane shakes his head at us as though disappointed.

"You're all puritans," he says, waving his hand in dismissal.

As we leave the classroom and start down the hallway, Tom says, "What the hell was that?" and with a brisk authority that makes me seethe, Jenny says, "He's a huge misogynist. My sister warned me."

Later, Jesse doesn't show at creative writing club and the classroom feels enormous with just me and Mr. Strane. I sit at the seminar table and he behind his desk, each of us staring at the other across a vast continent.

"There isn't much for you to do today," he says. "The lit journal is in good shape. We can start copyediting when Jesse's here to help."

"Should I go?"

"Not if you want to stay."

Of course I want to stay. I take my notebook from my backpack and open it to the poem I drafted the night before.

"What did you think of class today?" he asks. The low sun cuts through the now-skeletal red maple tree and into the classroom. Behind his desk, Mr. Strane is a shadow.

Before I can answer, he adds, "I ask because I saw your face. You looked like a startled little fawn. I expected the rest of them to be scandalized, but not you."

So he was looking at me. Scandalized. I think of Jenny calling him a misogynist, how narrow-minded and ordinary she sounded. I'm not like that. I don't ever want to be that.

"I wasn't. I liked the class." I shield my eyes so I can make out his features, his tender-condescending smile. I haven't seen that smile in weeks.

"I'm relieved," he says. "I was starting to wonder if I'd been wrong about you."

My breath catches at the thought of being so close to a serious misstep. One wrong reaction on my part could wreck this whole thing.

He reaches down then and opens his bottom desk drawer, pulls out a book, and my ears prick like a dog's. Pavlovian—we learned about that in my psychology elective last spring.

"Is that for me?" I ask.

He makes a face, like he isn't sure. "If I lend you this, you have to promise me not to let anyone know it was me who gave it to you."

I crane my neck, try to read the book's title. "Is it illegal or something?"

He laughs—really laughs, like when I called Sylvia Plath self-absorbed. "Vanessa, how do you always manage to have the perfect response even to things you don't understand?"

I scowl at that. I don't like the idea of him thinking there are things I don't understand. "What's the book?"

He brings it over, the cover still hidden. I grab it as soon as he sets it down. Flipping the paperback over, I see a pair of skinny legs in ankle socks and saddle shoes, a pleated skirt ending above two knobby knees. In big white letters across the legs: *Lolita.* I've heard the term somewhere before—an article about Fiona Apple, I think, a description of her as "Lolita-esque," meaning sexy and too young. I now understand why he laughed when I asked if the book was illegal.

"It's not poetry," he says, "but poetic prose. You'll appreciate the language, if nothing else."

I feel him watching me as I turn the novel over and skim the description. This is obviously another test.

"Looks interesting." I drop the book into my backpack and turn to my notebook. "Thanks."

"Let me know what you think of it."

"I will."

"And if anyone catches you with it, you didn't get it from me."

Rolling my eyes, I say, "I know how to keep a secret." That isn't necessarily true—before him, I hadn't ever had a real secret—but I know what he needs to hear. It's like he said, I always have the perfect response.

❧

Thanksgiving break. Five days of showers that last until the hot water runs out, of scrutinizing myself in front of the full-length mirror on the back of my bedroom door, plucking my eyebrows until Mom hides the tweezers, of trying to get the puppy to love me as much as Dad. I go for hikes every day, wearing a blaze-orange vest as I trek up the granite bluff that looms over the lake. Caves pock the face of it, crevices in the rock big enough for hawks to nest in and animals to hide.

Inside the biggest cave is an army-style cot. It's been there as long as I can remember, left behind by some long-ago rock climber. I stare at the cot's metal frame and rotten canvas bed and think of the first day of class when Mr. Strane said he knew Whalesback Lake, how he'd been here before. I imagine him finding me now, all alone and deep in the woods. He'd be free to do whatever he wanted with me, no chance of getting caught.

In the evenings I read *Lolita* in bed, mindlessly eating my way through a sleeve of saltines and propping up a pillow to hide the cover in case my parents open my bedroom door. While wind rattles the windowpane, I turn the pages and feel a slow burn within me, hot coals, deep red embers. It isn't only the plot, its story of a seemingly ordinary girl who is really a deadly demon in disguise and the man who loves her. It's that he gave it to me. There's now a whole new context to what we're doing, new insight into what he might want from me. What conclusion is there to draw besides the obvious? He is Humbert, and I am Dolores.

For Thanksgiving we go to my grandparents' house in Millinocket. It's unchanged from 1975, with its shag carpet and sunburst clocks, the smell of cigarettes and coffee brandy hanging in the air even with a turkey in the oven. My grandfather gives me a roll of Necco Wafers and a five-dollar bill; my grandmother asks if I've gained weight. We eat root vegetables and dinner rolls from the store, lemon meringue pie with browned peaks that Dad picks off when nobody's looking.

On the drive home the car lurches over frost heaves and through potholes, an endless wall of pitch-black woods on either side. The radio plays hits from the seventies and eighties, Dad tapping the steering wheel along to "My Sharona" while Mom sleeps, her head leaning against the window. *"Such a dirty mind / I always get it up for the touch of the younger kind."* I watch his fingers tap to the beat as the chorus comes around again. Does he even hear what the song is about, what he's humming along to? *"Get it up for the touch of the younger kind."* It's enough to make me crazy, seeing these things that no one else ever seems to notice.

The first night back after Thanksgiving break, I eat dinner at the empty end of a table, Lucy and Deanna gossiping a few seats away about some popular girl, a senior, who supposedly went to the Halloween dance on drugs. Aubrey Dana asks what kind of drugs.

Deanna hesitates, then answers, "Coke."

Aubrey shakes her head. "No one has coke here," she says.

Deanna doesn't argue; Aubrey is from New York, which makes her an authority.

It takes me a minute to realize they're talking about cocaine and not soda, the sort of thing that normally makes me feel like a yokel, but now their gossip strikes me as sad. Who cares if someone came to a dance on drugs? Don't they have better things to talk about? I stare down at my peanut butter sandwich and let myself detach, retreat into the ending of *Lolita* that I just reread, that final scene of Humbert bloodstained and dazed, and still in love with Lo, even after how much she hurt him and how much he hurt her. His feelings for her are endless and out of his control. How can they not be, when the whole world demonizes him for them? If he were able to stop loving her, he would. His life would be so much easier if he left her alone.

Picking at the crust of my sandwich, I try to see things from Mr. Strane's perspective. He's probably scared—no, terrified. I've been wrapped up in my own frustration and impatience, never considering all that was on the line for him or how much he's already risked touching my leg, saying he wanted to kiss me. He hadn't known what my reaction would be to these things. What if I'd been offended, told on him? Maybe all along he's been the brave one and I've been selfish.

Because, really, what risk is there for me? If I make a move toward him and he turns me down, I suffer nothing beyond a minor humiliation. Big deal. Life for me goes on uninterrupted. It isn't fair to expect him to be more vulnerable than he already has been. At the very least, I need to meet him in the middle, show him what I want and that I'm willing to let the world demonize me, too.

Back in my room, I lie in bed and flip through *Lolita* until I find the line I'm looking for on page 17. Humbert, describing the qualities of the nymphet hidden among ordinary girls: "she stands unrecognized by them and unconscious herself of her fantastic power."

I have power. Power to make it happen. Power over him. I was an idiot for not realizing this sooner.

Before American lit, I stop in the bathroom to check my face. I'm wearing makeup; I piled on every single product I own that morning and parted my hair on the side rather than in the middle. It's enough of a change that the face in the mirror seems unfamiliar—a girl from a magazine or a music video. Britney Spears tapping her foot against her desk as she waits for the bell to ring. The longer I stare at myself, the more my features fracture. A pair of green eyes drift away from a freckled nose; a pair of sticky pink lips separate and swim in different directions. One blink and everything scrambles back into place.

I spend so long in the bathroom I'm late to English for the first time ever. As I rush into the classroom, I feel eyes on me and assume they're Mr. Strane's, but when I look through my heavy eyelashes, I see it's Jenny, her pen frozen above her notes as she registers the changes in me, the makeup and hair.

We're reading Edgar Allan Poe that day, which is so perfectly appropriate I want to throw my head down on the table and laugh.

"Didn't he marry his cousin?" Tom asks.

"He did," Mr. Strane says. "Technically."

Hannah Levesque scrunches her nose. "Gross."

Mr. Strane says nothing about what I know would disgust the rest of them even more, that Virginia Clemm wasn't just Poe's cousin; she was thirteen years old. He has each of us read aloud a stanza from "Annabel Lee," and my voice is unsteady as I say the lines "I *was a child and* she *was a child.*" Images of *Lolita* crowd my head and mix with the memory of Mr. Strane whispering, *You and I are the same,* as he stroked my knee.

Toward the end of the period, he tips back his head, closes his eyes, and recites the poem "Alone" from memory, his deep, drawn-out voice making the lines *"I could not bring / My passions from a common spring"* sound like a song. Listening to him, I want to cry. I see him so clearly now, understand how lonely it must be for him, wanting the wrong thing, the bad thing, while living in a world that would surely villainize him if it knew.

At the end of class, after everyone else has left, I ask if I can shut the door and don't wait for him to answer before pulling it closed. It feels like the bravest thing I've ever done. He's at the chalkboard, eraser in hand, shirtsleeves pushed up past his elbows. He looks me up and down.

"You look a bit different today," he says.

I say nothing, just tug at my sweater sleeves and roll my ankles.

"It's as though you've aged five years over the break," he adds, setting down the eraser and wiping his hands. He gestures to the paper I'm holding. "Is that for me?"

I nod. "It's a poem."

When I give it to him, he starts to read it right away, doesn't lift his eyes even as he walks to his desk and sits down. Without asking, I follow and sit beside him. I finished the poem last night but tweaked the lines throughout the day, making them more like *Lolita,* more suggestive.

She waves the boats in from the sea.
One by one, they slide onto the sand-shore
with a thump that echoes
through her marrowed-out bones.
She shivers & shakes
as the sailors take her,

then cries through the aftercare,
the sailors feeding her mouthfuls of salted kelp,
saying they are sorry,
so sorry for what they've done.

Mr. Strane sets the poem on his desk and leans back in his chair, almost like he wants to distance himself from it. "You never title these," he says, his voice sounding far away. "You should title them." A minute passes and he doesn't move or speak, only stares down at the poem.

Sitting there in silence, I'm smacked with the awful feeling that he's tired of me, wants me to leave him alone. It makes me squeeze my eyes shut from embarrassment—for writing the blatantly sexy poem and thinking I could scheme and don a costume to get what I want, for reading too much into him loaning me a book and saying a few nice things. I saw what I wanted to see, convinced myself my fantasies were real. Sniffling like a little kid, I whisper that I'm sorry.

"Hey," he says, suddenly soft. "Hey, why are you sorry?"

"Because," I say, sucking in a breath. "Because I'm an idiot."

"Why say that?" His arm is around my shoulders, pulling me in. "You're nothing of the sort."

When I was nine, I fell from the last tree I ever tried to climb. Him holding me feels just like that fall—how the earth came up to meet me rather than the other way around, the way the ground seemed to swallow me in the moments after landing. He and I are so close, if I tilt my head a few degrees, my cheek presses against his shoulder. I breathe in the wool of his sweater, the coffee and chalk dust smell of his skin, my mouth mere inches from his neck.

We stay like that, his arm holding me and my head against his shoulder, while laughter drifts in from the hallway and the downtown church bells mark the half hour. My knees press into his thigh; the back of my hand grazes his pant leg. Breathing shallow breaths into his neck, I will him to do something.

Then a small motion: his thumb strokes my shoulder.

I lift my face so my mouth almost touches his neck and I feel him swallow once, twice. It's how he swallows—like he's pushing something down within him—that gives me the courage to press my lips against his skin. It's only a half kiss, but he shudders from it, and the feel of that makes me swell like a wave.

He kisses the top of my head then, his own half kiss, and again I press my mouth against his neck. It's a dialogue of half actions, neither of us fully committed. There's still a chance to turn away, change our minds. Half kisses can be forgotten but full kisses cannot. His hand squeezes my shoulder, tight and tighter, and something within my own body begins to rise. I struggle to force it down, worried that if I don't, I might leap forward, grab him by the throat, and ruin the whole thing.

Then, without warning, he lets go. He draws away from me and then we aren't touching at all. Behind his glasses, he blinks as though adjusting to new light. "We should talk about this," he says.

"Ok."

"This is serious."

"I know."

"We're breaking a lot of rules."

"I *know*," I say, annoyed at the idea of him thinking I don't realize this, that I haven't already spent hours trying to figure out exactly how serious this is.

He looks me over, his face bewildered and hard. Under his breath, he mutters, "This is unreal."

The second hand on the classroom clock ticks by. It's still faculty service hour. The door is closed, but technically someone could come in at any moment.

"So, what is it that you want to do?" he asks.

It's too big of a question. What I want depends on what he wants. "I don't know."

He turns toward the windows, crosses his arms over his chest. *I don't know* isn't a good answer. It's what a child would say, not someone willing and capable of making up her own mind.

"I like being with you," I say. He waits for me to offer more, and my eyes move around the classroom as I struggle for the right words. "I also like what we do."

"What do you mean, 'what we do'?" He wants me to say it, but I don't know what to call it.

I gesture at the space between our bodies. "This."

Smiling faintly, he says, "I like that, too. What about this?" He leans forward and touches the tips of his fingers to my knee. "Do you like this?"

Watching my face, his fingertips slide up my leg and keep sliding until they brush the crotch of my tights. Reflexively, my legs clamp together, trapping his hand.

"That was too far," he acknowledges.

I shake my head, relax my legs. "It's ok."

"It's not ok." His hand slips out from under my skirt and he slides like liquid out of his chair and onto the floor. Kneeling before me, he lays his head on my lap and says, "I'm going to ruin you."

It's the most unbelievable thing that has happened so far, more surreal than him saying he wanted to kiss me or his hand stroking my leg. *"I'm going to ruin you."* He says it with obvious torment, a glimpse into how much he's thought about it, wrestled with it. He wants to do the right thing, doesn't want to hurt me, but has resigned himself to the likelihood that he will.

With my hands hanging in midair above him, I take in his details: black hair, gray at the temples; the smooth grain of his beard ending at a clean-shaven line under his jaw. There's a small cut on his neck, slightly inflamed, and I imagine him that morning in his bathroom, razor in hand, while I stood barefoot in my dorm room, smearing makeup on my face.

"I want to be a positive presence in your life," he says. "Someone you can look back on and remember fondly, the funny old teacher who was pathetically in love with you but kept his hands to himself and was a good boy in the end."

His head still heavy in my lap, my legs start to shake, my armpits and the backs of my knees break into a sweat. *"Pathetically in love with you."* As soon as he says this, I become someone somebody else is in love with, and not just some dumb boy my own age but a man who has already lived an entire life, who has done and seen so much and still thinks I'm worthy of his love. I feel forced over a threshold, thrust out of my ordinary life into a place where it's possible for grown men to be so pathetically in love with me they fall at my feet.

"Some days I sit in your chair after you leave class. I rest my head on the table like I'm trying to breathe you in." He lifts his head from my lap, rubs his face, and sits back on his heels. "What the fuck is the matter with me? I can't tell you this. I'm going to give you nightmares."

He hefts himself back into his chair, and I know I have to offer something to convince him I'm not afraid. I need to match him, show he isn't alone. "I think about you all the time," I say.

For a moment, his face brightens. He catches himself and scoffs. "Like hell you do."

"All the time. I'm obsessed."

"That I find hard to believe. Beautiful girls don't fall in love with lecherous old men."

"You aren't lecherous."

"Not yet," he says, "but if I make another move toward you, I will be."

He needs more, so I give more. I tell him I write my stupid

poems just so he'll read them ("Your poems are not stupid," he says. "Please don't call them that."), that I spent all Thanksgiving break reading *Lolita* and feel changed because of it, that I dressed up today for him, that I shut the classroom door because I wanted us to be alone.

"And I thought we might . . ." I trail off.

"We might what?"

I roll my eyes, titter out a laugh. "You know."

"I don't."

Swiveling slightly in the chair, I say, "That we might, I don't know, kiss or something."

"You want me to kiss you?"

I lift my shoulders and duck my head so my hair falls over my face, too embarrassed to say it.

"Is that a yes?"

Behind my hair, I give a little grunt.

"Have you been kissed before?" He pushes back my hair so he can see me, and I shake my head no, too nervous to lie.

He gets up and locks the classroom door, turns off the lights so no one can look in through the windows. When he takes my face in his hands, I close my eyes and keep them closed. His lips are dry, like laundry stiff from the sun. His beard is softer than I expected, but his glasses hurt. They dig into my cheeks.

There's one close-lipped kiss, then another. He makes a wordless *hmm* sound and then there's an open kiss that goes on for a while. I can't focus on what is happening, my mind so far away it might as well belong to someone else. The whole time all I can think about is how weird it is that he has a tongue.

Afterward, my teeth won't stop chattering. I want to be fearless, to smirk and say something flirty and coy, but all I can do is wipe my nose on my sleeve and whisper, "I feel really weird."

He kisses my forehead, my temples, the corner of my jaw. "A good weird, I hope."

I know I should say yes, reassure him, give him no reason to doubt how much I want it, but I only stare off into middle distance until he leans forward and kisses me again.

I sit at my usual place at the seminar table, my palms flat on the tabletop to keep myself from touching the raw skin at the corners of my mouth. Other students filter in, unzipping their coats and pulling copies of *Ethan Frome* out of their backpacks. They don't know what happened, can never know, but still I want to scream it. Or, if I can't scream it, I want to press the heels of my hands against the table, break through the wood until the whole thing cracks apart and the splintered pieces fall in such a way that the secret spells out across the floor.

On the other side of the table, Tom leans back, stretching his arms behind his head so his shirt rides up, showing a couple inches of his stomach. Jenny's chair is empty. Before Tom came in, Hannah Levesque said something about them breaking up, gossip that would have sent me reeling two months ago. Now it barely registers. Two months feels like a lifetime.

During class, as Mr. Strane lectures on *Ethan Frome*, there's a slight tremble in his hands, a reluctance to look my way—or no, it's ridiculous now to think of him as "mister." But the thought of calling him by his first name seems wrong, too. At one point he touches his hand to his forehead, loses his train of thought, something I've never seen him do before.

"Right," he mumbles. "Where was I?"

The clock above the doorframe ticks two, three, four seconds. Hannah Levesque makes some painfully obvious point about the novel, and instead of brushing her off, Strane says, "Yes, exactly." Turning to the chalkboard, he writes in big letters, *Who is to blame?* and an ocean roars in my ears.

He talks about the whole plot of the novel even though we only had to read the first fifty pages for class. The allure of young Mattie and the moral conundrum the older, married Ethan finds himself in. Is Ethan's love for her really wrong? He lives in desolation. All he has is sickly Zeena upstairs. "People will risk everything for a little bit of something beautiful," Strane says, with so much sincerity in his voice there are ripples of laughter around the seminar table.

I should be used to this by now but it's still surreal—how he can talk about the books and also about me, and they have no idea. It's like when he touched me behind his desk while everyone else sat at the table, working on their thesis statements. Things happen right in front of them. It's like they're all too ordinary to notice.

Who is to blame? He underlines the question and looks to us for answers. He's struggling. I see that now. It isn't that he's nervous to be around me; he's wondering whether he did something wrong. If I were braver, I would raise my hand and say about Ethan Frome and about him, *He didn't do anything wrong.* Or I'd say, *Shouldn't Mattie share some of the blame, too?* But I sit silently, a scared little mouse.

At the end of class, *Who is to blame?* still stretches across the chalkboard. The other students file through the door, down the hallway, and out into the courtyard, but I take my time. I pull my backpack zipper, bend down and pretend to tie my shoes, slow as a sloth. He doesn't acknowledge me until the hallway outside the classroom is empty. No witnesses.

"How are you doing?" he asks.

I smile brightly, tug at my backpack straps. "I'm fine." I know I can't show even a hint of distress. If I do, he might decide I can't handle any more kisses.

"I was worried you might be feeling overwhelmed," he says.

"I'm not."

"Ok." He exhales. "Sounds like you're doing better than I am."

We decide I'll come by later, after faculty service hour when the humanities building is quiet. When I'm nearly out the door, he says, "You look lovely."

I can't stop the grin from taking over my face. I do look lovely—

dark green sweater, my best-fitting corduroys, my hair falling in waves over my shoulders. That was on purpose.

When I return to the classroom, the sun has set, and there aren't any window blinds so we turn off the lights, sit behind his desk, and kiss in the dark.

Ms. Thompson organizes a Secret Santa in the dorm and I draw Jenny's name, which seems like it should hurt. Instead all I feel is a vague annoyance. I take the ten dollars I'm meant to use on a gift and go to the grocery store, buy her a pound of generic-brand ground coffee, and spend the rest on snacks for myself. I don't even wrap the coffee; at the gift exchange I give it to her in the plastic grocery bag.

"What is this?" she asks, the first words she's spoken to me since last spring on the last day of the year—the *I guess I'll see you around* she tossed over her shoulder as she left our dorm room.

"It's your gift."

"You didn't wrap it?" She opens the bag with the tips of her fingers, like she's worried what might be inside.

"It's coffee," I say. "Because you were always drinking coffee or whatever."

She looks down at it, blinking so hard that for a moment I'm horrified, thinking she's about to cry. "Here." She thrusts an envelope at me. "I got your name, too."

Inside the envelope is a card and, inside that, a twenty-dollar gift certificate to the bookstore downtown. I hold the gift certificate in one hand and the card in the other, my eyes darting back and forth between them. Inside the card, she wrote, *Merry Christmas, Vanessa. I know we haven't kept in touch but I hope we can work on repairing our friendship.*

"Why did you do this?" I ask. "We were only supposed to spend ten dollars."

Ms. Thompson moves from pair to pair, commenting on all the gifts. When she reaches us, she sees Jenny's red cheeks, the vacuum-sealed bag of cheap coffee fallen out onto the floor, the guilt all over my face.

"Mmm, what a nice gift!" Ms. Thompson says, so enthusiastic I think she's talking about the gift certificate, but she means the coffee. "As far as I'm concerned, you can never have too much caffeine. Vanessa, what did you get?"

I hold up the gift certificate and Ms. Thompson gives a thin smile. "That's nice, too."

"I have homework to do," Jenny says. She picks up the coffee with two fingers, like it's something gross she doesn't want to touch, and leaves the common room. I want to say more, to shout after her that the only reason she wants anything to do with me is because Tom broke up with her, and that it's too late because I've moved on. I'm doing things now Jenny wouldn't even be able to imagine.

Ms. Thompson turns to me. "I think it was a thoughtful gift, Vanessa. It's not just about how much money you spend."

I realize then why she's being nice—she thinks I'm so poor that a three-dollar bag of coffee is all I can afford. The assumption is both funny and insulting, but I don't correct her.

"Ms. Thompson, what are you doing for Christmas?" Deanna asks.

"Going home to New Jersey for a while," she says. "Might take a trip to Vermont with friends."

"What about your boyfriend?" Lucy asks.

"Can't say I have one of those." Ms. Thompson steps away to check out some other Secret Santa gifts, and I watch how she clasps her hands behind her back and pretends not to hear Deanna whisper to Lucy, "I thought Mr. Strane was her boyfriend?"

One afternoon Strane tells me my name originated with Jonathan Swift, the Irish writer, and that Swift once knew a woman named

Esther Vanhomrigh, nickname Essa. "He broke her name apart and put it back together as something new," Strane said. "Van-essa became Vanessa. Became you."

I don't say it, but sometimes I feel like that's exactly what he's doing to me—breaking me apart, putting me back together as someone new.

He says the first Vanessa was in love with Swift and that she was twenty-two years younger. He was her tutor. Strane goes to the bookshelves behind his desk and finds a copy of the poem Swift wrote called "Cadenus and Vanessa." It's long, sixty pages, the whole thing about a young girl in love with her teacher. My heart gallops as I skim the poem, but I feel his eyes on me so I try not to let it show, shrugging my shoulders and saying in my laziest voice, "That's kind of funny, I guess."

Strane frowns. "I thought it eerie, not funny." He slides the book back onto the shelf and mumbles, "It got under my skin. Made me start thinking about fate."

I watch him sit at his desk and flip open his grade book. The tips of his ears are red, like he's embarrassed. Am I capable of embarrassing him? I forget sometimes he can be vulnerable, too.

"I know what you mean," I say.

He looks up from his book, light glinting off his glasses.

"I kind of feel like this whole thing is destiny."

"This whole thing," he repeats. "You mean what we do together?"

I nod. "Like maybe this is what I was born to do."

As my words register, his lips start to tremble like he's trying hard not to smile. "Go shut the door," he says. "Turn out the lights."

I use the pay phone in the Gould common room to call home the Sunday before Christmas break, and Mom says she has to pick me up on Tuesday rather than Wednesday, meaning an extra day of break, an extra day of no Strane. It's hard enough getting through a weekend without him; I don't know how I'll manage to survive three weeks, so when she tells me this, it feels like the floor opens up beneath me.

"You didn't even ask me! You can't just decide that you're going to pick me up a whole day early without asking me if it's ok." My panic gains momentum and I struggle not to cry. "I have responsibilities," I say. "There are *things I have to do.*"

"What things?" Mom asks. "Good lord, why are you so upset? Where is this coming from?"

Pressing my forehead against the wall, I take a breath and manage to get out, "There's a creative writing club meeting I can't miss."

"Oh." Mom exhales like she expected something more serious. "Well, I won't get there until six. That should give you enough time to go to your meeting."

She takes a bite of something and it crunches between her teeth. I hate how she eats while she talks to me, or cleans, or has conversations with Dad at the same time. Sometimes she'll take the phone with her into the bathroom and I don't realize until I hear a flush in the background.

"I didn't know you liked that club so much," she says.

I wipe my nose with my sweatshirt's dirty cuff. "It's not about me liking it. It's about taking my responsibilities seriously."

"Hmm." She takes another bite, and whatever it is rattles around in her teeth.

On Monday, when Strane and I sit in the dark classroom, I won't let him kiss me. I turn away and twist my legs out of his reach.

"What wrong?" he asks.

I shake my head, don't know how to explain. He seems completely unbothered by the upcoming break. He hasn't even brought it up.

"It's fine if you don't want me to touch you," he says. "Just tell me to stop."

He leans in close, peering at me, trying to make out my expression in the dark. I can see the darting shine of his eyes because he's not wearing his glasses—ever since I told him they hurt my face, he takes them off before we kiss.

"As much as I wish I could, I can't read your mind," he says.

His fingertips touch my knees and wait to see if I'll jerk away. When I don't, his hands creep farther up my thighs, over my hips, and around my waist, the casters of the chair squeaking as he pulls me close. I sigh, lean into him, his body like a mountain.

"It's just we're not going to be able to do this again for so long," I say. "Three whole weeks."

I feel him relax. "That's what you're sulking over?"

It's how he laughs that makes me start to cry, like I'm being ridiculous, but he thinks it's the idea of missing him that's making me so upset.

"I'm not going anywhere," he says, kissing my forehead. He calls me sensitive. "Like a . . ." He stops and softly laughs. "I was about to say like a little girl. I forget sometimes that's exactly what you are."

I turn my face deeper into him and whisper that I feel out of control. I want him to say he feels the same, but he just continues stroking my hair. Maybe he doesn't need to say it. I think of his head in my lap the afternoon we first kissed, how he moaned, *I'm going to ruin you.* Of course he's out of control; you have to be careening to do what we're doing.

He pulls away, kisses the corners of my mouth. "I've got an idea," he says.

The ground outside is covered in snow, reflecting enough light into the classroom so I can see his smile, the wrinkles that appear around his eyes. Up close, his face is disjointed, enormous. On the bridge of his nose there are indentations from his glasses that never go away.

"But you have to promise not to agree to what I'm proposing unless you absolutely want to," he says. "Ok?"

I sniff, wipe my eyes. "Ok."

"What if after Christmas break . . . say, the first Friday we're back . . ." He draws in a breath. "What if you came to my house?"

I blink in surprise. I assumed this would happen eventually, but this feels soon, though maybe not. We've been kissing for over two weeks.

When I say nothing, he continues. "I think it'd be nice to spend time together outside of this classroom. We could eat dinner, look at each other with the lights on. That'd be fun, right?"

Immediately, I'm afraid. I wish I weren't and, chewing on the inside of my cheek, I do my best to rationalize it away. I'm not afraid of him but rather of his body—the sheer size of it, the expectation that I do things to it. As long as we stay in the classroom, kissing is all we can do, but going to his house means anything can happen. That the obvious will happen. Meaning sex.

"How would I even get there?" I ask. "What about curfew?"

"Slip out of the dorm afterward. I can wait for you in the parking lot out back and whisk you away. Then in the morning, I'd get you back early enough that no one would be the wiser."

When I still hesitate, his body stiffens. His chair rolls backward, away from me, and cold air sweeps across my legs. "I'm not going to force you if you're not ready," he says.

"I'm ready."

"It doesn't seem like you are."

"I am," I insist. "I'll come over."

"But is that what you want?"

"Yeah."

"Is it really?"

"Yes."

He stares at me, the shine of his eyes moving back and forth. I gnaw harder on my cheek, thinking maybe he won't be mad at me if I hurt myself enough to ignite a fresh round of tears.

"Listen," he says, "I have no expectations. I'd be happy to sit on the couch with you and watch a movie. We don't even have to hold hands if you don't want to, ok? It's important that you never feel coerced. That's the only way I'll be able to live with myself."

"I don't feel coerced."

"You don't? Truly?"

I shake my head.

"Good. That's good." He reaches for my hands. "You're in charge here, Vanessa. You decide what we do."

I wonder if he really believes that. He touched me first, said he wanted to kiss me, told me he loved me. Every first step was taken by him. I don't feel forced, and I know I have the power to say no, but that isn't the same as being in charge. But maybe he has to believe that. Maybe there's a whole list of things he has to believe.

❧

For Christmas I get: a fifty-dollar bill; two sweaters, one lavender cable knit, the other white mohair; a new Fiona Apple CD to replace my scratched-up one; boots from the L.L.Bean outlet store, but you can only tell the stitching is messed up if you look closely; an electric kettle for my dorm room; a box of maple sugar candies; socks and underwear; a chocolate orange.

At home with my parents, I do my best to put Strane in a drawer and close it up tight. I resist the urge to stay in bed daydreaming and writing about him and instead do things that make me feel like the girl I used to be—reading by the woodstove; chopping figs and walnuts with Mom at the kitchen table; helping Dad haul home a tree, Babe the puppy bouncing alongside us like a furry yellow dolphin as we trudge through the snow. Most nights after Dad goes to bed and Babe follows him upstairs, Mom and I lie on the couch and watch TV. We like the same shows: period dramas,

Ally McBeal, The Daily Show. We laugh along with Jon Stewart, cringe when George W. Bush comes on-screen. The recount is long over now, Bush declared the winner.

"I still can't believe he stole the election," I say.

"They all steal elections," Mom says. "It's just not so bad when a Democrat does it."

While we watch TV and eat the expensive ginger lemon cookies Mom keeps hidden at the top of the pantry, she inches her feet toward me and tries to burrow them under my butt even though I hate it. When I grumble, she tells me to stop being prickly. "You used to be in my womb, you know."

I tell her about the note Jenny gave me with the Secret Santa present, about her and me repairing our friendship, and Mom smirks, jabs her finger at me. "I told you she'd try to do that. I hope you don't fall for it."

She falls asleep, her dishwater blond hair tangled across her face as the TV switches to infomercials. This is when Strane comes roaring back, when the house is still and I'm the only one awake. I stare at the screen with glazed eyes and feel him there with me, holding me, slipping his hand under my pajama bottoms. On the other end of the couch, my mother snores, jolting me out of the daydream, and I flee upstairs. My bedroom is the only safe space to let him in, where I can shut the door, lie on my bed, and imagine what it will feel like to be in his house, what it will feel like to have sex. What he'll look like when he takes off his clothes.

I dig through my old issues of *Seventeen*, searching for articles about having sex for the first time in case there's something I should do to prepare myself, but they all say the same inane stuff like, "Having sex is a big deal, don't feel pressured to do it, you have all the time in the world!" So I go online and find a message board thread titled "Advice on Losing Your V-Card," and the only piece of advice for girls is "Don't just lie there," but what does that even mean? Get on top? I try to imagine myself doing that to Strane, but it's too embarrassing; my whole body cringes at the thought. I close the browser, first checking the search history three times to make sure I deleted everything.

The night before we drive back to Browick, while my parents watch Tom Brokaw, I sneak into their room and open the top drawer of my mother's dresser, root around the bras and underwear until I find a silky black nightie with a yellowed tag still attached. Back in my bedroom, I try it on without anything underneath. It's a little long, reaching past my knees, but it's tight, the outline of my body visible in a way that seems grown-up and sexy. Staring in the mirror, I pile my hair on top of my head and let it fall around my face. I bite my bottom lip until it turns swollen and red. One of the straps falls down my arm and I imagine Strane, with his tender-condescending smile, slipping it back up my shoulder. In the morning, I stuff the nightgown into the bottom of my bag and can't stop smiling the whole drive back to Browick, pleased with how easy it is to get away with something, with anything.

On campus the snowbanks are taller, the Christmas decorations gone, and the dorms stink of the vinegar they use to wash the hardwood floors. Early Monday morning I go to the humanities building in search of Strane. At the sight of me, his face lights up, breaks into a grin, a hungry mouth. He locks the classroom door and presses me against the filing cabinet, kisses me so hard he practically gnaws at me, our teeth knocking against each other. His thigh pushes my legs apart and rubs against me—it feels good, but it happens so quickly I gasp, and at the sound he lets go and staggers backward, asks if he hurt me.

"I can't keep it together when I'm around you," he says. "I'm acting like a teenager."

He asks if we're still on for Friday. Says that over these past weeks, he thought about me constantly, was surprised at how much he missed me. At that, I narrow my eyes. Why surprised?

"Because really we don't know each other that well," he explains. "But, my god, you've gotten to me." When I ask him what he did for Christmas, he says, "Thought about you."

The week feels like a countdown, like slow footsteps down a long hallway. Once Friday night arrives, it hardly feels real to shove the black nightgown into my backpack while across the hall Mary Emmett belts out that five-hundred-twenty-five-thousand-six-hundred-minutes song from *Rent* with her door wide open and Jenny strides by in her bathrobe on her way to the shower. Strange to think that for them it's just another Friday night, how easily their ordinary lives go on, running parallel to my own.

At nine thirty I check in with Ms. Thompson, tell her I don't feel well and that I'm going to bed early, then wait until the hallway is clear and sneak out the back stairwell, the one with the broken alarm. Hurrying across campus, I see Strane's station wagon waiting with the headlights off in the lot behind the humanities building. When I throw open the passenger door and slide inside, he pulls me close, laughing in a way I haven't heard from him before—manic and gasping, as though he can't believe this is really happening.

His house is sparse and cleaner than I've ever seen my parents', the kitchen sink empty and shining, a dishrag drying on the faucet's long neck. A few days ago he asked what I like to eat, said he wanted to have my favorites on hand, and he shows me the three pints of expensive ice cream in the freezer, a six-pack of Cherry Coke in the fridge, two big bags of potato chips on the counter. There's a bottle of whiskey on the counter, too, along with a glass holding a mostly melted ice cube.

In the living room, there's no clutter on the coffee table, only a stack of coasters and two remote controls. The bookcases are neatly arranged, nothing thrown in sideways or upside down. As he leads me on a tour, I sip a soda and try to appear impressed but not too impressed, interested but not too interested. Really, though, I'm trembling all over.

His bedroom is the last room he shows me. We stand in the doorway, bubbles pinging inside my soda can, neither of us sure of the next move. I have to be back at Gould in six hours, but I've been here for only ten minutes. His bed stretches out before us, neatly made with a khaki comforter and pillows in tartan cases. It feels too soon.

"Are you tired?" he asks.

I shake my head. "Not really."

"Then maybe you shouldn't be drinking this." He takes the soda from my hands. "All that caffeine."

I suggest watching TV, hoping to remind him of the offer he'd made of sitting on the couch and watching a movie, holding hands.

"I'm sure to fall asleep if we do that," he says. "Why don't we just go ahead and get ready for bed?"

Turning to his dresser, he opens the top drawer, pulls something out. It's a pajama set, shorts and a tank top made from white cotton dotted with red strawberries. They're neatly folded with the tags still attached, brand new, bought especially for me.

"I thought you might forget to bring clothes to sleep in," he says, putting the pajamas in my hands. I say nothing about the black nightgown in the bottom of my backpack.

In the bathroom I try to make as little sound as possible as I peel off my clothes and break the tags off the pajamas. Before I put them on, I stare at my face in the mirror, peek in the shower at his bottle of shampoo and bar of soap, inspect everything on the counter. He has an electric toothbrush, an electric razor, and a digital scale that I stand on, curling my toes as the numbers flash—145, two pounds less than I was at Christmas.

Holding up the tank top, I wonder why he chose this particular set. Probably because he liked the print—he's said before that my hair and skin remind him of strawberries and cream. I picture him browsing a girls' clothing section, his big hands touching all the different pajamas, and the thought fills me with tenderness, similar to how I felt a few years ago when I saw a photo of that famous gorilla cradling her pet kitten, the vulnerability of someone so big handling something so delicate, trying their best to be careful and kind.

I open the bathroom door and step into the bedroom, shielding an arm across my chest. The lamp on the nightstand is on, a soft warm light. He sits on the edge of the bed, his shoulders hunched, hands clasped.

"Everything fit ok?"

I shiver and give a half nod. Outside the window a car drives by, the noise approaching then receding, a hush of silence.

He asks, "Can I see?" and I step toward him, close enough for him to wrap his fingers around my wrist and pull my arm down. As his eyes move over me, he sighs and says, "Oh no," like he's already sorry for what we're about to do.

He stands, folds down the comforter, and, under his breath, goes, "Ok, ok, ok." He says he'll stay dressed for now, which I know is meant to soothe me, maybe also himself. On his shirt, dark circles spread out from his armpits, just like during the convocation speech the first day of classes.

I slide into bed beside him and we lie on our backs under the covers, not touching, not talking. The ceiling is covered in cream and gold tiles that form a swirling pattern my eyes circle around and around. Beneath the down comforter, my hands and feet are warmer, but the tip of my nose stays cold.

"My room at home is always cold like this, too," I say.

"Is it?" He turns to me, grateful I've made this somewhat normal by speaking. He asks me to describe my bedroom, what it looks like, how it's arranged. I draw a map in the air.

"Here's the window facing the lake," I say, "and here's the window facing the mountain. Here's my closet and here's my bed." I tell him about my posters, the color of my bedspread. I say that in the summers, I wake sometimes in the middle of the night to the sound of loons screaming out on the lake, and that because the house isn't well insulated, ice forms on the walls in the winter.

"I hope someday I get to see it for myself," he says.

I laugh at the thought of him in my bedroom, how big he'd seem there, his head brushing the ceiling. "I don't think that'll ever happen."

"You never know," he says. "Opportunities come up."

He tells me about his childhood bedroom in Montana. It was cold in the winter, too, he says. He describes Butte, the old mining boomtown, once the richest place on earth and now a depressed brown basin cradled by mountains. He describes the abandoned headframes poking up between the houses, how downtown was built on the side of a hill and how at the top of that hill is a big pit of acid left over from the mining.

"That sounds horrible," I say.

"It does," he agrees, "but it's the sort of place that's difficult to understand until you see it for yourself. There's a strange beauty in it."

"Beauty in a pit of acid?"

He smiles. "Someday we'll go there. You'll see."

Under the comforter, he links his fingers through mine and continues talking, telling me about his younger sister, his parents; how his father was a copper miner, intimidating but kind, and his mother a teacher.

"What was she like?" I ask.

"Angry," he says. "She was a very angry woman."

I bite my lip, unsure what to say.

"She didn't care for me," he adds, "and I could never figure out why."

"Is she still alive?"

"They're both dead."

I start to say I'm sorry but he cuts me off, squeezes my hand. "It's fine," he says. "Ancient history."

We lie quiet for a while, our hands linked under the blankets. Breathing in and out, I close my eyes and try to pinpoint the scent of his bedroom. It's a thin, masculine smell, traces of soap and deodorant on the flannel sheets, cedar from the closet. It's strange to think this is where he lives like a normal person, sleeping and eating and doing all the monotonous everyday chores of living—washing the dishes, cleaning the bathroom, doing laundry. Does he do his own laundry? I try to picture him hauling clothes from washer to dryer, but the image dissolves as soon as I conjure it.

"Why didn't you ever get married?" I ask.

He glances over at me and I feel his hand loosen its grip on mine for a moment, long enough to tell me this was the wrong thing to ask.

"Marriage isn't for everyone," he says. "You'll figure that out as you get older."

"No, I get it," I say. "I never want to get married, either." I don't know if this is exactly true, but I'm trying to be generous. His worry is obvious, about me and what we're doing. The smallest movement makes him jump, like I'm an animal prone to bolt or bite.

He smiles; his body relaxes. I said the right thing. "Of course you don't. You know yourself enough to understand what you aren't made for," he says.

I want to ask what I am made for, but don't want to show I don't actually know myself, and don't want to push it now that he's again holding my hand and tilting his head toward mine like he's moving in for a kiss. He hasn't kissed me since I got here.

He asks again if I'm tired and I shake my head. "When you are," he says, "let me know and I can go to the living room."

The living room? I frown and try to figure out what he means. "Like you'll sleep on the couch?"

He lets go of my hand and starts to speak, stops, starts again.

"I'm ashamed of how I first touched you," he says, "back at the beginning of the year. That's not how I like to behave."

"I liked it, though."

"I know you liked it, but wasn't it confusing?" He turns to me. "It must have been. Having your teacher touch you out of nowhere. I didn't like doing that, acting without talking it through first. Talking through absolutely everything is the only way to redeem what we're doing."

He doesn't say it, but I know what's required of me here—to tell him how I feel and what I want. To be brave. I roll toward him, press my face into his neck. "I don't want you to sleep on the couch." I feel him smile.

"Ok," he says. "Is there anything else you want?"

I nuzzle against him, slide my leg over his. I can't say it. He asks if I want to be kissed, and when I nod into his neck, he takes a handful of my hair, draws my head back.

"My god," he says, "look at you."

I'm perfect, he says, so perfect I can't be real. He kisses me and other stuff starts to happen fast, things we haven't done before—pushing the tank top over my breasts, pinching and kneading, slipping his hand under the pajama shorts and cupping me down there.

For everything he does, he asks permission. "Can I?" before pulling the pajama top all the way over my head. "Is this ok?" before pushing my underwear over, slipping a finger inside so quickly that, for a moment, I'm stunned and my body plays dead. After a while he starts asking permission after he's already done the thing he's asking about. "Can I?" he asks, meaning can he tug the pajama shorts down, but they're already off. "Is this ok?" meaning is it ok for him to kneel between my legs, but he's already there, letting out a groan and saying, "I knew you'd be red here, too."

I don't understand what he's doing until he starts doing it. Kissing me there, going down on me. I'm not an idiot; I know it's something people do, but it hadn't occurred to me that it's something he would want. Wrapping his arms under me, he pulls me closer, and I dig my heels into the mattress, reach down and grab a fistful of his hair so hard it must hurt, but his kissing and licking and whatever else he does—how does he know exactly what to do to make me feel good? how does he know everything about me?—none of that stops. I bite my bottom lip to keep from crying out, and he makes a slurping sound, like sucking up the last of a soda through a straw, which would embarrass me if it didn't feel so good. I drape my arm across my eyes, fall into swirls of color, ocean waves rising to mountains, the sensation of being so small until I come, harder than when I do it to myself, so hard I see stars.

"Ok, stop," I say. "Stop, stop."

He recoils as though I kicked him away—sits back on his knees, still in his T-shirt and jeans, hair mussed and face shiny. "Did you come?" he asks. "Really, that fast?"

I squeeze my legs together and my eyes shut. I can't talk, can't think. Was that fast? How long did it even take? A minute or ten or twenty, I have no clue.

"You did, didn't you? Do you know how special that is?" he asks. "How rare?"

I open my eyes and watch him wipe his mouth with the back of his hand, then pause and hold that hand to his face, take a breath, and close his eyes.

He says he wishes he could do that to me every night. Pulling the comforter up with him, he lies down beside me and adds, "Every single night before you fall asleep."

Him cradling me feels almost as good as him going down on me, his chin resting on top of my head, his big body curled around mine. He smells like me. "We won't go further than that for now," he says, and I turn liquid-warm at the thought of sex being nothing but him doing that to me.

He reaches over and turns off the nightstand light, but I can't sleep. His arm grows heavy across my shoulders as I replay in my head the way he said "oh no" when he saw me in the pajamas, the way he wrapped his arms under my legs to pull me closer to his face when he went down on me. The way he, at one point, reached up and held my hand in the middle of it all.

I want him to do it again, but don't dare wake him to ask. Maybe he'll do it again in the morning before I leave. Maybe we'll be able to do it after school in his classroom sometimes, or go for drives off campus and do it in his car. My mind won't quiet. Even as I eventually doze, my brain still schemes.

When I wake a couple hours later, it's dark outside. Hallway light streams in through the bedroom doorway, across the floor. Beside me, Strane is awake, his mouth hot on my neck. I turn onto my back, grinning, expecting him to move his face down between my legs, but he's naked when I roll over. Pale skin covered in dark hair from his chest all the way down his legs, and in the center his penis, enormous and erect.

"Oh!" I say. "Ok! Wow. Ok." Small, stupid words. When he takes my wrist and guides my hand to it, I say them again. "Oh! Ok!" He closes my fingers around it, and I know that I'm meant to do the up-and-down stuff, and my hand immediately starts pumping away, dutiful as a robot, disconnected from my brain. It's loose skin sliding over a column of muscle, but rough, halting. It's like a dog hacking up garbage that's been sitting in its stomach for days, that violent, full-body gag.

"Slower, baby," he says. "A little slower." He shows me what he means, and I try to keep the pace even though my arm is starting to cramp. I want to tell him I'm tired, to roll over and never look at the thing ever again, but that would be selfish. He said me naked is the most beautiful thing he's ever seen. It would be cruel for me to counter that with disgust. It doesn't matter that my skin crawls from touching him. It doesn't matter. It's fine. *He did that to you, now you do this to him. You can handle a few minutes of this.*

When he guides my hand away from it, I worry he'll ask me to use my mouth next and I don't want that, I can't do that, but instead he says, "Do you want me to fuck you?" It's a question, but he isn't really asking.

I can't wrap my head around the change in him. Now I'm not even sure if he really said, *We won't go further than that for now*, or maybe "for now" meant something totally different from what I assumed. Do I want him to fuck me? Fuck me. The crudeness of it makes me turn my face into the pillow. His voice doesn't even sound the same, haggard and rough. I open my eyes and he's positioning himself between my legs, brow furrowed in concentration.

I try to stall, tell him I don't want to get pregnant.

"You won't," he says. "That's impossible."

I move my hips away. "What does that mean?"

"I had an operation, a vasectomy," he says. He holds himself with one hand and steadies me with the other. "You won't get pregnant. Just relax." He tries to push in, his thumb digging hard into my pelvis. It won't fit.

"You gotta calm down, honey," he says. "Take a deep breath."

I start to tear up, but he doesn't stop, just says I'm doing great as he keeps trying to get it in. He tells me to breathe in and out, and when I exhale, he thrusts hard and pushes a little farther inside. I start crying, really crying—still, he doesn't stop.

"You're doing great," he says. "Another deep breath, ok? It's ok if it hurts. It won't hurt forever. Just one more deep breath, ok? There we go. That's nice. That's so nice."

Afterward, he gets out of bed, a flash of belly and butt before I shut my eyes. He pulls on his underwear and the elastic band snaps like a whip crack, like something splitting in two. As he walks to the bathroom, he coughs hard and loud and I hear him spit into the sink. Under the blankets, I'm raw and slick, my legs slimy all the way down my thighs. My mind feels like the lake on a calm day, glassy and still. I'm nothing, no one, nowhere.

When he comes back into the bedroom, he looks like himself again, dressed in a T-shirt and sweatpants, his glasses on. He slides into bed, curls his body around mine. He whispers, "We made love, didn't we?" and I gauge the distance between "fuck" and "made love."

After a while, we have sex again and it's slower, easier. I don't come from it, but at least I'm not crying this time. I even like the weight of him on top of me, so heavy it slows my heart. He comes with a groan and a shudder takes over his body, radiating from his core. The feel of him trembling on top of me makes my muscles contract and squeeze him even tighter inside, and I understand then what people probably mean when they say that stuff about two becoming one.

He apologizes for finishing too quickly, for being clumsy. He says it's been a while since he was last intimate. I roll the word *intimate* around in my mouth and think of Ms. Thompson.

After we have sex the second time, I go to the bathroom and peek in his medicine cabinet, something I wouldn't think to do if I hadn't seen women in movies do it when they spend the night in a strange man's home. His cabinet is full of the usual Band-Aids and Neosporin, over-the-counter digestive stuff, plus two orange prescription bottles labeled with names I recognize from commercials, Viagra and Wellbutrin.

On the dark drive back to campus, the streetlights flashing yellow, he asks how I feel. "I hope you're not too overwhelmed," he says.

I know he wants the truth and that I should tell him I didn't like being woken up by him hard and practically pushing into me. That I wasn't ready to have sex this way. That it felt forced. But I'm not brave enough to say any of this—not even that I feel sick to my stomach when I think about him guiding my hand to his penis and don't understand why he didn't stop when I started to cry. That the thought *I want to go home* ran through my head the entire time we first did it.

"I feel fine," I say.

He watches me closely, like he wants to be sure I'm telling the truth. "That's good," he says. "That's what we want."

2017

Text from Mom: Hey you. Listen to what just happened. Middle of the night, I can't sleep, heard something outside, went downstairs and turned on the porch light, and there was a BEAR going through the garbage can!!! Scared the crap out of me. I screamed and ran upstairs and hid under the covers lol. Watching that British cooking show now to try to calm down. Lordy. Not much other news here. That woman Marjorie who lives on the other side of the lake has lung cancer. The one with the goats. Anyway, she's on her way out. Very sad. My car got recalled because of that thing with the door. Going to take 8–12 weeks. They gave me some piece of shit rental. Ugh. Horror after horror. Anyway, just checking in. Call your momma sometime.

Bleary-eyed and still in bed at ten A.M., I try to make sense of the text. I have no idea who Marjorie is, or what's wrong with Mom's car door, or what British cooking show she's talking about. Ever since Dad died, I'll wake up to texts like these. This one, at least, has regular punctuation; others are rambling stream-of-consciousness thoughts linked with ellipses, incoherent enough to make me worry.

I close the text, open Facebook, and check Taylor's profile for anything new. I type into the search bar names I've looked up so many times they pop up with the first letter: Jesse Ly, Jenny Murphy. Jesse lives in Boston, does something in marketing. Jenny's a surgeon in Philadelphia. In her photos, she already looks middle-aged, deep wrinkles around her eyes, brown hair laced with gray. Nothing posted about Strane in their profiles, but why would there be? They're adults living actual fulfilling lives. They have no reason to remember what happened back then, or even to remember me.

X-ing out of Facebook, I google "Henry Plough Atlantica College," and the first result is his faculty profile with the same decade-old photo of him in his office, the beers he and I would later drink together unopened on the bookshelf behind him. He was thirty-four then, only a couple years older than I am now. The second search result is an article from the Atlantica student newspaper dated May 2015, "Literature Professor Henry Plough Receives Teaching Award." It's a prize given every four years, the recipient decided by a student vote. Junior English major Emma Thibodeau says students are thrilled with the result: "Henry is an incredible professor, so inspiring and you can talk to him about anything. He's just an amazing person. His classes have changed my life."

I scroll to the bottom of the article where a cursor sits blinking in an empty text box. "*Want to leave a comment?*" I type, "Re: 'an amazing person'—Trust me, he's not," but the article is two years old and Henry didn't do anything that bad anyway, so what does it matter? I toss the phone across my bed, go back to sleep.

Strane calls when I'm walking to work, stoned from the bowl I smoked while getting ready. My phone vibrates in my hand, the screen flashing his name, and I stop in the middle of the sidewalk like a tourist, oblivious to the flow of pedestrian traffic. I bring the phone to my ear and someone smacks my shoulder, a girl in a jean jacket—no, two girls in matching jackets, one black-haired, one blond. They walk with their arms linked, backpacks bumping against their tailbones. They must be from the high school, sneaking out during lunch period to roam downtown. The black-haired girl, the one who ran into me, shoots me a look over her shoulder. "Sorry," she calls, her voice lazy and insincere.

On the phone, Strane says, "Did you hear me? I said I'm vindicated."

"You mean you're ok?"

"I'll be back in my classroom tomorrow." He laughs as though he can't believe it. "I thought for sure I was finished."

I stand on the sidewalk, my gaze still fixed on the two girls as they move down Congress Street, their undulating hair. Him back in the classroom, once again unscathed. Disappointment seeps into me as though I wanted to see him fall, a meanness that catches me off guard. Maybe I'm just stoned, my mind tumbling down a rabbit hole of feeling. I need to stop smoking before work. Need to grow up, let go, move on.

"I thought you'd be pleased," Strane says.

The girls disappear down a side street, and I exhale a breath I didn't realize I was holding. "I am. Of course I am. That's great." I start walking again, my legs unsteady. "I bet you're relieved."

"I'm a little more than relieved," he says. "I was making peace with the idea of spending the rest of my life in prison."

I stop myself from rolling my eyes at the exaggeration, as though he might somehow see me. Does he really believe he'd ever go to prison, a Harvard-educated, well-spoken white man? The fear feels unfounded and vaguely performative, but maybe it's cruel to criticize. He's been panicked, in crisis. He's earned the right to some melodrama. I can't understand what it feels like to stare down that kind of ruin. The risks he took were always greater than mine. *Just be nice for once in your life, Vanessa. Why do you always have to be so fucking mean?*

"We could celebrate," I say. "I can get Saturday off. There's a new Scandinavian restaurant everyone's crazy about."

Strane sucks in a breath. "Not sure that's going to work," he says. I open my mouth to offer something else—a different restaurant, a different day, to drive up to Norumbega rather than have him come here—but he adds, "I need to be cautious right now."

Cautious. I squint at the word, try to understand what he's really saying. "You're not going to get in trouble for being seen with me," I say. "I'm thirty-two years old."

"Vanessa."

"Nobody remembers."

"Of course they do," he says. Impatience sharpens his words. He shouldn't have to explain that even at thirty-two years old I'm still illicit, dangerous. I am living, breathing evidence of the worst thing he's ever done. People remember me. The whole reason he was on the brink of disaster is because people remember.

"It'd be best if we keep our distance for a while," he says. "Just until this all cools down."

I concentrate on breathing as I cross the street to the hotel, throwing a wave to the valet standing at the entrance to the parking garage, the housekeepers in the alley taking long drags from their cigarettes.

"Fine," I say. "If that's what you want."

A pause. "It's not what I want. It's just how it has to be."

I open the lobby door and my face is hit with a waft of air thick with jasmine and citrus. They literally pump the scent in through the vents. It's supposed to energize and rejuvenate the senses; the kind of attention to detail that makes this a luxury hotel.

"It's for the best," he says. "For both of us."

"I'm at work. I gotta go." I hang up on him without saying goodbye. In the moment, it's enough to make me feel I've won, but once I'm settled at my desk the pit in my stomach takes root and blooms into humiliation—discarded again at the first opportunity, tossed aside like trash. The same thing he did when I was twenty-two, when I was sixteen. It's a truth so blatant and bitter, not even I can sweeten it into something easier to swallow. He only wanted to make sure I'd stay quiet. He used me again. *How many times? What's it going to take, Vanessa?*

At my desk, I pull up Taylor's Facebook page. At the top of her feed sits a status update posted less than an hour ago: The school that once promised to nurture and protect me has sided with an abuser today. I'm disappointed but not surprised. Expanding the thread of comments, one with a couple dozen likes shows up first: I'm so, so sorry. Is there any other course of action you can take, or is this the end? Taylor's response turns my mouth dry.

In no way is this the end, she writes.

During my break, I go outside to the alley behind the hotel and dig a crumpled pack of cigarettes from the bottom of my purse. I smoke leaning against a fire escape, scrolling through my phone until I hear the scuff of shoes on pavement, a shush, a muffled laugh. Looking up, I see the two girls from my walk to work. They stand now at the far end of the alley, the blond girl clutching the black-haired one's arm.

"Go ask her," the blonde says. "Do it."

The black-haired girl takes a step toward me, stops, crosses her arms. "Hey," she calls. "Can we, um . . ." She looks over her shoulder to the blonde, who holds a fist against her mouth, grinning behind the cuff of her jean jacket.

"Do you have an extra cigarette?" the black-haired girl asks.

When I hold out two, they both rush forward. "They're a little stale," I say. That's ok, they say. That's totally fine. The blonde swings her backpack off one shoulder, pulls a lighter out of the front pocket. They light each other's, cheeks hollowing as they inhale. They're close enough for me to see the cat-eye points of their eyeliner, the tiny zits along their hairlines. When I'm around girls their age, the magic age Strane taught me to mythologize, I feel myself become him. Questions pile up in my mouth, ones designed to make them linger. I bite down hard to keep them from pouring out—what are your names, how old are you, do you want more cigarettes, or beer, or weed? It's so easy for me to imagine how it must've been for him, desperate enough to give a girl whatever she wanted to keep her close.

The girls thank me over their shoulders as they move back down the alley, their giddiness replaced with a languid cool thanks to the cigarettes between their fingers. Swaying their hips, they turn the corner, give me one last look, and are gone.

I stare at the spot where they disappeared, the setting sun glinting off a stream of water leaking from a dumpster, the windshield of an idling delivery van. I wonder what those girls saw when they looked at me, if they sensed a kinship, if the reason they dared ask me for a cigarette was because they could tell that, despite my age, really I'm one of them.

With an exhale of smoke, I pull out my phone and bring up Taylor's profile, but I see nothing. My mind is gone, galloping after the girls, wanting to know what Strane would think of them with their bummed cigarettes and tough attitudes. He'd probably find them coarse, too confident, risky. *You're so yielding*, he'd say as I let him move my body around. He made it a compliment, my passivity a precious and rare thing.

What would she do? It's a question that's more like a maze, one I can get lost in at the sight of any teenage girl. If her teacher tried to touch her, would she react the way she should, shove his hand away and flee? Or would she let her body go limp until he was through? I try sometimes to imagine another girl doing what I did—sink into the pleasure of it, crave it, build her life around it—but I can't. My brain hits a dead end, the maze swallowed by darkness. Unthinkable. Unspeakable.

I never would have done it if you weren't so willing, he'd said. It sounds like delusion. What girl would want what he did to me? But it's the truth, whether anyone believes it or not. Driven toward it, toward him, I was the kind of girl that isn't supposed to exist: one eager to hurl herself into the path of a pedophile.

But no, that word isn't right, never has been. It's a cop-out, a lie in the way it's wrong to call me a victim and nothing more. He was never so simple; neither was I.

Taking the long way back to the hotel lobby, I walk through

the lowest level of the parking garage into the basement, past the din of the laundry room's industrial-sized washers and dryers. The head of housekeeping stops me in the stairwell, asks if I mind bringing an extra set of towels to Mr. Goetz, the every-other-Monday businessman, in room 342.

"You sure you don't mind?" she asks as she hands me the towels. "He can be a sleaze to my girls, but he likes you."

Knocking on 342, I hear footsteps, then Mr. Goetz opens the door—shirtless and clutching a towel around his waist, wet hair, water droplets on his shoulders, dark hair on his chest, down the middle of his stomach.

At the sight of me, his face brightens. "Vanessa! Wasn't expecting you." He opens the door wider, nods for me to come inside. "Can you put the towels down on the bed?"

Hesitating at the threshold, I calculate the distance from the door to the bed and the distance from the bed to the credenza, where Mr. Goetz is using his free hand to open his wallet, the other still holding the towel. I don't want the door to close, don't want to be alone with him. I have to rush, lunging over to the bed and dropping the towels. I'm back at the door before it has a chance to shut.

"Hold on a second." Mr. Goetz holds out a twenty. I start to shake my head—it's too big of a tip for something as routine as fresh towels, suspiciously big, enough to make me want to run. He waves the bill at me like you would a piece of food to a wary stray. Stepping back into the room, I take the money and, as I do, he runs his fingers over mine. Gives me a wink. "Thanks, honey," he says.

Back in the lobby, safe behind the concierge desk, I take the twenty and shove it in my purse, tell myself I'll spend it on pepper spray, a pocketknife, something I can carry on me even if I never use it. Just to know it's there.

Then my phone buzzes: a new email.

To: vanessawye@gmail.com
From: jbailey@femzine.com
Subject: Browick School Story

Hi Vanessa,
My name is Janine Bailey and I'm a staff writer at *Femzine* currently working on a piece about the allegations of sexual abuse at the Browick School in Norumbega, Maine, where I understand you attended from 1999 to 2001.

I've interviewed a Browick graduate, Taylor Birch, who alleges she was sexually assaulted in 2006 by English teacher Jacob Strane, and your name was mentioned as another potential victim during my interview with Ms. Birch. Through my research, I've also received a separate anonymous tip regarding sexual abuse that allegedly occurred at the Browick School involving you and Mr. Strane.

Vanessa, I would love to talk with you. I'm committed to writing this piece with all the necessary sensitivity, and want to prioritize the survivors' stories while holding Jacob Strane and the Browick School accountable. With the current nationwide focus on stories of sexual assault, I think we have a real opportunity to make an impact here, especially if I were able to pair your story with Taylor's. You would, of course, have control over what would appear in the article regarding your experience. Think of this as the chance for you to tell your story on your own terms.

You can reach me at this email, or at (385) 843-0999. Call or text anytime.

Really hope to hear from you,
Janine

2001

Winter makes everyone weary this year. The cold is relentless, nights dipping to twenty below, and when the temperature goes above zero, it snows—days and days of it. After each storm, the snow banks grow until campus becomes a walled maze under a pale gray sky, and clothes that were new at Christmas quickly turn salt-stained and pilled as the reality of four more months of winter settles in. Teachers are impatient, even mean, giving faculty feedback so harsh we leave advisee meetings in tears. Over Martin Luther King Jr. Day weekend, the Gould janitor, fed up with us, locks the bathroom when a wad of hair clogs the shower drain for the millionth time, and Ms. Thompson has to use a paper clip to pick the lock. Students turn crazy, too. One night in the dining hall, Deanna and Lucy erupt into a screaming fight over a lost pair of shoes, Lucy grabbing a handful of Deanna's hair and refusing to let go.

Dorm parents are always on the lookout for signs of depression because a sophomore boy hanged himself in his room four winters ago. Ms. Thompson organizes a lot of themed activities to help us stave off the bad feelings: game nights and craft nights, baking parties and movie showings, each announced on a brightly colored flyer slipped under our doors. She encourages us to come by her apartment and use her light therapy box if we ever feel like we're "getting the SADs."

Through it all, I'm only half there. My brain feels split, one part in the moment, the other existing within all the things that have happened to me. Now that Strane and I are having sex, I no longer fit in the places I used to. Everything I write feels hollow; I stop offering to walk Ms. Thompson's dog. In class I feel disconnected, like I'm observing from a distance. During American lit

I watch Jenny switch seats at the seminar table so she's beside Hannah Levesque, who gazes at Jenny with wide-eyed adoration, the same expression I probably had all the time last year, and I feel a muted confusion, like I'm watching a movie with a disorienting plot. Truly, everything feels like a simulation, unreal. I have no choice but to pretend I'm the same as ever, but a canyon surrounds me now, sets me apart. I'm not sure if sex created the canyon or if it's been there all along and Strane finally made me see it. Strane says it's the latter. He says he sensed my difference as soon as he laid eyes on me.

"Haven't you always felt like an outsider, a misfit?" he asks. "I'll bet for as long as you can remember, you were called mature for your age. Weren't you?"

I think back to third grade, how it felt to bring home a report card with a teacher's note scribbled across the bottom: *Vanessa is very advanced, seems like she's eight years old going on thirty.* I'm not sure I was ever really a kid at all.

Twenty minutes before curfew, I walk into the Gould bathroom with my shower caddy and towel to find Jenny standing at the sink, her face smeared with soap. Living in the same dorm, she and I inevitably run into each other, but I've done my best to reduce the frequency, opting for the back stairwell so I don't walk past her room, taking my showers late in the evenings. We're forced together in American lit, but there I'm so focused on Strane that it's easy to ignore her. The rest of the class barely registers to me anymore.

So the sight of her in the bathroom wearing flip-flops and the same grungy bathrobe she had last year startles me so much, I reflexively start to duck back into the hallway. She stops me.

"You don't have to run off," she says, her voice languid as though bored. "Unless you really hate me that much?"

Her fingers rub her cheeks, massaging in the face wash. Her

hair has grown out from the bob she had at the start of the year, enough now for a messy bun at the base of her slender neck—she used to act self-conscious about it, complained that it made her head look like a ball balancing on a straw, a flower on a stem. She acted the same way about her skinny fingers, her size six feet, constantly drawing attention to the features I envied the most. Do I still envy her? I sometimes notice Strane watching her in class, his eyes tracing the line of her spine up to her bright brown hair. The little Cleopatra. "Your neck is perfect, Jenny," I would say. "You know it is." And she did know; she must have known. She just wanted to hear me say it.

"I don't hate you," I say.

Jenny glances at me in the mirror, a doubtful look. "Sure you don't."

I wonder if she would be hurt if I said I don't really feel anything at all toward her anymore. That I can't remember why losing her friendship had felt like losing the world, or why that friendship seemed so profound, never to be repeated. Now, it only strikes me as embarrassing, like any other outgrown phase. I think of how wrecked I was when she started going out with Tom and he began appearing everywhere, sitting with us at every meal, waiting outside our algebra class to spend the two minutes it took to walk from one building to the next with her. I denied being jealous, but of course I was, both of her and of him. I wanted it all—a boyfriend and a best friend, someone to love me enough that nobody could weasel their way between us. It was a pulsating, monstrous wanting beyond my control. I knew it was too much to feel, let alone show, yet I couldn't stop it from letting loose one Saturday afternoon, screaming at Jenny in the bakery downtown, crying like a toddler throwing a tantrum. She'd promised we would spend the day together, just us, a throwback to the pre-boyfriend days, but within an hour Tom appeared, pulling up a chair to our table and nuzzling his face into her neck. I couldn't take it anymore. I snapped.

That happened in late April, but the anger had been brewing within me for months, which explained Jenny's lack of shock, her immediate response like she'd been waiting for my dam to break. As soon as we were back in our room, she said, "Tom thinks you're too attached to me." When I asked her what that meant exactly, "too attached," she tried to shrug it off. "It's just something he said." I didn't care what Tom said about me; he was just some boy who barely spoke, his band T-shirts the only interesting thing about him. But it killed me that Jenny deemed it something worth repeating: "too attached." The implication of what being too attached to another girl might mean made my hair stand on end. I said, "That's not true," and Jenny flashed me the same doubtful look she gave me now. *Sure, Vanessa. Whatever you say.* I didn't argue further; I shut down, stopped speaking to her, and we fell into the silent standoff that had held until now. Deep down, I knew she was right; I did love her too much, and I couldn't imagine ever stopping. But less than a year later, here I am, not caring.

She leans over the sink, rinses off the soap, and pats her face dry as she says, "Can I ask you a question? Because I heard something about you."

I blink, jarred from my memories. "What did you hear?"

"I don't want to say it. It's really . . . I know it can't be true."

"Just tell me."

She presses her lips together, searching for the right words. Then in a low voice, she says, "Someone said you were having an affair with Mr. Strane."

She waits for my reaction, the expected denial, but I am too far away to speak. I'm watching her through the wrong end of a telescope—the towel still pressed to her cheek, her flushed neck. Finally, I manage the words "That's not true."

Jenny nods. "I figured." She turns back to the sink, sets down the towel, and picks up her toothbrush, turns on the water. In my ears, the sound of the tap amplifies to an ocean. The bathroom itself seems to turn watery, the tiled walls undulating.

She spits into the sink, turns off the tap, looks to me expectantly. "Right?" she prompts.

When had she been talking? While brushing her teeth? I shake my head; my mouth flops open. Jenny studies me, something unspooling behind her eyes.

"It is kind of weird," she says, "the way you always stay in his room after class."

Strane starts appearing everywhere, like he's trying to keep an eye on me. He shows up in the dining hall and watches me from the faculty table. He's in the library during study hour, browsing the bookcase directly in front of me. He walks past the open classroom door during my French class, stealing a glance at me each time. I know I'm being surveilled, but it also feels like being pursued, oppressive and flattering all at once.

One Saturday night I'm in bed, hair damp from the shower, homework laid out before me. The dorm is quiet; there's an indoor track meet, an away basketball game, and a ski meet at Sugarloaf. I'm dozing off when the sound of a knock jolts me out of bed, my books falling to the floor. Throwing open the door, I half expect Strane to be there, for him to grab my hand and lead me to his car, his house, his bed. But there is only the lit-up hallway of closed doors, empty in either direction.

Another afternoon he asks me where I went during lunch. It's five P.M. and we're in the office behind his classroom, the rest of the humanities building now empty and dark. The office is barely bigger than a closet, with just enough room for a table, a chair, and a tweed couch with threadbare arms. It had been full of boxes of old textbooks and long-gone students' papers, but he cleaned the room out specifically for us to use. It's the perfect hideaway—two locked doors between us and the hallway.

I tuck my feet up onto the couch. "I went back to my room. I had bio homework."

"I thought I saw you sneak off with someone," he says.

"Definitely not."

He settles into the other end of the couch, pulls my legs onto his lap, and plucks a paper from the to-be-graded stack on the table. We sit in silence for a while, him marking up the papers and me reading my history homework, until he says, "I just want to be sure that the boundaries you and I have established are holding strong."

I eye him, unsure what he's getting at.

"I know how tempting it might be to confide in a friend."

"I don't have friends."

He sets his pen and paper down on the table and takes my feet in his hands, rubbing them at first, and then he wraps his fingers around my ankles. "I trust you, I do. But do you understand how important it is that we keep this secret?"

"Duh."

"I need you to take this seriously."

"I am taking it seriously." I try to pull my feet away. He squeezes my ankles so I can't move.

"I wonder if you really understand the consequences we'd be hit with if we were exposed." I start to speak. He cuts me off. "Most likely, yes, I'd get fired. But you, too, would be sent packing. Browick wouldn't want you here after a scandal like that."

I shoot him a skeptical look. "They wouldn't kick me out. It wouldn't be my fault." Then, not wanting him to think I necessarily believe this, I add, "Meaning technically, because I'm underage."

"It wouldn't matter," he says. "Not to the higher-ups. They root out any and all troublemakers. That's how these places work."

He keeps going, his head tipped back, talking up at the ceiling:

"If we're lucky, it wouldn't go any further than the school, but if law enforcement caught wind of it, I'd almost certainly go to jail. And you'd end up in some foster home."

"Come on," I scoff. "I would not go to a foster home."

"You'd be surprised."

"You may forget this, but I do actually have parents."

"Yes, but the state doesn't like parents who let their child run around with a deviant. Because that's what they would brand me as, a so-called sex offender. After they arrested me, their next step would be to make you a ward of the state. You'd be shipped off to some hellhole—a group home of kids fresh out of juvie who would do god knows what to you. Your whole future would be out of your hands. You wouldn't make it to college if that happened. You probably wouldn't even graduate high school. You may not believe me, Vanessa, but you have no idea how cruel these systems can be. Give them a chance and they'll do everything in their power to ruin both our lives—"

When he starts talking like this, my brain can't keep up. It feels like he's exaggerating, but I get too overwhelmed and lose track of what I believe. He can make even the most outrageous things seem feasible. "I get it," I say. "I'll never tell anyone as long as I live. I'll die before I tell. Ok? I'll die. Can we please stop talking about this now?"

At that, he snaps out of it, blinking as though he just woke up. He holds out his arms for me to crawl into and cradles me against him. He says "I'm sorry" again and again, so many times the words stop making sense.

"I don't mean to scare you," he says. "There's just so much at stake."

"I know there is. I'm not stupid."

"I know you're not stupid. I know you're not."

The French classes take a weekend trip to Quebec City. We leave in the early morning, boarding a coach bus with plush seats and little TV screens. I sit by a window halfway back and dig my Discman out of my backpack, put in a CD, and try to appear like I don't care that I'm the only one without a seatmate.

For the first two hours, I stare out the window as the bus drives through foothills and farmland. When we reach the Canadian border, the landscape stays the same but the road signs switch to French. Madame Laurent shoots up out of her seat at the front of the bus and calls for our attention. "*Regardez!*" She points to each passing sign and prompts us to read them out loud. "*Ouest, arrêt . . .*"

Somewhere in rural Quebec we stop at a Tim Hortons for a bathroom break. There's a pay phone out front and I have two prepaid phone cards in my pocket from Strane with instructions to call if I get lonely. The receiver in my hand, I start to dial when Jesse Ly walks out of the Tim Hortons, wearing a long black coat that fans out around him, practically a cape, followed a ways behind by Mike and Joe Russo, who smirk, nudge each other, and don't even bother lowering their voices as they make fun of him. "Check out the Prince of Darkness," they say. "It's the Trench Coat Mafia." They don't call him gay, because that would go too far, but it feels like that's what they're really making fun of, not his coat. Jesse's face, his tipped-back chin and clenched jaw, shows he can hear them but is too proud to say anything. Dropping the phone receiver, I hurry over.

"Hey!" I grin at Jesse as though we're good friends. Behind us, the Russo twins stop laughing, which has less to do with me and more to do with Margo Atherton, who stands by the bus peeling off her sweatshirt, exposing six inches of stomach as her T-shirt rides up, but I still feel like I've done a good thing. Jesse says nothing as we board the bus and take our seats. Before we take off, though, he gathers up his stuff and moves down the aisle to me.

"Can I sit here?" he asks, pointing to the empty seat. I pull off my headphones, nod, and move my backpack out of the way. Jesse sits with a sigh, tips his head back. He stays like that until the bus shudders on and drives out of the parking lot, back onto the highway.

"Those guys are morons," I say.

His eyes snap open and he inhales sharply. "They're not so bad," he says, opening his novel and turning his body a little away from me.

"But they were being dicks to you," I say, as though he might not have realized.

"Really, it's ok," he says without looking up from the book. He clutches the pages, chipped black polish on his fingernails.

In Quebec City, Madame Laurent leads us through the cobblestone streets, pointing out the historical architecture—the Notre-Dame Quebec Cathedral, the Château Frontenac. Jesse and I barely acknowledge each other as we hang back from the rest of the group, watch the mimes perform on their big granite pedestals, ride the funicular from upper town to lower town and back again. He buys chintzy souvenirs: a watercolor of the Château Frontenac from an old woman on the street and a spoon with a scene from the Winter Carnival etched on the back, which he offers to me. We catch up with the group an hour later and I expect to be in trouble, but no one even noticed we were gone. For the rest of the afternoon, Jesse and I again sneak away, wandering the Old City streets without talking much, just nudging each other every once in a while to point out something funny or strange.

On the second day of the trip I try calling Strane from a pay phone, but there's no answer and I don't dare leave a message. Jesse doesn't ask me who I'm trying to call, doesn't need to.

"He's probably on campus," he says. "There's a coffeehouse open mic thing today in the library. They make all the humanities faculty go to them."

I stare at him as I slide the phone card back in my pocket.

"You don't have to worry," he says. "I'm not going to tell anyone."

"How do you know?"

He gives me a look, like, *Are you kidding?* "You're together all the time. It's fairly obvious what's going on. Plus, I saw it up close firsthand."

I think of what Strane said about foster homes and jails. I'm not sure what I've said counts as telling Jesse, but to be sure, I say, "It's not true." The words sound so pathetic he just gives me another look. Like, *Please.*

We leave on Sunday morning. An hour into the bus ride home, Jesse sighs and sets his novel upside down on his lap, looks over at me, motions for me to take off my headphones.

"You know it's a stupid thing to do, right?" he asks. "Like, *unbelievably* dumb."

"What is?"

He gives me a long look. "You and your teacher boyfriend."

My eyes skim the seats surrounding us, but everyone seems preoccupied—sleeping, or reading, or with their headphones on.

He continues. "It doesn't really bother me morally or anything. I'm just saying he'll probably ruin your life."

I ignore how cleanly his words cut and say it's worth the risk. I wonder how I sound to him, delusional, brave, or both. Jesse shakes his head.

"What?"

"You're an idiot," he says, "that's all."

"Gee, thanks."

"I don't mean that as an insult. I'm an idiot, too, in my own way."

Jesse saying I'm an idiot reminds me of Strane calling me a dark romantic—both seem to point to an inclination toward bad decision-making. The other day Strane referred to me as a "depressive," and I looked up the word: a person with a tendency toward melancholy.

A bad storm hits Norumbega and we wake to a glittering campus shrouded in a half inch of ice. Tree limbs bow under the weight, arching toward the ground, and the snow crust is so thick we can walk atop it without our boots breaking through. On a Saturday afternoon, on the couch in Strane's office, we have sex for the first time in sunlight. Afterward, I avoid looking at his naked body by watching dust motes swirl in the weak winter sun tinged green from the sea glass window. He traces road maps of blue veins on my skin, talks about how hungry I make him, that he'd eat me if he could. I wordlessly offer him my arm. *Go ahead.* He gives it only a soft-mouthed bite, but I would probably let him tear me apart. I'd let him do anything.

February comes and I am both better and worse at hiding things. I stop bringing up Strane during my Sunday night phone calls home, but I can't stay away from his classroom. I'm a permanent fixture there now. Even when other students come in for homework help during faculty service hour, I'm planted at the seminar table, pretending to be absorbed in my work but eavesdropping so intensely my ears burn.

One afternoon when we're alone, he takes a Polaroid camera from his briefcase and asks if he can take a photo of me at the seminar table. "I want to remember what you look like sitting there," he says. I immediately start to laugh from nerves. I touch my face and tug at my hair. I hate having my photo taken. "You can say no," he says, but I see the longing in his eyes, how important this must be. Refusing would break his heart. So I let him snap a few of me, both at the seminar table and sitting behind his desk, another on the couch in the office, my feet tucked up and my notebook open on my lap. He's so grateful, grinning as he watches them develop. He says he'll treasure them forever.

Another afternoon he brings me a new book to read—*Pale Fire*, Vladimir Nabokov. I start to flip through as soon as he gives it to me, but it doesn't look like a novel; the pages show a long poem, a series of footnotes.

"It's a difficult book," Strane explains. "Less accessible than *Lolita*. It's the type of novel that asks the reader to relinquish control. You have to experience it rather than try to understand it. Postmodernism . . ." He trails off, seeing the disappointment on my face. I wanted another *Lolita*.

"Let me show you something." He takes the paperback from my hands, flips to a page, and points to a stanza. "Look, it seems to reference you."

Come and be worshiped, come and be caressed,
My dark Vanessa, crimson-barred, my blest
My Admirable butterfly! Explain
How could you, in the gloam of Lilac Lane,
Have let uncouth, hysterical John Shade
Blubber your face, and ear, and shoulder blade?

My breath catches; my face goes hot.

"Uncanny, isn't it?" He smiles down at the page. "My dark Vanessa, worshipped and caressed." He smooths his hand down my hair, twirls a lock around his finger. Crimson-barred, maple-red hair. I think of what I said when he showed me the Jonathan Swift poem, about all this feeling destined. I hadn't really meant it then. I said it only to show him how happy and willing I was. But seeing my name on the page this time feels like a free fall, a loss of control. Maybe this really was predetermined. Maybe I was made for this.

We're still huddled over the book, Strane's hand resting on my back, when old, balding Mr. Noyes walks into the classroom. We dart off in opposite directions, me back to the seminar table and

Strane behind his desk, obviously caught. But Mr. Noyes seems unbothered. He laughs and says to Strane, "I see you've got a classroom pet," as though it's no big deal. It makes me wonder if we have to worry so much about getting caught. Maybe it wouldn't be the end of the world if the school finds out. They could give Strane a slap on the wrist, tell him to hold off until I graduate and turn eighteen.

When Mr. Noyes leaves, I ask Strane, "Have other students and teachers done this?"

"Done what?"

"This."

He looks up from his desk. "It's been known to happen."

He turns back to reading as the next question rests heavy on my tongue. Before I let it out, I look down at my hands. I imagine the answer laid out plainly on his face and don't want to see it. I don't really want to know.

"What about you? Have you, with another student?"

"Do you think I have?" he asks.

I look up, caught off guard. I don't know what I think. I know what I want to believe, what I have to believe, but I have no idea how those things align with what might've happened in all the years before me. He's been a teacher for almost as long as I've been alive.

Strane watches as I grapple for words, a smile creeping across his face. Finally, he says, "The answer is no. Even if I had moments of desire, it never would've seemed worth the risk. Not until you came along."

I try to hide how happy this makes me feel by rolling my eyes, but his words break my chest wide open and leave me helpless. There's nothing stopping him from reaching in and grabbing whatever he wants. I'm special. I'm special. I'm special.

I'm reading *Pale Fire* when Ms. Thompson knocks on my door for curfew check. She peeks her head around the door, her makeup off, hair tied up in a scrunchie; she sees me and checks my name off her list.

"Vanessa, hey." She steps into the room. "Remember to sign out before you leave on Friday, ok? You forgot before Christmas break."

She takes a step closer and I dog-ear the page I'm reading, close the novel. I feel light-headed from finding more evidence of myself in the text: the town where the main character lives is "New Wye."

"How's the homework?" she asks.

I've never asked Strane about Ms. Thompson. Since the Halloween dance, I haven't seen them together, and I remember how, after he and I had sex for the first time, he said it had been a while since he'd "been intimate." If they never had sex, then they were only friends, so there's no need for me to be jealous. I know all that. Still, when I'm around her a meanness takes over me, an urge to give her a glimpse of what I've done, what I'm capable of.

I set down *Pale Fire* so she can see the cover. "It's not homework. Or, I guess it kind of is. It's for Mr. Strane."

She gives me a smile, irritatingly benign. "You have Mr. Strane for English?"

"Yup." I look up through my eyelashes. "He's never talked to you about me?"

The wrinkles in her forehead deepen. The look lasts only for a second. If I wasn't on high alert, I wouldn't even notice it. "Can't say that he has," she says.

"That's surprising," I say. "He and I are pretty close."

I watch the suspicion bloom on her face, a sense of something amiss.

The next afternoon while Strane is at a faculty meeting, I sit behind his desk, something I would never dare to do otherwise.

The door is closed, no witnesses to see me thumb through his piles of ungraded assignments and lesson plans and pull open the long, skinny desk drawer that has the weird stuff in it: an opened bag of gumdrops, a pendant of St. Christopher on a broken chain, a bottle of antidiarrhea medicine that I shove to the back in disgust.

There usually isn't anything interesting on his computer, only a file of class documents and his rarely used school email, but when I interrupt the screensaver, an alert pops up on the task bar: (1) New Message from melissa.thompson@browick.edu. I click it open. The email is responding to another, three total in the chain.

To: jacob.strane@browick.edu
From: melissa.thompson@browick.edu
Subject: Student Concern

Hi Jake . . . I'd like to talk to you about this in person but thought I'd send an email . . . might be good to put this in writing anyway. I had an odd interaction with Vanessa Wye the other night that involved you. She was doing some homework for your class and mentioned that you and she are "close." It was how she said it . . . gave me a sense of some resentment there . . . even possessiveness? Definitely seems like she's got a crush on you . . . something to be aware of. I know you said she hangs around your classroom. Just be careful :) Melissa

To: melissa.thompson@browick.edu
From: jacob.strane@browick.edu
Subject: re: Student Concern

Melissa,

Appreciate the heads up. I'll keep an eye on it.

JS

To: jacob.strane@browick.edu
From: melissa.thompson@browick.edu
Subject: re: re: Student Concern

No problem . . . hope I didn't overstep . . . just picked up a vibe. Have a good break if I don't see you :) Melissa

I click out of the email chain, marking the most recent one from Ms. Thompson as unread. The curtness of his response makes me laugh out loud, as does Ms. Thompson's nervousness, her little smiley faces, the dot-dot-dots stringing together incomplete sentences. It occurs to me that maybe she isn't a smart person, or at least not as smart as me. I've never thought that about a teacher before.

Strane returns from the faculty meeting in a bad mood, drops his yellow legal pad on his desk and lets out a half sigh, half groan. "This place is going to hell," he mutters. Squinting at the computer monitor, he asks, "Did you touch this?" I shake my head. "Hmm." He grabs the mouse, clicks around. "Might need to put a password on this thing."

At the end of faculty service hour, when he's packing his briefcase, I say in a tone so painfully blasé it doesn't even sound like me, "You know Ms. Thompson is my dorm parent, right?"

I busy myself with putting on my coat so I don't have to look at him while he chooses his answer.

"I do know that," he says.

I drag my zipper up to my throat. "So, you and her are friends?"

"Sure."

"Because I remember seeing you together at the Halloween dance." I peek over at him, watch him wipe his glasses on his tie, put them back on.

"So you did read my email," he says. When I don't say anything, he crosses his arms and gives me one of his teacher looks. *Cut the bullshit.*

"Were you more than friends?" I ask.

"Vanessa."

"I'm just asking a question."

"You are," he agrees, "but it's a loaded question."

I pull my zipper up and down a few times. "I don't really care either way. It would just be nice to know."

"And why is that?"

"Because what if she senses there's something going on with you and me? She might get jealous and—"

"And what?"

"I don't know. Retaliate?"

"That's ridiculous."

"She wrote those emails."

Strane leans back in his chair. "I think the best solution to this problem is for you not to read my email."

I roll my eyes. He's being evasive, which means the truth isn't what I want to hear, and probably means he and Ms. Thompson were more than friends. They probably had sex.

I throw my backpack over one shoulder. "You know, I've seen her without makeup. She's not that pretty. Also, she's kind of fat."

"Come on," he chides, "that's not nice."

I glower at him. Of course it isn't nice; that's the whole point. "I'm leaving now. I guess I'll see you in a week."

Before I open the classroom door, he says, "You shouldn't be jealous."

"I'm not jealous."

"You are."

"I'm *not*."

He stands, moves around his desk and across the classroom toward me. He reaches over my shoulder and flips off the lights, takes my face in his hands, kisses my forehead. "Ok," he says softly. "Ok, you're not jealous."

I let him pull me in, my cheek resting against the middle of his chest. His heart echoes in my ear.

"I'm not envious of whatever dalliances you might've had before me," he says.

Dalliances. I mouth the word, wonder if it means what I hope it does—that even if he did do things with Ms. Thompson, he isn't doing them anymore, and whatever he did with her was never serious, not like what he's doing with me.

"I can't help what I did before I met you," he says, "and neither can you."

For me, there's nothing before him, nothing at all, but I know that's not the point. This is about him needing something from me. Not quite forgiveness, more like absolution, or maybe apathy. He needs me not to care about the things he's done.

"Ok," I say. "I won't be jealous anymore." It feels so generous, like I'm making a sacrifice for him. I've never felt so adult.

Last summer when I was at the height of my sulking, Mom tried to give me a pep talk about boys. She didn't understand what had actually happened with Jenny. She thought it had all been about Tom, that I'd liked him, that he'd chosen Jenny over me or something equally clichéd. It takes time for boys to see anything beyond what's right in front of them, she'd said, and then launched into some allegory about apples falling from trees and boys going for the easy-to-pick apples first but eventually learning that the best apples take a little more work. I wanted none of it.

"So you're saying girls are fruit that only exist for boys to eat?" I asked. "Sounds sexist."

"No," she says, "that's not what I'm saying at all."

"You're literally calling me a bad apple."

"I'm not," she says. "The other girls are bad apples."

"Why do any girls have to be bad apples? Why do we have to be apples at all?"

Mom took a deep breath, pressed the heel of her hand against her forehead. "My god, you're difficult," she says. "All I'm saying is it takes longer for boys to mature. I just don't want you to feel frustrated."

She meant to be reassuring, but her logic was easy to follow: boys never paid attention to me, therefore I wasn't pretty, and if I wasn't pretty, I'd have to wait a long time before anyone noticed me, because boys had to mature before they cared about anything else. In the meantime, apparently my only option was to wait. Like girls sitting in the bleachers at basketball games watching the boys play, or girls sitting on the couch watching boys play video games. Endless waiting.

It's funny to think how wrong Mom was about all that. Because there's another option for those brave enough to take it: bypass boys altogether, go straight to men. Men who will never make you wait; men who are starved and grateful for scraps of attention, who fall in love so hard they throw themselves at your feet.

When I'm home over February break, I go to the grocery store with Mom and, as an experiment, stare at every single man, even the ugly ones, especially the ugly ones. Who knows how long it's been since a girl last looked at them this way. I feel sorry for them, how desperate they must be, how lonely and sad. When the men notice me looking, they're visibly confused, brows knit as they try to figure me out. Only a few recognize what I am, a hardness taking over their faces as they match my stare.

Strane says he can't go a week without hearing from me. So one night halfway through break, after my parents go to bed, I bring the cordless phone up to my room, stuff pillows along the bottom of my bedroom door to block out the sound. My stomach flips as I dial his number. When he answers with a groggy hello, I say nothing, suddenly mortified at the thought of him rolling over and answering the phone like an old person who goes to bed at ten.

"Hello?" he says, impatience raising his voice. "Hello?"

I relent. "It's me."

He sighs and says my name, the *s* whistling through his teeth. He misses me. He wants me to tell him how my break has been, wants to know everything. I do my best to describe my days—walks with Babe, shopping trips into town, ice-skating as the afternoon sun sets on the frozen lake—while avoiding any mention of my parents, making it sound as though I do everything alone.

"What are you doing now?" he asks.

"I'm in my room." I wait for him to ask another question, but he's quiet. I wonder if he's fallen back asleep. "What are you doing?"

"Thinking."

"About what?"

"About you," he says. "And the time you were here in this bed. Do you remember how that felt?"

I say yes, though I know that what I felt and what he felt are probably two different things. If I shut my eyes, I feel the flannel sheets, the weight of the down duvet. His hand wrapped around my wrist, guiding it down.

"What are you wearing?" he asks.

My eyes dart to the door and I hold my breath, listening for any sounds from my parents' bedroom. "Pajamas."

"Like the ones I bought you?"

I say no, laugh at the thought of wearing something like those in front of my parents.

"Tell me what they're like," he says.

I look down at the pattern of dog faces, fire hydrants, and bones. "They're stupid," I say. "You wouldn't like them."

"Take them off," he says.

"It's too cold." I keep my voice light, feign naïveté, but I know what he wants me to do.

"Take them off."

He waits; I don't move. When he asks, "Did you?" I lie and say yes.

It goes on from there, him telling me what to do and me not doing any of it but letting him believe I am. I stay indifferent, a little annoyed, until he starts saying, "You're a baby, a little girl." Then something in me shifts. I don't touch myself, but I close my eyes and let my stomach flutter while I think about what he's doing and that he's thinking about me while he does it.

"Will you do something for me?" he asks. "I want you to say something. Just a few words. Will you do that? Will you say a few words for me?"

I open my eyes. "Ok."

"Ok? Ok. Ok." There's some muffling, like he's moving the phone from one ear to the other. "I want you to say 'I love you, Daddy.'"

For a second, I laugh. It's just so ridiculous. *Daddy.* I don't call my own father that, can't ever remember calling him that, but as I laugh my mind flies out of me and I don't find it funny anymore. I don't find it anything. I'm empty, gone.

"Go on," he says. "I love you, Daddy."

I say nothing, eyes fixed on my bedroom door.

"Just once." His voice haggard and rough.

I feel my lips move and static fills my head, white noise so loud I barely hear the sounds my mouth makes or the sounds of Strane—heavy breathing and groans. He asks me to say it again, and again my mouth forms the words, but it's just my body, not my brain.

I'm far away. I'm airborne, freewheeling, the way I was the day he touched me for the first time, back when I soared across campus like a comet with a maple-red tail. Now I fly out of the house, into the night, through the pines and across the frozen lake where the water moves and moans beneath the ice. He asks me to again say the words. I see myself in earmuffs and white skates, gliding across the surface, followed by a shadow underneath the foot-thick ice—Strane, swimming along the murky bottom, his screams muted to groans.

His labored breathing stops and I land back in my bedroom. He's finished; it's over. I try to imagine how it works when he does that, if he comes into his hand, or a towel, or straight onto the sheets. How gross it is for men, having the giveaway of a mess at the end. The thought *You're fucking disgusting* surges through me.

Strane clears his throat. "Well, I better let you go," he says.

After he hangs up, I throw the phone and it breaks open, batteries rolling across the floor. I lie in bed for a long time, awake but unmoving, eyes fixed on the blue shadows, my mind full of nothing, glassy and still enough to skate on.

Mom doesn't tell me that she heard me talking on the phone until we're driving back to Browick. When she says this, my hand grips the door handle, as though I might open it and hurl myself into the ditch.

"It sounded like you were talking to a boy," she says. "Were you?"

I stare straight ahead. It was mostly Strane doing the talking, but she could have picked up and listened in. My parents don't have a phone in their bedroom and I'd been using the only cordless. Maybe I hadn't heard her go downstairs?

"It's fine if you were," she adds. "And it's fine if you have a boyfriend. You don't need to keep it a secret."

"What did you hear?"

"Nothing, really."

I study her out of the corner of my eye. I can't tell if she's telling the truth. Why does she think I was talking to a boy if she didn't hear anything? My mind races alongside the car, trying to keep up. She must have heard something, but not enough to suspect anything unusual. If she heard Strane's deep, unmistakably grown-man voice, she would have freaked out right then, stormed into my room and ripped the phone from my hands. She wouldn't wait until we were alone in the car to bring it up so delicately.

I let out a slow breath and loosen my grip on the door handle. "Don't tell Dad."

"I won't," she says, her voice bright. She seems pleased, happy that I confided in her and shared my secret, or maybe she's relieved at the idea of me having a boyfriend, being social, fitting in.

"But I want you to tell me about him," she says.

She asks me his name, and for a second, I blank; I never call him by his first name. I could use a fake one, and probably should, but the temptation to say it out loud is too strong. "Jacob."

"Oh, I like that. Is he good-looking?"

I shrug, unsure what to say.

"That's ok," she says. "Looks aren't everything. It's more important that he's nice to you."

"He's nice to me."

"Good," she says. "That's the only thing I care about."

I lean against the headrest, close my eyes. It feels like getting an itch scratched, the relief of hearing her say that Strane being nice is the most important thing, more important than looks, and if treating me well is more important than looks, then it's more important than the age difference, or his being my teacher.

Mom starts asking more questions—what grade he's in, where he's from, what classes we have together—and my chest tightens; I shake my head and snap, "I don't want to talk about this anymore."

We're quiet for a mile and then she asks, "Are you having sex?"

"Mom!"

"If you are, you should be on the Pill. I'll make you an appointment." She stops, says quietly, more to herself than me, "No, you're only fifteen. That's too young." She looks over, her brow furrowed. "You're supervised there. It's not like some kind of free-for-all."

I sit unmoving, unblinking, unsure if she really wants me to reassure her. Yes, we're supervised. The teachers watch us very closely. It's suddenly sickening, this conversation, the deception, treating it all like a game.

Am I a monster? I wonder. *I must be. Otherwise I wouldn't be able to lie like this.*

"Should I make you an appointment?" she asks.

I think of Strane pressing my hip, holding me down, his operation, a vasectomy. I shake my head no and Mom sighs in relief.

"I just want you to be happy," she says. "Happy and surrounded by people who are nice to you."

"I am," I say. As the woods flash by, I venture further. "He tells me I'm perfect."

Mom presses her lips together, holding back a bigger smile. "First love is so special," she says. "You'll never forget it."

Strane is in a bad mood on the first day back, barely looking at me in class and ignoring my raised hand. We're reading *A Farewell to Arms*, and when Hannah Levesque calls the novel boring, Strane snaps that Hemingway would probably find her boring as well. He threatens Tom Hudson with a dress code violation because Tom's sweatshirt is unzipped, his Foo Fighters T-shirt on display. At the end of class, I try to take off with everyone else, for once having zero desire to linger. Before I reach the door, though, Strane calls my name. I stop and the other students move past me like a river current, Tom with his jaw set in anger, Hannah with her wounded expression, Jenny eyeing me as though she wants to say something, the words piled up behind her lips.

When the classroom empties, Strane closes the door, turns off the lights, and leads me into the office, where the radiator is on full blast, the sea glass window fogged over. He leans on the table rather than sitting on the love seat beside me, which seems deliberate, like he's sending a message. Switching on the electric kettle, he says nothing for the time it takes for the water to boil and to make himself a cup of tea; he doesn't offer me one.

When he finally speaks, his voice is clipped, professional. The mug of tea steaming in his hand, he says, "I know you're upset over what I asked you to do during our phone call." Except I'd practically forgotten about the phone call and what he'd asked me to say. Even when I try to recall it now, I can't quite remember. My brain veers away from the memory, repelled by a force beyond my control.

"I'm not upset," I say.

"Clearly you are."

I frown. This feels like a trick; he's the one who's upset, not me. "We don't have to talk about it."

"Yes," he says, "we do."

He does most of the talking, going on about how the break gave him time to think about all the ways in which I'm still a mystery to him. How he doesn't really know me. He's begun to wonder if he's been projecting himself onto me, tricking himself into thinking there's a connection between us when he's really seeing a reflection of himself.

"I even started to wonder if you enjoy making love, or if it's just a performance you put on for my benefit."

"I enjoy it," I say.

He heaves a sigh. "I want to believe you. Truly, I do."

He keeps going, pacing the short length of the office. "I feel so strongly toward you," he says. "Sometimes I worry I'll drop dead from it. It's stronger than anything I've ever felt for any woman. It's not even in the same universe of feeling." He stops, looks at me. "Does it frighten you to hear a man like me talk this way about you?"

A man like me. I shake my head.

"How does it make you feel?"

I look up at the ceiling as I try to come up with the right word. "Powerful?"

After that he relaxes a bit, set at ease by the idea of him making me feel powerful. He says fifteen years old is a strange thing, a real paradox. That in the middle of your adolescence, you're the bravest you'll ever be because of how the brain works at this age, the combination of malleability and arrogance.

"Right now," he says, "at fifteen, you probably feel older than you will at eighteen or twenty." He laughs and crouches before me, squeezes my hands. "My god, imagine you at twenty." He tucks a lock of hair behind my ear.

"Is that how you felt?" I ask. "When you were . . ." I don't say the rest of the sentence, *when you were my age,* because it sounds too much like something a kid would say, but he understands anyway.

"No, but boys are different. As teenagers, they're inconsequential. They don't become real people until adulthood. Girls become real so early. Fourteen, fifteen, sixteen. That's when your minds turn on. It's a gorgeous thing to witness."

Fourteen, fifteen, sixteen. He's like Humbert Humbert, assigning mythical significance to certain ages. I ask, "Don't you mean nine to fourteen?" I mean it in a teasing way, figure he'll understand the reference, but he looks at me like I've accused him of something horrible.

"Nine?" He jerks his head back. "I would never. Jesus, not *nine*."

"It's a joke," I say. "You know, like in *Lolita*. The age nymphets are supposed to be?"

"Is that what you think I am?" he asks. "A pedophile?"

When I don't answer, he stands, starts to pace again.

"You take that book too literally. I'm not that character. That's not what we are."

My cheeks burn at the criticism. It feels unfair; he's the one who gave me the novel. What did he expect?

"I am not attracted to children," he continues. "I mean, look at you, your body. You're nothing like a child."

I narrow my eyes. "What does that mean?"

He stops, momentarily snapped out of his anger, and I feel the power shift slightly back to me. "Well, what you look like," he says. "You're . . ."

"I'm what?" From the couch, I watch him fumble for words.

"I just mean you're fairly developed. More like a woman than not."

"So I'm fat."

"No. God, no. That's not what I'm saying. Of course not. Look at me, I'm fat." He smacks his stomach, tries to get me to laugh, and part of me wants to because I know that's not what he's saying, but it feels good to make him feel bad. He sits beside me, takes my face in his hands. "You're perfect," he says. "You're perfect, you're perfect, you're perfect."

We're quiet for a while, him gazing at me while I scowl up at the ceiling, not wanting to lose the upper hand so soon. I glance over at him and see a bead of sweat run down his cheek. I'm sweating, too—in my armpits, under my breasts.

He stares straight into me. "The thing I asked you to say on the phone? It was a fantasy. I wouldn't really do that. I wouldn't be that."

I say nothing and turn my face back toward the ceiling.

"Do you believe me?" he asks.

"I don't know. I guess so."

He reaches for me, pulls me onto his lap, wraps his arms around me and holds me so my face rests against his chest. Sometimes it's easier to talk this way, when we're not looking at each other.

"I know I'm a little dark," he says. "I can't help it. I've always been this way. It's a lonely way to live, but I'd made peace with that loneliness until you came along." He tugs on my hair. *You*. "When you started turning in those poems and chasing after me, at first I thought, ok, this girl has a crush. No big deal. I'll let her flirt and hang around the classroom a bit, nothing further than that. But the more time I spent with you, I started to think, my god, this girl is the same as me. Separate from others, craving dark things. Right? Aren't you? Don't you?"

He waits for my answer, for me to say yes, I am those things, but what he describes isn't how I've ever thought of myself, and his memory of me chasing after him seems wrong, too. He gave me books before I ever gave him poems. He was the one who said he wanted to kiss me good night, that my hair was the color of red maple leaves. That all happened before I even realized what was really going on. Then I think of him insisting that I'm the one in charge and that he doesn't care about the nonexistent dalliances I've had before him. There are things he needs to believe in order to live with himself, and it would be cruel for me to label these as lies.

"Think of the way you reacted when I first touched you," he says. "Any of those other girls in your class would have been horrified by me doing that, but not you."

He takes a handful of my hair and pulls my head back so he can see my face. His hold isn't rough, but it isn't soft, either.

"When we're together," he says, "it feels as though the dark things inside me rise to the surface and brush against the dark things inside you." His voice shakes with feeling and his eyes are big and glassy, full of love. He studies my face and I know what he's looking for—recognition, understanding, reassurance he's not alone.

I think of his knee pressing into me behind his desk, his hand stroking my leg. I didn't care that he hadn't asked if it was ok, or that he was my teacher, or that nine other people were in the room. As soon as it happened, I wanted it to happen again. A normal girl wouldn't have reacted that way. There is something dark about me, something that's always been there.

When I tell him yes, I feel that, too—the darkness in him, the darkness in me—he's all gratitude and adoration, his hand pulling tighter on my hair. Behind his glasses, his eyes dilate from wanting. He just wants and wants and wants. Sometimes when he's on top of me, when he's moaning with his eyes squeezed shut and not even noticing if I'm excited or sad or bored, I get the feeling all he really wants is to leave part of himself inside me, to stake his claim, not to impregnate me or anything like that, but something more permanent. He wants to make sure he'll always be there, no matter what. He wants to leave his fingerprints all over me, every piece of muscle and bone.

He pushes into me then, braces his legs against the arm of the couch and groans into my ear. It's strange to know that whenever I remember myself at fifteen, I'll think of this.

2017

There's an Oktoberfest event at the hotel, the courtyard full of kegs, plastic beer mugs, and middle-aged couples stuffing their faces with bratwurst. Meanwhile, I sit at the concierge desk picking apart a soft pretzel with my fingers, the guests far too drunk to need anything from me.

Most employees are drunk, too. The restaurant manager was nearly falling down when I first came in. He's in the back office now, gulping black coffee to sober up before the dinner rush. The valets park cars with loose limbs and unsteady eyes, and behind the front desk, even the owner's daughter, only seventeen, sneaks sips from a highball glass. I have two Sazeracs in me, just enough for a soft buzz.

Idly, I click around on the computer, cycling through the endless loop of email-Twitter-Facebook-email-Twitter-Facebook. The journalist wrote to me again, a polite but pushy follow-up—Hi Vanessa, I wanted to reach out to you again and reiterate how committed I am to getting your truth out there—strain in her words as she tries to appeal to the desire for retribution she assumes I have.

From the corner of my eye, I see a drunken guest stagger into the lobby, and I stare more intently at the computer screen, hunch my shoulders, and scowl, knowing he's less likely to bother me if I look like a hag. I hear the man say, "Hey there, honey," and my stomach drops, but his eyes are set on seventeen-year-old Inez behind the front desk. I turn back to the computer, the journalist's email. Getting your truth out there. My truth. As though I have any idea what that is.

Behind the front desk Inez tries to hide her glass, but the man sees. "Whaddya got there?" He peeks over the desk. "Drinking on the job? Bad girl."

It doesn't feel like my hand moving the mouse around the screen. Someone else guides it to the upper right corner, clicks "forward."

Inez's laugh is high and strained. The man takes this as encouragement and puts both elbows on the desk, leans in close. He squints at her name tag. "*Inez.* That's a pretty name."

"Uh, thanks."

"How old are you?"

"Twenty-one."

The man shakes his head, wags his finger. "There's no way you're twenty-one," he says. "Feels like just looking at you is enough to get me arrested."

My fingers move from key to key, typing jacob.strane@browick.edu into the recipient field as I watch the drunk man tell Inez how pretty she is, how she makes him wish he were thirty years younger. She scans the lobby for help, a thin smile plastered on her face, her eyes resting for a moment on me as I take the mouse, move the cursor to "send," and click.

The forwarded email takes off, the confirmation of message sent flashes at the top of the browser, and then—nothing happens. I don't know what I expect, for an alarm to be tripped, a crescendo of sirens, but the lobby remains the same, the drunk man still leering, Inez still eyeing me for help as I stare back, thinking, *What do you want from me? You really need me to rescue you? This is nothing. You're safe; he's on the other side of the desk and he's not going to get you. If you're that scared, go into the back office or flat-out tell him to leave. You should know how to handle this.*

Behind me, an elevator opens and a houseman emerges pushing a cart stacked with crates of wine for the courtyard event. Inez, seeing an opportunity, darts out from behind the front desk.

"Do you need help, Abdel?" she asks. The houseman shakes his head, but she grabs one end of the cart anyway. The drunken guest watches her disappear down the hallway, arms limp at his sides. Once she's gone, he looks over his shoulder, notices me for the first time.

"What are you looking at?" he asks, and then lumbers back outside into the courtyard.

Letting out a breath, I turn back to my computer screen and start the email-Twitter-Facebook loop all over again when my phone buzzes with a call from Strane. I watch it vibrate against the desk until it goes to voicemail. He tries again, then again, one after another. With each missed call, something within me gains momentum—a sense of smugness, a feeling of triumph. Maybe that journalist isn't wrong after all. Maybe there is vengeance lurking somewhere within me.

After my shift, I go to a bar. Perched on a stool in my work suit and sucking down whiskey and water, I scroll through my contacts, shooting off texts to see who might be willing to engage at eleven fifteen on a Monday night. Ira ignores me, as does the man I brought home a few weeks ago who left my apartment as soon as he could after I turned silent and unresponsive beneath him, my body curling into itself, hands hiding my face. Only one takes the bait: a fifty-one-year-old divorcé I slept with a few months ago. I didn't like how he spoke to me or how he treated the age gap like something out of a porno, calling himself Daddy and asking if I wanted a spanking. I tried to tell him to relax and be normal, but he didn't want to hear it, just clamped a hand over my mouth and said, *You want it like this, you want it, you know you do.*

Me: I'm drinking alone.

Him: Young girls shouldn't ever drink alone.

Me: Oh?

Him: Mmhmm. You should listen to me. I know what's best for you.

Between the texts, I receive another call from Strane—the seventh since I forwarded him the journalist's email. Hitting "ignore," I text the divorcé the address, and within fifteen minutes, he and I are sharing a cigarette in the alley behind the bar. I ask him how he's been; he asks me if I've been a bad girl.

I eye him as I take a drag and try to gauge how serious he is, if he expects me to answer.

"Because you look like you've been bad," he says.

I say nothing and look down at my phone. There's a text from Strane: I don't know what you're trying to communicate by sending me that email. As I watch, another appears: I don't have the patience for any games right now, Vanessa. Give me the courtesy of behaving like an adult. The divorcé moves toward me, backs me up against the brick wall of the bar. Shielded by the dumpsters, he presses his body into mine, tries to shove his hand under the waistband of my pants. At first I laugh and try to squirm away. When he doesn't stop, I shove him with the heels of my hands. He backs off but still looms over me, out of breath, his shoulders heaving. I flick my cigarette; ash spills onto his shoe.

"Relax," I say. "Just be cool, ok?" My phone starts to ring, and because the divorcé is there, or because I know I've worked Strane into a panic, which is all I really wanted, or because I'm drunk and therefore stupid, I swipe up to answer. "What do you want?"

"'What do you want?'" Strane says. "Is that really how you want to play this?"

I drop my cigarette and grind it out even though it's only half smoked, then immediately grope through my purse for another, waving off the divorcé when he offers me a lighter.

"Fine," the divorcé says. "I'll leave you alone. I can take a hint."

On the phone, Strane asks, "Who is that? Is someone there with you?"

"It's nothing," I say. "It's nobody."

The divorcé scoffs, turns on his heel like he's going back into the bar, then checks over his shoulder as if I'm going to stop him.

"Why did you forward me that email?" Strane asks. "What are you planning on doing?"

"I'm not planning anything," I say. "I just wanted you to see it."

They're both quiet, Strane on the phone and the divorcé holding the door open, waiting for me to tell him to stay. He's wearing the same clothes he had on when we hooked up before: black jeans, black T-shirt, black leather jacket, black combat boots—the uniform of the aging punks I always seem to end up going out with these days, men who claim to be turned on by strength but can only handle women who act like girls.

"I understand it might be tempting," Strane says, choosing each word with care, "to join in on the hysteria going on right now. And I know it would be easy for you to depict what happened between us as . . . inappropriate or abusive or whatever other label suits your mood. There's no doubt in my mind you'd be able to turn me into whatever you wanted . . ." He trails off, takes a breath. "But my god, Vanessa, do you really want this attached to you for the rest of your life? Because if you do this, if you come forward, it's going to stick to you—"

"Look, I'm not going to do anything," I say. "I'm not going to write her back, not going to tell. Ok? I'm not. I just wanted you to see what's going on, you know, on my end. You should realize this isn't only about you."

Through the phone, I feel the tide pull in his direction, a sudden gathering of feeling. He lets loose a bitter laugh. "That's what this is about?" he asks. "You needing attention and sympathy? Right now, in the midst of this shitstorm, that's the time you decide to act wounded?"

I start to apologize, but he cuts me off.

"You're comparing what I'm facing to you getting a couple of emails?" he asks, practically yelling. "Are you out of your fucking mind?"

He reminds me that, in this situation, I have it good. Don't I realize how much power I have? If the story of him and I came out, no one would blame me for a thing, not one fucking thing. It would all fall on him.

"I have to carry the weight of this alone," he says. "And all I'm asking is for you not to make it worse."

I end up crying, my forehead pressed against the brick alley wall. *I'm sorry. I don't know what's wrong with me. I'm sorry, you're right, you're right.* He cries, too. Says he's scared, that everything's starting to feel ominous. He's back teaching, but half the students transferred out of his classes, he was stripped of all his advisees, no one will look him in the eye. They're waiting for a reason to get rid of him.

"I need you on my side, Vanessa," he says. "I need you."

I go back inside, sit at the bar, and hang my head until the divorcé touches my shoulder. I bring him home, let him see the mess, let him do whatever he wants, I don't care. In the morning, he takes a hit off my weed while I pretend to be asleep. Even when he leaves, I don't open my eyes, don't move. I stay in bed until ten minutes before the start of my shift.

I don't see the article until I'm at work, sitting behind my desk. It's published on the front page of the Portland newspaper: "Longtime Boarding School Teacher Suspended Amid Further Allegations of Sexual Abuse." Five girls accusing him now, it says. Taylor Birch, plus four others: two recent graduates and two current students, all minors at the time of alleged abuse.

For the rest of my shift, my body carries on working. I use muscle memory to call restaurants, confirm reservations with guests, write out directions, wish everyone a lovely evening. Across the lobby, valets push luggage carts piled high with bags, and at the front desk Inez answers the phone in her high, sweet voice, "Thank you for calling the Old Port Hotel." Tucked away in the corner of the lobby, I am rigid and empty-headed, staring off into middle distance. The hotel owner passes by and notes how professional I look. He likes my posture, how there's nothing but empty appeasement behind my eyes.

The article says Strane groomed the girls. *Groomed.* I repeat the word over and over, try to understand what it means, but all I can think of is the lovely warm feeling I'd get when he stroked my hair.

2001

"Vanessa, you must be better about showing your steps," Mrs. Antonova says, smoothing the crumples out of my geometry homework for that week's tutoring session. "Otherwise how will I understand how you arrived at the answer?"

I mumble something like why should it matter so long as the answers are right, and Mrs. Antonova gives me a long look over her glasses. I should know why it matters; she's explained it many times.

"How do you feel about the test next Friday?" she asks.

"Same as I've felt about every other test."

"Vanessa! What is this attitude? This isn't you. Sit up straight, be respectful." She reaches forward and raps her pencil against my notebook that I still haven't opened. I sigh and push myself up out of my slouch, open the notebook.

"Should we go over the Pythagorean theorem again?" she asks.

"If you think I need it."

She takes off her glasses and sticks them up in her spun-sugar hair. "These sessions should not be me telling you what to do. What you need, we cover, ok? But I need you to meet me . . ." She gestures with one hand, groping for the word. "Halfway."

At the end of the session, I scramble to gather my things, wanting to get across campus to the humanities building so I can see Strane before his faculty meeting, but Mrs. Antonova stops me.

"Vanessa," she says, "I wanted to ask you."

I chew on the inside of my cheek while she collects her textbook, binder, tote bag.

"How are your other classes going?" she asks, pulling her pashmina off the back of the chair. She wraps it around her shoulders, combs the fringe with her fingers. It feels like she's moving slowly on purpose.

"They're fine."

She holds the classroom door open for me and asks, "What about your English grade?"

I grip my textbook tighter. "It's fine."

As we walk down the hallway, I pretend not to notice how she watches me. "I ask because I hear you spend a lot of time in Mr. Strane's room," she says. "Is that right?"

I swallow hard, counting each footstep. "I guess."

"You were in the creative writing club, but that meets only in the fall, yes? And English is a strength for you, so it can't be that you need the extra help."

I lift my shoulders, my best impression of nonchalance. "He and I are friends."

Mrs. Antonova studies me, deep wrinkles forming between her drawn-on eyebrows. "Friends," she repeats. "Does he tell you this? That you and him are friends?"

We round the corner, the double doors within sight now. "I'm sorry, Mrs. Antonova. I have a lot of homework," I say, trotting down the hallway, opening one of the double doors, and skipping down the steps. Over my shoulder, I thank her for all her help.

I don't tell Strane about Mrs. Antonova's questions, because I worry if I do, he'll say we need to be more careful and we already made plans for me to come over to his house on accepted student day, a Saturday of wide-eyed eighth graders and their parents wandering around campus in packs. Strane says it's a good night to do something clandestine, that special events inevitably bring confusion and things can slip through the cracks more easily.

At ten, I do the same routine as last time: check in with Ms. Thompson for curfew and sneak out the back stairwell with the broken alarm. As I run across campus, I hear noises coming from the dining hall—delivery trucks, metal slamming shut, men's voices through the dark. Strane's station wagon waits again with the headlights off in the faculty lot by the humanities building. He seems vulnerable waiting for me in his car, trapped in a little box. When I tap on the window, he jumps and presses a hand to his chest, and for a moment I just stand there, watching him through the window and thinking, *He could have a heart attack. He could die.*

At his house, I sit at the kitchen counter, banging my heels against the chair legs while he makes scrambled eggs and toast. I'm pretty sure eggs are the only thing he knows how to cook.

"Do you think anyone suspects something's going on with us?" I ask.

He gives me a surprised look. "Why do you ask?"

I shrug. "I dunno."

The toaster dings; the toast pops up. The slices are too dark, practically burnt, but I don't say anything. He spoons eggs on top of the toast and sets the plate in front of me.

"No, I don't think anyone's suspicious." He takes a beer from the fridge and drinks while he watches me eat. "Do you want people to be suspicious?"

I take a big bite to buy time before answering. Some questions he asks me are normal and some are tests. This one sounds like a test. Swallowing, I say, "I want them to know I'm special to you."

He smiles, reaches for my plate and picks up a piece of egg with his fingers, tosses it in his mouth. "Trust me," he says, "they definitely know that."

He surprises me with a movie for us to watch—*Lolita*, the old Kubrick one. It feels like his way of apologizing for saying I take the novel too literally. While we watch, he lets me drink a beer, and after, when we go to bed and I wear the strawberry pajamas again, I'm so floaty that when he asks me to get on my hands and knees so he can go down on me from behind, I don't act embarrassed at all, I just do it. After the sex is finished, he goes into the living room and brings back the Polaroid camera.

"Don't get dressed yet," he says.

I hold my arms over my chest and shake my head, my eyes wide.

Smiling gently, he reassures me it'll be for his eyes only. "I want to remember this moment," he says. "The way you look right now."

He takes the pictures. Afterward, I wrap myself in the comforter and Strane lays the photos across the mattress. Together we watch them develop, the bed and my body emerging from the dark. "My god, look at you," Strane says, his eyes darting from one to the other. He's entranced, transfixed.

I stare at the photos and try to see what he sees, but I look too weird in them—painfully pale against the unmade bed, my eyes unfocused, hair matted from sex. When he asks what I think, I say, "They remind me of that Fiona Apple music video."

He doesn't look up from the Polaroids. "Fiona who?"

"*Apple*. My favorite singer? Remember I had you listen to her once?" I also, a couple weeks ago, wrote some of her lyrics on a piece of notebook paper, folded it up, and left it on his desk on my way out of class. We were in the midst of a fight about me going away to college—I said I didn't want to, he said I shouldn't let myself be sidetracked, not by anyone or anything, including him, which made me cry, and then he said I was trying to manipulate him by crying. I thought the lyrics might help him understand how I felt, but he never said anything about it. I wonder if he even read them.

"Right, right." He gathers up all the photos. "Better put these in a safe hiding place."

He leaves the bedroom, goes downstairs, and I'm suddenly so annoyed I feel a burning in my chest, in my face and limbs. I pull the comforter over my head, breathe in the hot air, and remember how I said something about Britney Spears a few weeks ago and he had no idea who she was. "Is she some kind of pop act?" he asked. "I didn't realize your taste skewed that way." He made it seem like

I was stupid when he's the one who didn't even know who Britney Spears was.

Over April break, I turn sixteen. Babe goes to the vet to get spayed and comes home dopey with a shaved, stitched-up belly. I show my parents the list of colleges Strane picked out for me and we drive down to southern Maine to visit a couple there. As we wander the campuses, my father stares dumbfounded at the buildings, while my mother reads off information she found online: 40 percent of Bowdoin students participate in study abroad; one in four students continue on to graduate school. "What's the price tag for this place?" Dad asks. "Did you print off those figures?"

Halfway through the week, Strane comes to see me while my parents are at work, parking the station wagon in an overgrown boat access lane and hiking through the woods to our house. I wait in the living room, peeking around the doorway into the kitchen, waiting for him to appear in the window, and I let out a little shriek when he does, as though I'm scared, but I'm not really—how could I be? In his khaki jacket and clip-on sunglasses, he looks like someone's dad, some nondescript middle-aged dork, mild as milk.

As he cups his hands and peers in through the window, I grab Babe by the collar and throw open the door. Once he steps inside, she slips out of my hands. He grimaces as Babe jumps on him, her pink tongue flopping out the side of her mouth. I tell him to say no and she'll stop, but instead he shoves her too hard and she falls onto her back, the whites of her eyes flashing as she sulks away from him into her kennel. For a moment, I hate him.

He looks around the house, hands clasped behind his back like he's scared to touch anything, and I suddenly see everything from his perspective, how the house isn't clean like his, the layer of dog hair on the carpet, the old couch and its sagging cushions. Walking through the downstairs, he pauses at the little wooden houses balanced on the windowsills. Mom collects them; I give her one for Christmas every year. Strane stares at them and I imagine what he's thinking—that they're an ugly, stupid thing to collect. I think of the knickknacks on his bookcases, each one from a foreign country with a story behind it, and I think of what he said about my parents after their conference. *Decent people,* he called them. *Salt-of-the-earth types.* It reminds me of something I heard him say about another scholarship student, a senior in his AP class who was accepted to Wellesley but wasn't going because it was too expensive. He felt awful for her, but what could you do? *The poor girl doesn't come from much,* he said.

"It's boring down here," I say, grabbing his hand. "Let's go upstairs."

In my bedroom, he ducks as he steps through the doorway. He's so big he dominates the whole room, his head brushing against the slanted ceiling, his eyes taking in the poster-covered walls, the unmade bed.

"Oh," he breathes. "This is such a precious thing."

Because of Browick, my room is frozen in time, more a representation of who I was at thirteen than who I am now. I worry it might seem too much like a little girl's room, but that doesn't seem to bother Strane. He studies the bookcase crammed full of middle-grade novels I've long outgrown, the dresser cluttered with dried-out bottles of nail polish, Beanie Babies covered in dust. Lifting the lid of my jewelry box, he grins when the ballerina pops up and begins to spin. He opens a drawstring bag and pours worry dolls made of brown paper and string into his palm. He treats everything so delicately.

Before we have sex, he has me pretend to be asleep so he can crawl into bed and touch me as I feign waking up. When he pushes inside me, he clamps a hand over my mouth and says, "We have to be quiet," as though there were someone else in the house. While he pounds into me, so frantic and fast it feels like my brain rattles around in my skull, my limbs go limp and my mind slips out of me, retreats downstairs where Babe whines in her kennel, still wondering what she did wrong. After Strane finishes, he takes another Polaroid of me lying in bed, posing me first, arranging my hair over my breasts and opening the window shade so the light drapes across my body.

Later we go for a drive in his station wagon and cruise the highways that wind through the down east woods. His window is open; he lets his arm hang out. It's warm for April, seventy degrees, buds on the trees, weeds starting to grow along the roadside.

"I'll come see you during the summer just like this," he says. "I'll pick you up and we'll go for drives."

"Like Lolita and Humbert," I say without thinking, and then wince as I wait for his annoyance at the comparison, but he only smiles.

"I suppose that's fair." He looks over at me, slides his hand up my thigh. "You like the idea of that, don't you? Maybe one day I'll just keep driving rather than bring you home. I'll steal you away."

The closer we get to the coast, the busier the roads become. Strane doesn't seem afraid, though, so I'm not, either. We're outlaws on the lam, a couple of brazen criminals driving all the way to the easternmost tip of the state, a fishing village of people who don't bat an eye when we stop for sodas at the market and stroll down the pier discreetly hand in hand.

"Sixteen years old," he marvels. "Practically a woman now."

We set the self-timer on the Polaroid and balance it on the hood of the car. The photo comes out a little overexposed—Strane with his arm around me, the ocean a backdrop. It's the only photo that exists of the two of us. I want to ask if I can have it but figure he'll say no, so when he stops for gas I take it out of the glove compartment and slip it into my purse. I leave him the one of me on my bed. That's the one he really cares about anyway.

On the way home, he says he wants to kiss me a little while

longer, so he pulls off the highway onto a dirt logging road. The station wagon rocks over the gravel, mud splatters on the windshield. We drive a few miles through dense woods until the trees thin and then disappear altogether, revealing a rolling blueberry barren, a carpet of green dotted with white boulders. He parks, cuts the engine, and undoes his seat belt, reaches over and undoes mine.

"Get over here," he says.

As I climb over the console to straddle him, my back presses against the steering wheel and hits the horn, sending a spray of crows into the sky at the far edge of the barren. He cups my butt, the skirt of my dress hiked up around my waist, and a buzzing hums through the air. Out the car window, I see an apiary swarming with bees a couple hundred feet away. We're miles from anyone and anywhere, free to do whatever we want, our isolation as safe as it is dangerous. I don't know how to feel one without the other anymore.

He pushes my underwear aside. Two fingers in me. I'm still all sticky from the sex in my bedroom, the insides of my thighs starting to rash. My forehead presses into the crook of his neck, hot breath against his collarbone as he tries to make me come. He says he can feel it when I do. Some women lie about it, he says, but what my body does can't be faked. He says I get there fast. He can't believe how fast. It makes him want to make me get there over and over, to see how many times in a row I can handle, but I don't like that. It makes sex feel like some sort of game that only he's allowed to play.

As soon as it happens, I tell him to stop. I only have to say it once and he takes his hands off me like I'm something on fire. I move away from him, back over the console to the passenger seat, legs slick and chest heaving. He lifts his hand, the one that was working at me, and holds it to his face, breathes me in. I wonder how many times he's made me come. *Congratulations,* I want to say, *you did it yet again.* Tipping my head back, I watch the bees swarm and the tops of the far-off conifers sway.

"I don't know how I'm going to handle being away from you this summer," I say. I don't even know if I mean it. During breaks I've been fine without him. He's the one who says he can't go a week without talking to me or seeing me. It's just the sort of thing that slips out after sex, when I'm soft-belly vulnerable. But Strane takes it seriously. He's sensitive to any indication that I'm too attached, that he's affecting me in a way that might have long-term consequences.

"You'll be seeing plenty of me," he says. "You'll be sick of me by July."

When we're back on the road, he says it again. "You'll get sick of me." Then he adds, "You'll be the one to break my heart, you know. You're holding me in your little hands."

Break his heart? I try to imagine myself having that power, holding his heart, mine to abuse, but even when I picture it pulsing and pumping in my hands, it's still the boss of me, leading me around, jerking me this way and that with me clinging and unable to let go.

"Maybe you'll break me," I say.

"Impossible."

"Why impossible?"

"Because that isn't how these stories end," he says.

"Why does it have to end at all?"

He looks from the road to me, back to the road, his eyebrows cocked in alarm. "Vanessa, when we say goodbye, it won't be painful for you. You'll be ready to be rid of me. The rest of your life will stretch out ahead of you. It'll be exciting for you to move on."

I say nothing and stare out the windshield. I know that if I try to talk or move, I'll start to cry.

"I see so much in store for you," he says. "You're going to do incredible things. You'll write books, traipse around the world."

He keeps prophesizing, says I will have had a dozen lovers by the time I'm twenty. When I'm twenty-five, I'll be childless and still look like a girl, but at thirty, I'll be a woman, no more baby cheeks, with fine lines around my eyes. And, he says, I'll be married.

"I'm never getting married," I say. "Same as you. Remember?"

"You don't really want that."

"Yes, I do."

"You don't," he says flatly, his teacher voice taking over. "I'm no one to model yourself after."

"I don't want to talk about this anymore."

"Don't be upset."

"I'm not."

"You are. Look at you. You're crying."

I hunch my shoulders away from him and press my forehead against the window.

"It's just how it has to be," he says. "We aren't always going to fit together the way we do now."

"Please stop talking."

A mile goes by, the roar of eighteen-wheelers, the slow curve of an esker and the boggy lake below, a brown-black mass in the distance that could be a moose, could be nothing.

He says, "Vanessa, when you look back, you'll remember me as someone who loved you, just one of many. I guarantee your life is going to be so much bigger than me."

I let out a shaky breath. Maybe he's right. Maybe there's safety in what he says, a chance to walk away unscathed and unbound. Is it really impossible to imagine that I might emerge from this worldly and wise, a girl with a story to tell? Someday when people ask me, "Who was your first lover?" the truth will set me apart. Not some ordinary boy, but an older man: my teacher. He loved me so desperately I had to leave him behind. It was tragic, but I didn't have a choice. That's just how the world works.

Strane reaches for me as he drives, his fingers tracing my knee. He steals glances away from the road to check my face. He wants to make sure I like what he's doing. Does that feel good? Does that make me happy? My eyelids flutter as his hand moves up my thigh. He lives to please me. Even if we end up apart, right now, he worships me—his dark Vanessa. That should be enough. I'm lucky to have this, to be so loved.

❧

After April break, it's all downhill momentum. Warm days bring classes held outside and weekend trips to Mount Blue. Daffodils bloom and the Norumbega River rushes high, flooding the downtown streets. Creative writing club starts up again when the new issues of the lit journal come back from the printers, and as Jesse and I are sorting through the boxes, deciding where to drop the copies, Strane calls me into the office and kisses me hard, his tongue filling my whole mouth. It's reckless, bafflingly so; Jesse's right there, the office door not even closed all the way. When I return to the classroom, lips stinging and cheeks flushed, Jesse pretends not to notice, but he doesn't show for our next meeting.

"Where's Jesse?" I ask.

"He quit," Strane says. He smiles, seems pleased.

In English, we start a unit where we compare famous paintings to books we've read that year. Renoir's *Luncheon of the Boating Party* is *The Great Gatsby*, everyone lazy and drunk. Picasso's *Guernica* is *A Farewell to Arms*, the disjointed horrors of war. When Strane shows us Andrew Wyeth's *Christina's World*, the class agrees that it's most like *Ethan Frome* with its stark loneliness, the looming house on the hill. After class, I tell Strane that I see *Lolita* in the Wyeth painting and try to explain why—because the woman looks so beaten down with her skinny ankles, because the impassable distance between her and the house reminds me of the description of Lo at the end, pale, pregnant, and destined to die. Strane shakes his head and says for the millionth time that I assign too much significance to that novel. "We need to get you a new favorite book," he says.

He takes our class on a field trip to the town where Andrew Wyeth lived. We drive down the coast in a van so big that, sitting in the passenger seat beside him, the rest of the kids barely register. It's thrilling to leave campus with him, even with the entire class behind us, oblivious captives. What if he and I decided to seize the moment and run away together? We could leave them stranded at a rest stop, Jenny's hair whipping across her face as she watches us peel away.

But it's a bad time for a field trip, because he and I are in the midst of a fight over the idea of me spending another night at his house before summer break. He says we should hold off, not press our luck, and that I'll see him plenty over the summer, but when I ask for specific dates, he tells me I need to stop building my world around him. So on the drive, I give him the silent treatment and do things I know will annoy him—fiddle around with the radio, stick my feet up on the dash. He tries to ignore me, but I note his clenched jaw, how tight he grips the steering wheel. He says there's no reasoning with me when I get like this, when I act like a child.

Once in the town of Cushing, we tour the Olson House, the farmhouse at the top of the hill in *Christina's World.* The rooms are full of dusty, old-fashioned furniture and framed Wyeth paintings. But they aren't real, the tour guide explains. They're reproductions. They can't hang real ones because the salt air is too harsh and would ruin the canvases.

It's sixty-five degrees, warm and sunny enough to eat lunch outside. Strane lays out a blanket at the bottom of the hill, looking up at the farmhouse, the same perspective as *Christina's World.* After we eat, we do freewriting as he circles around us, hands clasped behind his back. I'm still committed to my anger and refuse to play along, leave my notebook and pen untouched on the ground while I lie on my back and gaze up at the sky.

"Vanessa," Strane says. "Sit up, get to work."

It's what he'd say to any other student acting out, but with me there's a weakness in his voice, a pleading note that surely the others can hear. *Vanessa, please don't do this to me.* I don't move.

When everyone else gets in the van for the drive to Browick, he grabs my arm and leads me around the back. "You've got to cut this out," he says.

"Let go." I try to jerk away, but he's holding me too tight.

"Acting like this isn't how you get what you want." He gives my arm a shake so rough it nearly knocks me over.

I glance up at the van's back windows, feeling split in two, one part out here with him, the other inside with everyone else, clicking in my seat belt and shoving my bag under the seat. If any of them looked out the back window, they would see his fingers digging into the soft skin of my upper arm and it would be enough to make someone start to suspect—more than enough. A thought slaps me, stings my skin: maybe he wants someone to see. I'm starting to understand that the longer you get away with something, the more reckless you become, until it's almost as if you want to get caught.

That night Jenny knocks on my door and asks if she can talk to me. From my bed, I watch her step inside and shut the door behind her. She takes in the mess of my room, the clothes strewn across the floor, the desk covered in loose papers and half-drunk mugs of tea blooming mold.

"Yes, I'm still disgusting," I say.

She shakes her head. "I didn't say that."

"You were thinking it."

"I wasn't." She pulls out my desk chair, but it's covered with a pile of clean laundry from a week ago that I never put away. I tell her to push it off, and she tips the chair, spilling the clothes onto the floor.

"What I want to talk about is serious," she says. "I just don't want you to get mad at me."

"Why would I get mad?"

"You're always mad at me, and I really don't understand what I did to deserve it." She glances down at her hands, adds, "We used to be friends."

I twist my face up, about to protest, but she takes a breath and says, "I saw Mr. Strane touch you on the field trip today."

At first I don't understand what she's talking about. *I saw Mr. Strane touch you.* It sounds too sexual. Strane didn't touch me on the field trip; we were mad at each other the whole time. But then I remember him grabbing my arm behind the van.

"Oh," I say. "It wasn't . . ."

She watches my face.

"It wasn't anything."

"Why did he do it?" she asks.

I shake my head. "I can't remember."

"Has he done it before?"

I don't know how to answer because I don't know what she's really asking, if this means that she now believes the rumor about Strane and I having an affair. She makes a face like she's dealing with someone helpless, the look she used to give me when she sensed I didn't know something she did about music or movies or the general ways the world worked. "I had a feeling," she says.

"You had a feeling what?"

"You don't have to feel bad. It's not your fault."

"*What* isn't my fault?"

"I know he's abusing you," she says.

My head jerks back. "Abusing me?"

"Vanessa—"

"Who told you that?"

"No one," she says. "I mean, I heard that rumor about you having sex with him for an A on a paper, but I didn't believe it. Even before I talked to you about it, I didn't believe it. You're not like that . . . you wouldn't do that. But then I saw what he did to you today, grabbing you, and I realized what's really going on."

The whole time she talks, I shake my head. "You're wrong."

"Vanessa, listen," she says. "He's horrible. My sister used to tell me he was a creep, that he'd harass girls when they wore skirts, stuff like that, but I had no idea he was this bad." She leans forward, her eyes hard. "We can get him fired. My dad is on the board of trustees this year. If I tell him about this, Strane is out."

I blink through the shock of her words—*fired, a creep, harassing girls.* How horrible it is to hear her call him Strane. "Why would I want to get him fired?"

"Why wouldn't you?" She seems genuinely confused. After a moment, her face turns gentle, pursed lips and upturned brows. "I know you're probably scared," she says, "but you don't have to be. He won't be able to hurt you anymore."

She stares at me, her face brimming with pity, and I wonder how it's possible that I once felt so much for her, yearned to be closer even as I slept beside her in the same small room, our bodies three feet apart. I think of her navy blue bathrobe hanging on the back of the door, the little boxes of raisins wrapped in cellophane that sat on the shelf above her desk, how she smeared lilac-scented lotion on her legs at night, the wet spots on her T-shirt from her freshly washed hair. Sometimes she binged on microwave pizzas, the shame pulsing out of her as she ate. I had noticed everything about her, every single thing she did, but why? What was it about her? She's so ordinary to me now, with a mind too narrow to understand anything about me and Strane.

"Why do you care so much about this?" I ask. "It has nothing to do with you."

"Of course it has to do with me," she says. "He shouldn't be here. He shouldn't be allowed near us. He's a predator."

I laugh out loud at the word *predator*. "Give me a break."

"Look, I actually care about this school, ok? Don't laugh at me for wanting to make it a better place."

"So you're saying I don't care about Browick?"

She hesitates. "No, but . . . I mean, it's not really the same with you. No one else in your family went here, you know? For you, it's like you come here and graduate and then that's it. You never think about it again. You never contribute."

"Contribute? Like give money?"

"No," she says quickly. "That is not what I said."

I shake my head. "You are such a snob."

She tries to backtrack, but I'm already putting my headphones on. They're not plugged into anything, the cord hanging off the bed, but it makes her stop talking. I watch her as she stands to leave, scoops up the laundry, puts it back on the chair. It's an act of kindness, but in the moment it enrages me, makes me tear off the headphones and ask, "So how's it going with Hannah?"

She stops. "What do you mean?"

"Are you two, like, besties now?"

Jenny blinks. "You don't have to be mean."

"You're the one who was always mean to her," I say. "You used to make fun of her to her *face*."

"Well, I was wrong," she snaps. "Hannah is fine. You, however, need serious help."

She goes to pull open the door and I add, "Nothing is going on with him and me. Anything you've heard is stupid gossip."

"It's not what I heard. I saw him touch you."

"You didn't see anything."

She squints at me, wraps her hand around the doorknob. "Yes," she says, "I did."

Strane has me recount what Jenny said to me word for word, and when I get to the part where she called him a creep, his eyes bug out like he can't believe anyone would ever accuse him of that. He calls her a "smug little bitch" and for a moment my body goes cold. I've never heard him use that word before.

"It'll be fine," he assures me. "So long as we both deny everything, everything will be perfectly fine. Rumors need proof to be taken seriously."

I try to point out that it isn't really a rumor, because Jenny saw him grab my arm. Strane only scoffs.

"Proves nothing," he says.

The next day in English, he asks us a question about *The Glass Menagerie* and calls on Jenny even though she doesn't raise her hand. Flustered, she looks down at her book. She wasn't paying attention, probably didn't even hear the question. She stammers out a few "ums," but instead of calling on someone else, Strane sits back in his chair and folds his hands like he's prepared to wait all day.

Tom starts to speak and Strane holds up his hand. "I'd like to hear from Jenny," he says.

We sit through another agonizing ten seconds. Finally, in a small voice, Jenny says, "I don't know," and Strane lifts his eyebrows and nods. Like *That's what I thought.*

At the end of class, I watch Jenny leave with Hannah, both of them whispering, Hannah throwing a glare over her shoulder at me. I approach Strane as he's erasing the chalkboard and say, "You shouldn't have done that to her."

"I would have thought you'd enjoy it."

"Embarrassing her will only make things worse."

He blinks at me, registering the criticism. "Well, I've taught kids like her for the past thirteen years. I know how to handle them." He drops the eraser on the chalk rail and wipes his hands. "And I'd really prefer if you didn't critique my teaching."

I apologize, but it's disingenuous and he knows it. When I say I have to go, that I have homework to do, he doesn't try to get me to stay.

Back in my room, I lie facedown on my bed and breathe into my pillow to calm myself out of hating him. Because in the moment, it does feel like that—like I hate him. Really, I just hate it when he gets angry at me, because that's when I feel things that probably shouldn't be there in the first place, shame and fear, a voice urging me to run.

It all falls apart over the course of one week. It starts on Wednesday, when I'm in French class and Strane opens the classroom door and asks Madame Laurent if he can borrow me. "Bring your backpack," he whispers. As we walk across campus to the administration building, he explains what's happening, but it's already obvious. Jenny wasn't in English class the past two days, and I've seen her around so I know she isn't sick. The previous night at dinner, I watched her with Hannah, their heads ducked together. When they came up for air, both turned straight toward me.

Strane says Jenny's father sent a letter to the school, but that it's all hearsay, no proof. It won't go anywhere. We just need to do exactly what we've talked about: deny everything. They can't hurt us if we both deny. An ocean roars in my ears. The more he talks, the further away he sounds.

"I already told Mrs. Giles none of this is true, but it's more important that you deny it." He watches my face as we walk. "Are you going to be able to do that?"

I nod. There are fifty steps to go before we reach the front door of the building, maybe less.

"You're very calm," Strane says. He stares into me, searching for a crack, the same way he looked at me in his station wagon after we had sex for the first time. As he opens the door, he says, "We'll get through this."

Mrs. Giles says she wants to believe us rather than what's in the letter—that's literally what she says from behind her enormous desk as Strane and I sit in the wooden chairs, like two kids in trouble.

"Honestly, I have a hard time imagining how this could be true," she says, picking up a piece of paper that I assume is the letter. Her eyes move over the lines. "'Ongoing sexual affair.' How could such a thing go on without anyone noticing?"

I don't understand what she means. Clearly, people have noticed. That's the whole reason Jenny's dad wrote the letter—people noticed.

Beside me, Strane says, "It really is absurd."

Mrs. Giles says she has a theory about what's behind all this. Every once in a while a rumor like this will manifest, and students, parents, other teachers catch wind of it and immediately take it as truth, regardless of how unbelievable the rumor might be.

"Everyone loves a scandal," she says, and then she and Strane exchange a knowing smile.

She says the rumors usually sprout from jealousy or a misinterpretation of innocent favoritism. That over the course of a career, teachers have many, many students, most of whom are, for lack of a better word, inconsequential. Students might be bright, accomplished individuals, but that doesn't necessarily mean a teacher will have a special connection with them. Every once in a while, however, a teacher will come across a student with whom he or she feels especially close.

"Teachers are human, after all, same as you are," Mrs. Giles says. "Tell me, you don't like all your teachers equally, do you, Vanessa?" I shake my head no. "Of course you don't. Some you prefer more than others. Teachers are the same with students. To a teacher, some students are just special."

Mrs. Giles leans back in her chair, folds her hands across her chest. "What I suspect happened is Jenny Murphy became jealous of the special treatment you received from Mr. Strane."

"One relevant point Vanessa shared with me," Strane says, "is she and Jenny roomed together last year and they didn't get along." He looks at me. "Isn't that right?"

Slowly, I nod.

Mrs. Giles throws up her hands. "Well, there you have it. Case closed."

She hands me a piece of paper—the letter from Jenny's father. "Now if you could read that over and then sign this." She hands me a second paper with a single typed line of text: "The parties below deny any truth to the contents of the letter written by Patrick Murphy on May 2, 2001." At the bottom are spaces for two signatures, mine and Strane's. My eyes skim over the letter, unable to focus. I sign the paper and then hand it to Strane, who does the same. Case closed.

Mrs. Giles smiles. "That should do it. Best to resolve these things as quickly as possible."

Shaky with relief, feeling like I might throw up, I stand and head toward the door, but Mrs. Giles stops me before I leave. "Vanessa, I'll have to call your parents to let them know about this," she says. "So make sure to call them this evening, ok?"

Bile rises in my throat. I hadn't considered this before. Of course she has to call them. I wonder if she'll call my house, leave a message on the answering machine, or if she'll call one of them at work—Dad at the hospital, Mom in her office at the insurance company.

As I leave the room, I hear Mrs. Giles say to Strane, "I'll let you know if I need anything else from you, but this should take care of it."

When I call home that evening, I offer a flood of explanations and platitudes: *everything's fine, nothing's going on, the whole thing is ridiculous, a stupid rumor, of course it's not true.* My parents are on different phones, both talking at once.

"You need to stop hanging out with these teachers, first of all," Mom says.

Teachers? Has there been more than one? Then I remember the

lie I told back at Thanksgiving, that it was my politics teacher who said my hair was the color of maple leaves.

Dad asks, "Do you want me to come get you?"

"I want to know exactly what's been going on there," Mom adds.

"No," I say. "I'm fine. And nothing's been going on. Everything's fine."

"You'd tell us if someone's been hurting you," Mom says. They both wait for me to confirm that, yes, I would tell them.

"Sure," I say. "But that's not what happened. Nothing's happened. How would it happen? You know how much supervision there is here. It's a lie Jenny Murphy came up with. Remember Jenny, how mean she was to me?"

"But why would she make something like this up? Get her father involved?" Mom asks.

Dad says, "This just doesn't sound right."

"She hates Mr. Strane, too. She has a vendetta against him. She's one of those entitled people who think anyone who doesn't suck up to her deserves to have his life ruined."

"I don't like this, Vanessa," Dad says.

"It's fine," I say. "You know I would tell you if anything was wrong."

He and I go quiet, wait for Mom.

"It's almost the end of the year," she says. "I guess it doesn't make sense to pull you out. But, Vanessa, you stay away from that teacher, ok? If he tries to talk to you, tell the headmaster."

"He's my teacher. He has to be able to talk to me."

"You know what I mean," she says. "Go to class and then leave."

"He's not even the problem."

"Vanessa," Dad barks. "Listen to your mother."

"I want you to call us every night," Mom says. "At six thirty, I expect the phone to ring. Understood?"

Staring across the common room, the television showing MTV

on mute, Carson Daly's spiked hair and black nail polish, I mumble, "Yes, ma'am." Mom sighs. She hates it when I call her that.

Strane says we need to back off for a while, be conscious of optics. No late afternoons in his office, long hours spent alone. "Even this is a risk," he says, meaning my skipping lunch to spend the free period in his classroom with the door wide open. We need to be careful, at least for the time being, as much as it kills him to keep his distance from me.

He's confident, though, that it'll all blow over soon. He keeps using that phrase, "blow over," like this is some bad weather. Summer will come and, with it, drives in his station wagon, open windows, and sea-salt air. He tells me to trust him, that by next fall, this will all be forgotten. I don't know if I believe him. A couple days pass and things seem ok, but whenever I'm within eyesight of Jenny, she shoots me a look of raw resentment. Strane thinks she's given up because she transferred out of his class, but I can tell she's still mad.

The bulletin board goes up listing every senior's plan for college the following year. I go to dinner and, while I'm waiting in line at the sandwich station, I notice Jenny and Hannah moving methodically around the dining hall. Jenny carries a pen and notebook, and as they approach each table, Hannah says something to the people sitting there, waits for a response, and then Jenny writes something down in the notebook. I notice, too, how many eyes turn toward me, then dart away, not wanting me to catch them staring.

I leave the line, and as I walk across the dining hall I hear Hannah ask, "Have any of you heard a rumor that Vanessa Wye and Mr. Strane are having an affair?"

It's a table of seniors. Brandon McLean, whose name I saw listed next to Dartmouth on the bulletin board, asks, "Who's Vanessa Wye?"

The girl sitting beside him—Alexis Cartwright, Williams College—points to me. "Isn't that her?"

The whole table turns. Jenny and Hannah do, too. I catch a glimpse of Jenny's notebook, a list of names, before she hides it against her chest.

Twenty-six. That's how many names are on Jenny's list. I sit across from Mrs. Giles, this time only her and me in the office, no secretary or Strane. Mrs. Giles hands me a copy of the list, and I read down the names, mostly sophomores, classmates, girls on my floor. No one I've ever talked to about Strane. Then I see the last name on the page—Jesse Ly.

"If you have anything you want to tell me," Mrs. Giles says, "now is the time to do it."

I'm not sure what she's expecting from me, if she still believes the rumor isn't true or if this list has changed her mind and now she's angry that I lied. She's angry about something.

I look up from the list. "I'm not sure what you want me to say."

"I'd like you to be honest with me."

I say nothing, not wanting to take a step in any direction.

"What if I tell you I've spoken with a student on this list who says you explicitly told them you were romantically involved with Mr. Strane?"

It takes me a moment to understand she doesn't mean "explicit" in a sexual sense, but that I told this person directly. Again, I say nothing. I don't know if she's telling the truth. It seems like the sort of bluff cops on TV shows use when trying to wrangle a confession out of someone. The smart move is always to stay silent, wait for your lawyer—though I don't know who the equivalent of a lawyer would be in my case. Strane? My parents?

Mrs. Giles takes a deep breath, touches her fingers to her temples. She doesn't want to be dealing with this. I don't want to deal with this, either. We should just forget it—that's what I want to say. Let's forget all about this. But I know we can't, not with Jenny leading the charge, and because of who her father is. The structure of Browick suddenly seems obvious, a blatant system of power and worth in which some people matter more than others, something I've always felt but haven't before been able to comprehend so plainly.

"We need to get to the bottom of this," she says.

"We are at the bottom," I say. "None of it is true. That's the bottom."

"So if I go get this student and bring them in here, will your story change?" she asks.

I blink as I realize she's trying to call my bluff, not the other way around. "It's not true," I say again.

"Fine." She gets up, leaves the office, the door still open.

The secretary pokes her head in, sees me and smiles. "Hang in there," she says.

A lump rises in my throat from this small scrap of kindness. I wonder if she believes me, what she thought during the last meeting with Mrs. Giles and Strane, while she sat scribbling down everything we said on her yellow legal pad.

A few minutes pass and Mrs. Giles comes back into the office with Jesse Ly trailing behind her. He sits in the chair beside mine, but he doesn't look at me. His face burns red, his neck, his ears. His chest heaves with each breath.

"Jesse," Mrs. Giles says, "I'm going to ask you the same question you answered before. Did Vanessa tell you that she and Mr. Strane were having an affair?"

Jesse shakes his head. "No," he says. "No, she never said that." His voice is high, frantic, the kind of voice you use when you're so desperate not to tell the truth, you don't care how obvious it is that you're lying.

Mrs. Giles again presses her fingertips to her temples. "That isn't what you said five minutes ago."

Jesse keeps shaking his head. *No, no, no.* He's distraught, so much so that I'm gripped with an overwhelming pity for him. I imagine reaching over and placing my hand over his, saying, *It's ok, you can tell her the truth.* But I only sit and watch, wondering if I'm ultimately to blame for him going through this moment of obvious pain, if it matters that I'm the one with more to lose.

"What did you tell her?" I ask quietly.

Jesse's eyes jump over to me. Still shaking his head, he says, "I didn't know this was going to happen. She just asked me—"

"Jesse," Mrs. Giles says. "Has Vanessa ever told you that she and Mr. Strane are romantically involved?"

He looks back and forth, from her to me. When his eyes sink to the floor, I know what's coming. I close my eyes and he says yes.

If I were weaker, this would be it. I've been trapped, confronted with my own inconsistency. The way Mrs. Giles stares me down, it's obvious she thinks this is over, that I'm about to break. But there's still a way out of this tunnel. I see the sliver of light. I just have to keep digging.

"I lied," I say. "It was all lies. What I told Jesse about Strane"—I correct myself—"Mr. Strane, none of it was true."

"You lied," Mrs. Giles repeats. "And why would you do that?"

I look her straight in the eye as I explain my reasons: because I was bored and lonely, because I had a crush on a teacher, because I have an overactive imagination. The longer I talk, the more confident I become, blaming myself, absolving Strane. It's such a good excuse, it explains away anything I said to Jesse, plus whatever rumors the twenty-five other names on the list heard. This should have been my story from the beginning.

"I know lying is a bad thing to do," I say, looking from Jesse to Mrs. Giles, "and for that I'm sorry. But that's the whole truth. There's nothing else to it."

It's a dizzy pleasure, like filling my lungs with fresh air after pulling the blankets off my face. I am smart and I am strong—more than anyone understands.

I skip lunch and go straight to Strane's classroom, knock on the door. He doesn't answer even though I can see the lights are on through the textured glass window. I tell myself he's just worried about the optics still, but during English, Mr. Noyes is there instead of Strane, and as soon as I step inside the classroom, he tells me I need to go to the administration building.

"What's going on?" I ask.

He holds up his hands. "I'm only the messenger," he says, but it's clear in the wary way he looks at me, like he doesn't want to be near me, that he knows something. I walk across campus, unsure if I should hurry or drag my feet, and when I reach the front steps of the admin building, looking up at the columns and the Browick seals on the double doors, Dad's truck pulls into the main campus entrance. I hold my hand up to shield my eyes and see they're both in there, Dad driving, Mom in the passenger seat with her hand clamped over her mouth. They turn into the parking lot, get out of the truck.

I hurry back down the steps and call, "What are you doing here?" At the sound of my voice, my mother's head whips around and she points a finger down at her feet, the way she calls to Babe when she's done something bad. *Get over here.* Just like the dog, I stop fifteen feet away and refuse to come any closer.

"Why are you here?" I ask again.

"Jesus, Vanessa, why do you think?" she snaps.

"Did Mrs. Giles call you? There's no reason for you to be here."

Dad is still in his work clothes, gray slacks and a blue pin-striped shirt with PHIL embroidered over the pocket. Despite everything else, embarrassment flares up in me. Couldn't he have changed?

He slams the truck door and strides over to me. "You ok?"

"I'm fine. Everything's fine."

He grabs my hand. "Tell me what happened."

"Nothing happened."

He stares straight into me, pleading, but I reveal nothing. My lower lip doesn't even tremble.

"Phil," Mom says. "Let's go."

I follow them into the building, up the stairs, and to the little room outside Mrs. Giles's office with the now-familiar secretary. I look to her for another smile, but she ignores me as she waves us in. Strane is in the office with Mrs. Giles, standing beside her desk, hands in his pockets, shoulders back. My chest aches from wanting to burrow into him. If I could I'd press myself into him and let his body consume me whole.

Mrs. Giles holds out her hand for my parents to shake. Strane holds out his hand, too, which Dad takes, but Mom just sits down, ignores him like he isn't even there.

"I think it's best if Vanessa isn't here for this," Mrs. Giles says. She looks to Strane and he gives a quick nod. "You can head back into the waiting room."

She gestures to the door, but I'm staring at Strane, noticing how his hair looks wet from the shower and that he's wearing his tweed blazer and a tie. *He's going to tell them,* I think. *He's turning himself in.*

"Don't," I say, but it barely comes out.

"Vanessa," Mom says. "Go."

The meeting lasts a half hour. I know this because the secretary turns on the radio, probably to keep me from overhearing what's being said in the office. "It's your two thirty afternoon coffee break," the DJ says, "a half hour of nonstop soft hits." While the secretary hums along, I think about how I'll always remember these songs because they were the ones playing when Strane confessed and sacrificed himself for me.

When it's over, they all emerge at once. Mrs. Giles and my parents stop in the waiting room. Strane keeps walking. He leaves without giving me a glance. I see Mom's flared nostrils and dilated eyes, Dad's mouth set in a straight line, looking how he did when he had to tell me our old dog died overnight.

"Come on," he says, taking my hand.

We sit on a bench outside, Mom staring at the ground, her arms crossed tight, while Dad does the talking. What he says is so far from what I expect, it takes me a while to swing back up and actually listen. He's not saying, *We know everything, it's not your fault.* He's saying that there's a code of ethics at Browick that students are held to, and I violated it by lying about a teacher and damaging his reputation.

"They take stuff like that pretty seriously here," Dad says.

"So it's not . . ." I look from one face to the other. "He didn't . . ."

Mom's head jerks up. "He didn't what?"

I swallow hard, shake my head. "Nothing."

Their explanation continues. I'm going to end the school year early. There are only a couple weeks left anyway. They're spending the night at the inn downtown, and, in the morning, I'll have to, as Dad puts it, "right my wrong." Mrs. Giles wants me to tell all the people on Jenny Murphy's list that the rumor about me and Mr. Strane is a lie and that I started the lie.

"Like, tell them one at a time?" I ask.

Dad shakes his head. "Sounds like everyone's going to get together so you can do it in one go."

"You don't have to do it," Mom says. "We can pack up your room and leave tonight."

"If Mrs. Giles wants me to do it, I have to," I say. "She's the headmaster."

Mom purses her lips, like she wants to say more.

"I'm still coming back next year, right?"

"Let's take this one step at a time," Dad says.

They take me out to dinner at the pizza place downtown. Between the three of us we can't even finish a pie. We pick at our slices, Mom using napkin after napkin to soak up the grease. Neither of them will look at me.

They offer to drive me back to campus, but I say no, I want to walk. Look at what a nice night it is, I say, still warm at dusk.

"I could use a peaceful few minutes before I go back up there," I say.

I expect them to refuse, but they seem too dazed to argue and let me go. They hug me goodbye outside the restaurant, Dad whispering, "I love you, Nessa," in my ear. They turn left toward the inn and I go right toward campus and the public library, toward Strane's house.

"I know this is stupid," I say when he opens the door, "but I had to see you."

He looks beyond me, to the street and sidewalk. "Vanessa, you can't be here."

"Let me come in. Five minutes."

"You need to leave."

I'm so frustrated, I scream and shove him with both hands, using all my weight, which doesn't move him but rattles him enough to shut the door and usher me around the side of the house so we're shielded from the street. As soon as we're secluded, I throw my arms around him, press against him as hard as I can.

"They're making me leave tomorrow," I say.

He takes a step back, unwinds my arms, and says nothing. I wait for his face to show something—anger or panic or regret for having let the situation reach this point—but he's completely blank. He shoves his hands in his pockets and looks over my shoulder, up at the house. He's like a stranger standing before me.

"They want me to talk in front of a bunch of people," I say. "I'm supposed to tell them I lied."

"I know," he says. He still won't look at me, his face set in a deep frown.

"Well, I don't know if I can do it." At that, his eyes flick down at me, a tiny victory, so I push it further. "Maybe I should tell them the truth."

He clears his throat but doesn't flinch. "From what I understand, you've already come pretty close to doing that," he says. "You told your mother about me. You told her I was your boyfriend."

At first I don't remember, then: the drive home from February break, after she heard me on the phone in the middle of the night. *What's his name?* she asked, the snow-covered fields and skeleton trees flying past the car windows. I answered with the truth—Jacob. But that was just a word, a common first name, not the same as a confession. She hadn't gleaned the truth from that one word. She couldn't have. If she did, she wouldn't have let Strane leave Mrs. Giles's office or agreed to this idea of me apologizing to a roomful of people.

"If you've decided you want to ruin me," Strane says, "I can't stop you. But I hope you understand what will happen if you do."

I try to say that I didn't really mean it, that of course I'm not going to tell, but his voice drowns out mine.

"Your name and photo will be in the papers," he says. "You'll be all over the news." He speaks slowly, carefully, like he wants to make sure I understand. "This will follow you around forever. You'll be branded for life."

I want to say, *Too late.* That I walk around every day feeling permanently marked by him, but maybe that's unfair. Hasn't he been trying hard to save me? Making me promise I'd move away for college, insisting that ultimately my life would be bigger than him. He wants more for me, an expanse of a future rather than a narrow road, but that can only happen if he remains a secret. Once the truth is out, he'll come to define my entire life; nothing else about me will matter. I see a half memory, like something from a dream: a hybrid girl, part myself and part Ms. Thompson—or maybe I'm remembering a news clip of Monica Lewinsky?—a young woman with tears rolling down her cheeks, trying to hold her head high through question after humiliating question of what happened: *Tell us exactly what he did to you.* It's easy to imagine how my life could become one long trail of wreckage leading directly back to my decision to tell.

"I'd rather end my life right now than go through that," Strane says. He looks down at me, his hands still in his pant pockets. He's casual even as he looks ruin in the eye. "But maybe you're stronger than I am."

At that, I start to cry, really cry, the kind I've never done in front of him before—hiccupping, awful, ugly crying with snot dripping from my nose. It comes on so fast, it knocks me over. I lean against the side of the house, brace my hands against my thighs, and try to breathe. The sobs won't stop. I wrap my arms around my middle, crouch on the ground, and smack the back of my head against the cedar shingles, like I'm trying to whack them out of me. Strane kneels before me, holds his hands behind my head, between me and the house, until I stop struggling against him, open my eyes.

"There you are," he says. He inhales, exhales, and my chest rises and falls along with him. His hands still cradle my head, his face close enough to kiss. Tears dry on my skin, tighten my cheeks, and his thumb strokes the soft spot behind my ear. He's grateful, he says, for what I've done so far. It's very brave to take responsibility and offer myself to the wolves. It's evidence of love. I probably love him more than anyone else ever has.

"I'm not going to tell," I say. "I don't want to. I never will."

"I know," he says. "I know you won't."

We work out together what I'll say in the meeting tomorrow, how I'll blame myself for the rumors, apologize for lying, and make clear that he did nothing wrong. It isn't fair, he says, that I'm being forced to do this, but clearing his name is the only way to get out of this alive. He kisses me on the forehead and the corners of my eyes the way he did when we kissed for the first time in his classroom, huddled behind his desk.

Before I leave, I glance over my shoulder and see him standing on the dark lawn, his silhouette illuminated by the light from the living room windows. Gratitude radiates out of him and into me, floods me with love. This, I think, is what it means to be selfless, to be good. How could I ever have thought of myself as helpless when I alone have the power to save him?

The next morning, the twenty-six people on Jenny's list meet in Mr. Sheldon's classroom. There aren't enough desks for everyone, so some kids lean against the back wall. I can't tell who's there; I only see faces bobbing and swaying, an ocean of buoys. Mrs. Giles has me stand next to her at the front of the room while I read the statement Strane and I came up with the night before.

"Any inappropriate rumors you might have heard about Mr. Strane and me are not true. I spread lies about him, which he did not deserve. I'm sorry for being deceitful."

The faces stare back at me, unconvinced.

"Does anyone have questions for Vanessa?" Mrs. Giles asks. One hand shoots up. Deanna Perkins.

"I just don't get why you would lie about this," Deanna says. "It doesn't make sense."

"Um." I look to Mrs. Giles, but she only stares back at me. Everyone is staring at me. "That isn't really a question."

Deanna rolls her eyes. "I'm just saying, why?"

"I don't know," I say.

Someone asks a question about why I'm in his room all the time. I say, "I'm never in his room," a lie so glaring, a couple people laugh. Someone else asks if there's something wrong with me "like, mentally," and I say, "I don't know, probably." As the questions continue, I realize the obvious: that I can't come back, not after this.

"Ok," Mrs. Giles says, "that's enough."

Everyone is given a slip of paper with three questions. One, who did you hear this rumor from? Two, when did you hear it? Three, have you told your parents about it? When I leave, all twenty-six heads are bent, filling out the survey, except for Jenny's. She sits with her arms crossed, staring at her desk.

I get back to Gould and find my parents packing up my room. The bed is stripped, the closet empty. Mom blindly dumps my stuff into a garbage bag—trash, papers, anything on the floor.

"How did it go?" Dad asks.

"It?"

"The, you know . . ." He trails off, unsure what to call it. "The meeting."

I don't answer. I don't know how it went, can't even process what really happened. Watching Mom, I say, "You're throwing away important stuff."

"It's garbage," she says.

"No, you're putting school things in there, stuff I need."

She stands back and lets me rifle through the garbage bag. I find an essay with Strane's comments, a handout he gave us on Emily Dickinson. I clutch the papers to my chest, not wanting them to see what it is I'm saving.

Dad zips my big suitcase, stuffed with clothes. "I'll start bringing stuff down," he says, stepping out into the hallway.

"We're leaving now?" I turn to Mom.

"Come on," she says. "Help me clean this out." She opens my bottom desk drawer and gasps. It's full of trash: crumpled papers, food wrappers, used tissues, a blackened banana peel. I'd filled it in a panic a few weeks ago right before room inspections and forgotten to clean it out. "Vanessa, for god's sake!"

"Just let me do it if you're going to yell at me." I grab the bag from her.

"Why won't you just throw things away?" she asks. "I mean, Jesus, Vanessa, that's trash. *Garbage.* What kind of person hoards garbage in a drawer?"

I focus on breathing as I empty the desk drawer into the trash bag.

"It's not sanitary and it's not normal. You scare me sometimes, you know that? These things you do, Vanessa, they don't make sense."

"There." I shove the drawer back into the desk. "All clean."

"We should disinfect it."

"Mom, it's fine."

She looks around the room. It's still a mess, though it's hard to tell what mess is mine and what is from packing everything up.

"If we're leaving now," I say, "I need to go do something."

"Where do you need to go?"

"Ten minutes."

She shakes her head. "You're not going anywhere. You're staying here and helping us clean this room."

"I have to say goodbye to people."

"Who do you need to say goodbye to, Vanessa? It's not like you have any goddamn friends."

She watches as my eyes smart with tears but doesn't look sorry. She looks like she's waiting. That's how everyone's been looking at me this whole week—like they're waiting for me to break. She turns back to the mess, yanking open the top dresser drawer and pulling out fistfuls of clothes. When she does, something falls, slides across the floor between us: the Polaroid of Strane and me on the village pier. For a moment, she and I stare down at it, equally stunned.

"What . . ." Mom crouches down, reaches for it. "Is that—"

I swoop down, grab the photo and press it facedown to my chest. "It's nothing."

"What is that?" she asks, reaching for me now. I back away.

"It's nothing," I say.

"Vanessa, give it to me." She holds out her hand like there's a chance I might give it up that easily, like I'm a child. I say again that it's nothing. It's nothing, ok? Over and over, my voice rising into a panic until it reaches a scream so forceful Mom steps away from me. The high note seems to linger, ringing through the half-emptied room.

"That was him," she says. "You and him."

Staring at the floor, shaken from the scream, I whisper, "It wasn't."

"Vanessa, I *saw* it."

My fingers curl against the Polaroid. I imagine Strane here in the room, how he'd calm her down. *It's nothing,* he'd say, his voice soothing as a balm. *You didn't see what you thought you did.* He could convince her of anything, same as me. He'd guide her to the desk chair and make her a cup of tea. He'd slip the photo into his pocket, a movement so subtle and quick she wouldn't even notice.

"Why are you protecting him?" Mom asks. She breathes hard, her eyes searching. It's not a question of anger; she truly doesn't understand. She's baffled by me, by all of this. "He hurt you," she says.

I shake my head; I tell her the truth. "He didn't."

Dad comes back then, his face sweaty. He hefts a duffel bag full of books over one shoulder and, as he's looking for something else to carry, notices Mom and I in our standoff, my hand still pressing the Polaroid to my chest. To Mom, he says, "Everything ok here?"

There's a beat of total silence, the dorm at midmorning empty except for us. Mom lets her eyes slide away from me. "Everything's fine," she says.

We pack up the rest of my room. It takes four trips to bring everything down. There's a moment before I get in the truck when my feet burn to run—across campus, down the hill into downtown, to Strane's house. I imagine breaking in, climbing into his bed, hiding beneath the covers. We could have run away. I said that to him last night before I left his house. "Let's get in your car right now and drive off." But he said no, that wouldn't work. "The only way to get through this is to face the consequences and do our best to live through them."

As Dad lifts the last garbage bag into the truck bed, Mom touches my shoulder. “We can still go tell them,” she says. “Right now, we can go in—”

Dad opens the door, hoists himself into the driver’s seat. “You ready?”

I jerk my shoulder out of Mom’s grasp and she watches me climb into the cab.

The whole drive home, I lie across the back bench seat. I watch the trees, the silvery underbellies of leaves, the power lines and signs for the interstate. In the truck bed, the tarp covering all my stuff flaps in the wind. My parents stare straight ahead, their anger and grief palpable enough to taste. I open my mouth to let it all in and swallow it whole, where deep in my belly it turns into blame.

2017

Mom calls as I'm walking home from the grocery store, my bag weighed down with pints of ice cream and bottles of wine. She asks, "Do you want to come home for Thanksgiving?" sounding exasperated, as though she's asked me this many times before when we haven't spoken about the holiday at all.

"I assumed you would want me to," I say.

"It's up to you."

"Do you not want me to come?"

"No, I do."

"Then what is it?"

A long pause. "I don't want to cook."

"You don't have to."

"It won't feel right if I don't."

"Mom," I say, "you do not have to cook." I adjust the grocery bag on my shoulder and hope she can't hear the clanking bottles. "You know what we should do? Get some of that frozen fried chicken that comes in the blue box. We can just eat that. Remember how we used to have it every Friday night?"

She laughs. "I haven't had that in years."

I walk down Congress Street, past the bus depot, the statue of Longfellow staring down every passerby. I can hear the news playing in the background of the phone call: a pundit's voice, then Trump's.

Mom groans and the background noise is gone. "I mute him whenever he comes on."

"I don't understand how you can watch that all day."

"I know, I know."

My building comes into view. I'm about to wrap things up as she says, "You know, I saw your old school in the news the other day."

I don't stop walking, but I stop thinking, stop looking. I walk past my building, cross the next street and keep going. I hold my breath and wait to see if she'll push further. She only said *your old school*, not *that man*.

"Well anyway," she says with a sigh, "that place always was a hellhole."

In the wake of the article about the other girls, Browick suspends Strane without pay and opens another investigation. This time the state police are involved, too. Or at least I think these things are true; they're morsels I've picked up from Taylor's Facebook posts and the comment section of the article, where pieces of seemingly legitimate information hide among rumors, rants, and hand-wringing. People screaming, IT'S SIMPLE, JUST CASTRATE ALL PEDOPHILES; others giving a more subdued benefit of the doubt, stuff like, Shouldn't we all be innocent before proven guilty, let justice run its course, you can't always trust these accusations, especially when they come from teenage girls with their vivid imaginations, their emotional unreliability. It's head spinning and endless, and I don't really know what's going on because Strane hasn't told me. My phone sits silent for days.

It takes all my self-control not to reach out. I write him texts, delete them, and write them again. I draft emails, bring up his number and poise my finger to call, but I won't let myself. Despite the years of deferment, of allowing him to lecture me on what's true, what's puritanical hysteria, and what's blatant lie, I do still have a grasp on reality. I haven't been gaslighted into senselessness. I know I should be angry, and though that emotion sits on the other side of the canyon, far out of reach, I do my best to act as though I feel it. I sit and stay quiet, let my silence speak while I watch Taylor share the article again and again, captioning it with raised-fist emojis and words that read like nails in a coffin: Hide all you want, but the truth will always find you.

When he does contact me, it's an early-morning call, the phone ringing beneath my pillow, sending a vibration across the mattress that sounds in my dream like the drone of a motor on the lake, the rough muted hum I'd hear when swimming underwater as a speedboat passed. When I answer, I'm still in the dream, tasting lake water, watching the sunrays cut through the dark, all the way to the rotten leaves and fallen branches, all that endless muck.

On the phone, Strane exhales a shaky breath, the haggard kind you take after crying. "It's all over," he says. "But know that I loved you. Even if I was a monster, I did love you." He's outside. I hear wind, a wall of sound garbling his words.

Sitting up, I look to the window. It's before sunrise, the sky a gradient of black to violet. "I've been waiting for you to call me."

"I know."

"Why didn't you tell me? I had to read about it in the newspaper. You could have told me."

"I didn't know it was coming," he says. "I had no idea."

"Who are these girls?"

"I don't know. They're just girls. They're nobody. Vanessa, I don't know what this is. I don't even know what I'm supposed to have done."

"They're saying you molested them."

He's quiet, probably taken aback to hear the word come out of me. I've been gentle with him for so long.

"Tell me it's not true," I say. "Swear to me." I listen to the white noise of the wind.

"You think it could be true," he says. It isn't a question but a realization, like he's taken a step backward and can now see the doubt that's begun to sidle up alongside the limits of my loyalty.

"What did you do to them?" I ask.

"What are you imagining? What do you think I'm capable of?"

"You did something. Why would they say this if you didn't do anything?"

"It's an epidemic," he says. "There's no logic to it."

"But they're just girls." My voice cracks, a sob chokes out, and it feels like observing someone else cry, a woman playing the role of me. I remember my college roommate Bridget saying, after I first told her about Strane, *Your life is like a movie*. She didn't understand the horror of watching your body star in something your mind didn't agree to. She meant it as a compliment. Isn't that what all teenage girls want? Endlessly bored, aching for an audience.

Strane tells me not to try to make sense of this, that it'll drive me crazy. "What is *this*?" I ask. "What is *it*?" I need a scene to slip into, a description of where they were in the classroom, behind his desk or at the seminar table, what the light looked like, what hand he used, but I'm crying too hard and he's telling me to listen, to please stop crying and listen to him.

He says, "It wasn't the same with them, do you understand? It wasn't like how it was with you. I loved you, Vanessa. I loved you."

When he hangs up, I know what's next. I remember the threat I made to Ira when, exasperated with my inertia, he'd said he was going to report Strane himself. "Ira, if you do that," I said, my voice steady and cold, "if you tell anyone anything about him, you will never see me again. I'll disappear."

Staring at the phone, I tell myself the urge to call 911 is irrational, unwarranted, but really I'm scared. I don't know how to explain any of this—who I am, who he is—without giving away the whole story. I tell myself it wouldn't help, that I don't even know where he is—outside, someplace windy. This isn't enough to go on. Then I see a text from him, sent just before the call. You can do whatever you want, he wrote. If you want to tell, you should.

I type a response, my fingers flying across the screen: I don't want to tell. I never will. I watch the message deliver and then sit unread.

I fall back asleep, first fitful and then deep like the dead, and I don't wake up until quarter past eleven, when they've already dragged the river for his body. By five P.M., the Portland newspaper posts an article.

Longtime Browick Schoolteacher Found Dead in Norumbega River

NORUMBEGA—Jacob Strane, 59, of Norumbega, a longtime teacher at the Browick School, died early Saturday morning.

The Norumbega County Sheriff's Department reported that Strane's body was found midmorning in the Norumbega River near the Narrows Bridge.

"The gentleman jumped off the bridge. We recovered his body this morning," the Sheriff's Department stated. "We received a call at 6:05 AM about a possible jumper, and that person then witnessed the gentleman jump. There's no indication of any foul play."

Strane was born in Butte, Montana, and taught English at the Norumbega boarding school for thirty years and was a well-known member of the community. Last Thursday, this paper reported Strane was under investigation after five Browick students came forward with allegations of sexual abuse against the teacher, the allegations ranging in date from 2006 to 2016.

The Sheriff's Department stated that while Strane's death has been ruled a suicide, an investigation is ongoing.

The article includes a photo from a recent school picture day, Strane sitting before a blue background, wearing a tie I recognize and even remember the feel of—navy with little embroidered diamonds. He looks so old, hair thin and gray, face clean-shaven and sallow, all loose neck and hooded eyes. He looks small. Not small like a boy, but like an old man, brittle and worn down. He doesn't look straight at the camera but somewhere off to the left, with a puzzled expression, mouth slightly open. He looks confused, like he doesn't fully comprehend what has happened or what he's done.

The next day, a box arrives in the mail postmarked the day

before he jumped from the bridge. Inside I find Polaroids, letters, cards, and photocopies of essays I wrote for his class, everything resting on a bed of yellowed cotton—the strawberry pajamas he bought for me the first time we slept together. There's no note, but I need no explanation. It's all the evidence, every last bit he had.

The story spreads across the state. Local TV news runs a segment with quick shots of the Browick campus, students walking on pathways shaded by pine trees, white clapboard dorms, the administration building with its columned facade. There's a lingering shot of the humanities building. Then the same photo of Strane and, beneath it, his misspelled name: JACOB STRAIN.

Time disappears as I scroll through comment sections, Facebook posts, Twitter threads, my phone dinging every so often from the Google Alert I've set for his name. On my laptop, I keep fifteen tabs open at a time, jumping from one to the other, and when I've caught up on all the comments, I watch the news clip. The first time I watched it, I had to run to the bathroom and throw up, but I've forced myself to sit through it so many times, I turn numb to it. No reaction when Strane's photo flashes on-screen. When the newscaster says "allegations from five different students," I don't even flinch.

After about twenty-four hours, the story travels south. It's picked up by papers in Boston and New York, and then people start writing think pieces. In an attempt to complicate the current cultural trend of allegations, they give the articles titles like "Has This Reckoning Gone Too Far?" and "When Allegations Turn Deadly" and "It's Time to Talk About the Danger of Accusations Without Due Process." The think pieces feature Taylor alongside Strane, and out of her they craft an archetype of the overzealous accuser, a millennial social justice warrior who never stopped to think about the consequences of her actions. Some defend Taylor on social media, but the louder voices vilify her. They call her selfish, heartless, a murderer—because his death is her doing; she drove him to suicide. The host of a men's rights podcast devotes an entire episode to the story, calls Strane a victim of the tyranny of feminism, and his listeners go after Taylor. They get her phone number, her home and work addresses. Taylor posts on Facebook screenshots of emails and texts from anonymous men threatening to rape her, to kill her and cut up her body. Then, a few hours later, she vanishes. Her profile goes on lockdown, all the public content gone. It happens so fast.

Meanwhile, I keep calling out of work, days lost to my open laptop, my nightstand crowded with food wrappers and empty bottles. I drink, smoke, and study Strane's photos of me as a baby-faced, thin-limbed teen. In them I look impossibly young, topless and grinning in one, holding my arms out toward the camera. In another I'm slouching in the passenger seat of his station wagon, shooting the camera a glare. In another I'm lying facedown on his bed, the sheet pulled up to my waist. I remember inspecting that last photo after he took it and thinking it strange that he thought it was sexy, but I tried to see it that way, too. I had told myself it was like something out of a music video.

I grab my laptop, google "Fiona Apple Criminal," bring up the video, and there's teenage Fiona, sullen and lithe. She sings about being a bad girl, and I think of the divorcé asking me this in the alley behind the bar: *Have you been a bad girl? You look like you've been bad.* I remember Strane lamenting how I turned him into a criminal. I saw such power in that. I could have sent him to jail, and in my brattiest moments, I'd imagined it—Strane in a lonely little cell, with nothing to do but think about me.

The video ends and I gather the pictures, dump them back into the box. That fucking box. Ordinary girls have shoeboxes of love letters and dried-out corsages; I get a stack of child porn. If I were smart, I'd burn everything, especially the photos, because I know how they'd look to a normal person, like something confiscated from a sex-trafficking ring, evidence of an obvious crime—but I could never. It would be like setting myself on fire.

I wonder if it's possible for me to be arrested for having photos of myself. I wonder if maybe this is me turning into a predator, if the way I get excited around teenage girls says something about me. I think about how abusive people are always abused as kids. They say it's a cycle, avoidable if you're willing to do the work. But I'm too lazy to take out the trash, too lazy to clean. No, none of this even applies to me. I wasn't abused, not like that.

Stop thinking. Let yourself grieve—but how can I grieve when there hasn't been an obituary, nothing about a funeral, only these articles written by strangers? I don't know who would even arrange a funeral, maybe his sister who lives in Idaho? But even if there is a funeral, who would go? I couldn't go. People would see me, and then they'd know. *Tell me what happened,* they'd say. *Tell us what he did to you.*

My brain starts to skip, my bedroom suddenly seems lit by a strobe, so I take an Ativan, smoke a bowl, and lie back. I always let the pill sink in before I decide whether to do another lap. I never go overboard. I'm careful, which is how I know my problem is mild, if I even have a problem, which I maybe don't.

It's fine. The drinking, the pot, the Ativan, even Strane—it's perfectly fine. It's nothing. It's normal. All interesting women had older lovers when they were young. It's a rite of passage. You go in a girl and come out not quite a woman but closer, a girl more conscious of herself and her own power. Self-awareness is a good thing. It leads to confidence, knowing one's place in the world. He made me see myself in a way a boy my own age never could. No one can convince me that I would have been better off if I'd been like the other girls at school, giving blow jobs and hand jobs, all that endless labor, before being deemed a slut and thrown away. At least Strane loved me. At least I knew how it felt to be worshipped. He fell at my feet before he even kissed me.

Another cycle—drink, smoke, swallow. I want to be low enough to slip beneath the surface and swim without needing air. He's the only person who ever understood that desire. Not to die, but to already be dead. I remember trying to explain it to Ira. Just a glimpse was enough to make him worry, and worry never leads to anything good. Worry makes people butt in where they don't belong. Any time I've ever heard the words "Vanessa, I worry about you," my life has been blown apart.

Whiskey, pot, no more Ativan. I know my limits. I've got a good head on my shoulders, despite all this. I can take care of myself. Look at me—I'm ok. I'm fine.

I reach for my laptop, replay the video. Teen girls writhe around in their underwear while faceless men guide their heads and hands down. Fiona Apple was raped when she was twelve years old. I remember her talking about it in interviews back when I was twelve years old. She spoke about it so openly, the r-word coming out of her as though it were the same as any other. It happened outside her apartment; the whole time the man did what he did, she could hear her dog barking through the door. I remember crying over that detail while hugging our old shepherd dog, hot tears that I buried into his fur. I had no reason to care about rape then—I was a lucky kid, safe and securely loved—but that story hit me hard. Somehow I sensed what was coming for me even then. Really, though, what girl doesn't? It looms over you, that threat of violence. They drill the danger into your head until it starts to feel inevitable. You grow up wondering when it's finally going to happen.

I google "Fiona Apple interviews" and read until my eyes blur. A line from a 1997 *SPIN* article about the same music video makes me choke out a laughing sob: "Watching it, you feel as creepy as Humbert Humbert." If I tug on any string hard enough, *Lolita* will emerge from the unraveling. Later in the article, Fiona asks the interviewer a series of questions about her rapist, her rape:

"How much strength does it take to hurt a little girl? How much strength does it take for the girl to get over it? Which one of them do you think is stronger?" The questions hang there, the answers obvious—she's the strong one. I'm strong, too, stronger than anyone has ever given me credit for.

Not that I've been raped. Not *raped* raped. Strane hurt me sometimes, but never like that. Though I could claim he raped me and I'm sure I'd be believed. I could participate in this movement of women upon women upon women lining the walls with every bad thing that's ever happened to them, but I'm not going to lie to fit in. I'm not going to call myself a victim. Women like Taylor find comfort in that label and that's great for them, but I'm the one he called when he was on the brink. He said it himself—with me, it was different. He loved me, he loved me.

When I walk into Ruby's office, she takes one look at me and says, "You're not doing ok."

I try to raise my eyes to meet hers but make it only to the orange pashmina wrapped around her shoulders.

"What's happened?"

I lick my lips. "I'm grieving. I lost someone important to me."

She brings her hand to her chest. "Not your mother."

"No," I say. "Someone else."

She waits for me to explain; her frown deepens as the seconds pass. I'm usually so direct, coming into her office prepared with a handful of topics I want to touch on. She's never had to pry anything from me.

I take a breath. "If I tell you about something illegal, are you required to report it?"

She answers slowly, caught off guard. "It depends. If you told me you murdered someone, I'd have to report it."

"I didn't murder anyone."

"I didn't think so."

She waits for me to elaborate and it suddenly feels ridiculous, being so coy.

"The grief I'm going through is connected to abuse," I say. "Or things that other people consider abusive. I don't think it was abuse. I just want to make sure you won't tell anyone if I don't want you to."

"Are we talking about abuse that happened to you?"

I nod, my eyes fixed on the window over her shoulder.

"I can't share anything you tell me without your explicit permission," she says.

"What if it happened when I was underage?"

Her eyes flutter, a few rapid blinks. "Doesn't matter. You're an adult now."

I take my phone out of my bag and hand it over, the article about Strane's suicide already loaded. Ruby's face darkens as she scrolls. "This is connected to you?"

"That was the teacher, the one who . . ." I falter, wanting to explain, but the words aren't there. They don't exist. "I mentioned him once. I don't know if you remember."

It was months ago, when she and I were still getting to know each other. Back then, at the end of sessions, she would ask me casual questions, like a cooldown lap after a long workout—where did I grow up, what do I do for fun—normal boring stuff. One week, she asked me about writing, about studying it in college, what age I really got into it. She asked, "Were you encouraged by any specific teachers?" It was an innocuous question, but it broke my face apart. Not from crying but giddiness—gasping, teenage giggling. I hid behind my hands and peeked out through my fingers while Ruby looked on, stunned.

Eventually, I managed to say, "There was one teacher who was very encouraging, but it was complicated." And when I said that, a heavier gravity settled into the office. It was as though Strane had used my body to reveal himself.

"There's a story there, then," Ruby said.

Still squirming, I nodded.

Then, very quietly, she asked, "Did you fall in love with him?" I don't know how I answered. I must have said yes one way or another, and then we moved on, talked about something else, but I was struck by that question. I still am. The implied agency—did I fall in love with him? I don't think anyone I've confided in has ever asked me that. Only if I slept with him, how it started, or how it ended, never if I loved him. After that session ended, we didn't talk about it again.

Across from me, Ruby's mouth falls open. "This was him?"

"I'm sorry," I say. "I know this is a big thing to spring on you."

"Don't apologize." She reads for a moment longer, then sets the phone facedown on the little table between us and looks me in the eye. Asks me where I want to start.

She's patient as the words drip out of me. I do my best to give a brief synopsis—how it started, how it continued. I don't talk about feelings, about what it did to me, but the facts are enough to horrify her. Though I'm not sure I'd recognize the horror if I weren't so good at reading her. She keeps it contained to her eyes.

At the end of the hour, she calls me brave—for confiding, for trusting. "I'm honored," she says, "that you chose to share this with me."

Leaving her office, I wonder when I made the decision, if I arrived with the resolve to tell somewhere in my mind, if it was within my control at all.

On the walk home, I'm propelled by the mania of confession, the sudden lightness that follows an unburdening. I sidestep a cluster of tourists, one saying to another, "I've never seen so many cigarette butts. I thought this place was supposed to be beautiful." I think of how, throughout the whole session, Ruby treated me like a skittish animal ready to bolt, her carefulness an echo of Strane's slow approach. How cautious he was, first angling his knee against my thigh, such a small thing that could have been an accident, then his hand on my knee, a little pat, a friendly thing people do to each other. *Pat-pat-pat.* I'd seen teachers give students hugs before, no big deal. It only accelerated after that, once he knew I was ok with it—and isn't that what consent is, always being asked what you want? Did I want him to kiss me? Did I want him to touch me? Did I want him to fuck me? Slowly guided into the fire—why is everyone so scared to admit how good that can feel? To be groomed is to be loved and handled like a precious, delicate thing.

Once I'm in the stale air of my apartment, the mania levels out and then drops as I take in the mundane mess of my unmade bed and kitchen counters covered in food wrappers, the calendar on my refrigerator that Ruby had me make months ago, each day taken up by some embarrassingly basic chore—do laundry, take out the trash, buy groceries, pay rent—things that probably come naturally to most people. If it weren't for seeing these tasks written out plainly before me, I'd walk around in dirty clothes, live on potato chips from the corner store.

The line of Polaroids stretches across my living room, the strawberry pajamas draped over the radiator. I wonder what level of crazy I've reached and how much further I could go, how many more steps until I become a woman who boards up the windows to live uninterrupted in the filth of her past. I told Ruby I'd already imagined this—him dying, how it might happen, how it would feel. He was twenty-seven years older; I was prepared. But I pictured him withered and helpless, gazing up at me from a deathbed. He'd leave me something real: his house, his car, or just money. Like Humbert at the very end, giving Lo that envelope stuffed with cash, a tangible payment for all he'd put her through.

At one point during the session, Ruby said it seemed like I had so much built up inside me, I was ready to burst. She called my mind *on fire* from wanting to talk.

"We'll have to be careful," she said, "and not do too much too soon."

But standing in my living room, I imagine what it might feel like to be reckless. My breath catches at the thought of what would happen if I spilled a line of gasoline over all this evidence, from thirty-two all the way back to fifteen. The wreckage I'd cause if I dropped a match and let it burn.

2001

*It's early June, the first sunny day after two weeks of rain. The black-*flies are gone, but the mosquitoes are thick, swarming around us as we drag the swimming float across the yard into the lake. Dad and I sit on opposite sides, each with a paddle, guiding it past the boulders into deep water, where Dad attaches it to the anchor, takes off the buoy. We sit for a while on the float, Dad with one foot dangling in the water, me with my knees pulled up to my chest, shielding my old saggy bathing suit, its elastic rotted, the stretched-out straps knotted to keep them from falling down my arms. Onshore, Babe paces and pants, her leash tethered to the trunk of a pine tree. Neither of us is eager to swim back home. There haven't been enough hot days; the water's still cold.

Staring across the lake, sunlight streaming in rays straight to the bottom, I can see the sunken logs left from a hundred years ago, back when the lake and the woods surrounding it were owned by a lumber mill. Closer to shore, sunfish guard their egg nests, perfect circles of sand laboriously cleared with their tail fins. Damselflies dart over the water, their long bodies fused, looking for a safe place to mate. Two of them land on my forearm, electric blue bodies, transparent wings.

"Seems like you're doing better," Dad says.

That's how we talk about Strane now, Browick, everything that happened—evasive references. This is the closest anyone ever comes to mentioning it. Dad keeps his eyes on Babe back onshore, doesn't look over to check my response. I notice he does that a lot now, avoids looking at me, and I know it's because of what happened, but I tell myself it's because I lived away at school for two years, because I'm older, because what father wants to look at his teenage daughter in a saggy swimsuit.

I say nothing, stare down at the damselflies. I do feel better, or at least better than I did a month ago when I left Browick, but admitting it feels too much like moving on.

"Might as well get this over with." He stands, dives into the water. When his head pokes back up, he lets out a whoop. "Judas Priest, that's cold." He looks toward me. "You getting in?"

"I'll wait a few minutes."

"Suit yourself."

I watch him move through the water back to shore, where Babe waits, ready to lick the droplets off his shins. I close my eyes and hear the water lapping against the sides of the float, the *dee-dee-dee* calls of the chickadee, the wood thrush and mourning dove. When I was younger, my parents used to say I sounded like a mourning dove, always sulking, always so damn sad.

When I dive in, the cold is such a shock that for a split second I can't swim, can't move, my body careening toward the green-black bottom, but then—the gentle pull back to the surface, my face turned upward, toward the sun.

As I walk across the yard to the house, my stomach sinks when I see Mom's car in the driveway. Home from work, she's picked up a pizza. "Grab a plate," Dad says. He folds his slice in half, takes a big bite.

Mom drops her purse onto the counter, kicks off her shoes, and notices me in my swimsuit and with wet hair. "Vanessa, for god's sake, get a towel. You're dripping all over the floor."

I ignore her and inspect the pizza, globs of sausage and cheese. Even though I'm so hungry my hands are shaky, I make a face. "Yuck. Look at that grease. Disgusting."

"Fine," Mom says. "Don't eat it."

Sensing a fight, Dad moves out of the kitchen, into the living room and the escape of the TV.

"What should I eat instead? Everything in this house is inedible."

She touches two fingers to her forehead. "Vanessa, please. I'm not in the mood."

I throw open a cupboard door, take out a can. "Corned beef hash that's"—I check the date—"two years expired. Wow. Yum."

Mom grabs the can, throws it in the garbage. She turns, goes into the bathroom, and slams the door.

Later, when I'm in bed with my notebook, writing down the scenes that never stop replaying in my head—Strane touching me for the first time behind his desk, the nights I spent at his house, the afternoons in his office—Mom comes up with two slices of pizza. She sets the plate on my nightstand, sits on the edge of the bed.

"Maybe we could take a trip down the coast this weekend," she says.

"And do what?" I mumble. I don't look up from my notebook, but I can feel her hurt. She's trying to pull me back into being a kid, back when she and I never needed to *do* anything, when we'd just get in the car and head out, happy to be together.

She looks down at the notebook pages, tilts her head to see what I'm writing. *Classroom* and *desk* and *Strane* repeat over and over.

I flip over the notebook. "Do you mind?"

"Vanessa," she sighs.

We stare each other down, her eyes traveling my face, searching for the changes in me, or maybe for a sign of something familiar. She knows. That's all I can think whenever she looks at me—she *knows.* At first I was scared she would contact Browick or the police, or at least tell Dad. For weeks, every time the phone rang, my body braced itself for the inevitable fallout. But it never happened. She's keeping my secret.

"If nothing happened," she says, "you need to figure out a way to let it go."

She pats my hand as she gets up, ignores how I jerk out of reach.

She leaves my bedroom door open halfway and I get up to shove it closed.

Let it go. When I first realized she wasn't going to tell anyone, I was relieved, but now, it's started to flatten out into something like disappointment. Because the deal seems to be, *if you want me to keep this secret, then we have to pretend it never happened*—and I can't do that. I'll remember everything as hard as I can. I'll live inside these memories until I can see him again.

The summer stretches on. At night, I lie in bed and listen to the loons scream. During the day, while my parents are at work, I walk the dirt road and pick wild raspberries to cook in pancakes that I drench in syrup and eat until I feel sick. I lie in the yard, facedown in the crabgrass, and listen to Babe lope around in the lake, looking for fish. The spray of water droplets on my back as she shakes herself dry, her nose nudging the back of my neck as though to ask if I'm ok.

I choose to think of this as the lull in my story, a period of banishment that tests my loyalties but will ultimately make me stronger. I've accepted that I cannot contact Strane, at least not any time soon. Even if my parents weren't checking the caller ID and phone bill, I imagine lines being tapped, emails monitored. One phone call from me and he could be fired. The cops could show up at his door. It's strange to think of myself as that dangerous, but look at what already happened—I barely opened my mouth and brought us to the brink of disaster.

All I can do is suffer through. Paddle the canoe into the middle of the lake and let it drift back to shore, read *Lolita* for the millionth time and scrutinize Strane's faded annotations. Stare down page 140, when Humbert and Lo are in the car the morning after they have sex for the first time, where a line is underlined in what looks like fresher ink: "It was something quite special, that feeling: an oppressive, hideous constraint as if I were sitting with the small ghost of somebody I had just killed." Think of Strane driving me back to campus after the first night at his house, how closely he studied me when he asked if I was ok. Scrawl in my notebook, *"Jailbait" means having the power to turn a man into a criminal with just one touch.*

I dread August, because once the Browick move-in date passes, I can no longer pretend there's a chance this will fix itself, that I might wake up that morning to the truck packed, my parents crying out, "Surprise! It's all been worked out. Of course you're going back!" On the morning of move-in day, I wake to an empty house, my parents both at work. A note on the kitchen counter tells me to vacuum, do the dishes, brush Babe, water the tomato and zucchini plants. Still in my sleep shorts and T-shirt, I throw on sneakers and take off into the woods. I run straight up the bluff, underbrush scraping my shins. When I reach the top, gasping for breath, I look out over the lake, the mountain, that long, low whale's back rising from the earth. The endless woods interrupted only by a wisp of highway, big rigs gliding like toys on a track. I think of stepping into an empty dorm room, the sun draped across a bare mattress, finding someone else's initials carved on the windowsill. I imagine a new class taking their seats around the seminar table while Strane looks on, thinking of me.

My new high school is a long one-story building that was hurriedly built in the sixties to accommodate all the baby boomers and hasn't been updated since. It shares a parking lot with a strip mall that has a discount grocery store, a laundromat, a telemarketing center where people sell credit cards, and a diner that still allows people to smoke.

It's the opposite of Browick in every possible way. Carpeted classrooms, pep rallies, kids in T-shirts and jeans, voc classes, cafeteria trays of chicken nuggets and slab pizza, classrooms so crowded they can't fit another desk. On the drive in that morning, Mom says it's good I'm starting on the first day of a new school year, that I'll blend right in, but as I walk the hallways it's clear I've been marked. Kids I recognize from middle school avert their eyes, while others openly stare. In Honors French 4, the textbook full of lessons I've already learned, two boys in the row beside me whisper about a new girl they've heard about, a junior, a transfer, a slut who boned a teacher.

At first, I can only blink blindly down at my textbook. *Boned?*

Then rage rushes through me. Because these boys have no idea the girl they're talking about is sitting next to them, because I have only two choices and neither is fair—sit and say nothing, or cause a scene and out myself. Maybe the boys assume I'm a senior like them, but more likely is that it doesn't even cross their minds that I'm the girl in question. From the outside, I must seem ordinary, barefaced and dressed in size ten corduroys. *You?* they'd ask in disbelief, unable to reconcile me with the slut they had imagined.

On my fourth day, two girls fall into step beside me on the way to the cafeteria. One I know from middle school, Jade Reynolds. Her brown hair is bleached a brassy orange, and she's ditched the wide-leg jeans and barbell necklaces she used to wear but kept the kohl-rimmed eyes. The other girl, Charley, I recognize from my chemistry class. She's tall, smells of cigarettes, has hair so bleached it's almost white. Her hooked nose makes her eyes look slightly crossed, like a Siamese cat.

Jade smiles at me as we walk, a smile that's less about being nice and more about peering straight into me. "Vanessa, hi," she says brightly, drawing out her words. "Do you want to eat with us?"

My shoulders hunch reflexively. I shake my head, sensing a trap. "That's ok."

Jade ducks her head. "Are you sure?" She keeps smiling that strange searching smile.

"Come on," Charley says, her voice rough. "Nobody wants to eat alone."

In the cafeteria, the girls head straight to a table in the corner. I barely sit down before Jade leans across the table, her brown eyes wide.

"So," she says. "Why did you transfer here?"

"I didn't like it," I say. "Boarding school was too expensive."

Jade and Charley exchange a look.

"We heard you had sex with a teacher," Jade says.

In a way, it's a relief to hear the question leveled at me directly—a relief, too, to imagine the story snaking its way across the state, refusing to be left behind. My parents can pretend it never happened but it did, it *did.*

"Was he hot?" Charley asks. "I'd fuck a hot teacher."

They watch me curiously as I struggle to answer. Like with the boys in French class, I know what they imagine is way off—a handsome young teacher, like something out of a movie. I wonder what they'd think of me if they saw Strane with his belly and wire-framed glasses.

"So you really did?" Jade asks, a note of incredulity in her voice. She isn't convinced. I lift my shoulders, not quite affirmation but not a denial, and Charley nods like she understands.

The girls share a package of peanut butter crackers Jade produces from her backpack, both pulling the crackers apart and scraping the peanut butter off with their teeth. Their eyes follow the teacher circling the cafeteria. When the teacher ducks down to talk to a table across the room, Jade and Charley shoot up.

"Come on," Charley says. "Bring your backpack."

They hurry out of the cafeteria and down the hallway, turn a corner into a smaller wing of the school and then out a door that opens onto a walkway leading to a temporary classroom. They duck under the walkway railing and jump onto the grass below.

When I hesitate, Charley reaches up and smacks my ankle hard. "Jump before someone sees you."

We run across the grass to the parking lot and the strip mall, where people push carts teeming with bags out of the grocery store. A man leaning against an empty taxi watches us as he takes a drag off a cigarette.

Charley grabs my sleeve and leads me into the grocery store. I drift along, following them through the aisles. The employees eye us. It's obvious we're from the high school; our backpacks are dead giveaways. Charley and Jade meander up and down a few aisles before heading for the makeup section.

"I like this," Jade says, inspecting the bottom of a lipstick. She holds the tube out to Charley, who flips it over and reads the color name, "Wine with Everything."

Jade hands the lipstick to me. "It's nice," I say, handing it back.

"No," she whispers. "Put it in your pocket."

I clasp my hand around the lipstick, realizing what this is all about. In one fluid motion, Charley shoves three bottles of nail polish into her backpack. Jade slips two lipsticks and an eyeliner into her pocket.

"That's enough for now," Charley says.

I follow them across the store, back toward the doors. When we cut through an empty register lane, I drop the lipstick among the candy bars.

In a parallel universe, I'm still at Browick. I have another single in Gould, bigger this time, with more natural light. Instead of chemistry, U.S. history, and algebra, I take courses in stellar astronomy, the sociology of rock and roll, the art of math. I have a directed reading with Strane and we meet in the afternoons, in his office, to talk about the books he tells me to read. Thoughts flow from him straight into me, our brains and bodies connected.

I dig through my bedroom closet and find the glossy brochures I brought home as an eighth grader who saw galaxies in her future. I cut up the pages and glue them on the cover of my journal—dining hall tables set with tablecloths for parents' visiting weekend, students bent over books in the library, the autumn campus awash in golden light and fiery leaves, maple red. An L.L.Bean catalog comes in the mail and I cut that up, too. The men are all stand-ins for Strane, dressed in tweed blazers, flannel shirts, and hiking boots, holding mugs of steaming black coffee. I miss him so much, I exhaust myself from it. I drag myself from class to class, breaking the days down into manageable units. If not hours, then minutes. If I think about how many days lie before me, I end up obsessing over things I know I shouldn't. Like, maybe being dead isn't the worst thing. Maybe it wouldn't be so bad.

On the third week, the Twin Towers fall, and all day at school, we watch the news. Miniature American flags start appearing on cars, pinned to people's jackets, in convenience stores next to the cash registers. Fox News plays on the TV in the cafeteria, and every evening my parents watch hours of CNN, the same shots of smoke billowing from the towers, George W. with a megaphone at Ground Zero, pundits speculating about where the anthrax letters are coming from. My new English teacher hangs an illustration of a crying bald eagle on the front of her desk, and in the corner of the whiteboard, she writes the words *NEVER FORGET.* Yet all I can think about is Strane, my own loss. In my notebook, I write, *Our country was attacked. It is a tragic day.* Close the front cover, open it again and add, *And yet all I care about is myself. I am selfish and bad.* I hope the words will shame me. They do nothing.

During lunch, Charley, Jade, and I smoke cigarettes around the back of the strip mall, hidden between two dumpsters piled high with cardboard. Jade wants Charley to skip chemistry so they can go somewhere—the mall, maybe? I don't know. I'm not really listening. The real reason Jade wants Charley to skip is because she's jealous, hates that Charley and I have a class together without her. Fifty whole minutes she doesn't have access to.

"I can't skip," Charley says, flicking her cigarette. There's a tattoo of a tiny heart on her middle finger—a stick and poke, she said. Her mother's boyfriend did it. "We have a quiz today. Right, Vanessa?"

I move my head in a part shake, part nod. I have no idea.

Jade glares out at the grocery store loading docks, the backed-in eighteen-wheelers delivering food. "Figures," she mutters.

"Oh my god, *relax*." Charley laughs. "We'll go after school. God, you're so fuckin' uptight."

Jade exhales a cloud of smoke, nostrils flared.

In chemistry, Charley whispers that she's horny for Will Coviello, wants him so bad she's willing to give him a blow job and she *never* gives blow jobs. I hardly hear her because I'm so engrossed in the inside cover of my notebook, where I've written out Strane's schedule from memory. Right now, he's teaching sophomore English, sitting at the seminar table, someone else in my chair.

"Isn't that sad?" Charley asks. "Do you think I'm pathetic?"

I don't look up from my notebook. "I think you should do whatever you want with whoever you want."

I look ahead to the next class period on Strane's schedule—a free hour. I picture him in the office, reclined on the tweed sofa, a stack of ungraded homework on his lap, his thoughts drifting to me.

"See, that's why I like you," Charley says. "You're so chill. We should hang out. Like, for real. Outside of school."

I glance up from my notebook.

"What about Friday? You can come to the bowling alley."

"I don't really like bowling."

She rolls her eyes. "We don't actually *bowl*."

I ask what it is that they do there, but Charley only grins, ducks her head down toward the gas valve, puckers her lips, moves to turn it on. I grab her hand and she laughs, raspy and loud.

On Friday night, Charley drives all the way out to my house to pick me up, comes inside and introduces herself to my parents. Her hair is pulled back into a neat ponytail and she's wearing a ring that hides her tattoo.

She tells my mom she's had her license for a year, a lie that comes out so smooth, it fools even me. I see my parents exchanging glances, how Mom wrings her hands, but I know they don't want to tell me I can't go. At least I'm making friends, starting to fit in.

Once Charley and I are walking up the driveway, out of earshot, she says, "Christ, you really live out in the fuckin' boonies."

"I know, I hate it."

"I would, too. You know, last year I dated a guy who lived out here." She says his name, but I don't recognize it. "He was a little older," she explains.

Her car squeals as she pulls out of the driveway, and I picture Mom wincing at the sound. "Yeah, sorry," Charley says, "muffler's bad." She drives with one hand on the wheel, the other holding a cigarette, her window cracked to let out the smoke. She wears gloves with the fingertips cut off, her coat covered in cat hair. She asks me questions about myself, about what I think of different people at school, about having gone to Browick. She says she's obsessed with the idea of boarding school.

"Was it crazy?" she asks. "It must've been. Full of rich kids, right?"

"Not everyone was rich."

"Were there drugs everywhere?"

"No," I say. "It wasn't like that. It was . . ." I think of the white clapboard campus, the autumn oak trees, the snow banks higher than our heads, the teachers in jeans and flannel shirts—Strane, draped in shadow, as he watched me from behind his desk. I shake my head. "It's hard to describe."

Charley sticks the tip of her cigarette out the window. "Well, you're lucky. Even if you were only there a couple years. My mom would never be able to swing that."

"I had a scholarship," I say quickly.

"Yeah, but even then, my mom wouldn't have let me go. She loves me too much. I mean, letting your kid move away as a freshman? At fourteen? That's crazy." She takes a drag, exhales, and adds, "Sorry. I'm sure your mom loves you. It's just different, I guess, with mine. We're close. It's just her and me."

I wave her off, say that it's fine, but what she said stings. Maybe it hurts because it might be true. Maybe I wasn't loved enough. Maybe that lack of love shaped the loneliness he saw in me.

"Will's supposed to be there tonight," she says, such a sudden subject change I start to ask Will who, but then remember what she said in chemistry. *Will Coviello is so hot, I'll give him a blow job. Watch me, I'll do it.* I've known Will Coviello since I was in kindergarten. He's a year older, a senior, lives in a big house with a tennis court out front. Girls used to call him Prince William in middle school.

When we get to the bowling alley, Jade is already there, wearing a satiny camisole without a bra. The bowling alley is dimly lit, with long tables set back from the lanes where a bunch of kids from school sit, their faces recognizable but most of their names out of reach. There's a sports bar attached to the bowling alley, an open doorway separating the two so jukebox music drifts in, the smell of beer.

Charley sits next to Jade. "Have you seen Will?" When Jade nods and points toward the doors, Charley takes off so fast she almost knocks over a chair.

Without Charley around, Jade won't speak to me. She stares pointedly over my shoulders, refuses to look at me. Her eyeliner cuts across her eyelids into sharp points. I haven't seen her wear it like that before.

Men with drinks in their hands wander out of the bar and into the bowling alley, their eyes skimming the dim room. A man in a camo jacket sees our table and gestures to his friend. The other man just shakes his head and holds up his hands, as if to say, *I don't want anything to do with that.*

I watch the man in the jacket come over, notice how he zeroes in on Jade and her slutty top. He pulls up a chair beside her, sets his drink on the table. "Hope you don't mind if I sit here," he says. His accent turns *here* into two syllables. *He-yah.* "It's so crowded, there's nowhere else for me to go."

It's a joke; there are plenty of seats. Jade is supposed to laugh, but she won't even look over at him. She sits with her back stick straight and arms crossed over her chest. In a tiny voice, she says, "It's fine."

The man isn't bad looking, despite his grubby hands. He's who the boys at school will grow up into—thick Maine accent and a pickup truck. "How old are you?" I ask. The question comes out more forceful than I intend, makes me sound accusing, but he doesn't seem put off. He turns toward me, his attention immediately shifting away from Jade.

He says to me, "I feel like I should be asking you the same question."

"I asked first."

He smirks. "I'll tell you, but I'll make you work for it. I graduated high school in nineteen eighty-three."

I think for a moment; Strane graduated high school in 1976. "You're thirty-six."

The man raises his eyebrows, sips his drink. "You disgusted?"

"Why would I be disgusted?"

"Because thirty-six is old." He laughs. "How old are you?"

"How old do you think I am?"

He looks me over. "Eighteen."

"Sixteen."

He laughs again, shakes his head. "Christ."

"Is that bad?" It's a stupid question and I know it. Of course it's bad. The badness of it is written all over his face. I flick my eyes over to Jade and she stares at me as though she's never seen me before, like she has no idea who I am.

A senior girl at the other end of the table leans toward us. "Hey, can I have a sip of your drink?" she asks. The man grimaces a little, a small show of acknowledgment that it's wrong, but slides the glass down the table. The girl takes one sip and then shrieks out a giggle, as though instantly drunk.

"Ok, ok." The man reaches for his drink. "I don't wanna get kicked out."

"What's your name?" I ask.

"Craig." He nudges the glass toward me. "You want a taste?"

"What is it?"

"Whiskey and Coke."

I reach for it. "I love whiskey."

"And what's your name, sixteen-year-old-who-loves-whiskey?"

I shake my hair back from my face. "Vanessa." I say it with a sigh, as though I'm bored to tears, as though a fire isn't burning in me. I wonder if this counts as cheating, how angry Strane would be if he walked in and saw this scene.

Charley comes back over, her face flushed, hair messed up. She takes a long swallow from Jade's can of soda.

"What happened?" Jade asks.

Charley waves her hand; she doesn't want to talk about it. "Let's get out of here. I want to go home and pass out." She looks at me, suddenly remembering. "Shit, I need to drive you home."

Craig watches intently. "You need a ride?" he asks me.

I balk, my limbs tingling.

"Who are you?" Charley asks.

"I'm Craig." He holds his hand out for her to shake. Charley just stares him down.

"Right." She looks to me. "You're not leaving with him. I'll drive you home."

I give Craig a sheepish smile and try not to look too relieved.

"Does she always tell you what to do?" he asks. I shake my head and he leans in toward me. "So what if I wanted to talk to you sometime? How would I do that?"

He wants a phone number, but I know my parents would probably call the police at the sound of his voice. "Do you have Instant Messenger?"

"Like AOL? Sure, I've got that."

Charley watches as I fish a pen from the bottom of my bag and write my screen name on the palm of his hand. "You really like old guys, don't you?" she asks as we walk out the door. "Sorry if I cock-blocked you. I didn't think you really wanted to let him drive you home."

"I didn't. I just like the attention. He's obviously a loser."

She laughs, opens her car door and gets inside, leans across and unlocks the passenger door. "You know, you're surprisingly screwed up."

On the drive to my house, Charley plays the same Missy Elliott song over and over, the dashboard glowing her face blue as she raps along: *"Ain't no shame, ladies, do your thing / just make sure you're ahead of the game."*

By Monday everyone knows Charley gave Will a blow job, but he won't speak to her now and Jade hears from Ben Sargent that Will called Charley white trash.

"Men are shit," Charley says as we smoke cigarettes behind the grocery store, huddled between the dumpsters. Jade nods in agreement and I do, too, but only for show. I stayed up late Saturday and Sunday chatting with Craig, and my head still rings from all the compliments he gave me. I'm so pretty, so hot, unbelievably sexy. Since he met me Friday night, I'm the only thing he's thought about. He'll do anything to see me again.

Charley says that men are shit, but really she means boys. She wipes away tears before they have a chance to fall, and I know she's mad and that it must hurt like hell, but a part of me can't help but think: what did she expect?

❧

Craig is nothing like Strane. He's a veteran, was in Desert Storm, and now works construction. He doesn't read, didn't go to college, and doesn't have anything to say when I try to talk about the things I care about. The worst thing about him is how much he likes guns—not just hunting rifles but handguns. When I say I think guns are idiotic, he writes, You won't think that when someone breaks into your bedroom in the middle of the night. Being armed will probably seem pretty smart then.

Who's going to break into my bedroom? I shoot back. You?

Maybe.

With Craig, it's only chatting online, which makes it ok even when he acts like a creep. I haven't seen him since that night at the bowling alley, and I'm not in any rush to, but he says he wants to see me. He talks all the time about how he wants to take me out.

Where would we even go? I ask, like I'm stupid. Whenever the conversation veers off in a direction I don't like, I play dumb, which means I play dumb so often, he thinks I actually am.

What do you mean, where? Craig writes. To the movies, dinner. Haven't you ever been on a date before?

Ok, but I'm sixteen.

You could pass for eighteen.

He doesn't understand how this works, doesn't get that I don't want to pass for eighteen and that I have zero interest in going to the movies as though he were a boy my own age.

The weather cools to a raw gray. The leaves change and fall, the woods turn sparse with skeletal trees. I learn things about myself: that if I limit myself to five hours of sleep, I'm too tired to care what happens around me; if I wait until dinnertime to eat anything, hunger pains drown out any other feelings. Christmas comes and goes, another new year; the TV news still screams about anthrax and war. At school, the rumors about me have long died down. My parents stop locking the cordless phone in their bedroom every night.

I keep chatting with Craig, but his compliments turn stale and the feeling he gave me when I first met him dries up. Now when we chat, all I can think about is what Strane would think of him and what Strane would think of me for spending my time talking to him.

Craig207: Can I admit something? I had a one-night stand on Saturday.
dark_vanessa: why are you telling me this?
Craig207: Because I think you should know that I thought about you the whole time.
dark_vanessa: hmmm
Craig207: I pretended she was you.

Craig207: So you still haven't heard from that teacher?
dark_vanessa: it's not safe for us to talk.
Craig207: You talk to me. How is that different?
dark_vanessa: you and I haven't done anything. we're just talking.
Craig207: You know I want to do more than talk.
Craig207: He's really the only guy you've been with?
Craig207: Hello? You there?

Craig207: Look, I've been pretty patient, but I'm reaching my breaking point. I've had it with this endless talking.
Craig207: When can I see you?
dark_vanessa: um not sure. maybe next week?
Craig207: You said next week is February break.
dark_vanessa: oh yeah. I dunno. it's hard.
Craig207: It doesn't have to be hard. We can make this happen tomorrow.
Craig207: I work half a mile away from the high school. I'll pick you up.

dark_vanessa: that wouldn't work.

Craig207: It will work. I'll prove it.

dark_vanessa: what does that mean?

Craig207: You'll see

dark_vanessa: what are you saying???

Craig207: You get out around 2, right? That's usually when I see all the buses lining up out front.

dark_vanessa: what are you going to do just show up or something?

Craig207: You'll see then how easy it is

dark_vanessa: please do not do that.

Craig207: You don't like the idea that the man you've been toying with might finally take some action?

dark_vanessa: I'm serious

Craig207: See ya

I block his screen name, delete all our chats and emails, and fake sick the next day, grateful that at least I never told him exactly where I live so there's no chance he'll find me at home. When I return to school, I carry my house key so it sticks out between my fingers as I walk from the school doors to the bus. I imagine him grabbing me from behind, forcing me into his truck, and then who knows what. Rape and murder me, probably. Carry my corpse to the movies so we can finally have that stupid date he always went on about. After a week passes and nothing happens, I stop holding my key like a weapon and unblock his screen name to see if he'll message me. He doesn't. He's gone. I tell myself I'm relieved.

In early March, my copy of *Lolita* goes missing from my nightstand. I tear my room apart searching for it; the thought of losing it has me almost out of my mind with panic. It wasn't just my copy; it was Strane's—his notes in the margins, traces of him on the pages.

I don't really believe my parents took it, but I don't know how else it could have disappeared. Downstairs, Mom sits alone at the dining room table. It's covered in bills, a calculator with a spool of paper. Dad's in town buying sugaring supplies for the upcoming weekends of boiling down maple sap on the woodstove, filling the house with sweet steam.

"Did you go in my room?" I ask.

She looks up from the calculator, her face serene.

"Something's missing," I say. "Did you take it?"

"What is it that's missing?" she asks.

I take a breath. "A book."

She blinks, looks back down to the bills. "What book?"

I clench my jaw; my stomach tightens. It feels like she wants to see if I'll say it. "It doesn't matter," I say. "It was mine. You have no right to take it."

"Well, I don't know what you're talking about," she says. "I didn't take anything from your room."

My heart pounds as I watch her shuffle the papers. She writes down a list of numbers and then punches those numbers into the calculator. When a sum appears, she sighs.

"You think you're protecting me but it's too late," I say.

She looks up, her eyes sharp, a crack in the cool expression.

"Maybe some of this was your fault," I say. "Did you ever consider that?"

"I'm not getting into this with you right now," she says.

"Most mothers don't let their kid move out at fourteen. You realize that, right?"

"You didn't *move out*," she says sharply. "You went away to school."

"Well, all my friends think it's weird that you let me do that," I say. "Most mothers love their kids too much to send them away, but not you I guess."

She stares at me, her face drains of color and the next moment it's swallowed by a flush. Boiling red, flared nostrils, maybe the first time I've ever seen in her that kind of anger. For a moment I imagine her leaping up from the table and lunging at me, her hands around my neck.

"You begged us to let you go there," she says, her voice shaking from the effort to remain calm.

"I didn't beg."

"You gave us a goddamn presentation about it."

I shake my head. "You're exaggerating," I say, though she's not. I did give a presentation; I did beg.

"You can't do that," she says. "You don't get to change the facts to suit the story you want to tell."

"What does that mean?"

She takes a breath as though to speak. Then she exhales, lets it go. She stands, moves into the kitchen—to get away from me, I know, but I follow her. A few steps behind, I ask again, "What does that mean? Mom, what is that supposed to mean?" To drown me out, she turns the water on full blast and clangs the dishes in the sink, but I don't stop. The question keeps coming out of me, berating and outside my control, outside myself.

The plate in her hands slips, or maybe it's slammed on purpose. Either way, it breaks—shards into the sink. I go quiet, my hands tingling as though I'm the one who shattered the plate.

"You lied to me, Vanessa," she says. Her hand, red from the hot water and slick with soap, turns off the tap and then balls into a fist. Water darkens her shirt as she pounds that fist against her own heart. "You told me you had a boyfriend. You sat there and you lied to me and you let me think . . ."

She trails off and clamps the wet hand over her eyes, like she can't bear to remember it. That drive back to Browick, her saying, *All I care about is that he's nice to you.* Asking me if I was having sex, if I needed to go on the Pill. *First love is so special,* she said. *You'll never forget it.*

Again she says, "You lied to me."

She waits, expecting an apology. I let the words hang in the air between us. I feel emptied out and stripped bare, but I don't feel sorry, not for anything.

She's right; I did lie. I sat there and let her believe what she wanted and felt no remorse. It didn't even really feel like lying, more like shaping the truth to fit what she needed to hear, an act of contortion I learned from Strane—and I was good at it, able to manipulate the truth so covertly she had no idea what I'd done. Maybe I should have felt guilt afterward, but all I remember feeling is pride for getting away with it, for knowing how to protect her, him, myself, everyone at once.

"I never imagined you being capable of that," she says.

I lift my shoulders; my voice comes out like a croak. "Maybe you don't really know me."

She blinks, registering both what I said and what I haven't. "Maybe you're right," she says. "Maybe I don't."

Wiping her hands, she leaves the sink of dirty dishes, the broken plate. On her way out of the kitchen she pauses in the doorway. "You know, sometimes I'm ashamed that you're my kid," she says.

I stand for a while in the middle of the kitchen, my ears following the groan of the stairs as she climbs, my parents' bedroom door opening and closing, her footsteps directly above me, the creak of the metal frame as she gets into bed. The walls and floors here are so thin, the house so cheaply built, you can hear anything if you listen hard enough, a constant threat of exposure.

I plunge my hand into the sink and grope blindly for pieces of the broken plate, not caring if I slice myself open. I leave the shards lined up on the counter, dripping water and soap suds. Later, when I'm lying in my own bed still checking myself for hurt—was it so bad, what she said to me? it feels worse than what I deserved—she tosses the shards into the trash and I hear the clatter of ceramic from all the way up in my attic bedroom. The next day I find *Lolita* back on my bookshelf.

Charley's mom gets a job in New Hampshire, the third time they've moved in four years. On her last day at school, she sneaks beers in her backpack and we drink them behind the grocery store, our burps echoing against the dumpsters. After school, Charley gives me a ride home, still buzzed, running every red light on our way out of town while I laugh and lean my head against the window, thinking, *If this is how I die, it wouldn't be so bad.*

"I wish you weren't leaving," I say as she turns onto the lake road. "I won't have any friends without you."

"There's Jade," she says, peering at the dark road, trying to avoid the potholes.

"Ugh, no thanks. She's the fuckin' worst." My bluntness surprises me; I've never shit-talked Jade to Charley before, but what does it matter now?

Charley smirks. "Yeah, she can be. And she does kind of hate you." She stops the car at the top of my driveway. "I'd come in, but I don't want your parents to smell beer on me. Though you probably smell like it, too."

"Wait a sec." I dig through my backpack for the toothpaste I began carrying around once I started smoking cigarettes. I suck a little bit into my mouth, swish it around.

"Look at you." Charley laughs. "Surprisingly screwed up *and* brilliant."

I hug her for a long time and, in my giddiness, want to kiss her but control the urge, force myself to climb out of the car. Before I shut the door, I duck down and say, "Hey, thanks for not letting me leave with that guy at the bowling alley."

She frowns, trying to remember. Her eyebrows lift. "Oh, right! No problem. He was clearly going to murder you."

As she backs out of the driveway, she rolls down the window and calls, "Keep in touch!" I nod and call back, "I will!" but it means nothing. I don't have her address or new phone number. Even later, with Facebook and Twitter, I'll never be able to find her.

For a while, Jade and I try to hang out, trudging alongside each other to the grocery store during lunch, trying to convince the other to shoplift and growing incensed when she won't. One morning, I'm in the cafeteria before first period, scrambling to finish my algebra homework, when she marches up to me.

"So I saw that guy Craig at the bowling alley on Saturday," she says.

I look up. She's smiling, can barely keep her lips closed. She looks like she's about to spill out all over the place.

"He said to tell you that you're a cunt." She waits, eyes wide, for my reaction. I feel my face burn and I imagine hurling my algebra book at her, knocking her over, yanking on her brassy bleached hair.

But I just roll my eyes and mumble something about him being a gun-loving pedophile, then turn back to my homework. After that, Jade starts hanging out with a popular group, the kids she was friends with in middle school. She dyes her hair brown and joins the tennis team. When we pass in the hallway, she stares straight ahead.

Rather than deal with finding a new place to sit in the cafeteria, I give up altogether and start spending lunch period at the diner in the strip mall. Every day I order coffee and pie while I read or finish homework, imagining that I look mysterious and adult sitting in a booth all by myself. Sometimes I feel men looking at me from their counter stools, and sometimes I meet their gaze, but it always ends there.

At home, deep in the woods, in the middle of nowhere, the internet is my only way out. Online, I search endlessly, googling different combinations of Strane's name and Browick, in quotations and without, but find only his faculty profile and something about him volunteering at a community literacy program in 1995. Then, in mid-March, a new result appears: he won a national teaching award, attended a ceremony in New York. There's a photo of him onstage accepting the plaque, a big grin on his face, white teeth shining through black beard. I don't recognize his shoes and his hair is shorter than I've ever seen it. Embarrassment creeps up my spine as I realize he probably wasn't thinking about me at all in that moment. There isn't a single moment when I'm not thinking about him.

At night, I stay up late talking with strangers on Instant Messenger. I search the same list of key words—*lolita, nabokov, teacher*—and I message all the men who show up in the results. If they start getting creepy like Craig, I sign off. It's not about that. I just like how they happily listen while I tell them everything that happened with Strane. You're a very special girl, they type, for being able to appreciate the love of a man like that. If the men ask for a photo of me, I send an image of Kirsten Dunst from the movie *The Virgin Suicides* and none of them ever call me out on it, which makes me wonder if these men are stupid or just ok with me being a liar. If they send me a photo, I tell them they're handsome and they all believe me, even the ones who are clearly ugly. I save all their pictures in a folder titled MATH HOMEWORK so my parents won't look in it, and sometimes I sit clicking through photo after photo, sad homely face after sad homely face, and think that if Strane had sent me a photo before I really knew him, he'd fit right in.

Mud season turns to blackfly season. The lake ice thaws slowly, first turning gray, then blue, and then dissolving to cold water. The snow in the yard melts, but deep in the woods, drifts still nestle against boulders, crusty snow piles peppered with pine needles and spruce cones. In April, a week before my seventeenth birthday, Mom asks if I want to have a party.

"And invite who?"

"Your friends," she says.

"What friends?"

"You have friends."

"That's news to me."

"You do," she insists.

It almost makes me feel sorry for her, picturing what she imagines my life at school is like, smiling faces in the hallways, a lunch table of nice girls with good grades, when in reality it's me staring at the ground as I walk and drinking black coffee in a diner with a bunch of retirees.

We end up going out to eat at Olive Garden for my birthday, a brick of lasagna followed by a brick of tiramisu pierced with a candle. My present is an eight-week driver's education course, a gesture that shows Browick is even further behind us.

"And maybe, once you pass," Dad says, "we'll find you a car."

Mom's eyebrows shoot up.

"Eventually," he clarifies.

I thank them and try not to act too excited by the thought of the places a car can take me.

❧

That summer, Dad helps me get a filing clerk job at the hospital in town—eight bucks an hour, three days a week. I'm assigned to the urology archives, a long windowless room of floor-to-ceiling shelves crammed with medical charts that are shipped in from all over the state. Every morning when I arrive, a pile of charts waits to be filed, along with a list of patients whose charts I need to pull, either because they have upcoming appointments or because they died so long ago the chart can now be destroyed.

The hospital is understaffed, so entire days pass without the lead clerk checking on me. Even though I'm not supposed to, I spend most of my time reading charts. There are so many—even if I worked at the hospital for the rest of my life, I wouldn't be able to get through them all. Finding an interesting one is a guessing game of running my fingers along their color-coded stickers, tugging out a random one and hoping for a good story. You really can't predict which ones are going to be good. Thick charts can read like novels, with years of symptoms, operations, and complications in blue carbon copy and faded ink. Sometimes the thin ones are the most devastating, a tragedy compacted into a handful of appointments and a red stamp on the front cover: DECEASED.

Almost all the urology patients are men, most middle-aged or older. They're men who pee blood or aren't peeing at all, men who pass stones and grow tumors. The charts have grainy X-rays of kidneys and bladders lit up with dye, diagrams of penises and testicles annotated with the doctor's scrawl. In one chart, I find a photograph of bladder stones in a gloved palm like three spiky grains of sand. The transcript shows the doctor's question, *How long has there been blood in your urine?* and the patient's answer, *Six days.*

At lunch, I eat in the cafeteria armed with a book so I have an excuse not to sit with Dad. It feels better with some breathing room between us, because in some ways, he's a different person at the hospital. His accent becomes thicker, and I hear him laugh at gross jokes that he'd be offended by if Mom were around. Plus, he has a ton of friends. People's faces light up at the sight of him. I had no idea he was so popular.

On my first day, when he went around introducing me to what seemed like every single person, I asked him, "How does everyone know you?" He just laughed and said, "Helps if you've got your name on your shirt," pointing to the PHIL embroidered above his breast pocket, but it's more than that—even doctors smile when they see Dad coming, and they never smile, and some people already knew stuff about me, how old I am, that I like to write. They still think I go to Browick, which makes sense. I assume he told everyone when I was accepted, and he wouldn't have gone around announcing it when I was kicked out.

Dad and I really don't have much to say to each other, which is ok. In the truck, he keeps the radio turned up so it's too loud to talk, and once we're at home, he settles into his chair and turns on the TV. In the afternoons he likes to watch shows from when he was a kid, *The Andy Griffith Show* and *Bonanza,* while I go for long walks with Babe around the lakeshore and up the bluff to the cave where the abandoned cot still sits rotting. I try to stay out of the house until Mom gets home. Not that being with her is any easier, but when they're together, they forget about me, and I can slip up into my bedroom and shut the door.

Dad tells me I should start saving now for college textbooks. Instead, I blow my first two paychecks on a digital camera and, on my days off, take self-portraits in the woods, wearing floral dresses and knee socks. In the photos, ferns brush my thighs and sunlight streams through my hair, making me look like a wood nymph, like Persephone wandering her meadow, waiting for Hades to come. I draft an email to Strane with a dozen JPEGs attached and hover the mouse over "send," but when I imagine the ruin that could come to him, I can't do it.

Midsummer, he appears in the form of a chart waiting to be filed, included in an archive shipment from western Maine. STRANE, JACOB. BORN NOVEMBER 10, 1957. Inside are the records of the vasectomy he had in 1991, notes from the initial consultation appointment, written in the doctor's handwriting: *33 y.o. patient is unmarried but insistent in not wanting children.* There are notes from the actual surgery, from the follow-up appointment: *Patient was instructed to apply ice to the scrotum once a day and to wear scrotal support for two weeks.* At "scrotal support," I slap the chart shut, mortified at the phrase even if I'm unsure exactly what it means.

I open it again, read it all the way through—his vitals, his stats, six foot four, 280 pounds. His signature in three different places. I pull apart two pages stuck together by a decade-old ink blot and imagine the pen leaking onto his hands. I can see his fingers, his calluses and flat, bitten-down nails. How they looked resting on my thigh the first time he touched me.

The story of his chart is undramatic but still surreal, his recovery described as him holding a bag of ice to his groin. I try to picture it—he had the surgery in July, so the ice must have been melting and there would've been wet spots on his shorts, a sweating glass of a cold drink beside him, an orange bottle of painkillers that clicked as he tapped them out into his palm. At the time, I was how old? I count in my head: six, a first grader, barely a person and nine years away from being in bed with him, squirming under his hands as he told me to calm down, that I couldn't get pregnant, he'd had a vasectomy.

I want to steal the chart, but when they hired me, I had to sign pages of confidentiality agreements, bolded statements about the legal consequences of sharing medical records. I make do with visiting the chart every day, pulling it out from its spot on the bottom shelf and transcribing the notes into my journal, underlining the phrase *unmarried but insistent in not wanting children.* It makes me think of the only part of *Lolita* I truly hate, the passage where Humbert imagines first having daughters with Lo, then making granddaughters with those daughters. It makes me remember, too, the thing I've almost forgotten—him asking me to call him Daddy on the phone while he jerked off on the other end.

But these thoughts are like water-smoothed stones I pick up and study with cool eyes, then let fall back into the lake. In the quiet of the hospital, the oscillating fan stirs my hair as the thoughts sink to the bottom of my brain and disappear beneath the muck. I close the chart, pick up another stack, file it away.

2017

One of the front desk clerks called out sick, leaving Inez stranded on a sold-out Saturday night, so I abandon the concierge desk to help her. When I was first hired eight years ago, it was for a front desk position, and I still remember the basics. Inez has to teach me the updated computer system, her voice rising into a question as she explains the sequence for making a reservation, checking in a guest. I can't tell if she's nervous around me or merely annoyed. If I say something self-deprecating after screwing up, she exhales a quick succession of "you're fine, you're fine, you're fine."

The hours fly by despite my brain fog, or maybe because of it. The bartender brings me a dark and stormy and Inez breaks into a grin when I offer her a sip, the two of us crouching behind the desk as we pass it back and forth. I forget how it can be to work alongside someone, the camaraderie that emerges when dealing with customers: the repeat guest who insists we have put her in a different room this time, even though we let her come around the desk and see her reservation history and that it's always been room 237; the couple who brushes off our warning that the cheaper street-facing room will be loud and then an hour later comes to the lobby upset about the noise. Inez is good at dealing with the complainers, bats her eyes and clutches her hand over her heart as she says, "I am so sorry. I am just *so sorry*." She lays it on so thick it throws the guests off guard; they almost always end up assuring her that it's ok, no big deal, and when they leave, Inez mutters a string of obscenities under her breath.

"I thought you were just the boss's daughter," I say, "but you're actually good at this."

She squints at me, deciding whether to be insulted.

I add, "You're better than I am. I can't fake sympathy," and her face melts into a smile, won over by the flattery.

"When people are angry, they're looking for a fight," she says. "You act submissive, they back off."

"Yeah, that's the same strategy I use with men." I look to see her reaction, if she'll smirk in recognition, but her brow only furrows, vaguely confused.

I watch her click around on her computer, the screen lighting her face. She's seventeen but looks much older, airbrushed makeup and flat-ironed hair ending in a perfectly blunt line. Wearing a string of pearls and a white silk blouse under her suit, she appears put together, already better at being a woman than I am.

"You're very insightful," I say. "You seem mature for your age."

She gives me a sideways glance, her guard still half up. "Uh, thanks." She turns back to the computer, hunches her shoulders so I can't see the screen.

At nine thirty, after the rush dies down, a man approaches the desk—fortysomething, handsome, short. His reservation is for one night, a Jacuzzi suite facing the garden courtyard. He's requested a special turndown to be waiting upon his arrival: dimmed lights, bubble bath, rose petals on the bed, champagne on ice.

As I check him in, I tell him everything is ready and waiting in the room. "Assuming you still want the turndown," I say, glancing around the lobby. He seems to be alone.

The man smiles at Inez. Even though I'm the one checking him in, he hasn't stopped smiling at her since he stepped up to the desk. "That's perfect," he says.

He pockets the key card, heads back toward the elevators. Inez turns to file his registration slip, and I watch the man pause halfway across the lobby, hold out his hand. A woman rises from one of the wingback chairs. She glances over her shoulder at the front desk, locks eyes with me, and I see she's not a woman at all. She's a teenager in Converse sneakers and an oversized sweater with sleeves that fall past her wrists. While they wait for an elevator, the man nuzzles his face into her neck and the girl hiccups a laugh.

"Did you see that?" I ask Inez after they get on the elevator. "The girl he was with. She looked fourteen."

She shakes her head. "I didn't see." She looks down the list of check-ins, all highlighted green. Everyone's in their rooms; we can relax. "I'm going to eat," she says.

I think of the done-up room, the rose petals on the bed, the churning bath bubbles, the girl's uneasy giggle as he pulls the baggy sweater off her body. As Inez heads for the kitchen, I picture myself making a key and going up to the room, bursting inside, digging my nails into the man as I yank him off the girl. But what would that do other than cause a scene and get me fired? She looked willing, happy. It's not like he was dragging her up there. Standing behind the desk, I swallow the last of my drink and watch Inez come back with a plate of pasta. She shovels it into her mouth as she walks, flecks of red sauce on her white blouse.

While she eats in the back office, a man comes up to the desk and says he has a reservation. I search the system as he looms over me with crossed arms, his face all overgrown eyebrows and gin blossom nose. He heaves a sigh, wanting to be sure I'm aware of how annoyed he is, how incompetent I am. *Do you realize there's a girl getting raped upstairs,* I think, *and there's nothing anyone can do about it?*

"There's no reservation under your name," I say. "Are you sure you're at the right hotel?"

"Of course I'm sure." He produces from his pocket a folded piece of paper. "There, see?"

I look it over and see it's a confirmation for a hotel in Portland, Oregon. When I point out his mistake, apologizing as though it's somehow my fault, the man gapes at the paper, then at me, and then at his wife, who sits across the lobby surrounded by their bags.

"We flew up here from Florida," he mumbles. "What are we going to do?"

The city is booked up for the night, yet I manage to find them a room at a hotel by the airport, and the man, too stunned to thank me, ushers his wife across the lobby, back to the valet, who brings around their rental car. As they drive off, I let my body slump against the desk. My head falls into my hands. Deep breath.

When the phone rings, I pick up without opening my eyes, recite the hotel's greeting.

"Hi there," the voice says, hesitant and female. "I'm looking for Vanessa Wye."

I open my eyes and look out across the quiet lobby. Inez emerges from the back office and gestures to me—*one second*—as she heads toward the staff bathroom.

"Hello?" The voice waits. "Is this Vanessa?"

I reach for the phone switchboard, the red button to cancel the call.

"Don't hang up," the voice says. "This is Janine Bailey, from *Femzine*? I sent you a couple emails hoping we could connect. I thought I'd try you at work in a last-ditch effort."

I hold my finger against the "cancel call" button but don't press down. My voice cracks as I tell her, "You already tried calling me. You left a voicemail."

"You're right," she says. "I did."

"And now you're calling again. This time at my work."

"I know," she says. "I realize I'm being pushy, but let me ask you a question. How much have you been following this story?"

I say nothing, unsure what she means.

"Taylor Birch—you know Taylor, don't you? She's really been through hell these past few weeks. Have you seen the abuse she's been subjected to? The men's rights activists, trolls on Twitter. She's gotten death threats—"

"Yeah," I say. "I saw something about that."

There's a click, and then her voice is louder, closer, like she's taken me off speakerphone. "I'm going to be straight with you, Vanessa," she says. "I know your history. And while I can't force you to come forward, I want to make sure you understand how much your story could help Taylor. I mean, you really have the opportunity to help the entire movement here."

"What do you mean, you know my history?"

Her voice jumps half an octave as she says, "Well, Taylor told me what she knew . . . rumors, details Jacob Strane shared over the years."

My head jerks back—*years?*

"And, well . . ." Janine lets out a laugh. "Taylor also sent me a link to a blog? That she said was yours? I gave it a read. Couldn't stop reading it, really. Captivating stuff. You're a wonderful writer."

Stunned, I type the old URL into my browser. After everything that happened in college, I made the blog private, inaccessible without a password. Now it loads with every post visible, reverted back to its default public setting. I can't remember the last time I checked to make sure it was locked—it could have been sitting out in the open for years. Scrolling down the page, I see "S.," my transparent code for Strane, scattered across the blocks of text.

"It shouldn't have been accessible," I say as I bring up the login screen, try to remember the decade-old password. "I don't know what happened."

"I'd like to reference it in the article."

"No," I say. "I can say no, right?"

"I'd prefer to have your permission," she says, "but the blog was public."

"Well, I'm deleting it now anyway."

"And you're free to do that, but I took screenshots."

I stare at the computer screen; the password recovery options tell me to check my old Atlantica email address that I haven't had access to for years. "What are you saying?"

"I'd prefer to have your permission," she says again, "but I have an obligation to write the best article I possibly can. We can work together on this, ok? You tell me what you're comfortable with and we'll start from there. Would you be willing to do that, Vanessa?"

Words pile up in my mouth—*stop calling me, stop emailing me, and stop saying my name as though you know me*—but I can't be biting, not now that she's seen the blog with its posts telling our story in my own words.

"Maybe," I say. "I don't know. I need to think about it."

Janine exhales a rush of breath against my ear. "Vanessa, I really hope you do. We owe it to each other to do whatever we can. We're all in this together."

I glare across the lobby and force myself to agree. "Sure, absolutely, you're so right."

"Trust me, I know how hard this is." Janine lowers her voice. "I'm a survivor, too."

That word, with its cloying empathy; that patronizing, flattening word that makes my whole body cringe no matter the context—it pushes too far. My lips curl up over my teeth as I spit out, "You don't know anything about me," and I hang up the phone, bolt across the lobby to the empty staff bathroom, and throw up into a toilet, curling my arms around the bowl until the wave passes, my stomach empties out, and I'm coughing up bile.

I'm still catching my breath on the floor and checking my blazer for vomit when the bathroom door opens and I hear my name. Inez.

"Vanessa? Are you ok?"

I wipe my mouth with the back of my hand. "Yup, I'm fine," I say. "Just a stomach thing."

The door closes, then opens again.

"Are you sure?" she asks.

"I'm fine."

"Because I could cover for—"

"Would you just give me some fucking space?" I press my cheek against the metal stall as her footsteps hurry away, back to the desk where, for the rest of the shift, her glassy eyes threaten to cry.

A few years ago, I saw Taylor's face staring at me from a light pole while I waited to cross Congress Street. It was a flyer, an advertisement for a poetry reading at a bar. I knew she wrote poems and published some. I read everything I could get my hands on, ordering copies of the journals, routinely checking her seldom-updated website. I looked for traces of Strane in her writing, but all I found in the poems were quiet images of luna moths in incandescent light, a six-stanza meditation on her uterus. It's something I could never wrap my head around, the idea that she could go through life writing about anything other than Strane if what he did to her was really so bad.

I've never understood anything about her, no matter how hard I try. A few years ago I figured out where she worked, the neighborhood she lived in. Based on an Instagram of the view from her kitchen window, I figured out her exact building. I never stalked her, not exactly; the closest I ever let myself get was walking by her work, passing the building around lunchtime, checking each coming and going blond head. But when wasn't I checking for her, scanning faces in restaurants and coffee shops, supermarkets and corner stores? I imagined her sometimes behind me as I walked the city. The thought of her watching made my body buzz, the same feeling I'd get when I imagined Strane's eyes on me.

When I went to her reading, I stood at the back of the dimly lit bar, my red hair tucked up and hidden under a beanie. I stayed only long enough to see her walk to the microphone and start to speak. Her great big grin and wild, gesticulating hands. She was fine—that's what I told myself as I walked home, my cheeks flushed with something between jealousy and relief. She looked ordinary, happy, untouched. That night, I dug through old folders, found marked-up college essays, poems from high school. A paper I wrote on the role of rape in *Titus Andronicus* with Henry Plough's comments at the end: *Vanessa, your writing is astounding.* I remember scoffing at the grade, knowing it was nothing to take seriously, only another round of praise from a teacher who wanted to coax me closer. But maybe he meant it. And maybe Strane—with all his compliments, his insistence that the way I saw the world was extraordinary—meant it, too. For all his faults, he was a good teacher, trained in spotting potential.

I search Twitter for Strane's name and mostly find Taylor's, a mix of feminist defenses and sexist attacks. One tweet includes a photo of her at fourteen, skinny and smiling through braces in her field hockey uniform, the text screaming, THIS IS HOW OLD TAYLOR BIRCH WAS WHEN JACOB STRANE ASSAULTED HER. I try to imagine the same line paired with the Polaroids Strane took of me at fifteen, my heavy-lidded eyes and swollen lips, or with the photos I took of myself at seventeen, standing before a backdrop of birch trees, lifting my skirt as I stared at the camera, looking like a Lolita and knowing exactly what I wanted, what I was. I wonder how much victimhood they'd be willing to grant a girl like me.

2002

*Senior year starts, and within the first week, I show up at the counsel-*or's office with my college applications filled out and a draft of an entrance essay I worked on all summer. I kept the list of schools Strane wrote for me, but the guidance counselor has me expand the list. I need safeties, she says. Why don't we take a look at some state schools?

The strip mall diner closed over the summer, so I eat in the cafeteria, sitting with Wendy and Maria, girls from my English class. Maria is on exchange from Chile and lives with Wendy's family. They're exactly the kind of girls my parents want me to be friends with—studious, sweet, no boyfriends. At lunch, we eat low-fat yogurt and apple slices with two measured tablespoons of peanut butter while we quiz each other with flash cards, compare homework, and obsess over college applications. Wendy is hoping for University of Vermont, and Maria wants to stay in the States for college, too. Her dream is anywhere in Boston.

Life goes on and on. I get my license but no car. Babe comes home with porcupine quills all over her muzzle, and Mom and I have to hold her down while Dad pulls out each one with needle-nose pliers. Dad is elected union rep at the hospital. Mom gets an A in her history class at the community college. The leaves change. I get decent SAT scores and finish another draft of my college application essay. In English, there's a lesson on Robert Frost, but the teacher makes no mention of sex. Maria and Wendy share a bagel at lunch, tearing pieces off with their fingers. A boy in my physics class asks me to the water semiformal and I say yes out of curiosity, but he has oniony breath and the thought of him touching me makes me want to die. In the dark auditorium, when the boy leans in to kiss me during a slow dance, I blurt out that I have a boyfriend.

"Since when?" he asks, eyebrows cocked.

Since always, I think. *You don't know anything about me.*

"He's older," I say. "You wouldn't know him. Sorry, I should've told you sooner."

For the rest of the dance, the boy doesn't speak to me, and at the end of the night, he says he can't drive me home, that I live too far and he's too tired. I have to call Dad to pick me up, and on the ride home he asks what went wrong, what happened, did the boy try something, did he hurt me? I say, "Nothing happened. It was nothing," all the while hoping he doesn't realize how familiar our words are, his questions and my denial.

After a series of thin envelopes from colleges, half-hearted wait-lists and outright rejections, in March a fat envelope from Atlantica College, a school the guidance counselor convinced me to add. I tear into it, my parents watching with proud smiles. *Congratulations, we are delighted.* Brochures and forms pour out asking if I want to live on campus, do I have a dorm preference, and which meal plan do I want? There's an invitation to an accepted student day and a handwritten note from my future advisor, a poetry professor with half a dozen published collections. *Your poems are extraordinary,* she writes. *I'm so looking forward to working with you.* My hands shake as I flip through everything. Even though Atlantica is technically a state school and not prestigious, getting accepted still feels so much like Browick, I'm thrown back in time.

That night, after my parents go to bed, I grab the cordless phone and step outside onto the snowy yard, the moon illuminating the frozen lake.

It's no surprise that Strane doesn't answer. When the answering machine kicks in, I want to hang up and try again. Maybe if I keep calling, he'll pick up out of pure exasperation. Even if he screams at me to leave him alone, at least I'll get to hear his voice. I imagine him watching the caller ID, the flashing WYE, PHIL &

JAN. There's no way for him to know it's not my parents calling to tell him they know everything and are going to make him pay, send him to prison. I hope he's terrified, even if only for a moment. I love him, but when I think of that photo of him accepting the award in New York, the Association of New England Boarding Schools recognizing Jacob Strane as a distinguished teacher of the year, I want to hurt him.

His recorded voice speaks—"You've reached Jacob Strane . . ."—and I see him standing in his living room: his bare feet and T-shirt, his belly sloping over his underwear, his eyes on the machine. The beep pierces my ear and I stare across the lake, the long mountain purple against the blue-black sky.

"It's me," I say. "I know you can't talk to me, but I wanted to tell you I got into Atlantica College. Starting on August twenty-first, that's where I'll be. And I'll be eighteen then, so . . ."

I pause and hear the answering machine tape roll. I imagine it playing as evidence in a courtroom, Strane seated behind a table next to a lawyer, his head hanging in shame.

"I hope you're waiting for me," I say, "because I'm waiting for you."

The weather warms and everything feels easier with the Atlantica acceptance in my pocket. It's a sweetener for the bitterness of exile, a light at the end of this tunnel of shit. Despite the warnings teachers give that college acceptances can hypothetically be revoked, my grades fall to bare-effort Bs and Cs. Once or twice a week, I blow off afternoon classes to walk through the woods between the high school and the interstate, mud seeping into my sneakers as I watch the cars through the bare trees and smoke the cigarettes I pay a boy in my math class to buy for me. One afternoon, I see a deer dart out into the road and five cars, one after another, pile into a wreck. It takes just seconds for it to happen.

April, two days before my birthday, an alert pops up when I'm checking my email: jenny9876 has sent you a chat request—do you accept? I click "yes" so hard the mouse slips out from under my hand.

jenny9876: Hey Vanessa. It's Jenny.
jenny9876: Hello?
jenny9876: Please answer if you're there.

I watch the messages pop up, the line of text at the bottom of the chat window flashing jenny9876 is typing . . . jenny9876 is typing. Then it stops. I try to picture her—the line of her neck, gleaming brown hair. It's April break at Browick; she must be at home in Boston. My fingers hover over the keyboard, but I don't want to start typing until I'm ready, don't want to let her see me start and stop and start again, a giveaway that I'm struggling.

dark_vanessa: what
jenny9876: Hey!
jenny9876: I'm so glad you're there
jenny9876: How are you?
dark_vanessa: why are you messaging me?

She says she knows I must hate her because of what happened at Browick. That it's been a long time and maybe I don't even care anymore, but she still feels guilty. With graduation approaching, she's been thinking about me a lot. How I'm not there and he still is—the unfairness of that.

jenny9876: I want you to know when I went to Mrs. Giles, I didn't know what was going to happen.
jenny9876: This might sound naive, but I really thought he was going to get fired.
jenny9876: I only did what I did because I was so worried about you.

She tells me she's sorry, but all I care about is Strane. As she apologizes, I try to type out questions, no longer caring that she can see my false starts, my scramble for words. She moves on to talking about college—how she's headed to Brown, that she's heard good things about Atlantica—but I don't want to talk about college; I want to ask her about the length of his hair, if it's overgrown and unkempt, if his clothes are frumpy—the only visible markers of his mental state I can think of, because I can't expect her to tell me what I really want to know: Is he depressed? Does he miss me? I end up asking simply, Do you see him a lot? and her hate for him launches forth, palpable through the screen.

jenny9876: Yeah, I see him. I wish I didn't. I can't stand him. He walks around campus looking like a broken man but he has no reason to. You're the one who suffered.

dark_vanessa: what do you mean? like he looks sad?

jenny9876: Miserable. Which is pretty ridiculous considering how he threw you under the bus.

dark_vanessa: what do you mean?

jenny9876 is typing . . . jenny9876 is typing . . .

jenny9876: Maybe you don't know.

dark_vanessa: know what?

jenny9876: That he was the one who got you kicked out. He pressured Mrs. Giles into doing it.

jenny9876: I probably shouldn't be talking about this.

jenny9876: I'm not even really supposed to know.

dark_vanessa: ???

jenny9876 is typing . . . jenny9876 is typing . . .

jenny9876: Ok so last year, me and some other people started a new club called Students for Social Justice, and one of the big things we wanted to work on was getting Browick to have an actual sexual harassment policy because they didn't have one on record at all (which is really irresponsible and technically illegal). And so last winter, I met with Mrs. Giles about it because the administration wouldn't do anything to help us, and when I met with her, I sort of used you as an example of a situation we wanted to prevent from happening again.

jenny9876: Because even though there was that meeting where you had to take responsibility for everything, everyone knows what really happened. They know you were victimized by him.

jenny9876: Anyway, when I met with Mrs. Giles she said I had it wrong, that you hadn't been mistreated and that the school did nothing wrong. She showed me a couple of memos Strane had written about you and in them he pretty much claimed you made everything up.

jenny9876: Which is so frustrating because I know you didn't. I don't know exactly what happened between you two but I saw him grab you.

dark_vanessa: memos?

jenny9876: Yeah. There were two. One was about how you had destroyed his reputation and that Browick was no place for liars. I remember he called you "a bright but emotionally troubled girl." He said you had violated the school code of ethics and should be expelled for it.

jenny9876: The other memo was from earlier. Maybe January 2001? It was about you having a crush on him and hanging around his classroom. There was something about him wanting a paper trail in case your behavior got out of hand. It seemed like something he wrote to cover his tracks in case he got caught.

After that, my brain launches off into the air, into the woods, needing the distance to understand. January 2001. When he and I were driving through the flashing yellow streetlights to his house, when he was giving me the strawberry pajamas—he lied to the school about me then. I was delirious, not yet able to grasp what was happening; he was strategizing and looking ten steps ahead. At the end, when it fell apart and he convinced me to stand in front of that room of people and call myself a liar, what was it that he said? "Vanessa, they decided you have to leave and there's no changing their minds. It's done." I thought "they" meant Mrs. Giles, the administration, the institution of Browick itself. I thought it was him and me against them.

Before she signs off, Jenny asks me what really happened. Hands shaky, I start to type out, he used me then threw me away, then think better and delete it, the specter of firing and police and Strane thrown in prison still too frightening.

dark_vanessa: nothing happened

The day after my birthday, I tell my parents I have to go to the library in town for a school project that doesn't exist. It's the first time I've ever asked to take the car on my own. They're in the yard, cleaning the garden before planting annuals, their arms filthy with dirt up to their elbows. Mom hesitates, but Dad waves his hand. *Go ahead.*

"You've got to go out on your own sometime," he says.

When I'm halfway to the car, keys in hand, Mom calls to me. My heart skips, half hoping she'll tell me to stop.

"Will you buy some milk while you're out?" she asks.

As I drive, the logic I constructed while in exile bows under this new weight and threatens to collapse. I'm not sure what, other than desperation, made me believe he wanted to get in touch and was waiting until I turned eighteen. He made no explicit promise, not even during the last conversation we had. He assured me that everything would be ok, and I took "ok" to mean one thing, but who knows what it meant to him. "Ok" could simply mean unscathed, unfired, and unjailed. My hands grow slick on the steering wheel. How easy it is to be tricked into building a narrative out of air, out of nothing.

Once in town, I turn onto the small highway heading west to Norumbega, trying to work through my memories to find anything real. The times I told people at school that I had a secret older boyfriend—my body cringes when I think of it. I knew it wasn't entirely true, but it felt true enough to lie about. He was waiting for me, even if the boyfriend label didn't really fit. The whole time, I'd been discarded, unwanted. Maybe he's moved on completely, is in love and having sex with someone else, a woman, a student.

My brain shorts out at the thought—a flash of bright light and pain. The car swerves into the soft shoulder, then back onto the road.

Norumbega is unchanged: the tree-lined river, the bookstore, the head shop, the pizza place, the bakery, Browick's hilltop campus glinting above downtown. I park in his driveway, behind the station wagon. The same one we drove from campus to his house, then later through the down east woods, his free hand resting between my legs. So much time has passed, but it feels just like two years ago; I'm wearing the same clothes, look the same, or maybe I've gotten older and not realized it. Is there a chance he might not recognize me? I remember the shade of disappointment on his face when I turned sixteen. *Practically a woman now*. Maybe I've been hardened and aged. I feel tough, or at least tougher than I was. But why? I haven't actually been through anything. I saw a car crash through the trees, talked to some men online, came close to being kidnapped by a loser with a gun collection, ate a lot of pie in a diner by myself. Maybe that all adds up to a kind of wisdom. I wonder whether I'd even fall for it if he were my teacher now.

Like a cop, I bang on his front door rather than knock because I want to scare him, and I half expect him not to answer, to stand unmoving in the middle of his living room and hold his breath until I give up and leave. It's possible he doesn't want to see me ever again; maybe that was his goal when he had me sent away, to thrust me out of his life along with all the life-ruining repercussions I embody.

But no—he opens the door right away, like he was waiting on the other side. He throws it open wide, reveals himself, looking older and younger at the same time, more gray in his beard, longer hair. His arms are tan. He wears a T-shirt and shorts, boat shoes with no socks, pale legs covered in dark hair.

"My god," he says. "Look at you."

He brings me inside, his hand on my back. The scent of his house, something I hadn't thought to miss, fills my head, and I hold up my hands to ward it off. He asks if I want anything to drink, gestures to the living room and tells me to sit down. He opens the refrigerator, pulls out two bottles of beer. It's barely past noon.

"Happy birthday," he says as he hands me a bottle.

I don't take it. "I know what you did," I say, trying to hold on to the anger, but the words come out as squeaks. I'm a mouse already on the verge of tears. He touches his hand to my face to soothe me. I jerk away, and as I do I think of the line from *Lolita,* when Humbert finds Lo after so many years: "I'll die if you touch me."

"You had them kick me out," I say.

I expect his face to go pale and slack, the look of someone caught, but he barely flinches. He just blinks a few times, like he's trying to find an entry point into my anger. Once he gets there, he smiles.

"You're upset," he says.

"I'm pissed."

"Ok."

"You're the one who got me kicked out. You threw me away."

"I didn't throw you away," he says gently.

"But you got me kicked out."

"We did that together." He smiles with a furrowed brow, like he's confused, like I'm being ridiculous. "Don't you remember?"

He tries to jog my memory, says that I told him I'd take care of everything, that he can still see the determined look on my face, resolved to take the fall. "I couldn't have stopped you even if I'd wanted to," he says.

"I don't remember saying that."

"Well, regardless, you did. I remember it perfectly." He takes a drink of beer, wipes his mouth on his wrist, and adds, "You were very brave."

I try to remember the last conversation he and I had before I left—in his backyard, night falling around us. How panicked I was, begging him to tell me it would be ok, that I hadn't ruined everything. He seemed horrified by me; that's what I remember most about that conversation: his look of repulsion as he watched me fall apart, hiccups and snotty nose. I don't remember saying I'd take care of anything. I just remember him saying we would be ok.

"I didn't know I was going to get expelled," I say. "You never told me that was going to happen."

He lifts his shoulders. *My bad, oh well.* "Even if it wasn't spelled out, it must have been obvious that was the only way we were going to wrangle our way out of the utter hell that threatened us."

"You mean it was the only way you were going to get away with not going to jail."

"Well, yes," he agrees. "That was absolutely part of my thinking. Of course it was."

"But what about me?"

"What about you? Look at you. Aren't you ok? You certainly look ok. You look beautiful."

My body reacts even if I don't want it to. An intake of breath so sharp, air whistles through my teeth.

"Look," he says, "I understand that you're angry, that you feel hurt. But I did the best I could. I was terrified, you know? So instincts kicked in. I wanted to protect myself, sure, but you were at the forefront of my mind as well. Getting you away from Browick saved you from an investigation that might've wrecked you. Your name in the papers, a notoriety you have no control over following you like a pall. You wouldn't have wanted that. You wouldn't have survived it." His eyes travel over me. "All this time, I assumed you understood why I did it. I even thought you'd forgiven me. Wishful thinking, I guess. I could've projected too much wisdom onto you. I know I did that at times."

Something cold trickles down my spine—embarrassment, shame. Maybe I'm being dense, simple-minded.

"Here." He puts a beer bottle in my hand. Numbly, I say I'm not old enough. He smiles and says, "Sure you are."

We sit in the living room, on opposite ends of the couch. Little things are different—the pile of junk mail moved from the kitchen counter onto the coffee table, a new pair of hiking boots lie kicked off by the door. Otherwise, it's the same—the furniture, the prints on the walls, the position of the books on the shelves, the scent of everything. I can't get away from the smell of him.

"So," he says, "you're heading to Atlantica soon. That will be a good place for you."

"What does that mean? That I'm too stupid for a good school?"

"Vanessa."

"I couldn't get into any of the ones you picked out for me. We can't all go to Harvard."

He watches me take a long swallow of the beer. The familiar floaty fizz travels down my throat. I haven't drunk alcohol since Charley moved away.

"And what are you doing with yourself this summer?" he asks.

"Working."

"Where?"

I lift my shoulders. The hospital cut its budget so I can't go back there. "My dad has a friend who says I can work at this car parts warehouse."

He tries to hide his surprise, but I see how his brows jump. "Honest work," he says. "Nothing wrong with that."

I take another long swallow.

"You're quiet," he says.

"I don't know what to say."

"You can say anything."

I shake my head. "I don't feel like I know you anymore."

"You'll always know me," he says. "I haven't changed. I'm too old for that."

"I've changed."

"I'm sure you have."

"I'm not naive like I was when you knew me."

He tilts his head. "I don't remember you ever being naive."

I take another drink, a third of the bottle gone in two swallows, and he finishes his, goes to the fridge for another. He gets one for me, too.

"How long are you going to be angry with me?" he asks.

"You don't think I should be?"

"I want you to explain why you feel this way."

"Because I lost things that were important to me," I say. "While you lost nothing."

"That's not true. To many, I lost my reputation."

I scoff. "Big deal. I lost that, plus tons more."

"Like what?"

Tucking the beer between my legs, I count off on my fingers. "I lost Browick, my parents' trust. There were rumors at my new school as soon as I got there. I never even had a chance to be normal. It traumatized me."

He makes a face at *traumatized.* "You sound like you've been seeing a psychiatrist."

"I'm just trying to make you understand what I've gone through."

"Ok."

"Because it isn't fair."

"What isn't fair?"

"That I went through all that and you didn't."

"I agree that it's not fair that you suffered, but me suffering alongside you wouldn't have made it fair. It only would've resulted in more suffering."

"What about justice?"

"Justice," he scoffs, his expression suddenly hard. "You're looking to bring me to justice? To do that, honey, you have to believe that I unduly harmed you. Do you believe that?"

I fix my eyes on the unopened beer bottle sweating on the coffee table.

"Because if you believe that," he continues, "tell me now and I'll turn myself in. If you think I should go to prison, lose all my freedoms, and be branded a monster for the rest of my life just because I had the bad luck of falling in love with a teenager, then please, let me know right now."

I don't think that. That isn't what I mean by justice. I just want to know he's been miserable, a broken man like Jenny described. Because here, in front of me, he doesn't look broken. He looks happy, the teaching award propped up on the bookcase.

"If you think it hasn't been painful for me, you're wrong," he says, as though he knows my thoughts. Maybe he does, always has. "It's been agony."

"I don't believe you," I say.

He leans toward me, touches my knee. "Let me show you something." He gets up, goes upstairs. The ceiling creaks as he walks down the hallway into his bedroom. He returns with two envelopes, one a letter addressed to me, dated July 2001. The first lines turn my stomach inside out: *Vanessa, I wonder if you remember me, last November, moaning into your soft warm lap, "I'm going to ruin you"? My question for you now is, did I? Do you feel destroyed?*

There's no safe way to get this to you, but guilt may make me willing to risk it. I need to know you're ok. Inside the other envelope is a birthday card. He's signed the inside *Love, JS.*

"I was going to work up the nerve to mail the card this week," he says. "My plan was to drive to Augusta and drop it in a mailbox there so your parents wouldn't see a Norumbega stamp."

I toss both envelopes on the coffee table as though I'm unimpressed, force myself to roll my eyes. That isn't enough. I need more evidence of his agony—pages and pages of it.

He sits beside me on the couch and says, "Nessa, think about this. By leaving, you got to escape. Meanwhile, I had to spend my days in a place that only reminded me of you. Every day, I had to teach in the room where we met, watch other students sit at your spot at the table. I don't even use my office anymore."

"You don't?"

He shakes his head. "It's full of junk now. Has been since you left."

I can't shrug off that detail. His office sitting unused seems a testament to the power my ghost has wielded. Every day, I haunted him. And he's right about me being able to escape; the public high school hallways and classrooms offer zero reminders of him, something I had viewed with endless grief, but maybe I had it easier by being thrown into an unfamiliar environment. Maybe there were benefits to what I went through compared with what he endured.

I drink the second beer. When he sets a third on the coffee table, I protest, say I have to drive home, but take a long swallow anyway. My tolerance for alcohol is shot; after only two, my face is flushed, my eyes slow. The more I drink, the further I drift from the anger I came in with. My rage is left onshore while I'm pulled into deep water, floating on my back, little waves lapping against my ears.

He asks what I've done over the past two years, and, to my horror, I hear myself tell him about Craig, the men I talked to online, the boy who took me to the semiformal. "They all made me sick," I say.

He smiles wide. There's no hint of jealousy in his reaction; he seems pleased that I tried and failed.

"What about you?" I ask, my voice stumbling, too loud.

He doesn't answer. He's all smiles as he evades. "You know what I've been up to," he says. "Doing the same thing as always, right here."

"But I'm asking about who you've been doing it *with*." I take a swig, smack my lips against the bottle. "Is Ms. Thompson still here?"

He gives me his tender-condescending look. I'm being charming. My demand for answers is cute. "I like your dress," he says. "I think I recognize it."

"I wore it for you." I hate myself for saying it. There is no need to be so honest, yet I can't stop. I tell him I talked to Jenny, that she called him a broken man. "She's the one who told me about you getting me kicked out. She knew everything. She read the letter you wrote to Mrs. Giles about how I was 'emotionally troubled.'" I hook my fingers into air quotes.

He stares at me. "She read what?"

I smile, can't help it. Finally, something got under his skin.

"How did she read that document?" he asks. I laugh at how he says *document*.

"She said Mrs. Giles showed it to her."

"That's outrageous. Totally unacceptable."

"Well, I think it's good," I say. "Because now I know how conniving you really were."

He studies me, trying to gauge how much I know, how serious I am.

"You called me 'troubled' in that letter. Right? Like I was crazy. A stupid little girl. I get why you did that. It was an easy way to protect yourself, right? Teenage girls are crazy. Everyone knows that."

"I think you've had enough to drink," he says.

I wipe my mouth with the back of my hand. "You know what else I know?"

Again, he just stares. I see the impatience in his clenched jaw. If I push much further, he could cut me off, grab the bottle out of my hand, force me out the door.

"I know about the other letter. The one you wrote way back at the beginning of everything. How I had a big crush on you, and that you wanted to leave a paper trail in case I did something inappropriate and it got out of hand. You'd barely even fucked me and you were already thinking about how to cover your tracks."

His face might've gone pale, except my eyes lag, won't focus.

"But I guess I understand that, too," I say. "To you, I was disposable—"

"That's not true."

"—like garbage."

"No."

I wait for him to say more, but that's all he has. *No.* I stand and take a half dozen steps to the door before he stops me.

"Let me leave," I say. It's a clear bluff; I don't even have my shoes on.

"Baby, you're drunk."

"Big deal."

"You need to lie down." He guides me upstairs, down the hallway, into the bedroom—the same khaki comforter and tartan sheets.

"You shouldn't use flannel sheets in the summer." I flop down on my back, again floating on the lake, the bed rocking with the waves. "Don't touch me," I bark when he tries to pull my dress strap down my shoulder. "I'll die if you touch me."

I roll onto my side, away from him, facing the wall, and listen to him stand over me. Endless minutes of his sighs, "fucks" muttered under his breath. Then the floorboards creak. He goes back into the living room.

No, I think. *Come back.*

I want him to keep watching, to remain vigilant beside me. I think about getting up and faking a faint, letting my body collapse onto the floor, imagining that he'd run to me, pick me up, stroke my cheek to bring me back to life. Or I could make myself cry. I know the sound of me sobbing will bring him running, turn him tender, even if that tenderness will inevitably turn hard, an erection digging into my thigh. I want the moments before sex. I want him to take care of me. But I'm too drowsy, my limbs too heavy to do anything but sleep.

I wake to him getting into bed. My eyes fly open and I see the pattern of sunlight and shadows has shifted across the wall. When I stir, he stops, but when my eyes flutter shut and I don't move again, he eases himself onto the mattress. I lie there, eyes closed, hearing and feeling everything, his breathing, his body.

When I wake again, I'm on my back, my dress bunched around my waist, my underwear off. He kneels on the floor, head between my legs, his face buried in me. His arms are wrapped around my thighs so I can't move away. He looks up and locks eyes with mine. My head lolls and he keeps going.

I see my body from above, ant-small, pale limbs floating on the lake, the water now past my ears. It laps at my cheeks, almost to my mouth, almost drowning. Beneath me are monsters, leeches and eels, toothy fish, turtles with jaws strong enough to snap an ankle. He keeps going. He wants me to come, even if it means rubbing me raw. A reel starts to play in my mind, a parade of images projected onto my eyelids: loaves of bread dough rising on a warm kitchen counter, a conveyor belt moving groceries while my mother looks on, holding her checkbook, a time lapse of roots extending into soil. My parents washing the dirt from their arms, looking at the clock, neither one of them yet asking out loud, "Where's Vanessa?" because acknowledging I've been gone too long will let in the first pinprick of fear.

When Strane moves up onto the bed and pushes into me, one hand guiding his penis, the reel snaps. My eyes fly open. "Don't."

He freezes. "You want me to stop?"

My head rolls against the pillow. He waits a beat longer and then slowly starts to move in and out.

The waves pull me farther from shore. The rhythm he keeps helps the reel start again, his steady in-out-in-out. Was he always this heavy and slow? Beads of sweat slide off his shoulders onto my cheeks. I don't remember it being like this.

I shut my eyes and again see loaves of bread rising, groceries moving forever forward, endless bags of sugar, boxes of cereal, broccoli crowns, and cartons of milk disappearing into the horizon. *Pick up some milk while you're out?* Mom liked that, asking me to run an errand for the first time. Maybe it made her feel better about letting me take the car. Everything will be ok, I'll come back home safe. I had to; I was getting the milk.

Strane groans. He had been braced up on his hands; now he lets himself fall on top of me. His arms snake under my shoulders, his breath in my ear.

Between breaths, he says, "I want you to come."

I want you to stop, I think. But I don't say it out loud—I can't. I can't talk, can't see. Even if I force my eyes open, they won't focus. My head is cotton, my mouth gravel. I'm thirsty, I'm sick, I'm nothing. He keeps going, faster now, which means he's close, only a minute or so left. A thought shoots through me—is this rape? Is he raping me?

When he comes, he says my name over and over. He pulls out, rolls onto his back. Every part of him is slick with sweat, even his forearms, his feet.

"Unbelievable," he says. "This wasn't where I expected my day to end up."

I lean over and vomit onto the floor, the splatter-slap of sick hitting hardwood. It's beer and bile; I'd been too anxious to eat anything all day.

Strane sits up on his elbows and stares down at the vomit. "Jesus, Vanessa."

"I'm sorry."

"I mean, it's ok. It's fine." He pushes himself off the bed, pulls on his pants, and steps around the sick. Goes into the bathroom, returns with a spray bottle and rag, gets on his hands and knees and cleans the floor. I keep my eyes shut tight through the smell of ammonia and pine, my stomach still churning, the bed undulating beneath me.

When he climbs back into bed, he's all over me despite my just having puked, and his hands smelling like cleaner. "You'll be ok," he says. "You're drunk, that's all. Stay here and sleep it off." His mouth and hands take me in, testing what's changed. He pinches my stomach where it's grown softer, and my brain brings up a fractured memory, maybe only a dream—in the office behind his classroom, me naked on the love seat, him fully clothed, inspecting my body with the impartial interest of a scientist, squeezing my stomach, dragging his finger along the tracks of my veins. It hurt then and it hurts now, his heavy limbs and sandpaper hands, a knee prying my legs apart. How can he be ready again? The bottle of Viagra in the bathroom cabinet, puke crusting together a lock of my hair. Him on top, his body so big it could smother me if he weren't careful. But he is careful and he is good and he loves me and I want this. I still feel torn in two when he pushes inside, will probably always feel this way, but I want it. I have to.

I don't get home until quarter to midnight. I come into the kitchen and Mom's waiting. She grabs the keys out of my hand.

"Never again," she says.

I stand with my arms limp at my sides, messy hair and red-rimmed eyes. "Aren't you going to ask where I've been?" I say.

She stares at me, into me. She sees everything. “If I did,” she says, “would you tell me the truth?”

⁂

I cry at graduation along with everyone else, but my tears are from the relief of having survived what I still think of as my penance. Our graduation is held in the gym and the fluorescent lights make us look jaundiced. The principal won’t let anyone clap as we walk across the stage, says it makes the ceremony too long and it isn’t fair that some students would get loud cheers and others might not get any at all. Browick’s graduation is on the same Saturday afternoon, and during mine, I imagine theirs: chairs arranged on the lawn outside the dining hall, the headmaster and faculty standing in the grove of white pines, distant church bells chiming. I walk across the silent stage to receive my diploma and close my eyes, imagine the sun on my face, that I’m wearing Browick’s thick white gown with the crimson sash. The principal shakes my hand limply, gives me the same “well done” he gives everyone else. The whole thing feels meaningless, but what does it matter? I’m not really here in this stuffy gym with the sounds of squeaking folding chairs and cleared throats, the rustle of programs fanning faces jeweled with sweat. I’m walking across the carpet of orange-dead needles, accepting hugs from Browick faculty, even from Mrs. Giles. In my fantasy she never kicked me out; she has no reason to think ill of me at all. Strane hands me my diploma, standing by the same tree where, two and a half years ago, he told me he wanted to put me to bed and kiss me good night. His fingers touch mine as he passes it to me, imperceptible to anyone else, but the thrill of it sends me airborne into the nothing-nowhere-no-one feeling I’d get when I left his classroom, red hot with secrets.

In the gym, I clutch my diploma as I walk back to my chair.

Shoes scuffle on the floor. The principal shoots a glare at the lone parent who dares to clap.

After the ceremony, everyone spills out into the parking lot and takes photos, positioning the camera so the strip mall isn't visible in the background. Dad tells me to smile, but I can't force my face to listen.

"Come on, at least pretend to be happy," he says.

I part my lips and show my teeth and end up looking like an animal ready to bite.

All summer I work at the auto parts warehouse, filling orders for starters and struts while classic rock radio blares over the white noise of the conveyor belts. Twice a week at the end of my shift, Strane waits for me in the parking lot. I try to dig the grit out from under my fingernails before climbing into the station wagon. He likes my steel-toed boots, the muscles in my arms. He says a summer of manual labor is good for me, that it'll make me value college all the more.

Every so often, anger hits me, but I tell myself what's done is done—Browick, his role in my leaving, all of it in the past. I do my best not to feel resentful when I remember what he used to say about helping me apply to summer internships in Boston, or when I see his Harvard robes hanging on his closet door, left there from the Browick graduation. Atlantica is a respectable choice, he says, nothing to be ashamed of.

At work on a Friday afternoon in the warehouse, Jackson Browne plays while I start on a pallet of chassis parts. The man filling orders in the next section belts out a line of song as "The Load-Out" gives way to "Stay." My utility knife slips as I tear open the plastic wrap, leaving a six-inch slice on my forearm that, before the rush of blood, is gently parted skin, a painless peek through the curtains. The man in the next section glances over, sees me with my hand clamped over the wound, blood seeping through my fingers and dripping onto the concrete floor.

"Shit!" He scrambles to unzip his sweatshirt as he runs over. He ties it around my arm.

"I cut myself," I say.

"You think?" The man shakes his head at my helplessness, cinches the sweatshirt tighter. Sooty warehouse dust lines his knuckles. "How long were you going to stand there before you said something?"

The days Strane picks me up from work, we drive around like teenagers with nowhere to go, and when he drives me back home, he drops me off at the top of the dirt road. My mother asks me where I've been and I tell her, "With Maria and Wendy." The girls I used to sit with at lunch, the ones I haven't spoken to since graduation.

"I didn't realize you were such good friends," Mom says. She could push further, ask why they never come inside when they drop me off, why she's never even met them at all. I'm eighteen and moving to Atlantica at the end of August, which I'd point out if she dared question me. But she never does. She says ok and lets it drop. The freedom leaves me adrift, unsure of what she knows, what she suspects. "I don't want to pull those old books off the shelf," she says when her sister calls to hash out something that happened when they were kids. There's a wall around her; I build one around me.

Strane asks if I'm still angry. We're in his bed, the flannel sheets damp beneath our sweaty bodies. I stare at the open window, listening to the sounds of cars and pedestrians, the perfect stillness of his house. I'm tired of him asking me this, his insatiable need for reassurance. *No, I'm not angry. Yes, I forgive you. Yes, I want this. No, I don't think you're a monster.*

"Would I be here if I didn't want this?" I ask, as though the answer were obvious. I ignore what hangs in the air above us, my anger, my humiliation and hurt. They seem like the real monsters, all those unspeakable things.

2017

At my next session with Ruby, before I even sit down, I ask if she's been contacted by anyone looking for information on me. I called Ira last night asking the same thing, while his new girlfriend hissed in the background, "Is that her? Why is she calling you? Ira, hang up the phone."

"Who would be looking for information on you?" Ruby asks.

"Like a journalist."

She stares, bewildered, as I take out my phone and pull up the emails. "I'm not being paranoid, ok? This is actually happening to me. Look."

She takes the phone, begins to read. "I don't understand—"

I grab it from her hand. "Maybe it doesn't seem like a big deal, but it's not just emails, ok? She's been calling me, harassing me."

"Vanessa, take a breath."

"Do you not believe me?"

"I believe you," she says. "But I need you to slow down and tell me what's going on."

I sit, press the heels of my hands against my eyes and try my best to explain the emails and calls, the unearthed blog I finally managed to delete, how the journalist still has screenshots saved. My brain is jumpy, won't stay focused even for the length of a sentence. Ruby still gets the gist of it, though, her face opening up in sympathy.

"This is so intrusive," she says. "Surely this isn't ethical on the part of the journalist." She suggests I write to Janine's boss, or even go to the police, but at the mention of cops, I grab the arms of my chair and yell out, "No!" For a moment, Ruby actually looks scared.

"I'm sorry," I say. "I'm panicking. I'm not myself."

"That's ok," she says. "It's an understandable reaction. This is one of your worst fears coming true."

"I saw her, you know. Outside the hotel."

"The journalist?"

"No, the other her. Taylor, the one who accused Strane. She's harassing me, too. I should show up at her work, see how she likes it."

I describe what I saw last night as dusk began to fall, the woman standing across the street, how she stared up at the hotel, right into the lobby window I was looking out of, staring at *me,* her blond hair whipping across her face. As I talk, Ruby watches me with a pained expression, like she wants to believe me but can't.

"I don't know," I say. "Maybe I imagined it. That happens sometimes."

"You imagine things?"

I lift my shoulders. "It's like my brain superimposes onto strangers the faces I want to see."

She says that sounds difficult and I shrug again. She asks how often this happens and I say it depends. Months will pass without it happening at all, and then months where it happens every day. It's the same with the nightmares—they come in waves, brought on by something not always easy to predict. I know to stay away from any books or movies set in a boarding school, but then I'll be blindsided by something as benign as a reference to maple trees, or the feeling of flannel against my skin.

"I sound like I'm crazy," I say.

"No, not crazy," Ruby says. "Traumatized."

I think about the other things I could tell her, the drinking and smoking to get me through the day, the nights when my apartment feels like a maze so impossible to navigate I end up sleeping on the bathroom floor. I know how easily I could make my most shameful behaviors add up to a diagnosis. I've lost entire nights to reading about post-traumatic stress, mentally checking off each symptom, but there's a strange letdown at the thought of everything inside me being summed up so easily. And what's next—treatment, medication, moving past it all? That might seem like a happy ending for some, but for me there's only the edge of this canyon, the churning water below.

"Do you think I should let that journalist write about me?" I ask.

"That's a choice only you can make."

"Obviously. And I've already made up my mind. There's no way I'm agreeing to it. I just want to know if you think I should."

"I think it would cause you severe stress," Ruby says. "I'd worry the symptoms you described would become even more intense to the point where it would be difficult for you to function."

"But I'm talking on a moral level. Because isn't it supposed to be worth all the stress? That's what people keep saying, that you need to speak out no matter the cost."

"No," she says firmly. "That's wrong. It's a dangerous amount of pressure to put on someone dealing with trauma."

"Then why do they keep saying it? Because it's not just this journalist. It's every woman who comes forward. But if someone doesn't want to come forward and tell the world every bad thing that's happened to her, then she's what? Weak? Selfish?" I throw up my hand, wave it away. "The whole thing is bullshit. I fucking hate it."

"You're angry," Ruby says. "I don't think I've ever seen you truly angry before."

I blink, breathe through my nose. I say I feel a little defensive, and she asks defensive how.

"I feel backed into a corner," I say. "Like all of a sudden, not wanting to expose myself means I'm enabling rapists. And I shouldn't even be part of this conversation at all! I wasn't abused, not like other women are claiming to have been."

"Do you understand that someone could have been in a relationship similar to yours and consider it to have been abusive?"

"Sure," I say. "I'm not brainwashed. I know the reasons why teenagers aren't supposed to be with middle-aged men."

"What are the reasons?" she asks.

I roll my eyes and list off: "The power imbalance, teenage brains not being fully developed, whatever. All that crap."

"Why didn't those reasons apply to you?"

I give Ruby a sidelong look, letting her know I see where she's trying to lead me. "Look," I say, "this is the truth, ok? Strane was good to me. He was careful and kind and good. But obviously not all men are like that. Some are predatory, especially with girls. And when I was young, being with him was still really hard, despite how good he was."

"Why was it hard?"

"Because the whole world was working against us! We had to lie and hide, and there were things he couldn't protect me from."

"Like what?"

"Like when I got kicked out."

When I say that, Ruby squints, her brow furrows. "Kicked out of what?"

I forgot I hadn't told her. I know the phrase "kicked out" hits hard and gives the wrong impression. It makes it sound as though I had no agency in the situation, like I was caught doing something bad and then told to pack my bags. But I had a choice. I chose to lie.

So I tell Ruby it was complicated, that maybe "kicked out" isn't the right way to describe it. I tell her the story: the rumors and meetings, Jenny's list, the last morning with the packed classroom and me standing at the chalkboard. I've never told it with such detail, don't know if I've even thought about it this way before—chronologically, one event leading to the next. It's usually fractured, memories like shattered glass.

At a couple points, Ruby interrupts me. "They did what?" she asks. "They *what*?" She's appalled at things I've never paid attention to before, like how Strane was the one who pulled me out of class for the first meeting with Mrs. Giles, the fact that no one reported it to the state.

"What, like child protective services?" I ask. "Come on. It wasn't like that."

"Any time a teacher suspects a child is being abused, they're mandated to report it."

"I worked in child protective services when I first moved to Portland," I say, "and the kids who ended up in that system had been through actual abuse. Horrific stuff. What happened to me wasn't anything like that." I sit back, cross my arms. "This is why I hate talking about it. I end up making it sound way worse than it actually was."

She studies me, deep lines in her forehead. "Knowing you, Vanessa, I think you're more likely to minimize than exaggerate."

She starts talking in an authoritative tone I've never heard before, practically scolding. She says it's humiliating what Browick forced me to do. That being instructed to demean yourself in front of your peers is enough to cause post-traumatic stress, regardless of anything else I went through.

"Being forced into helplessness by one other person is terrible," she says, "but being humiliated in front of a crowd . . . I don't want to say that it's worse, but it is different. It's severely dehumanizing, especially for a child."

When I start to correct her use of "child," she amends herself: "For someone whose brain wasn't fully developed." Then she meets my gaze, waits to see if I'll challenge my own words. When I don't, she asks if Strane stayed on at Browick after all that, if he knew what happened in that meeting.

"He knew. He helped me plan what I was going to say. It was the only way to repair his reputation."

"Did he know you were going to get kicked out?"

I lift my shoulders, unwilling to lie but unable to say yes, he knew, he wanted it to happen.

"You know," Ruby says, "earlier you described this as something he didn't have the power to protect you from, but it sounds like he was actually the cause of it."

For a moment my breath gets knocked out of me, but I recover quickly, shrugging like it's nothing. "It was a complicated situation. He did the best he could."

"Did he feel guilty about it?"

"About having me kicked out?"

"That," she says, "and making you lie, take the fall."

"I think he thought it was unfortunate but something that had to be done. What was the alternative, him going to prison?"

"Yes," she says firmly, "that would have been an alternative, and it would have been a just one because what he did to you is a crime."

"Neither of us would have survived him going to prison."

Ruby watches me and there's a shifting of gears behind her eyes, the marking of a mental note. It's more subtle than scribbling on a notepad the way a TV therapist might, yet still detectable. She observes me so closely, puts everything I say and do into a larger context, which of course reminds me of Strane—how could it not? How his eyes bore into me during class, constantly calculating. Ruby once told me that I'm her favorite client because there's always another layer to peel back, something else to unearth, and hearing this was as thrilling as hearing, *You're my best student.* Like Strane calling me precious and rare, Henry Plough saying I'm an enigma, impossible to understand.

She asks then what I think she's wanted to ask me all along. "Do you believe the girls who accused him?"

I don't hesitate in saying no. I flick my eyes to her face, catch her fast-blinking surprise.

"You think they're lying," she says.

"Not exactly. I think they got carried away."

"Carried away how?"

"In this hysteria that's going on," I say. "The constant accusations. Like, it's a movement, right? That's what people are calling it. And when you see a movement with so much momentum, it's natural to want to join, but to be accepted into this one you need something horrible to have happened to you. Exaggeration is inevitable. Plus, it's all so vague. These terms are easy to manipulate. Assault can be anything. He could have just patted them on the leg or something."

"But if he was innocent, how do you make sense of him taking his own life?" she asks.

"He always said he'd rather be dead than live life branded as a pedophile. When these accusations came out, he knew everyone would assume he was guilty."

"Are you angry with him?"

"For killing himself? No. I understand why he did it, and I know that I'm at least partially to blame."

She starts to say no, that isn't true, but I cut her off.

"I know, I know—it isn't my fault, I get it. But I'm the reason he had all these rumors attached to him in the first place. If he hadn't already had the reputation of being a teacher who sleeps with students, I doubt Taylor would have accused him of anything, and if she hadn't come forward, the other girls wouldn't have, either. Once a teacher gets accused of this, everything he says and does is seen through a filter, to the point where even innocuous behavior is interpreted as something sinister." I go on and on, parroting his arguments, the part of him left inside me suddenly risen and fully alive.

"Think about it," I say. "If a normal man pats a girl on the knee, no big deal. But if a man who's been accused of being a pedophile does it? People are going to react disproportionately. So, no, I'm not mad at him. I'm mad at them. I'm mad at the world that turned him into a monster when all he did was have the bad luck of falling in love with me."

Ruby crosses her arms and stares down at her lap, as though she's trying to calm herself.

"I know how this all sounds," I say. "I'm sure you think I'm terrible."

"I don't think you're terrible," she says quietly, still gazing down at her lap.

"Then what do you think?"

She takes a deep breath, meets my eyes. "Honestly, Vanessa, what I'm hearing is that he was a very weak man, and even as a girl, you knew you were stronger than him. You knew he couldn't handle being exposed and that's why you took the fall. You're still trying to protect him."

I bite down on the inside of my cheek because I won't let my body do what it really wants—to contort itself inward, to curl so tight my bones snap. "I don't want to talk about him anymore."

"Ok."

"I'm still grieving, you know. On top of everything else, I'm mourning the loss."

"It must be hard."

"It is. It's excruciating." I swallow down the tightness in my throat. "I let him die. You should know that, just in case you start feeling sorry for me. He called me right before he did it, and I knew what he was going to do and I did nothing to stop him."

"It wasn't your fault," Ruby says.

"Yeah, you keep saying that. Nothing ever seems to be my fault."

She says nothing, staring at me with that same pained expression. I know what she thinks, that I'm pathetic, intent on creating my own doom.

"I tortured him," I say. "I don't think you understand how much I contributed to everything. His whole life descended into hell because of me."

"He was a grown man and you were fifteen," she says. "What could you have possibly done to torture him?"

For a moment I'm speechless, unable to come up with an answer besides, *I walked into his classroom. I existed. I was born.*

Tipping my head back, I say, "He was so in love with me, he used to sit in my chair after I left the classroom. He'd put his face down on the table and try to breathe me in." It's a detail I've trotted out before, always meant as evidence of his uncontrollable love for me, but saying it now, I hear it as she does, as anyone would—deluded and deranged.

"Vanessa," she says gently, "you didn't ask for that. You were just trying to go to school."

I stare out the window over her shoulder, at the harbor, the swarming gulls, the slate-gray water and sky, but I only see myself, barely sixteen with tears in my eyes, standing in front of a room of people, calling myself a liar, a bad girl deserving of punishment. Ruby's far-off voice asks me where I've gone, but she knows that it's the truth that has spooked me, the expanse of it, the starkness. It offers nowhere to hide.

2006

It's early September, senior year of college about to begin, and I'm cleaning my apartment with the windows thrown open. The sounds of seasonal transformation drift in from the downtown streets below, the loudspeaker from the trolley tours mixed with the moaning brakes of a moving van, the final wave of tourists in town for the last of the warm weather and cheaper hotel rooms. The center of town has shifted toward campus, and until May, Atlantica will belong to the college. Bridget, my roommate, is due to arrive from Rhode Island the following day and classes begin the day after that. I've lived here all summer, cleaning hotel rooms for cash and getting stoned and wasting time online at night—except when Strane comes over, which he's done only a handful of times. He blames the long drive, but really he just hates the dingy apartment. The first time he visited, he took one look around and said, "Vanessa, this is the kind of place people go to kill themselves." He's forty-eight and I'm twenty-one, and mostly it's the same as it was six years ago. The big threats are gone—no one's going to get thrown in jail or lose their job—but I still lie to my parents about him. Bridget is the only friend who knows he exists. When he and I are together, it's either at his house or in my apartment with the shades drawn. He takes me out in public sometimes, but only places where there's little chance we'll be recognized—the secrecy, once a necessity, now seems a product of shame.

I'm in the bathroom wiping down the sides of the shower, something I only do when he's coming, when my phone trills with an incoming call: JACOB STRANE.

I hit "answer," my fingers pruned from the cleaner. "Hey, are you—?"

"Can't do it tonight," he says. "Too much going on here."

I move into the living room while he goes on about being re-appointed department chair, his mounting responsibilities. "The department's a mess," he says. "We've got someone on maternity leave and the new teacher they hired is completely clueless. On top of that, they're implementing some new school-wide counseling program, hired some girl barely older than you to instruct us how to handle students' feelings. It's insulting. I've been doing this for two decades."

I begin to pace the length of the living room, following the path of the oscillating fan. The only furniture we have is a duct-taped papasan chair, a coffee table made of milk crates, and my parents' old TV stand. We'll have a couch soon; Bridget says she knows someone getting rid of one for free.

"But this was the last chance for us to be together."

"Are you leaving on an extended voyage I don't know about?"

"My roommate's moving in tomorrow."

"Ah." He clicks his tongue. "Well, you've got a bedroom. The door closes."

I let out a tiny slip of a sigh.

"Please don't sulk," he says.

"I'm not." But I am, my limbs heavy, my bottom lip jutting out. I spent the whole morning clearing the empty bottles and coffee cups out of my bedroom, washing the dishes, wiping the hair out of the bathtub. Plus I want to be with him. That's the real source of my disappointment. It's been two weeks.

Into the phone, I mumble, "I'm needy." It's the closest I can get to saying what I feel, which isn't horniness, because it isn't really about sex. It's him looking at me, adoring me, telling me what I am and giving me what I need to get through the day-to-day drudgery of pretending I'm like everybody else.

I hear him smile—the quick exhale, a soft sound from the back of his throat. *I'm needy*. He likes that. "I'll get out there soon," he says.

Bridget arrives the following afternoon, dropping her bags in the middle of the living room floor. With shining eyes, she asks, "Is he here?" She's anxious to meet Strane; I'm not sure she's convinced he's real. I told her a vague version of the story last spring at the bar after we signed our lease. She's an English major, same as me, and we'd had classes together for three years, but we weren't good friends. Living together was an arrangement of convenience. She'd found a two-bedroom apartment; I needed a place. Yet over the course of one night at the bar, I went from mentioning that I'd gone to Browick for "about a year"—usually that's as close as I came to the truth—to giving her a disjointed history of the whole mess five drinks later. I told her that he singled me out and fell in love, that I was expelled because I wouldn't betray him, but we ended up back together because we can't stay away from each other, despite the age difference, despite everything. She was the perfect listener, widening her eyes at the most intense plot points, nodding empathetically at the difficult moments, and through it all showing no hint of judgment. Since then, she had never been the first to mention Strane, always followed my lead. Even now, asking *Is he here?* was only because I texted her the day before with an apologetic warning: I hope you won't be too alarmed if a middle-aged man is in the apartment when you get here tomorrow. That was the first time I ever tried turning him into a joke and it felt good, surprisingly so.

Is he here? I shake my head but don't explain why and Bridget doesn't ask.

We move in the rest of her stuff, black garbage bags full of clothes and pillows and bedsheets, a trash can stuffed with shoes, a crockpot full of DVDs. We pick up the couch—literally pick it up—and carry it four blocks while cars pass by and honk at us. We rest halfway, dropping the couch on the sidewalk and draping ourselves across it, stretching our legs and shielding our eyes from the sun. Once we haul it up into the apartment, we push it against a living room wall and spend the rest of the afternoon drinking sugary wine and watching *The Hills.* We swig straight from our respective bottles, wipe our lips with the backs of our hands, and sing along to the theme song, episode after episode.

When the sky darkens and the wine runs out, we go to the corner store for more to drink while we get ready for the bar. Rilo Kiley blares from Bridget's bedroom on the other end of the apartment as I flat-iron my hair and line my eyes. At one point, she appears in my bedroom doorway with a pair of scissors.

"I'm giving you bangs," she says.

I sit on the edge of the bathtub while she snips at my hair with the paint-stained scissors, her laptop open to a photo of Jenny Lewis for reference. "Perfect," she says, stepping aside so I can look in the mirror. I look like a little girl, two big eyes peering out from beneath a blunt fringe.

"You look amazing," Bridget says.

I turn from side to side and wonder what Strane will think.

At the bar, I perch on a stool and guzzle pints, while Bridget is sidetracked by boys who pull her in for hugs as an excuse to lay their hands on her. She's beautiful: high cheekbones and long honey hair, a gap between her front teeth that I've seen men go cross-eyed over. Meanwhile, I'm pretty but not beautiful, smart but not cool. I'm acerbic, salty, too intense. When Bridget's fiancé met me, he said just being around me felt like a kick in the balls.

❧

Atlantica College is morning fog and salt-drenched air, seals sunning their speckled bodies on the pink granite shore, whaler mansions converted into classrooms, a giant humpback skull hanging in the cafeteria. The school mascot is a horseshoe crab, and we're all aware of how ridiculous this is, the bookstore stocked with sweatshirts that read GOT CRABS? across the back. There aren't any sports teams, the students call the president by her first name, and professors wear Teva sandals and T-shirts and bring their dogs to class. I love the college, don't want to graduate, don't want to leave.

Strane says I need to contextualize my reluctance to grow up, that everyone my age is drawn to self-victimization. "And that mentality is especially difficult for young women to resist," he says. "The world has a vested interest in keeping you helpless." He says as a culture we treat victimhood as an extension of childhood. So when a woman chooses victimhood, she is therefore freed from personal responsibility, which then compels others to take care of her, which is why once a woman chooses victimhood, she will continue to choose it again and again.

I still feel different from others, dark and deeply bad, same as I did at fifteen, but I've tried to gain a better understanding of the reasons. I've become an expert of the age-gap trope, consuming books, films, anything featuring a romance between an adult and legal child. I search endlessly for myself but never find anything truly accurate. Girls in those stories are always victims, and I am not—and it doesn't have anything to do with what Strane did or didn't do to me when I was younger. I'm not a victim because I've never wanted to be, and if I don't want to be, then I'm not. That's how it works. The difference between rape and sex is state of mind. *You can't rape the willing, right?* My freshman year roommate said that when I tried to stop her from going home drunk with some guy she met at a party. You can't rape the willing. It's a terrible joke, sure, but it makes sense.

And even if Strane did hurt me, all girls have old wounds. When I first came to Atlantica, I lived in a women's dorm that was like Browick but more fraught, alcohol and pot easily available, minimal supervision. Open doors lined the hallways, and girls wandered from room to room late into the night, confessing secrets, laying their hearts bare. Girls I met only hours before wept beside me on my bed, telling me about their distant mothers and mean fathers and how their boyfriends cheated on them and that the world was a terrible place. None of them had had affairs with older men and they were still screwed up. If I had never met Strane, I doubt I would've turned out all that different. Some boy would've used me, taken me for granted, ripped my heart out. At least Strane gave me a better story to tell than theirs.

Sometimes it's easier to think of it that way—as a story. Last fall I took a fiction writing workshop, and all semester I turned in pieces about Strane. While the stories were critiqued by the class, I took notes on what everyone said, copied down all their comments, even the stupid ones, the mean ones. If someone said, "I mean, she's obviously a slut. Who has sex with a teacher? Who does something like that?" I wrote those questions in my notebook and then added my own: *(Why did I do it? Because I'm a slut?)*

I left that class feeling battered and bruised, but it seemed like penance, a deserved humiliation. Maybe there's a comparison to be made between sitting silently through those brutal workshops and standing in that Browick classroom as questions were hurled at me, but I try not to let myself linger on thoughts like these. I keep my head down, keep going.

The professor teaching my capstone lit seminar is new. Henry Plough. I noticed his nameplate on the office next to my advisor's the other day, the door ajar, showing an empty room with a desk and two chairs. At the first seminar meeting, I sit at the far end of the table, hungover, maybe still drunk, my skin and hair stinking of beer.

As I watch the other students filter in, each face familiar, my brain seems to spasm, a flash of light and wall of sound, an instant headache so strong I press my fingers against my eyes. When I open them again, Jenny Murphy is there—Jenny the former roommate, the fleeting best friend, the life ruiner. She sits at the seminar table, chin resting on her fist, her brown bobbed hair and the long line of her neck exactly the same. Has she transferred? My body trembles as I wait for her to notice me. How funny that neither of us has aged. I don't look a day over fifteen, either, the same freckled face and long red hair.

I'm still fixated on her when Henry Plough comes into the classroom carrying a textbook, a leather bag slung over his shoulder. Dragging my eyes away from Jenny, I take him in, this new professor. At first glance, he is Strane, all beard and glasses, heavy footsteps and wide shoulders. Then the revisions reveal themselves: not dominatingly tall but average height, his hair and beard blond rather than black, brown eyes instead of gray, glasses horn-rimmed not wire frame. He's slimmer, smaller, and he's young—that's the last thing I notice. No gray hairs, smooth skin beneath his beard, midthirties. He's Strane in the pupal stage, still soft.

Henry Plough drops his copy of the textbook onto the seminar table and it thuds loudly, making everyone wince.

"Sorry, didn't mean to do that."

He picks it back up, holds it in his hands for a moment, unsure what to do, then sets it back down on the table carefully.

"I guess I should get started," he says, "now that my awkward entrance is out of the way."

From the start, his demeanor is all wrong—affable and self-deprecating; nothing about him strikes a chord of terror like Strane did on the first day, filling the blackboard with notes on a poem no one dared admit they hadn't read. And yet as Henry Plough goes through the roster, his eyes moving up and down the length of the seminar table, taking each of us in, I am back in Strane's classroom, feeling his eyes drink me in. A breeze drifts in through the open window, and the salt air smells of burned dust from the radiator in Strane's office. The scream of a seagull turns into the Norumbega church bells marking the half hour.

At the other end of the table, Jenny finally looks my way. Our eyes meet and I see it's not Jenny at all, just a girl with a round face and brown hair who I've had classes with before.

Henry Plough reaches the end of the roster. As always, I'm last.

"Vanessa Wye?" It sounds so imploring on the first day of a new semester. Vanessa, why?

I raise two fingers, too shaken to lift my arm. At the other end of the table, the girl I thought was Jenny uncaps her pen and the storm surge within me retreats, leaving behind garbage and tangled strands of rotten kelp. I feel a familiar fear: maybe I'm crazy, narcissistic, delusional. Someone so stuck in her own brain, she turns unwilling bystanders into ghosts.

Henry Plough studies my face as though to memorize it. In his grade book, he puts a mark next to my name.

For the rest of the seminar, I sit hunched in my seat, daring to look at him only in glances. My brain keeps drifting out the window; I can't tell if it's trying to escape or get a wider view. After class I walk home alone along a shoreline path, sea mist frizzing my hair. It's a pitch-black night and I'm wearing my earbuds, music turned up so loud I don't stand a chance against anyone who might want to grab me from behind—senselessly stupid behavior. I'd never admit to this, but the thought of a monster's breath on the back of my neck gives me a thrill. It propels me forward, the epitome of asking for it.

Strane comes to see me that Friday night. I wait for him in front of my building, sitting on the stoop of the bagel shop that fills our apartment with the smell of yeast and coffee every morning. It's a warm evening: girls in sundresses walk to the bars; a boy from my poetry class sails by on a longboard, drinking a beer. When Strane's station wagon appears, it turns down the alley rather than parking on the street where it's more likely to be seen. He's still paranoid, even though there aren't any Browick alums at Atlantica.

After a minute, he emerges from the dark alley and grins under the glow of a streetlight, holds out his arms. "Get over here."

He's wearing stonewashed jeans and white tennis shoes. Dad clothes. When weeks pass between visits, I get caught off guard and end up burying my face in his chest just so I don't have to look at his ruddy nose and graying beard, stomach falling over his waistband.

He leads the way up the dark stairwell to my apartment like it's his place and not mine. "You have a couch now," he says as we step inside. "That's an improvement."

He turns to me with a smirk, but his face softens as he takes me in. Out on the street, in the dark, he couldn't see how pretty I am in my sundress, with my new bangs, winged eyeliner, and rose-stained lips.

"Look at you," he says. "Like a French girl from nineteen sixty-five."

His approval is all it takes for my body to buckle and his ugly clothes to turn not so ugly, or at least not important. He's always going to be old. He has to be. That's the only way I can stay young and dripping with beauty.

Before I open the door to my bedroom, I warn, "I didn't get a chance to clean, so be nice."

I turn on the lights and he surveys the mess: the piles of clothes, coffee mugs and empty wine bottles on the floor beside my bed, a cracked eye shadow palette ground into the carpet.

"I will never understand how you live in this," he says.

"I like it," I say, using both hands to shove my clothes off the bed. That's not really true, but I don't want to hear his lecture about messy environments reflecting messy minds.

We lie down, him on his back and me on my side squeezed between him and the wall. He asks about my classes and I go through the list, hesitating when I get to Henry Plough's. "Then there's that capstone seminar."

"Who's the professor?"

"Henry Plough. He's new."

"Where'd he get his doctorate?"

"I have no idea. It's not like they put it on the syllabus."

Strane frowns, vaguely disapproving. "Have you given thoughts to your plans?"

Plans. Postgraduation. My parents want me to move south, to Portland, Boston, beyond. "There's nothing for you up here," Dad jokes, "only nursing homes and rehab centers, because everyone north of Augusta is elderly or an addict." Strane wants me to leave, too, says I should broaden my horizons and get out into the world, but then he'll add something like, "Don't know what I'll do without you. Probably give in to my baser instincts."

I wiggle my head, noncommittal. "Eh, a little. Hey, wanna smoke?" I crawl over him, grab the jewelry box where I keep my pot. He watches with a frown as I go through the steps of loading a bowl, but he takes a long hit when I offer the pipe.

"Didn't anticipate having a twenty-one-year-old girlfriend meant a midlife round of substance abuse," he says, his voice thin with an exhale of smoke, "though I guess I should have seen it coming."

I take a hit, inhaling so hard my throat burns. I hate how excited I get when he calls me his girlfriend.

We smoke the bowl and drink a mostly full bottle of wine left on the floor next to the bed. I turn on my little TV, and for five excruciating minutes we watch a reality show about men getting arrested after trying to meet up with teenage girls from chat rooms who were actually cops in disguise. I put on a movie instead. All I have are films that hit equally close to home—both versions of *Lolita*, *Pretty Baby*, *American Beauty*, *Lost in Translation*—but at least they focus on the beauty of it all, frame it as a love story.

When Strane takes off my dress and rolls me onto my back, I'm so high I feel blurred, like swirling smoke, but as he starts to go down on me, everything crashes into focus. I clamp my legs shut. "I don't want that."

"Nessa, come on." He rests his face against my clamped thighs, gazes up at me. "Let me."

I lift my eyes to the ceiling and shake my head. I haven't let him go down on me for at least a year now, maybe longer. It wouldn't kill me or anything, but it would admit a kind of defeat.

He continues. "You're turning down pleasure."

I tense every muscle in my body. Light as a feather, stiff as a board.

"Are you punishing yourself?"

My thoughts tumble down a wormhole, dulled edges and gentle curves. I see the night ocean, waves hitting the granite shore. Strane is there, standing on a slab of pink granite, his hands cupped around his mouth. *Let me do it. Let me pleasure you.* He keeps calling, but I'm out of reach. I'm a speckled seal swimming past the breakers, a seabird with a wingspan so strong I can fly for miles. I'm the new moon, hidden and safe from him, from everyone.

"You're stubborn," he says, moving on top of me and nudging my legs apart with his knee. "So stupidly stubborn."

He tries to push in, and then has to reach down to stroke himself; he keeps going soft. I could help, but I'm still feather light, board stiff. Plus, it isn't my problem. If a forty-eight-year-old man can't get hard for a twenty-one-year-old girl, can he get hard for anything? For a fifteen-year-old, maybe. Sometimes at his house in Norumbega, we pretend it's the first time again. *You gotta relax, honey. I can't get in if you don't relax. Deep breaths.*

He starts to move in and out of me, and I shut my eyes to watch the familiar images play on loop: loaves of bread rising, groceries traveling down a conveyor belt, a time lapse of white roots extending into soft earth. The longer the reel plays, the more my skin crawls. My chest starts to heave. Even with my eyes open, all I see are the images. I know he's on top of me, fucking me, but I can't see him. This keeps happening. The last time I tried to explain to him what this feels like, he told me it sounded like hysterical blindness. *Just calm down. You gotta relax, honey.*

I grab at my own throat. I need him to choke me; it's the only thing that will bring me back. “Do it hard,” I say. “Really rough.” He does it only if I beg, a stream of gasping “pleases” until he relents, presses half-heartedly on my throat. It’s enough for the apartment to reappear, his face looming over me, sweat sliding down his cheeks.

Afterward, he says, “I don’t like doing that, Vanessa.”

I sit up, scoot down the bed, and grab my dress from the floor. I have to pee and don’t like walking around naked in front of him, and I also don’t know when Bridget’s coming back.

He adds, “There’s something very troubling about it.”

“Define ‘it,’” I say, slipping the dress over my head.

“This violence you want me to do to you. It’s . . .” He grimaces. “It’s awfully dark, even for me.”

Before we fall asleep, the lights out and *Pretty Baby* playing on mute, Bridget returns from the bar. We listen to her walk around the living room and then, stumbling slightly, into the bathroom. The water turns on full blast, not quite covering the sound of her puking.

“Should we help her?” Strane whispers.

“She’s fine,” I say, though if he weren’t here, I would check on her. I don’t know if it’s that I don’t want him near her or the other way around.

After a while, she moves into the kitchen. A cupboard door opens and there’s a crinkle of plastic from her hand reaching into a box of cereal. It’s the kind of night when she and I usually camp out on the couch and watch late-night infomercials until we pass out.

Under the blankets, Strane’s hand moves across my thigh.

“Does she know I’m here?” he whispers. His hand between my legs, he works at me as we listen to Bridget move through the apartment.

In the morning, I wake in bed alone. I think he’s left until I hear footsteps out in the living room and the bathroom door open. Then

Bridget's voice high with surprise, "Oh, I'm sorry!" and Strane's rushed "No, no, it's fine. I was just leaving."

I listen as they introduce themselves. Strane calls himself "Jacob" as though he were normal, as though any of this were normal, while I lie frozen in bed, suddenly terrified, like a girl in a horror film seeing claws creeping out from under the closet door. When he comes back into the bedroom, I pretend to be asleep. Even when he touches my shoulder and says my name, I don't open my eyes.

"I know you're awake," he says. "I met your roommate. Seems like a nice girl. I like that gap in her smile."

I bury my face deeper into the comforter.

"I'm leaving now. Can I get a kiss goodbye?"

I snake my arm out from under the covers and hold up my hand for a high five, which he ignores. I listen to his heavy footsteps move through the apartment, and when I hear him say goodbye to Bridget, I cover my face with my hands.

I open my eyes and she's standing in my bedroom doorway, her arms crossed. "Stinks like sex in here," she says.

I sit up, pulling the covers with me. "I know he's gross."

"He's not gross."

"He's old. He's so old."

She laughs, tosses her hair. "Really, he wasn't that bad."

I get dressed and we go to the coffee shop downstairs for bacon and egg bagels and black coffees. At a table by the window, I watch a couple walking an enormous curly-haired dog, pink tongue flopping out of its panting mouth.

Bridget says, "So you've been with him since you were fifteen?"

I suck coffee through my teeth, scald my tongue. It's not like her to pry. We give each other distance, refer to it jokingly as the "no-judgment zone," the space in which I watch her hook up with guys despite her fiancé back home in Rhode Island and I do whatever it is I do with Strane.

"Off and on," I say.

"He was the first you had sex with?"

I nod, my eyes on the window, still watching the couple and the curly-coated dog. "First and only."

At that, her eyes bug out. "Wait, seriously? No one else?"

I lift my shoulders and suck down more coffee, burning my throat. There's satisfaction in seeing my life contort another person's face into shock and awe, but a second too long and their awe turns to gawking.

"I can't imagine what that must've been like," she says.

I try to hide how my eyes smart with tears. I shouldn't be upset. This is nothing. She's just curious. This is what having a friend is like. You talk about boys, your wild teenage past.

"Were you scared?"

Picking at my bagel, I shake my head. Why would I have been scared? He was so careful with me. I think of the public high school, of Charley and Will Coviello, who called her white trash and never spoke to her again after she gave him a blow job. How he came back into the bowling alley with that smirk on his face, so pleased to have gotten what he wanted. Being subjected to that kind of humiliation would have been scary. Not Strane, who sank to his knees before me, who told me I was the love of his life.

I flick my eyes to Bridget, stare her down. "He worshipped me. I was lucky."

Fall comes on suddenly. The hotels close up and the visa workers go home. The trees turn the second week of September, clusters of yellow leaves stark against an overcast sky. Mornings are cold, wet with fog, and I wake with damp bedsheets twisted around my ankles.

At the end of September, in the lull before Henry Plough's seminar starts, a girl I've had writing workshops with since freshman year takes her seat at the seminar table and sets down a pile of books. She wears cowboy boots and short skirts and sends her work out to lit journals, and my advisor once described her as "destined for Iowa." On the top of the stack of books is *Pale Fire*, Vladimir Nabokov. I freeze at the sight of the novel. *"Come and be worshiped, come and be caressed, / My dark Vanessa."*

Henry points to it. "Great choice there," he says. "That's one of my favorites."

The girl grins. Her cheeks flush instantly from the attention. "It's for twentieth-century lit. I'm writing a paper on it, which is"—she widens her eyes—"intimidating."

The boy beside her asks what it's about and I listen, thumping and hot, as she tries to explain and falters. Henry starts to speak, but I cut in louder.

"There isn't really a plot," I say. "Or, at least, that's not how it's meant to be read. The novel is a poem and footnotes, and the footnotes tell their own story, but the character writing those footnotes is unreliable so the whole thing is unreliable. It's a novel that resists meaning and demands that the reader relinquish control . . ."

I trail off, feeling the swell of anxiety that comes whenever I talk like this—like Strane is channeling himself through me. Coming from him, this kind of talk sounds brilliant, but it just makes me seem like a bitch, haughty and harsh.

"Well anyway," the girl says, "it's not my favorite Nabokov. I read *The True Life of Sebastian Knight* and liked it a lot better."

Quietly, I correct her: "*Real Life*."

With a roll of her eyes she turns away from me, but at the front of the seminar table, as the rest of the class enters and takes their seats, Henry watches me with a faint smile, contemplating.

When I get home from class, I make myself dinner and read *Titus Andronicus* for next week, the start of the Shakespeare unit. It's a brutal, bloody play of severed hands and heads cooked in pies. Lavinia, the general's daughter, is gang-raped and subsequently mutilated. The men who rape her cut out her tongue so she can't speak and cut off her hands so she can't write. Still, she's so desperate to tell, she learns how to hold a stick in her mouth and scratches out the men's names in the dirt.

When I reach that part of the play, I stop reading and grab Strane's old copy of *Lolita* from my bookcase and thumb through until I find the section I'm looking for on page 165: Lo laughing at a newspaper column advising kids that if a strange man offers you candy, you should say no and scratch his license plate number on the side of the road. I pencil *Lavinia?* in the margin and dog-ear the page. I try to pick up *Titus Andronicus* again, but my brain won't focus.

I open my laptop and bring up the blog I created three years ago. It's technically public but anonymous—I use pseudonyms and google myself every few weeks to make sure it doesn't come up in the search results. Maintaining this blog is like walking alone at night with my headphones on, like going to the bar with the sole intention of getting so drunk I can't see straight, things I remember my Psychology 101 textbook referring to as "risky behavior."

September 28, 2006
He mentioned Nabokov today, so I feel I should document this burgeoning thing.

I don't know what to call it. Really, "it" is nothing, a narrative born of my own depraved brain—but how can I not jump to that familiar story when the characters, the setting, and so many of the details are the same? (In the classroom, the professor's eyes drift to the end of the seminar table, to the red-haired girl whose voice trembles whenever she's called on to read.)

This is absurd. I *am absurd, projecting all this onto a man I know nothing about except what he looks like standing in front of a chalkboard and the most mundane facts anyone could scrounge up with a Google search. I feel like I've plucked him out of the classroom, like I'm doing to him what S. did to me. But isn't the professor supposed to be S. in this scenario?*

I've started dressing like I did at fifteen on the days I know I'll see him—baby doll dresses and Converse sneakers, my hair in braids—as though the sight of me doing my best nymphet impression might make him realize what I am and what I'm capable of, which is to say . . . I am probably legitimately actually INSANE.

"One of my favorites," he said today, about Pale Fire *(not* Lolita*—can you imagine if he'd said that about* Lolita*?). Not a big deal. An innocuous comment. All English professors love that novel. But I hear this professor say it, the one I've decided is special, and suddenly it becomes revelatory.*

I hear Pale Fire *and all I can think of is S. giving me his own copy, telling me to turn to page 37. How it felt to find my own name on the page:* My dark Vanessa.

And just like that, my mind draws a new connection between the characters. Sometimes it really does feel like a curse, the meaning I can attach to anything.

❧

There are three bars in Atlantica: one where students go, with microbrews on tap and clean floors; a tavern with pool tables and jars of pickled eggs; and a bar-slash-oyster shack, perched on the edge of a pier, where drunken fishermen get into knife fights. Bridget and I only ever go to the student bar, but she heard the tavern has dancing on Saturday nights.

"We won't know anyone there," she says. "We'll be free."

She's right; we are the only Atlantica students there and probably ten years younger than everyone else, though the lights are so dim it's hard to tell. We do shots of chilled tequila and carry beer bottles onto the dance floor, swigging as we gyrate to Kanye, Beyoncé, Shakira. We're so giddy that we grab at each other, red and honey hair falling over our faces and into our drinks. A man asks if we do everything together, and we're having so much fun, we don't act offended; we just laugh: "Maybe!" When the DJ starts to play techno, we leave the dance floor to catch our breath and sidle up to the bar, where more shots appear before us, paid for by a man in a Red Sox hat and camo jacket.

"I like the way you two move," the man says, and for a terrifying second, it's Craig, that creep from the bowling alley in high school; then I blink and see he's a stranger with pockmarked cheeks and bad breath. He hovers over us until we go dance just to escape him. Toward the end of the night, when Bridget's in the bathroom and I'm leaning against the bar, so much tequila in me my eyes won't focus, the man reappears. I can't see him but I can smell him—beer and cigarettes and something else, a rot that hits my face as he slides a hand across my ass. "Your friend is the pretty one," he says, "but you look like you'd be more fun."

I wait a second, two, three, gripped with the same senseless feeling I had at ten years old, when I jammed my finger in my mom's car door and, instead of screaming in pain, I stood there thinking, *I wonder how long I can stand this?* Then I swat his hand away and tell him to fuck off: he calls me a bitch. Bridget comes back from the bathroom and takes out her keys, jangles her little bottle of Mace at him, and he calls her a crazy bitch. The whole walk home, she and I are giddy with fear, holding hands and looking over our shoulders.

Back at the apartment, Bridget passes out on the couch, her arm cradling a half-eaten bowl of mac and cheese. I shut myself in the bathroom and call Strane. It goes to voicemail, so I call again and again until he answers, his voice thick with sleep.

"I know it's late," I say.

"Are you drunk?"

"Define 'drunk.'"

He sighs. "You're drunk."

"Someone touched me."

"What?"

"A man. At a bar. He grabbed my butt."

There's silence on the other line, like he's waiting for me to get to the point.

"He didn't ask me. He just did it."

"You don't have to confess anything to me," he says. "You're young. You're allowed to have fun."

He asks if I'm being safe, tells me to call him in the morning, looks out for me like a parent, knows more about me than my actual parents, who I speak to only in generalities during our twenty-minute phone calls on Sunday nights.

On the tile floor, a towel bunched under my head, I mumble, "Sorry I'm such a mess."

"It's fine," he says. But I want him to tell me that I'm not a mess at all. I am beautiful, precious, and rare.

"Well, it's your fault, you know," I say.

A pause. "Ok."

"Everything wrong with me originated with you."

"Let's not do this."

"You created this mess."

"Baby, go to bed."

"Am I wrong?" I ask. "Tell me I'm wrong." I stare up at a water stain stretching across the ceiling.

Finally, he says, "I know it's what you believe."

During the class discussion devoted to *The Tempest,* Henry tells us all to pair up. Within seconds, everyone has figured it out through imperceptible gestures and glances. They drag their chairs closer together while I stand and look around for someone else without a partner. As I scan the room, I catch Henry watching me, his face tender.

"Vanessa, over here." Amy Doucette waves her hand. When I sit, she leans toward me and whispers, "I didn't do the reading. Did you?"

I give a shrugging nod and lie: "I skimmed it." Really, I read it twice and called Strane to talk about it. He told me if I wanted to impress the professor, I should either refer to the play as postcolonial or make a joke about Francis Bacon having written it. When I asked who Francis Bacon was, he wouldn't tell me. "I'm not doing all the work for you," he said. "Look it up."

Now, as I describe the plot to Amy, I see Henry making his way from pair to pair out of the corner of my eye. When he's close to us, my voice jumps, unnaturally high and bright: "But it doesn't really matter what the play's about anyway, because Shakespeare didn't write it, Francis Bacon did!"

Henry lets out a laugh—a real one, from the belly and loud.

At the end of class, he stops me on my way out the door and hands me my essay on Lavinia from *Titus Andronicus.* I focused on her torn-out tongue and torn-off hands, her subsequent silence, the failure of language in the face of rape.

"Great job with that," he says. "And I liked your joke. From class, not the paper." He blushes, continuing, "I didn't see any jokes in your paper, but maybe I missed them."

"No, there weren't any jokes."

"Right," he says, the flush now all the way down his neck.

I'm so nervous around him, all my body wants to do is bolt. I shove the essay in my jacket pocket and throw my backpack over one shoulder, but he stops me, asking, "You're a senior, right? Are you applying to graduate school?"

It's such a sudden question, I laugh in surprise. "I don't know. Haven't planned on it."

"You should consider it," Henry says. "Based on that work alone"—he gestures to the paper stuffed in my pocket—"you'd be a strong candidate."

I read over the paper as I walk home, scrutinizing first Henry's marginal comments and then the sentences of mine he commented on, trying to find this supposed potential. I wrote the paper quickly, three typos in the first paragraph, a flimsy conclusion. Strane would have given it a B.

The first week in November, Strane makes a reservation at an expensive restaurant down the coast and books us a hotel room. He tells me to dress up, so I wear a black silk dress with thin straps, the only nice thing I own. The restaurant is Michelin-starred, Strane says, and I pretend to know what that means. It's in a remodeled barn with weathered wooden walls and exposed beams, white tablecloths and brown leather club chairs. The menu is all stuff like scallops with asparagus flan, tenderloin crusted with foie gras. Nothing has a price.

"I don't know what any of this is." I mean it as bratty, but he takes it as insecure. When the waiter comes, Strane orders for both of us—rabbit loin wrapped in prosciutto, salmon and pomegranate sauce, champagne panna cotta for dessert. Everything arrives on enormous white plates, a perfect little construction in the center, barely recognizable as food.

"How do you like it?" he asks.

"Good, I guess."

"You guess?"

He gives me a look like I'm being ungrateful, which I am, but I don't have it in me to play the doe-eyed girl from the sticks, awed at a glimpse of the high-class world. He took me to a restaurant like this in Portland for my birthday. I acted sweet then, moaning over the food, whispering, *I feel so fancy,* across the table. Now, I poke at the panna cotta and shiver in my summer dress, my bare arms broken out in goose bumps.

He pours more wine into both our glasses. "Have you thought any more about what you're going to do after graduation?"

"That's a terrible question."

"It's only a terrible question if you have no plan."

I pull the spoon from between my lips. "I need more time to figure it out."

"You have seven months to figure it out," he says.

"No, I mean like an extra year. Maybe I should fail all my classes on purpose to buy some time."

He gives me the look again.

"I was thinking," I say slowly, twirling my spoon in the panna cotta, turning it into mush, "if I don't figure something out, could I stay with you? Just as a backup plan."

"No."

"You're not even thinking about it."

"I don't need to think about it. The idea is ridiculous."

I sit back in my chair, cross my arms.

He leans toward me, ducks his head, and in a low voice says, "You cannot move in with me."

"I didn't say *move in*."

"What would your parents think?"

I shrug. "They wouldn't need to know."

"They wouldn't need to know," he repeats, shaking his head. "Well, people in Norumbega would certainly notice. And what would they think if they saw you living with me? I'm still trying to get myself out from under what happened back then, not get sucked back in."

"Fine," I say. "It's fine."

"You'll be ok," he says. "You don't need me."

"It's *fine*. Forget I ever mentioned it."

Impatience simmers beneath his words. He's annoyed I'd ask such a thing, that I would even want it, and I'm annoyed, too—that I'm still so devoted to him, still a child. I've come nowhere close to fulfilling the prophecy he laid out for me years ago, a dozen lovers at twenty, a life in which he was one of many. At twenty-one, there's still only him.

When the check comes, I grab it first, just to see the total: $317. The thought of so much money on one meal is nauseating, but I say nothing as I slide the bill across the table.

After dinner, we go to a cocktail lounge around the corner from the hotel. The bar has darkened windows and heavy doors, dim lights inside. We sit off in a corner at a small table, and the waiter stares at my ID for so long Strane grows annoyed and says, "All right, I think that's enough." Beside us, two middle-aged couples sit talking about traveling abroad, Scandinavia, the Baltics, St. Petersburg. One of the men keeps saying to the other, "You need to go there. It's nothing like here. This place is a shithole. You need to go *there*." I can't tell what he thinks is the shithole—Maine, America, or maybe just the cocktail lounge.

Strane and I sit close, our knees touching. While we eavesdrop on the couples, he slides his hand onto my thigh. "Do you like your drink?" He ordered us each a Sazerac. It all tastes like whiskey to me.

His hand slides farther between my legs, his thumb brushing the crotch of my underwear. He has an erection; I can tell by how he shifts his hips and clears his throat. I know, too, that he likes touching me next to the men his age and their old wives.

I drink another Sazerac, and another, and another. Strane's hand doesn't leave my legs.

"You're all goose pimples," he murmurs. "What kind of girl doesn't wear stockings in November?"

I want to correct him and say, *You mean tights—nobody says "stockings," this isn't the nineteen fifties,* but before I can, he answers his own question.

"A bad girl, that's what kind."

In the hotel lobby, I hang back while he checks into our room. I inspect the empty concierge desk, accidentally brush a pile of brochures onto the floor. On the elevator up to the room, Strane says, "I think that man at the front desk winked at me." He kisses me as it dings for our floor, like he wants someone to be waiting on the other side, but the doors open onto an empty hallway.

"I'm going to be sick." I grab a handle, push down hard. "Come on, open up."

"That's not our room. Why did you let yourself get this drunk?" He ushers me down the hallway and into the room, where I make a beeline for the bathroom, sinking to the floor and curling my arms around the toilet. Strane watches from the doorway.

"A hundred-fifty-dollar dinner down the drain," he says.

I'm too drunk for sex but he still tries. My head lolls against the pillows as he pushes my legs apart. The last thing I remember is telling him not to go down on me. He must have listened; I wake up with my underwear on.

In the morning, as he drives me back to Atlantica, the radio plays Bruce Springsteen. "Red Headed Woman." Strane sneaks glances at me, smiling slyly at the lyrics, trying to get me to smile, too.

Well, listen up, stud
Your life's been wasted
Till you've got down on your knees and tasted
A red headed woman.

I lean forward, turn it off. "That's disgusting."

After a few miles of silence, he says, "I forgot to tell you, that new counselor at Browick is married to a professor at your college."

I'm too hungover to care. "How thrilling," I mumble, my cheek pressed against the cool window, the coastline flying by.

Henry's office is on the fourth floor of the biggest building on campus, concrete and brutalist, the eyesore of Atlantica. Most departments are housed there; the fourth floor belongs to English professors, open office doors revealing desks and armchairs and overstuffed bookshelves. Every single one reminds me of Strane's—the scratchy sofa and seafoam glass. Whenever I walk this hallway, time feels flat, like it's folded onto itself over and over, a piece of paper into a crane.

Henry's door is ajar, and through the few inches I see he's at his desk, watching something on his laptop. When I knock lightly on the doorframe, he jumps, hitting the space bar on his keyboard to pause the video.

"Vanessa," he says, pulling open the door. There's a timbre to his voice like he's pleased to see me standing there and not anyone else. His office is still as bare as it was when I glimpsed inside before the semester began. No rug on the floor, nothing on the walls, but clutter has begun to emerge. Loose papers spread across the desk, books lie haphazard on the shelves, and a dusty black backpack hangs by one strap from the filing cabinet.

"Are you busy?" I ask. "I can come back another time."

"No, no. Just trying to get some work done." We both glance at the video paused on his laptop, a guy with a guitar frozen mid-strum. "Emphasis on 'trying,'" he adds, and gestures to the extra chair. Before I sit, I gauge the distance of the chair from his desk—close but far enough away that he can't reach over and suddenly touch me.

"I have an idea for my final paper," I say, "but it would mean bringing in a text we didn't read in class."

"What were you thinking?"

"Um, Nabokov? How Shakespeare shows up in *Lolita*?"

During my freshman year, in a class on unreliable narrators, I called *Lolita* a love story and the professor cut me off, saying, "Calling this novel a love story indicates an unconscionable misreading on your part." She wouldn't even let me finish what I was trying to say. Ever since then, I haven't dared bring it up in any of my classes.

But Henry just crosses his arms and leans back in his chair. He asks what connections I see between *Lolita* and the plays we've read, so I explain the parallels I've found: Lavinia from *Titus* scratching her rapists' names in the dirt and raped, orphaned Lo scoffing at the suggestion she do the same thing if strange men offer her candy; how *Henry IV*'s Falstaff lures Hal away from his family the way a pedophile lures a wayward child; the virginal symbolism of *Othello*'s strawberry handkerchief and the strawberry-print pajamas Humbert gives Lo.

At the last point, Henry frowns. "I don't remember that detail of the pajamas."

I stop, mentally thumb through the novel, trying to recall the exact scene, if it's before Lo's mother died, or if it's at the first hotel Lo and Humbert stay at together, at the very beginning of their first road trip. Then my body jumps. I remember Strane taking the pajamas out of a dresser drawer, the feel of the fabric between my fingers, trying them on in his bathroom, the harsh lights and cold tile floor. Like a scene from a movie I watched years ago, something observed from a safe distance.

I blink. From his chair, Henry watches me with gentle eyes, lips softly parted.

"Are you ok?" he asks.

"I might be remembering that one wrong," I say.

He says that it's fine and the whole thing sounds great, excellent, far and away the best paper topic he's heard so far, and he's heard from almost everyone.

"You know," he says, "my favorite line in *Lolita* is about the dandelions."

I think for a moment, try to place it . . . dandelions, dandelions. I can picture the line on the page, toward the beginning of the novel, when they're in Ramsdale, Lo's mother still alive. "Most of the dandelions had changed from suns to moons."

"The moons," I say.

Henry nods. "Changed from suns to moons."

For a second, it's like our brains are connected, like a wire snaked out of mine and planted itself into his, both of us seeing the same image, seeded and full in our heads. It seems strange that his favorite line in the whole sordid novel is something so chaste. Not any of the descriptions of Lolita's supple little body or Humbert's attempts at self-justification, but an unexpectedly lovely image of a front yard weed.

Henry shakes his head and the wire between us snaps, the moment over.

"Well, anyway," he says. "It's a good line."

November 17, 2006

Just back from talking with the Professor about Lolita *for a half hour. He told me his favorite line ("Most of the dandelions had changed from suns to moons," pg. 73). At one point, he said "nymphet," and hearing that word made me want to tear him open and eat him.*

He picked up on something strange about me, how deeply I know the novel. When I referenced some little detail—Humbert's attraction to his first wife because of how her foot looked in a black velvet slipper—the Professor asked, "Are you reading this for another class, or . . . ?" Meaning, how do I know the book so well? I told him it's mine. That it belongs to me.

I said, "You know how sometimes there's a book that's yours*?" And he nodded, like he understood exactly.*

I'm sure his intentions are pure, that he thinks I'm a bright girl with good insights, but then there are moments like this:

before I left his office he watched me pull on my coat. I couldn't find my sleeve, stumbled a little as I groped around for it. He made a small movement then, like he was about to help me, but stopped himself, controlled himself. His eyes, though, were soft, so soft. S. is the only other person who's ever looked at me that way.

Am I being greedy or delusional? Another affair with a teacher, give me a break. Lightning doesn't strike twice, etc. But if it did happen, would it even be considered the same sort of thing? The basic facts are much more palatable: twenty-one instead of fifteen, thirty-four instead of forty-two. Two consenting adults. Scandal or relationship, who's to say?

Obviously I'm getting ahead of myself, but I also know what I am, what I could become.

At my poetry press internship, we prepare for the arrival of a prominent poet who is coming to town for his book release. Jim, the other intern, and I spend two weeks designing press materials, showing the press materials to our boss and the assistant director of the press, then redesigning, and redesigning again. When asked if I want to drive to Portland to pick up the poet from the airport, I grab the chance. I plan out what I'll wear, make a list of conversation topics for the hour drive back to campus. I even print off copies of my best poems in the dream case scenario that he takes an interest in me, though it feels embarrassingly presumptuous.

On the day before the poet arrives, Eileen, the director of the press, finds me in the kitchen, filling the electric kettle with water.

"Vanessa, hi," she says, stretching out her vowels so long it sounds as though she's offering consolation for some tragedy. I didn't even realize she remembered my name. She hasn't spoken to me since my interview last spring.

"So Robert will be here tomorrow," she says, "and I know you said you'd pick him up from the airport, but Robert can be a bit, you know . . ." She looks at me expectantly. When I only stare back at her, she continues in a whisper. "He can be kind of forward. You know—handsy."

I blink in surprise, still holding the electric kettle. "Oh, ok."

"There was an incident at the last event we held for him, though 'incident' is too strong a word. It was nothing, really. But it might be best for you to steer clear. Just to be safe. Do you understand what I'm getting at?"

My face burning, I nod so hard the water sloshes around inside the kettle. Eileen blushes, too. She seems mortified to be telling me this.

"So should I not pick him up from the airport?" I ask, assuming she'll say no, don't be silly, of course I should, but instead Eileen grimaces, like she doesn't want to say yes but has to anyway.

"I think that's for the best. I thought I'd ask James if he'd be willing."

I almost ask, *James?* but realize she means Jim.

"Thank you for being so understanding, Vanessa," Eileen says. "It really means a lot."

For the rest of the afternoon, I sort through submissions, reading but retaining nothing, my heart racing and teeth chattering. The way Eileen said "it might be best for you to steer clear" makes my skin crawl. I can't stop hearing it. The way she said "you," like I'm a liability.

For the rest of the semester, I let my pot run out, stop drinking so much. It happens by accident, a realization that I've been sober for a week and a half without even trying. I do the dishes, clean the bathroom. I even do laundry on a regular basis and don't let it get to the point where I have to wear bikini bottoms as underwear.

I see Henry Plough on campus all the time. Three times a week, we pass each other in the student center. While I'm reshelving books at my library job, he appears around a corner and nearly collides with the cart. He's three people ahead of me in line at the coffee shop beneath my apartment, and my stomach flips at him being so close to where I sleep. Sometimes, when we pass each other, I pounce on him, ask stupid questions I already know the answers to about the seminar. One day as I walk by him, I reach over and playfully punch his arm, and he grins in surprise. Other days, when it feels like I've been acting too desperate, I ignore him, pretend I don't know him. If he says hi, I narrow my eyes.

His term paper is my last one, finished Friday afternoon of finals week. With the paper still warm from the printer, I hurry across campus, past the empty parking lots and darkened buildings, to catch him in his office. Inside, the English department hallway is a line of closed doors—including Henry's, but I know he's in there. I checked before I came in and saw his lit-up window.

Rather than knock, I slip my essay under the door, hoping he'll see it, notice my name on the first page, and lunge for the door. I hold my breath and the knob turns, then opens.

"Vanessa." He says my name in that awestruck way. Plucking my essay off the floor, he asks, "How did this turn out? I've been looking forward to reading it."

I lift my shoulders. "Your expectations shouldn't be too high."

He flips through the first couple of pages. "Of course my expectations are high. Everything you turn in is wonderful."

I linger in the doorway, unsure what to do. Now that my paper is done and the semester finished, I don't have any excuses to talk to him. He sits turned toward me, leaning slightly forward, the body language of someone who wants you to stay. I need to hear him say it. Our eyes lock.

"You can sit," he says. It's an invitation, but still leaves it up to me.

I choose to sit, to stay, and we're silent for a moment, until I smile and gesture—generously, I think—to the now-overloaded bookshelves above his desk. "Your office is such a mess."

He relaxes. "It is a mess."

"I shouldn't criticize," I say. "I'm messy, too."

He looks around at the stack of manila folders that threatens to spill over, the uninstalled printer on the edge of his desk and its mess of cords. "I tell myself I prefer it this way, but that's probably just self-delusion."

I bite my bottom lip, remembering all the times I've said the same thing to Strane. My eyes dart around the office, fall on the tallest bookshelf where two unopened beers sit among the books. "You're hiding booze in here."

He looks to where I'm pointing. "If I'm trying to hide it, I'm doing a pretty bad job." He stands, turns the bottles so I can see their labels: SHAKESPEARE STOUT.

"Ah," I say. "Nerd beer."

He grins. "In my defense, they were a gift."

"What are you saving them for?"

"I'm not sure I'm saving them for anything."

It's obvious what the next thing out of my mouth will be. He seems to hold his breath waiting for me to say the words:

"What about right now?"

I say it so jokingly, it should be easy for him to respond, *Vanessa, I don't think that's a good idea.* Maybe if another student asked him, it would be. But he doesn't even pretend to deliberate. He just holds up his hands, as though I've twisted his arm and he can't fight anymore.

"Why not?" he says.

Then I'm taking out my keys because I have a bottle opener key chain, and we're clinking bottles, the fizz from the warm beer going all the way up my nose. Watching him drink is like peering behind a curtain. I see him at a bar, at home, sitting on the couch, lying in bed. I wonder if he grades papers late at night, if he keeps mine at the bottom of the pile, purposely saved for last.

No—he isn't like that. He's good, outright boyish, flashing me a sheepish grin before tipping back the bottle. I'm the one with ulterior motives. *I'm* the corruptor, luring him into a trap. I almost tell him to smarten up, stop being so trusting. *Henry, you can't drink beers in your office with a student. Do you understand how stupid this is, how easily it could get you into trouble?*

He asks if I'm taking his gothic seminar next semester and I say I'm not sure, that I haven't signed up for anything yet.

"You should get on that," he says. "You're running out of time."

"I always leave it until the last minute. I'm a fuckup." I throw back the bottle and take a long swallow. *Fuckup.* I like how it feels to describe myself as that to Henry, who has spent so much time praising my brain.

"Sorry for being crass," I add.

"It's fine," he says, and I see a slight change in his expression, a shade of concern.

He asks questions about my other classes, my future plans. Have I thought any more about graduate school? It's too late to apply for the fall, but I can get a head start on applications for next year.

"I don't know," I say. "My parents didn't even go to college." I'm not sure what that has to do with anything, but Henry nods like he understands.

"Neither did mine," he says.

If I decide to apply, he says, he'll help me navigate the process, and my brain catches on his choice of verb—*navigate.* I see a map spread out across a desk, our heads huddled together. *We'll figure this out, Vanessa. You and me.*

"I remember how daunting it was when I first thought about applying," Henry says. "It felt like embarking on totally unfamiliar territory. You know, before coming here I was at a prep school for a year, and it was strange, teaching those kids. Sometimes it seemed as though entitlement was instilled in them at birth."

"I went to a school like that," I say. "For a couple years, anyway."

He asks which school, and when I say Browick, he seems rattled.

He sets his beer bottle on the desk, clasps his hands together. "The Browick School?" he asks. "In Norumbega?"

"You've heard of it?"

He nods. "Strange coincidence. I, uh . . ."

I wait for him and beer settles in my mouth, for a moment my throat too tight to swallow. "I have a friend who works there," he says.

Nausea surges up my throat, and my hands tremble so badly, I knock over my bottle as I try to set it down. It's nearly empty, but a little spills onto the floor.

"Oh god, I'm sorry," I say, righting the bottle, knocking it over again, then giving up and tossing it into the garbage can.

"Hey, it's fine."

"It spilled."

"It's fine." He laughs like I'm being silly, but when I push my hair back from my face, he sees I'm crying, but it's not normal crying. This is just tears showing up on my cheeks. I'm not even sure they're coming from my eyes when I cry like this. It feels more like being wrung out, like a sponge.

"This is so embarrassing," I say, wiping my nose with the back of my hand. "I'm an idiot."

"Don't." He shakes his head, baffled. "Don't say that. You're fine."

"What does your friend do? Is he a teacher?"

"No," he says. "She's a—"

"'She'? It's a she?"

He nods, looking so concerned, I imagine I could confess anything and he would hear it. I can feel his kindness already, before I say a word.

"Do you know anyone else who works there?" I ask.

"No one," he says. "Vanessa, what's wrong?"

"I was raped by a teacher there," I say. "I was fifteen." I'm shocked at how smoothly the lie comes out of me, though I don't know if I'm lying or just not telling the truth. "He's still there," I add. "So when you said that you knew someone, it just . . . I panicked."

Henry brings his hands to his face, to his mouth. He picks his beer back up, sets it down again. Finally, he says, "I'm stunned."

I open my mouth to clarify, to explain that I'm exaggerating, I shouldn't use that word, but he speaks first.

"I have a sister," he says. "Something similar happened to her."

He looks to me, big sorrowful eyes, each of his features a gentler version of Strane's. It's easy to imagine him sinking to his knees, lowering his head into my lap, not to lament how he will inevitably ruin me but instead to mourn that another man already has.

"I'm sorry, Vanessa," he says. "Though I know that might be a useless thing to hear. I'm just so sorry."

We're quiet for a moment, him leaning forward as if he wants to comfort me—his kindness like bathwater, lapping my shoulders, milky and warm. This is more than I deserve.

My eyes fixed on the floor, I say, "Please don't tell your friend about this."

Henry shakes his head. "I wouldn't dream of it."

On the day after Christmas, I drive to Strane's house, blasting Fiona Apple and singing my throat on fire. I slouch in my seat as I pass through the downtown streets of Norumbega, leave the car in the library parking lot across from his house, and run to his front door with my hood covering my recognizable hair—precautions dictated by Strane that I've followed for so long, I do them without thinking.

Once inside, I'm shifty, darting away from his hands and not looking him in the eye. I worry he knows what I said to Henry. There's the possibility Henry told his friend and his friend told someone else at Browick; it wouldn't take much for the gossip to loop back around to Strane. There's also what I know is impossible but nevertheless half believe: that he knows everything I say and do, that he has the ability to peer inside my mind.

When he surprises me with a wrapped present, I don't take it at first, worried it's a trap, that I'll open the box to find a note saying, *I know what you did.* He's never given me a Christmas present before.

"Go on," he says with a laugh, nudging the gift against my chest.

I stare down at it, a clothing-sized box wrapped in thick gold paper and red ribbon, the work of a retail employee. "But I didn't get you anything,"

"I wouldn't expect you to."

I peel off the paper. Inside is a thick sweater, dark blue with a cream Fair Isle design around the neck. "Wow." I lift it from the box. "I love it."

"You sound surprised."

I slip the sweater over my head. "I didn't realize you paid attention to what kinds of clothes I wear." A stupid thing to say. Of course he pays attention. He knows everything about me, everything I've ever been and will be.

He makes us pasta and red sauce—no eggs and toast for once—and sets our plates on the bar, arranges the silverware and folded napkins like it's a date. He asks what I'm taking next semester, withholding his usual criticism about the course descriptions and reading lists. When I tell him about my finals and the paper I wrote for Henry's class, he interrupts me.

"That's the professor," he says. "Specializes in British lit, came from Texas? That's him. His wife is that new counselor they brought in for the students."

I bite down, hard, on my tongue. "Wife?"

"Penelope. Fresh out of grad school, got an LCS—whatever that social work degree is."

My breathing stops, caught between inhale and exhale.

Strane taps his fork against the rim of my plate. "You all right?"

I nod, force myself to swallow. *I have a friend who works there.* Friend. He said that. Or am I remembering it wrong? But why would he lie? Maybe he felt so sorry for me that he didn't want to bring even the idea of another woman into the room. But he mentioned his sister—and besides, the lie would have happened before I said anything about being raped. So why would he lie?

I ask what she's like, the most banal question I can think of, because I don't dare ask the ones I really want answers to—what does she look like, is she smart, what kind of clothes does she wear, does she talk about him?—but even though I hold back, Strane still knows. He sees it in me, my ears pricked and hackles raised.

"Vanessa, stay away from him," he says.

I screw up my face, fake indignation. "What are you talking about?"

"Be a good girl," he says. "You know what you're capable of."

After we eat and the dishes are in the sink, he stops me when I move toward the stairs, up to his bedroom.

"I have to tell you something," he says. "Come in here."

As he guides me into the living room, I think again that this is it, the confrontation about what I said. That's why Strane mentioned Henry—he's taking it slow, luring me into it. But as he sits me down on the couch, he warns that what he's about to tell me will sound worse than it actually is, that it's a misunderstanding, an unfortunate circumstance.

What he says is so at odds with what I'm expecting, I interrupt, "Wait, so this isn't about anything I did?"

"No, Vanessa," he says. "Not everything is about you." He sighs, rakes his hand through his hair. "I'm sorry," he adds. "I'm nervous, though I don't know why. If anyone's going to be understanding, it's you."

He says there's been an incident at Browick. It happened back in October, in his classroom during faculty service hour. He was meeting one-on-one with a student who had questions about an essay. She always had questions about everything, this girl. At first he thought she was merely anxious, a grade worrier, but as she started hanging around the classroom more, he realized she had a crush on him. Truthfully, it reminded him of me—her giddy demeanor, her unguarded adoration.

On this October afternoon, they were sitting at the seminar table, side by side, while he went over her essay draft. She was flustered, practically trembling from anxiety—about the grade, about being so close to him—and at some point during the conference he reached down and patted her knee. He meant it to be reassuring. He was trying to be kind. But the girl took that touch and twisted it into something ugly. She started telling her friends that he'd made a pass at her and that he wanted to have sex with her, that he was sexually harassing her.

I throw up my hand, cutting him off. "Which hand did you use?"

He blinks in surprise.

"When you touched her. Which hand?"

"Why does that matter?"

"Show me," I say. "I want to see exactly what you did."

There on the couch, I make him demonstrate. I scoot away from him, leaving a chaste distance, and press my knees together and sit up straight—the nervous pose my body remembers from those times I sat beside him at the very beginning of things. I watch his hand reach down, pat my knee. It's familiar enough to make me gag.

"It was nothing," he says.

I shove his hand away. "It's not nothing. That's how it started with me, with you touching my leg."

"That's not true."

"Yes, it is."

"It's not. You and I started long before I ever laid a hand on you."

He says this so forcefully, I can tell he's said it to himself many times before. But if it didn't start when he first touched me, when did it? When he told me, drunk at the Halloween dance, that he wanted to put me to bed and kiss me good night, or when I began inventing reasons to talk to him after class so I could get him alone and feel his eyes on me? When he wrote on my poem draft, *Vanessa, this one scares me a little,* or on the first day of classes, when I watched him give the convocation speech, his face dripping with sweat? Maybe the start can't be pinned down at all. Maybe the universe forced us together, rendering us both powerless, blameless.

"It's not even comparable," he says. "This student is nothing to me, the so-called physical contact was nothing. It was a matter of seconds. I certainly don't deserve to have my life destroyed over it."

"Why would this destroy your life?"

He sighs, sits back on the couch. "The administration caught wind of it. They're saying they need to do an investigation. Over a pat on the knee! It's puritanical hysteria. We might as well be living in Salem."

I stare him down, try to get him to flinch, but he looks innocent—the lines in his forehead creased in concern, his eyes enormous behind his glasses. Still, I want to be angry. He says the touch was insignificant, but I know how heavy with meaning a touch like that can be.

"Why are you even telling me?" I ask. "Do you want me to tell you it's ok? That I forgive you? Because I don't."

"No," he says, "I'm not asking you to forgive me. There's nothing to forgive. I'm sharing this because I want you to understand that I'm still living with the consequences of loving you."

For a split second, my eyes start to roll. I stop myself, but he still sees.

"Mock me all you like," he says, "but before you, no one would have jumped to conclusions like this. They never would have believed this girl's word over mine. These are my colleagues, people I've worked with for twenty years. That history means nothing now that my name has been dragged through the mud. Everyone assumes the worst about me. I've got eyes on me at all times, constant suspicion. And an uproar over this! My god, a friendly pat on the knee is something I do without thinking. Now it's evidence of my depravity."

Exactly how many girls have you touched? The question sits hot on my tongue, yet I don't say it. I swallow it, burning my throat all the way down, another stomach ember.

"Loving you branded me a deviant," he says. "Nothing else about me matters anymore. One transgression will define me for the rest of my life."

We sit in silence, the sounds of his house amplified—the refrigerator hum, the hiss of the steam heat.

I tell him I'm sorry. I don't want to say it but feel I have to, like he needs to hear it so badly, he's pulling the words out of me like teeth. *I'm sorry you'll never get out from under the long shadow I cast. I'm sorry what we did together was so horrific, there's no path back from it.*

He forgives me, says it's all right, then reaches over and pats my knee, until he realizes what he's doing, stops, and curls his hand into a fist.

When we go to bed on his flannel sheets, we keep our clothes on and I think of this girl he touched, faceless and bodiless, a specter of an accusation and a harbinger of the obvious: that I am getting older, and each passing day brings girls into the world who are younger than me, who might someday end up in his classroom. I imagine them, their bright hair and downy arms, until I'm exhausted, but as soon as my mind tempers down, I recall what he said about Henry, about his wife. Another wing of the labyrinth to get lost in, remembering what I told Henry about Strane, the r-word I used, how he must have gone home that night and told his wife everything. I made him promise not to tell, but the promise was only an extension of his lie. Of course he'd tell his wife. He'd have to—and who would she have to tell? If she's a counselor, would she be obligated to report it? My mouth goes dry at how easily it could all come back around. I can't get out of this. I was stupid to think I could say something, anything, without it eventually getting back to Strane.

Around midnight, we hear sirens. First faintly, then closer and closer, until it sounds like they're outside the house. For a moment I'm sure they're coming for us, that police are about to burst through the door. Strane gets out of bed and peers out the window into the night.

"I can't see anything." He grabs a sweater and heads out of the bedroom, down the stairs to the front door. When he opens it, smoke wafts in with the frigid air, so pungent it soars upstairs, fills the house.

He calls up to me, "There's a fire down the block. A big one." After a couple minutes, he returns wearing his parka and boots. "Come on, let's go see it up close."

We dress in so many layers we become anonymous, only our eyes showing above our scarves. Walking down the snow-packed sidewalks, he and I could be anyone, could be ordinary. We follow the sirens and smoke, not finding the fire until we turn a corner and see the five-story Masonic temple both ablaze and encased in ice. Six fire trucks park around the perimeter of the building, all hoses on full blast, but the night is too cold. The water, every last bit of it, freezes as soon as it hits the building's limestone exterior while the flames rage inside. The longer the firefighters try to douse the building, the thicker the ice shell grows.

While we watch, Strane reaches for my mittened hand and holds it tight. The firefighters eventually give up and, like us, stand back and watch the building burn—a small crowd gathers, a news truck arrives. Strane and I stay for a long time, holding hands, both of us blinking back tears that collect in crystals on our eyelashes.

Later, in his bed, body and mind exhausted, I ask, "Is there more you're not telling me about that girl?" When he doesn't answer, I ask it plainly: "Did you fuck her?"

"Christ, Vanessa."

"It's ok if you did," I say. "I'll forgive you. I just need to know."

He rolls toward me, holds my face in both hands. "I touched her. That's all I did."

I close my eyes as he strokes my hair and calls her terrible names: *a liar, a little bitch, an emotionally troubled girl.* I wonder what he would call me if he knew all the things I've called him in my mind over the years, if he finds out what I told Henry. But I say nothing. My silence is so reliable. He has no reason not to trust me.

At three in the morning, I wake and slip out from underneath his heavy arm, pad barefoot on the cold wood floors out of the bedroom, downstairs to the kitchen where his laptop sits on the counter. I open it and the browser loads his Browick email inbox. Weekly newsletters, minutes from faculty meetings—I scroll until I see the subject "Student Harassment Report." I freeze when I hear something, one hand hovering over the trackpad, the other poised to slap the laptop closed. When silence settles again, I click open the email and scan the text. It's from the board of trustees, written in language formal to the point of impenetrable, but I don't want to know the details anyway. I'm just looking for a name. I scroll up and down, eyes darting back and forth across the screen, and then I see it on the second line: Taylor Birch, the student making the claims. I close the email and sneak back upstairs into bed, under his arm.

2017

Taylor works in a new building five blocks from the hotel, a shock of glass and steel amid the limestone and brick. I know the name of the company, Creative Coop, and that it's described as a creative work space, but I can't figure out what anyone does there. Inside, it's all natural light and leather couches, expansive tables where people sit with open laptops. Everyone is smiling and young, or if not, then cool in a way that masquerades as youth—trendy haircuts, eccentric glasses, normcore clothes. I stand gripping my purse until a girl with round wire-framed glasses asks me, "Are you looking for someone?"

My eyes dart around the room. It's too big, too many people. I hear myself say her name.

"Taylor? Let's see." The girl turns and scans the room. "There she is."

I look where she points: bent over a laptop, thin shoulders and pale hair. The girl calls, "Taylor!" and her head lifts. The shock on her face sends me backward toward the door.

"I'm sorry," I say. "I made a mistake."

I'm already outside and half a block away when I hear her call my name. Taylor stands in the middle of the sidewalk, white blond braid hanging over her shoulder. She's wearing a turtleneck sweater with sleeves so long they fall past her wrists, no coat. As we study each other, she reaches up, fingertips poking out of her sweater sleeve, and tugs at the end of her braid. Suddenly, I see her as he might have—fourteen and unsure of herself, worrying the ends of her hair as he gazed at her from behind his desk.

"I can't believe it's really you," she says.

I came prepared with rehearsed lines, sharp ones. I wanted to slice her to the bone, but there's too much adrenaline pulsing in me. It turns my voice shaky and high as I tell her to leave me alone.

"Both you and that journalist," I say. "She keeps calling me."

"Ok," Taylor says. "She shouldn't have done that."

"I have nothing to say to her."

"I'm sorry. Really, I am. I told her not to be pushy."

"I don't want to be in the article, ok? Tell her that. And tell her not to write about the blog. I don't want any of this to touch me."

Taylor watches me, loose wisps floating around her face.

"I just want to be left alone," I say. I throw all my strength into the words, but they emerge like a plea. This is all wrong; I sound like a child.

I turn on my heel to go. Again, she calls my name.

"Can we just talk to each other?" she asks.

We go to a coffee shop, the one where I met Strane three weeks ago. Standing in line, I take in the up-close details of her, the thin silver rings on her fingers, a mascara smudge below her left eye. The scent of sandalwood clings to her clothes. She pays for my coffee, her hands shaking as she takes out her credit card.

"You don't need to do that," I say.

"I do," she says.

The barista starts the espresso machine, a din of grinding and steam, and after a minute our drinks arrive side by side, identical tulips drawn in the foam. We sit near the window, a buffer of empty tables around us.

"So you work at that hotel," she says. "That must be fun."

I scoff out a laugh and a blush immediately takes over Taylor's face.

"I'm sorry," she says. "That's a stupid thing to say."

She says she's nervous, calls herself awkward. Her hands are still shaking, her eyes looking everywhere but at me. It takes effort to stop myself from reaching across the table and telling her it's fine.

"What about you?" I ask. "What kind of company is that exactly?"

She flashes a smile, relieved at the easy question. "It's not a company," she says. "It's a cooperative work space for artists."

I nod like I understand what that means. "I didn't realize you were an artist."

"Well, not a visual artist. I'm a poet." She lifts her coffee and takes a sip, leaving a pale pink stain on the rim.

"So being a poet is what you do?" I ask. "Like, for money?"

Taylor holds her hand up to her mouth, like she's burned her tongue. "Oh no," she says, "there's no money in that. I have side hustles. Freelance writing projects, web design, consulting. Lots of things." She sets down the coffee, clasps her hands. "Ok, I'm just going to go ahead and ask. When did it end with you and him?"

The question catches me off guard, so pointed and yet banal. "I don't know," I say. "It's hard to pinpoint." Her shoulders seem to fall in disappointment.

"Well, he ended things with me in January oh-seven," she says, "when the rumor really started to circulate around school. I always wondered if he cut things off with you then, too."

I try to keep my face arranged in a patient smile as I think back to that year. January? I remember his confession, the burning building encased in ice.

"Obviously I didn't have it as bad as you," Taylor continues. "He didn't get me kicked out or anything. But still, he made me transfer out of his class, stopped acknowledging me. I felt abandoned. It was awful—so, so traumatizing."

I nod along, not knowing what to make of her, what she says or how willing she is to say it. I ask, "So you weren't in touch with him at all over the past ten years?" I already know the answer—of course she wasn't—but after she twists up her face and replies, "God no!" she asks, "Were you?" And that's what I want, the chance to say yes, to differentiate myself, to draw a line and make clear that we are not the same at all.

"We were in contact right up until the end," I say. "He called me right before he jumped. I'm pretty sure I was the last person he talked to."

She leans forward; the table rattles. "What did he say?"

"That he knew he'd been a monster, but he loved me." I wait for realization to cross her face—that she'd been wrong about him, about me, and about whatever it was he did to her, but she only snorts.

"Yeah, that sounds like him." She gulps her coffee, throwing back the mug as though it were a shot. Wiping her lips, she notices my expression. "I'm sorry," she says. "I don't mean to mock. It's just so typical, you know? That way he'd berate himself to make you feel sorry for him."

My head tips back as though the weight of my brain has suddenly changed. He did do that. He did it all the time. I'm not sure I've ever summed him up so neatly.

"Can I ask you another question?" Taylor asks.

I barely hear her, my brain busy righting what she's thrown off balance. It must've been a guess, what she said, extrapolated from some moment of him slipping out of the teacher role and revealing himself. It's hardly profound, describing him that way. Beating yourself up in the hopes of gaining sympathy—what person doesn't do that every now and then?

"How much did you know about me at the time?" she asks.

Still far away, I answer, "Nothing."

"Nothing?"

I blink and she comes into focus, her face so sharp it hurts to see. "I knew you existed. But he said you were . . ." I almost say again *nothing*. "A rumor."

She nods. "That's what he called you at first, too." She tucks her chin, lowers her voice into an impression of Strane: "'A rumor that follows me like a black cloud.'"

It's stunning how much she sounds like him, his exact cadence and the metaphor I remember him using to describe me, the image it always put in my head of him relentlessly pursued by the threat of rain. "So you knew about me?"

"Of course," she says. "Everyone knew about you. You were practically an urban legend, the girl he'd had an affair with who disappeared after it all came out. But the story was so vague. No one knew the truth. So I believed him at first, when he said the story wasn't true. It's embarrassing to admit now, because of course it was true. Of course he'd done it before. I was just . . ." She lifts her shoulders. "I was so young."

She goes on, explaining how eventually he told her the truth about me but waited until she was "fully groomed." He called me his deepest secret, said he loved me but I'd outgrown him, we didn't fit together anymore the way we did when I was Taylor's age.

"He seemed genuinely brokenhearted," she says. "This is really screwed up, but he had me read *Lolita* at the beginning of things. You've read it, right? The way he talked about you reminded me of the first girl Humbert Humbert is in love with, the one who dies and supposedly makes him a pedophile. At the time, I thought a man being wounded like that was *romantic*. Looking back, the whole thing was just deranged."

I try to pick up my coffee, but I'm trembling too much so it just clatters back down, spills all over my hands. Taylor jumps up and grabs some napkins, still talking as she wipes the table. She explains how she eventually suspected Strane was still seeing me—that she snooped on his phone and saw all the calls and texts, figured out the truth.

"I used to get so jealous when I knew he was going to see you." She stands over me, sliding a soppy napkin across the table, the end of her braid grazing my arm.

"Did you have sex with him?" I ask.

She stares down at me unblinking.

"I mean, did he have sex with you? Force you? Or . . ." I shake my head. "I don't know what I'm supposed to call it."

Tossing the napkins in the garbage, she sits back down. "No," she says. "He didn't."

"What about the other girls?"

She shakes her head no.

I exhale loudly, relieved. "So what exactly did he do to you?"

"He abused me."

"But . . ." I look around the coffee shop, as though the people sitting at other tables might be able to help. "What does that mean? Did he kiss you, or . . ."

"I don't want to focus on the details," Taylor says. "It's not helpful."

"Helpful?"

"To the cause."

"What cause?"

She tilts her head and squints, the same look Strane used to give me when I was floundering. For a moment, I think she's again doing an impression of him. "The cause of holding him accountable."

"But he's dead. What do you want to do to him, drag his body through the streets?"

Her eyes widen.

"I'm sorry," I say. "That came out wrong."

She closes her eyes and inhales, holds the breath, and then lets it go. "It's fine. This is hard to talk about. We're both doing the best we can."

She starts to talk about the article, how the goal of it is to bring to light all the ways the system failed us. "They all knew," she says, "and they did nothing to stop him." I assume she means Browick, the administration, but don't ask questions. She talks so fast;

it's hard to keep up. Another goal of the article, she says, is to connect with other survivors.

"You mean in general?" I ask.

"No," she says. "Survivors of him."

"There are others?"

"There has to be. I mean, he taught for thirty years." She cups her hands around her empty mug, purses her lips. "So I know you said you don't want to be in the article." I open my mouth, but she continues. "You can be completely anonymous. No one would know it's you. I know it's scary, but think of the good it would do. Vanessa, what you went through . . ." She ducks her head, looks straight at me. "It's the kind of story that has the power to change the way people think."

I shake my head. "I can't."

"I know it's scary," she says again. "The idea terrified me at first."

"No," I say, "it's not that."

She waits for me to explain, her eyes darting.

"I don't consider myself to have been abused," I say. "Definitely not the way you all do."

Her pale eyebrows shoot up in surprise. "You don't think you were abused?"

The air seems sucked out of the coffee shop, noises amplified, colors muted. "I don't think of myself as a victim," I say. "I knew what I was getting into. I wanted it."

"You were fifteen."

"Even at fifteen."

I go on, justifying myself, words spilling out of me, the same old lines. He and I were two dark people who craved the same things; our relationship was terrible but never abusive. The more alarmed Taylor's expression becomes, the more I dig in. When I say what he and I had was the kind of thing great love stories are made of, she holds her hand up to her mouth, like she's about to be sick.

"And if I'm being totally honest," I say, "I think what you and this journalist are doing is pretty fucked up."

Her face scrunches in disbelief. "Are you serious?"

"It seems dishonest. There are things you say about him that don't line up with what I know was true."

"You think I'm lying?"

"I think you're making him out to be something worse than he was."

"How can you say that when you know what he did to me?"

"But I don't know what he did to you," I say. "You won't tell me."

Her eyes flutter shut. She presses her palms on the table, as though calming herself down. Slowly, she says, "You know he was a pedophile."

"No," I say, "he wasn't."

"You were fifteen," she says. "I was *fourteen*."

"That's not pedophilia," I say. She stares at me agog. I clear my throat and say, carefully, "The more correct term is ephebophile."

And with that, the wire connecting her and me goes slack. She holds up her hands as though to say, *I'm done*. She says she needs to go back to work, won't look at me as she gathers her empty coffee cup and phone.

I follow her out of the shop, tripping a little over the doorway. I have a sudden urge to reach out, to grab her braid and not let go. Outside, the sidewalk is empty save for a man with his hands shoved in his coat pockets and eyes fixed on the ground, whistling one steady single note as he walks toward us. Taylor watches the man, her face so furious I think she's going to snap at him to shut up, but as he passes by, she whirls around, jabs her finger at me.

"I used to think about you all the time back when he was abusing me," she says. "I thought you were the only person who could understand what I was going through. I thought . . ." She takes a breath, lets her arm drop. "Who cares what I thought. I was wrong, obviously wrong." She starts to walk off, stops, and adds, "I received death threats after I came forward. Did you know that? People posted my address online and said they were going to rape and murder me."

"Yes," I say, "I know that."

"It's selfish to watch the rest of us not be believed and do nothing to help. If you came forward, no one would be able to ignore you. They'd have to believe you and then they'd believe us, too."

"But I don't understand what that would give you. He's dead. He's not going to apologize. He'll never admit he did anything wrong."

"It's not about him," she says. "If you came forward, Browick would have to admit that it happened. They'd be held responsible. It could change how that school is run."

She looks at me expectantly. I lift my shoulders and she huffs a frustrated sigh.

"I feel sorry for you," she says.

As she starts to walk away, I reach out. My fingers brush her back. "Tell me what he did to you," I say. "Don't say he abused you. Tell me what happened."

She turns, her eyes wild.

"Did he kiss you? Did he bring you into his office?"

"Office?" she repeats, and I close my eyes, relieved at her confusion. "Why does it matter so much to you?" she asks.

I open my mouth, the word *because* poised to come out—*because—because whatever happened to you couldn't have been so bad, because it's ridiculous for you to demand so much when I'm the one who bore the brunt of him. I'm the one marked for life.*

"He groped me, ok?" she says. "In the classroom, behind his desk."

I breathe out and turn limp, swaying as I stand. Like Strane under the spruce tree at the Halloween dance. *You know what I want to do to you?* At that point, he'd only touched me—groped behind his desk.

"But he violated me in other ways," she says. "It doesn't have to be physical to be abuse."

"What about the other girls?" I ask.

"He groped them, too."

"That's all he did?"

She scoffs, "Yeah, I guess that's all."

So he touched them. It was what he'd confessed to me all along, starting that night at his house, when he held my face in his hands and said, *I touched her. That's all.* I was relieved then. I wait now for the relief to find me again but there's nothing, not even outrage or shock. Because by hearing her say it, nothing is changed. I already knew.

"I know how different it was with you," she says. "But it started the same way, right? Calling you up to his desk. You wrote about it on your blog. I remember when I first found it. Reading it was like reading myself."

"You read it back then?"

She nods. "I found it bookmarked on his computer. I used to leave you anonymous comments sometimes. I was too scared to use my name."

I say I had no idea—about the comments, her reading.

"Well, what did you know?" she asks. "Did you really not know about me?" She's already asked the question and I've already answered, but it means something different now. She's asking if I knew what he did to her.

I tell the truth. "I knew," I say. "I knew about you." He told me but called her nothing and I didn't argue. I forgave him, and I offered forgiveness for something so much worse, something he hadn't even done. What was a hand on the leg compared to what he'd done to me? I didn't think it mattered, and even now, with her standing before me, it's hard to understand the damage it could have caused. *Was it really that bad, what he did to you? Was it worth all this?*

"It might seem small to you," she says. "But it was enough to wreck me."

She leaves me standing in the middle of the sidewalk, her braid bouncing against her back as she strides away. I walk home through the square, the giant Christmas tree being strung with lights, the high school kids on their lunch period loitering around, boys with their hoods up and groups of teenage girls in jean jackets and scuffed sneakers. Their chipped nail polish and ponytails and laughter and—I squeeze my eyes shut so tightly I see sparks and stars. He's still inside me, trying to keep me seeing them the same way he did, a series of nameless girls sitting at a seminar table. He needs me to remember they were nothing. He could barely differentiate between them. They never mattered to him. They were nothing compared to me.

I loved you, he says. *My dark Vanessa.*

In Ruby's office, I ask, "Do you think I'm selfish?"

It's late, not our normal day or session time. I'd texted her, I'm having an emergency, something she has always told me I could do but I never imagined I'd need it.

"I think there are ways forward that don't require stripping yourself bare," Ruby says. "Better ways."

From her armchair, she watches me and waits, her endless patience. Out the window, the sky is a range of blue, azure to cobalt to midnight. I tip my head back so my hair falls away from my face, and to the ceiling I say, "You didn't answer the question."

"No, I don't think you're selfish."

I straighten my head. "You should. I've known this whole time what he did to that girl. Eleven years ago, he told me he touched her. He didn't lie. He didn't hide it from me. I just didn't care."

Her expression doesn't change; only her fluttering lashes show I've affected her.

"I knew about the other girls, too," I say. "I knew he was touching them. For years he would call me late at night and we'd—we'd talk about the things we did when I was younger. Sex stuff. But he'd talk about other girls, too, ones in his classes. He'd describe calling them up to his desk. He was telling me what he was doing. And I didn't care."

Ruby's face is still unflinching.

"I could have made him stop," I say. "I knew he couldn't control himself. If I'd left him alone, he probably would have been able to stop. I forced him to relive it when he didn't want to."

"What he did to you or to anyone else wasn't your fault."

"But I knew he was weak. Remember? You said that yourself. And you're right, I did know. He told me he couldn't be around me because I brought out darkness in him, but I wouldn't leave him alone."

"Vanessa, listen to yourself."

"I could have stopped him."

"Ok," she says, "even if you could have stopped him, it wasn't your responsibility and it wouldn't have changed anything for you. Because stopping him wouldn't have changed the fact that you were abused."

"I wasn't abused."

"Vanessa—"

"No, listen to me. Don't act like I don't know what I'm saying. He never forced me, ok? He made sure I said yes to everything, especially when I was younger. He was careful. He was good. He loved me." I say that over and over, a refrain that turns meaningless so quickly. *He loved me, he loved me.*

I hold my head in my hands and Ruby tells me to breathe. I hear Strane's voice instead of hers, telling me to take deep breaths so he can get farther inside. *That's nice,* he said. *That's so nice.*

"I'm so fucking tired of this," I whisper.

Ruby's crouching on the floor in front of me, her hands on my shoulders, the first time she's ever touched me. "What are you tired of?" she asks.

"Hearing him, seeing him, everything I do being laced with him."

We're quiet. My breathing steadies and she stands, her hands dropping away from me.

Gently, she says, "If you think back to the first incident—"

"No, I can't." I throw my head against the back of the chair, press myself into the cushion. "I can't go back there."

"You don't have to go back," she says. "You can stay in the room. Just think of one moment, the first one between the two of you that could be considered intimate. When you look back on that first memory, who was the initiator, you or him?"

She waits, but I can't say it. *Him.* He called me up to his desk and touched me while the rest of the class did their homework. I sat beside him, stared out the window, and let him do what he wanted. And I didn't understand it, didn't ask for it.

I exhale, hang my head. "I can't."

"That's fine," she says. "Take it slow."

"I just feel . . ." I press the heels of my hands into my thighs. "I can't lose the thing I've held on to for so long. You know?" My face twists up from the pain of pushing it out. "I just really need it to be a love story. You know? I really, really need it to be that."

"I know," she says.

"Because if it isn't a love story, then what is it?"

I look to her glassy eyes, her face of wide-open empathy.

"It's my life," I say. "This has been my whole life."

She stands over me as I say I'm sad, I'm so sad, small, simple words, the only ones that make sense as I clutch my chest like a child and point to where it hurts.

2007

Spring semester I start drinking again, a crowd of empty bottles on my nightstand. If I'm not in class, I'm in bed with my laptop, the fan whirring and screen glowing late into the night. I scroll through photos of Britney Spears in the midst of a breakdown, shaving her head, attacking paparazzi with an umbrella and caged-animal eyes. Gossip blogs post the same pictures over and over with headlines like "Former Teen Pop Princess Goes Off the Deep End!," followed by pages of gleeful comments: What a train wreck! . . . So sad how they always end up like this . . . I bet she'll be dead by the end of the month.

At night, I keep my phone on the windowsill next to my bed, and in the morning, the first thing I do is check to see how many times Strane has called. When I'm out at the bar with Bridget and feel my phone vibrate, I dig it out of my bag and hold it up so she can see his flashing name. "I feel bad," I say, "but I just can't talk to him." I've told her about the investigation, called it a "witch hunt" as Strane did, made it clear that he didn't really do anything bad, but that I'm still angry. Don't I have the right to be mad? "Of course you do," Bridget says.

I start checking Taylor Birch's Facebook profile every day, clicking through her public photos, both disgusted and pleased at how ordinary she appears with her braces and stringy white blond hair. Only one photo gives me pause: her grinning in a field hockey uniform, kilt ending halfway down her tanned thighs, BROWICK in maroon lettering across her flat chest. But then I remember Strane describing my fifteen-year-old body, how he called it fairly developed, more woman than not. I think of Ms. Thompson, her womanly body. I shouldn't be so eager to turn him into a monster.

I don't need the credits, but I take Henry's gothic seminar anyway. In class, he turns to me when the other students drag their feet through discussions. A silence falls over the room and his eyes skim the rest of them, landing always on me. "Vanessa?" he prompts. "Your thoughts?" He relies on me to always have something to say about the stories of obsessive women and monstrous men.

After every class, there's some pretense for me to follow him into his office—he has a book he wants to lend me, he nominated me for a departmental award, he wants to talk to me about an assistant job that's available next year, something for me to do while I work on grad school applications—but once we're alone, it devolves into talking, laughing. Laughing! I laugh more with him than I ever have with Strane, who I'm still ignoring, whose phone calls have started coming every night, voicemails asking me to please, please call him, but I don't want to hear how he's hanging by a thread. I want Henry, to sit in his office and point to a postcard tacked to the wall, the only thing he's hung up, and ask for the story behind it and have him tell me it's from Germany, that he went to a conference there and lost his luggage and had to wander around in sweatpants. I want to hear him call me funny, charming, brilliant, the best student he's ever had; for him to describe what he sees in store for me. "When you're in graduate school," he says, "you'll be one of those hip teaching assistants, the kind who holds her office hours in a coffee shop." It's a small thing but enough for my breath to catch. I can see myself at the head of my own classroom, telling my own students what to read and write. Maybe that's what this has always been about—not wanting these men but wanting to be them.

In my blog, I document everything he says to me, every look, every grin. Fixated on the question of what it means, I tally it all up as though this will give me an answer. We eat lunch together in the student union, he responds to my emails at one in the morning, matching me joke for joke and signing his name "Henry," while emails to the whole class are "H. Plough." On my blog, I type it might mean nothing but it should mean something over and over until the lines fill the whole screen. He tells me about having memorized "Jabberwocky" for fun when he was ten years old, and I see him as a boy the way I never could with Strane. But that's what he is, boyish, at least, if not an outright boy, grinning when I tease him, that flush taking over his face. He references *Simpsons* episodes in his emails, mentions some song popular in his grad school days. "You don't know Belle and Sebastian?" he asks, surprised. He makes me a CD and as I scour the lyrics for clues, the version of me that lives in his mind reveals herself.

But he doesn't touch me. There's nothing close to a touch, not even a handshake. It's just endless looking—in his office, during class. As soon as I open my mouth to speak, his face turns tender and he praises everything I say to the point where the other students exchange annoyed looks, like *There she goes again*. It all feels familiar, a trajectory I remember so well I have to clench my fists to stop from tearing into him when we're alone. I tell myself it's all in my head and that this is how normal teachers treat their best students, a little special attention, nothing to lose your mind over. It's just that I'm depraved, my mind so warped by Strane that I misinterpret innocent favoritism as sexual interest. But then again—making me a CD? Calling me into his office every day? It doesn't feel normal, not in my body, and my body knows even if my mind gets confused. Sometimes it feels like he's waiting for me to move toward him, but I don't have the courage I had at fifteen, I fear rejection, and besides, he's not giving me enough, no pat on the knee or leaf held up to my hair. My most brazen behavior: going braless one day under a silk camisole, but then I'm disgusted when he stares—so what is it that I want? I don't know, I don't know.

Late at night, when I'm too drunk to stop myself, I open my laptop and type the Browick address into my browser, bring up the staff profiles. Penelope Martinez got her bachelor's degree from the University of Texas in 2004, which makes her twenty-four. That's how old Ms. Thompson was when she and Strane were doing whatever they did. Why did no one think that was wrong at the time, a twenty-four-year-old girl and a forty-two-year-old man? "Girl" because she was more like a girl than a woman back then, with her scrunchies and hooded sweatshirts. Penelope looks like a girl, too—glossy dark hair, button nose, and thin shoulders. She's fresh-faced and youthful, Strane's type. I imagine him walking beside her through campus, hands clasped behind his back, making her smile. I wonder what she would do if he tried to touch her. What she did the first time Henry touched her. I don't know when they got together, but no matter what he would've been a decade older, big clumsy hands and hot breath through his beard.

One afternoon Henry and I are talking in his office when his phone rings. As soon as he answers, I know it's her. He turns away from me, gives clipped replies to her questions, an edge in his voice that makes me feel like I'm intruding, but when I rise to leave he holds out a hand and mouths, *Hold on.*

"I have to go," he says, exasperated, into the phone. "I'm with a student." He hangs up without saying goodbye and it feels like a triumph.

He's never come clean about her being his wife and not a "friend." He never mentions her at all—why would he? Why would he not? There's zero evidence of her, no wedding ring, no photo in his office. Maybe she's mean to him, maybe she's boring, maybe he's unhappy. Maybe since meeting me, he's had moments of thinking, *I should have waited.* I force myself to think about her because it seems like the moral thing to do, but she's only a fuzzy figure on the periphery. Penelope. I wonder if Henry calls her that or if he uses a nickname. I look up her staff profile on the Browick website again, imagine the possibility that she might be talking to Strane at the exact moment I'm talking to Henry. Strane, who calls and calls, who says he needs me, that this radio silence is cruel and uncalled for. Maybe my neglect is making him so lonely he has to resort to flirting with the pretty young counselor. I bet she's easy to talk to, easier than I ever was. I imagine her sitting through his rants with a patient, unwavering smile. The perfect listener. He'd love that. My brain keeps going to the point I almost forget it's all in my head: Strane making Penelope laugh as I make Henry laugh; Henry at home, up late in the living room, writing me an email as Penelope sits in the bedroom writing to Strane.

Yet it always comes back to this hard reality: Henry must know I would let him touch me but he never tries. That, I know, is the most meaningful detail. It negates everything else.

February 13, 2007

It's been six weeks since I spoke to S., when he told me that people are out to get him and that one of his enemies might try to contact me. I swore my loyalty, and I'll stick to that loyalty forever (what's the alternative? turning on him? unthinkable), but ever since that night at his house, I haven't been able to stomach him. I have an inbox of voicemails. He wants to take me out to dinner, he wants to know how I'm doing, he wants to see me, he wants me. I listen to a few seconds of each and then throw my phone across the room. This is the first time it's ever really felt like he's chasing after me. No coincidence that it comes after a confession, on his part, of bad behavior.

I can't bring myself to write out what he did, though being evasive makes his action seem horrific. It's not as though he killed anyone. He didn't even really hurt anyone, though "hurt" is such a subjective thing. Think of all the thoughtless pain we inflict. A mosquito on your arm; you don't even hesitate to smack it dead.

After class, Henry says he needs to ask me something. "I thought about emailing you," he says, "but figured it would be better to do it in person."

When we get to his office, he shuts the door. I watch him rub his face, take a deep breath.

"This is uncomfortable for me," he says.

"Should I be nervous?" I ask.

"No," he says quickly. "Or, I don't know. It's just, I caught wind of a rumor about your old high school, something about an English teacher being inappropriate with a student. I heard the story secondhand, don't know any real facts, but I thought . . . well. I don't know what to think."

I swallow hard. "Did your friend tell you about this? The one who works there?"

He nods. "She did, yes."

I wait through a long beat of silence, plenty of time for him to offer the truth.

"I guess I feel a little responsible," he says, "knowing what I know."

"But it's none of your business." He gives me a startled look and I add, "I mean that in a good way. You don't need to worry about it. It's not your problem."

I try to smile like my throat isn't squeezing into a fist, cutting off my air. I imagine Taylor Birch crying on a sofa, confessing to Penelope the sympathetic counselor—*Mr. Strane touched me, why did he do it, why won't he do it again*—but my brain goes too far, ends up back in Strane's office. Hissing radiator, seafoam glass.

"Look," I say, "it's a boarding school. Rumors like that happen all the time. If your friend hasn't been there very long, she might not know what to take seriously and what to ignore. She'll learn."

"What I heard sounded pretty serious," Henry says.

"But you said you heard it secondhand," I say. "I know what actually happened, ok? He told me. He said he touched her leg and that's all."

"Oh," Henry says, surprised. "I didn't think—I mean, I didn't realize—you're still in contact with him?"

My mouth goes dry as I realize my misstep. A good victim

wouldn't still talk to her rapist. Strane and I still being in contact throws into question everything I've let Henry believe. "It's complicated," I say.

"Sure," he says. "Of course."

"Because what he did to me wasn't *rape* rape."

"You don't need to explain," he says.

We sit in silence, my eyes lowered to the floor, him gazing at me.

"You really don't need to worry," I say. "What happened to that girl is nothing like what happened to me."

He says ok, that he believes me, and we let it go.

The first week of March a manila envelope arrives in the mail, addressed to me in Strane's blocky hand. Inside, I find a three-page letter and a stapled packet of documents: a photocopy of the statement he and I signed on the day we were found out, dated May 3, 2001; handwritten notes from the meeting he and Mrs. Giles had with my parents; a poem about a mermaid and an island of stranded sailors that I vaguely remember writing; a copy of the withdrawal form with my signature at the bottom; a letter about me, Strane, and our rumored ongoing affair, addressed to Mrs. Giles, written in a hand I don't recognize until I see the name at the bottom—Patrick Murphy, Jenny's dad, the letter that set the whole thing in motion.

I lay all the documents across my bed, one paper after another. In the letter addressed to me, Strane writes,

> Vanessa,
>
> I'm not doing well over here. I'm not sure how to take your silence, if you're trying to communicate something by not communicating, if you're angry, if you want to punish me. You should know I'm punishing myself plenty already.
>
> The harassment mess is ongoing. I'm hopeful it'll be sorted out soon, but it might get worse before it gets better. There

remains a possibility someone might contact you with the aim of using you against me. I hope I can still count on you.

Maybe I'm a fool to put this in writing. The power you hold over my life is immense. I wonder how it must feel to go about your day, masquerading as an average college girl, all the while knowing you could destroy a man with one well-placed phone call. But I still trust you. I wouldn't send an incriminating letter if I didn't.

Look at the documents I've enclosed here, the wreckage of six years ago. You were so brave then, more a warrior than a girl. You were my own Joan of Arc, refusing to give in even as the flames licked your feet. Does that bravery exist in you still? Look at these papers, evidence of how much you loved me. Do you recognize yourself?

I transcribe the letter and post it on my blog without any context or explanation other than, at the bottom of the post, in all caps: CAN YOU IMAGINE HOW IT WOULD FEEL TO HAVE THIS ARRIVE IN YOUR MAILBOX? A question posed to nobody, anybody. I rarely ever get replies to my posts, have no regular readership, but the next morning, I wake to an anonymous comment, left at 2:21 A.M.: Cut him out of your life, Vanessa. You don't deserve this.

I delete the post, but more comments start to appear, always in the middle of the night, waiting for me when I wake up. A line-by-line critique when I post a draft of a poem; Gorgeous left in response to a series of selfies. I reply, Who are you? but never receive a response. After that, the comments stop.

❦

From my bedroom doorway, Bridget asks, "Are you coming?"

It's the start of Spring Fling, a week of day drinking and blowing off classes. There's a party that afternoon on the pier.

I look up from my laptop. "Hey, look at this." Turning the screen, I show her Taylor Birch's latest photo: a close-up selfie, her lips turned downward, eyes rimmed with black liner. When Bridget doesn't react, I say, "That's the girl who's accusing him."

"What about it?"

"It's just so ridiculous." I laugh. "The face she's making! I want to comment and tell her to cheer up."

Bridget gives me a long look, her lips pursed. Finally, she says, "Vanessa, she's a kid."

I turn the laptop away from her, feel my cheeks burn as I x out of the page.

"You really shouldn't check her profile so much," she says. "It's only going to upset you."

I snap the laptop shut.

"And making fun of her seems kind of mean."

"Yeah, I get it," I say. "Thanks for the input."

She watches me get out of bed and stomp around my room, root through the piles of clothes on the floor. "So, are you coming?" she asks.

It's only sixty-five degrees, but for April in Maine that's as good as summer. There are cases of PBR stacked on the pier, hot dogs cooking on hibachi grills. Girls sunbathe in bikini tops, and three guys in board shorts climb over pink granite to wade up to their knees in the frigid water. Bridget finds a tray of Jell-O shots and we down three each, sucking them between our teeth. Someone asks about my postgraduation plans and I love having an answer: "I'm going to be Henry Plough's assistant while I work on grad school applications." At the sound of Henry's name, a girl turns, touches my shoulder—Amy Doucette, from the capstone seminar.

"Are you talking about Henry Plough?" she asks. She's tanked; her eyes won't stop sliding around. "God, he's so hot. Not physically, obviously, but intellectually. I want to crack his head open and take a big bite out of his brain. You know?" She laughs, slaps my arm. "Vanessa knows."

"What is that supposed to mean?" I ask, but she's already turned away, her attention stolen by an enormous watermelon being broken open the same way she said she wanted to break open Henry's skull. "It's had two bottles of vodka soaked into it," someone says. No one has a knife or plates, so people just grab handfuls, boozy juice dripping onto the pier.

I guzzle a can of warm beer and watch the waves through the gaps in the floorboards. Bridget comes over, a hot dog in each hand, offers me one. When I shake my head and say that I'm going to go, her shoulders drop.

"Why can't you just have fun for once in your life?" she asks, but she sees the hurt on my face, understands she's gone too far. As I leave, I hear her call, "I was kidding! Vanessa, don't be mad!"

At first I head back home, but the thought of spending another drunken afternoon in bed makes me take a sharp turn toward Henry's building, knowing he's on campus Monday afternoons. I have his entire schedule memorized: when he's on campus, when he's teaching, and when he's in his office, most likely alone.

The door is ajar, his office empty. On his desk sits a stack of papers and his wide-open laptop. I imagine plopping down in his chair and opening the desk drawers, sifting through everything inside.

He finds me standing over his desk. "Vanessa."

I turn. His arms are weighed down with spiral notebooks, student journals from English composition, the things he hates most to grade. I know so much about him. It's not normal to know this much.

As he sets the journals on his desk, I sink into the extra chair, hold my head in my hands.

"Did something happen to you?" he asks.

"No, I'm just drunk." I tip my head back and see the grin on his face.

"You get drunk and your instincts tell you to come here? I'm flattered."

I groan, press my palms against my eyes. "You shouldn't be nice to me. I'm being inappropriate."

Hurt flashes across his face. That was the wrong thing to say. I know better than anyone that calling too much attention to what we're doing can ruin the whole thing.

Reaching into my pocket, I pull out my phone, hold it out for him as I scroll through the missed calls. "Do you see that? That's how many times he's been calling me. He won't leave me alone. I'm going crazy."

I don't explain who "he" is because I don't need to. Strane is probably at the forefront of Henry's mind every time he looks at me. I wonder if they've met. I've imagined them shaking hands, the traces of me left on Strane's body transmitted onto Henry—the closest I've come to touching him.

Henry stares hard at my phone. "He's harassing you," he says. "Can you block his number?"

I shake my head, though I have no idea. I probably could, but I want the calls to keep coming. They're the breath on the back of my neck. I also know that Henry's sympathy hinges on me doing and wanting the right things, taking all possible steps to protect myself.

"How's this for harassment?" I say. "A few weeks ago, he mailed me a bunch of papers from when I was kicked out of Browick—"

"What?" Henry gapes at me. "I didn't realize you were kicked out."

Is that another lie? Technically, I withdrew—there was even a copy of the withdrawal form in the envelope Strane sent—but it feels more true to say I was kicked out, because it wasn't my choice, even if it was my fault.

I listen to myself go on and tell the story, how I took the blame because I didn't want to send Strane to jail, about the meetings and standing in front of the room and calling myself a liar, answering questions like it was a press conference. As he listens,

Henry's mouth falls open, sympathy emanates out of him, and the more affected he looks, the more I want to talk. A momentum gains within me, an increased righteousness, a sense that I lived through something horrible, a disaster so stark it split my life in two. And now, in the aftershock of survival comes the desire to tell. Shouldn't I be able to tell this story if I want to? Even if I manipulate the truth and obscure the details, don't I deserve to see the evidence of what Strane did to me on another person's sympathetic face?

"Why would he do this?" Henry asks. "Is anything happening now to make him send you these things?"

"I've been ignoring him," I say, "because of what's been going on."

"The complaint against him?"

I nod. "He's worried I'm going to tell on him."

"Would you consider doing that?" Henry asks.

I don't answer, which is as good as saying no. Rolling my phone between my hands, I say, "You must think I'm terrible."

"I don't."

"It's just really complicated."

"You don't have to explain."

"I don't want you to think I'm selfish."

"I don't think that. In my eyes you're strong, ok? You are incredibly, incredibly strong."

He calls Strane psychologically deluded, says he's trying to control me, make me feel like I'm fifteen again, that what he did to me and continues to do is beyond the pale. When Henry says this, I see a stark white sky and an endless expanse of scorched earth, a silhouette barely visible behind a wall of smoke, Strane tracing blue veins on pale skin, dust motes swirling in the weak winter sun.

"I'm never going to tell on him," I say, "no matter how bad he is."

Henry's features go soft—soft and so, so sad. I feel in that moment that if I moved toward him, he'd let me do whatever I want. He wouldn't say no. He's close enough to reach, his knee pointed toward me, waiting. I imagine his arms opening, drawing me in. My mouth inches from his neck, his body shuddering as I pressed my lips against him. He would let me. He'd let me do anything.

I don't move; he exhales a sigh.

"Vanessa, I worry about you," he says.

On the Friday before spring break, Bridget comes home with a kitten wrapped in a towel. Calico and green-eyed, a flea-dusted belly and crooked tail. "I found her in the alley by the bagel shop dumpster," Bridget says.

I hold my fingers to the kitten's nose, let her bite my thumb. "She smells like fish."

"She had her head in a tub of lox."

We give the kitten a bath, name her Minou. As the sun sets, we drive to the Wal-Mart in Ellsworth for a litter box and cat food, tucking the kitten into a tote bag Bridget carries over her shoulder because we don't dare leave her alone. On the drive home, while Minou mews in my lap, my phone starts to ring over and over—Strane.

Bridget laughs when I hit "ignore" for the fourth time in a row. "You're so mean," she says. "I almost feel sorry for him."

The phone buzzes a new voicemail and she gasps in sarcastic shock. We're so giddy about the kitten, it makes everything seem up for grabs, like we could tease each other about anything and just laugh and laugh.

"You're not even going to listen?" she says. "It could be an emergency."

"I promise, it's not."

"You don't know that! You should listen."

To prove my point, I play it on speaker, expecting a thick-throated plea for me to call him back, upset that he hasn't heard from me—did I ever get the package he sent? Instead, it's a wall of garbled sound, wind and static overlaid with his voice, angry:

"Vanessa, I'm on my way to your apartment. Answer your fucking phone." Then a click, voicemail over.

Carefully, Bridget says, "That sounds like an emergency."

I dial his number and he picks up after half a ring. "Are you home? I'm a half hour away."

"Yes," I say. "Or, no. I'm not home right this second. We found a kitten. We had to buy a litter box."

"You what?"

I shake my head. "Nothing, never mind. Why are you coming here?"

He barks out a laugh. "I think you know why."

Bridget keeps looking over, eyes darting between me and the road. Illuminated by the dashboard, I see her mouth: *Everything ok?*

"I don't know why," I say. "I have no idea what's going on. But you can't just decide to come—"

"Did he already tell you what happened?"

My eyes search the windshield, the tunnel the headlights make along the dark highway. I feel a prick on the back of my neck at how Strane spits out *he*. "Who?"

Strane laughs again. I can see him, eyes hard, jaw clenched, a bitter anger I've seen him direct only at other people. The thought of that anger turned on me feels like soft earth giving way beneath my feet.

"Don't play dumb," he says. "I'll be there in ten minutes."

I try to point out that he just said he's a half hour away, but he's already hung up, the screen flashing CALL ENDED. Beside me, Bridget asks, "Are you ok?"

"He's coming to the apartment."

"Why?"

"I don't know."

"Did something happen?"

"I don't know, Bridget," I snap. "I'm sure you could hear the whole fucking conversation. He wasn't exactly generous with details."

We drive in silence, our easygoing camaraderie now sucked out of the car. From my lap, Minou mews, pitiful little sounds that would enrage only a monster—but that must be what I am, because all I want to do is clamp my hands over the kitten's tiny face and scream at it, at Bridget, at everyone, to just shut up for a second and let me think.

Bridget says she'll go out for the night so Strane and I can have the apartment to ourselves. Really, it's clear she just wants to get away from me and my weird old boyfriend and the fraught cloud that constantly hangs over me. It's like I heard her say to a guy she brought home a couple weeks ago: *Oh, Vanessa is always in crisis mode, the kind of girl who attracts drama.*

After she leaves, I sit on the couch, Minou on my knees and my laptop open on the coffee table. Every few minutes I lean forward to refresh, as though an email might appear explaining this all away. When I hear the building door open and heavy steps clomp up the stairs, I push Minou off, grab my phone. He pounds on the apartment door, the kitten disappears behind the couch, and my thumb strokes the keypad, the idea of calling 911 as much of a fantasy as the idea that an email from Henry might arrive in my inbox. Calling wouldn't solve anything. Asking for help would mean answering the dispatcher's unanswerable questions, demanding I explain the inexplicable. *Who is this man banging on your apartment door? How do you know him? What, exactly, is your relationship to him? I need the whole story, ma'am.* My choices: wade through seven years of this swamp and throw myself at the mercy of a skeptical third party who might not even believe me, or open the door and hope it won't be too bad.

When I let him in, he's out of breath and hunches over just inside the door, hands braced on his thighs, every inhale a wheeze.

I take a step toward him, worried he's about to drop. He holds up a hand.

"Don't come near me," he says.

Righting himself, he throws his coat on the papasan chair, looks around at the dirty towels spilling out from the bathroom doorway, the bowl crusted with mac and cheese on the coffee table. He moves into the kitchen, opening cupboards.

"You don't have any clean glasses?" he asks. "Not one?"

I point to the stack of plastic cups on the counter and he shoots me a glare—*lazy, wasteful girl*—and fills one with tap water. I watch him drink, counting the seconds until his anger refuels, but when he empties the cup, he just leans against the counter, deflated.

"You really don't know why I'm here?" he asks.

I shake my head as his eyes bore into me. I haven't seen him since Christmas, when he told me about Taylor Birch. Over the months there's been a change in him, his face somehow altered. I search until I find it: his glasses. They're frameless now, nearly invisible. A pang hits my heart at the thought of him changing something so integral without telling me.

"I came here straight from a Browick faculty event," he says. "Or a fundraiser. Hell, I don't know what it was. I wasn't even going to go. You know how I hate those things, but I thought another night sequestered at home might do me in." He sighs, rubs his eyes. "Sick and tired of being treated like a leper."

"What happened?"

He drops his hand. "I was sitting with some colleagues, including Penelope." He checks my face for a reaction, notices how I suck in my breath. "See, you know what I'm going to say. Don't act dumb with me. Don't . . ." He slams his palms against the counter and takes a lunging step at me, hands out like he's going to grab me by the shoulders, and then he stops short, clenches his fists.

The curtains are wide open, the need to protect us drilled into me so deeply it's all I can think about—that anyone passing by on the street could glance up and get a clear view inside. When I move to draw the blinds, he grabs my arm.

"You told her husband," he says. "Your professor. You told him I raped you."

As he lets go, he pushes me. It's not that hard but enough that I stumble backward into the trash can that belongs under the sink but has been sitting in the middle of the kitchen floor for god knows how long. I fall and the hood over the stove rattles the way it does on windy days. Strane doesn't move as I scramble to my feet. He asks if he hurt me.

I shake my head. "I'm fine," I say, even though my tailbone feels bruised. I look again to the window, the rapt audience of witnesses I imagine out there in the dark. "Why was she talking to you about me? The wife, I mean. Penelope."

"She said nothing about you. It was her husband. Her husband who glared at me for an hour and a half and then followed me to the bathroom—"

There's a tipping point within me, a sudden crash. "Henry was there? You met him?"

Strane stops, caught off guard by how I say the other man's name, the way I exhale it, like a sigh after sex. His face, for a moment, weakens.

"What did he say?" I ask.

And with that, he's again hardened, furrowed brow and flashing eyes. "No," he says flatly. "I'm asking questions here. You tell me why you did it. Why you felt compelled to tell a man whose wife works with me that I raped you." His voice chokes on *raped*, the word so repulsive it makes him gag. "Tell me why you did it."

"I was trying to explain what happened when I left Browick. I don't know. It came out."

"Why would you need to explain that to him?"

"He said something about having taught at a prep school, I said I'd gone to one, he said he had a friend who worked at Browick. It came up naturally, ok? I didn't go out of my way to tell him."

"So someone mentions Browick and you immediately start blabbing about rape? For god's sake, Vanessa, what is wrong with you?"

I curl into myself as he goes on. Don't I understand what that kind of accusation could do to him? It's slander, a literal crime, enough to take down any man, let alone one who's already hanging by a thread. If the wrong people caught wind of this, he'd be finished, thrown in jail for the rest of his life.

"And you know this. That's what I can't understand. You know what an accusation could do to me, and yet . . ." He throws up his hands. "I can't wrap my head around it, the deceit that requires, the cruelty."

I want to defend myself, except I don't know if anything he says is wrong. Even if the word first slipped out by accident, I never corrected it. I kept the lie going, showing Henry the dozens of missed calls, letting him call Strane "deluded" and "beyond the pale," all because I wanted to be wounded and delicate, a girl deserving of tenderness. But I think, too, of those memos Strane wrote to cover his tracks. I was oblivious back then, doing my best to follow his lead, and he saw no problem framing me as a troubled girl with a crush, knowing what it would do to me. If I'm deceitful and cruel, so is he.

I ask, "Why did you wait months to tell me about what happened with that girl?"

"No," Strane says. "Don't try to turn this around on me."

"But that's what this is all about, right? You're mad because you're already in trouble for groping another girl—"

"Groping? Jesus, what a word."

"That's what it's called when you touch a kid."

He grabs the plastic cup, turns on the faucet. "There's no talking to you when you're like this, determined to paint me as a villain."

"Sorry," I say, "it's kind of hard to avoid."

He drinks, wipes his mouth with the back of his hand. "You're right. It's easy to make me into a bad man. It's the easiest thing in the world. But that's just as much your fault as it is mine. Unless you truly have convinced yourself that I raped you." He tosses the half-full cup into the sink, braces himself against the counter. "Raped while writhing in orgasm. Give me a fucking break."

I clench my fists, digging my fingernails into my palms, and will my brain to stay in the room, in my body. "Why didn't you want to have children?"

He turns. "What?"

"You were in your thirties when you had a vasectomy. That's so young."

He blinks, trying to figure out if he ever told me how old he was when he had the surgery, how I could know this if he never did.

"I saw your medical chart," I say. "When I worked at that hospital in high school, I found it in the archives."

He starts moving toward me.

"The doctor's notes said you were adamant about not wanting kids."

He comes closer, backing me up into my bedroom. "Why are you asking me this?" he asks. "What are you trying to say?"

In my room, my calves hit the side of my bed. I don't want to say it. I don't know how. It's not a single question, rather a haze of unspeakable things: not understanding why he touched another girl in the same way he touched me if he hadn't wanted her the same way he wanted me. Why his hands shook when he gave me the strawberry pajamas, why it felt as though by giving them to me he was revealing something he'd spent his whole life trying to hide. When he asked me to call him Daddy on the phone, how it felt like one of his tests. I did it because I didn't want to fail, didn't want to be narrow-minded or scandalized, and afterward, he'd hung up as soon as he could, like he'd revealed too much of himself. I felt shame pulsate out of him that night. It had soared through the phone, straight into me.

"Don't turn me into a monster because you're looking for a way out," he says. "You know that's not what I am."

"I don't know what I know," I say.

He reminds me of what I've done. It's not fair to think of myself as blameless in all this. I'm the one who came back, showing up on his doorstep after two years apart. I could have forgotten about him, moved on with my life.

"Why did you come back if I hurt you?" he asks.

"It didn't feel finished," I say. "I still felt tied to you."

"But I didn't encourage you, not even when you called. Do you remember that? Your little voice coming out of the answering machine. I stood there, didn't let myself do anything."

He starts to cry then, as though on cue, bloodshot eyes filling with tears.

"Wasn't I careful?" he asks. "Always checking you were ok?"

"Yes," I say, "you were careful."

"I wrestled with it. You have no idea how much. But you were so sure of yourself. You knew what you wanted. Do you remember? You asked me to kiss you. I tried to make sure you really wanted it. You'd get annoyed with me, but still I made sure."

Tears run down his cheeks, disappear into his beard, and I try to steady myself through the softening that comes from seeing him cry.

"You said yes," he says.

I nod. "I know I did."

"Then when did I rape you? Tell me when I did that. Because I've been—" He sucks in a shaky breath, rubs his eyes with the heels of his hands. "I've been trying and I can't understand . . ."

He follows me down onto the bed, hides his face against me, wet haggard breaths against my chest until that feeling subsides and another takes over, his mouth moving to my neck, his hands hiking up the skirt of my dress. I let him do what he wants—remove everything, lay me across the bed—even though everywhere he touches hurts. He spreads my legs, buries his face into me, and there are tears in my eyes, on my cheeks. It's my birthday in two days. I'll be twenty-two. Seven years of my life defined by this. When I look back, I won't see anything else.

In the middle of it, I hear the building door open and two sets of footsteps clomp up the stairs. There's Bridget's laugh rising up the stairwell, the sound of a stumble. "Are you ok?" a boy asks as the apartment door opens. "Do I have to carry you?"

"I'm so drunk," Bridget says. Her laughter fills the living room. "I'm drunk, I'm drunk, I'm drunk!"

There's the clang of keys hitting the floor, the boy following her into her bedroom, a door slamming shut. I try to hold on to the sound of her laugh, but she turns on her music so loud that even if I screamed, they wouldn't hear.

As Strane works at me, part of me leaves the bedroom and wanders into the kitchen, where the cup he drank from lies tipped over in the sink. The faucet drips; the refrigerator hums. The kitten pads in from the living room, wanting to be held. Standing by the window, the broken-off part of me takes the kitten in her arms, gazes down at the quiet street below. It's started to storm, a streetlight's orange glow illuminating the sheets of rain, and the broken-off part of me watches it fall, humming softly to herself to block out the sounds coming from the bedroom. Every so often, she holds her breath and listens to check if it's still happening. When she hears the metal scrape of the bed frame, the slap of skin on skin, she holds the kitten closer, turns back to the rain.

In the morning Strane goes down to the bagel shop for coffees. I sit up in bed, holding my steaming cup and staring off into middle distance, while he recounts in detail everything that happened at the Browick event—parents, alumni, faculty, drinking wine and eating hors d'oeuvres in the auditorium. He noticed Henry glaring at him but thought nothing of it until he went to take a piss and found Henry waiting in the hallway afterward, like a drunk in a bar looking for a fight.

"He told me we have a student in common," Strane says. "Then he said your name. He said he knew I was harassing you and shoved me against the wall. Said he knew what I did to you. Called me a rapist." After saying the word, he presses his lips together, takes a deep breath.

I bring the coffee to my lips and try to imagine Henry so out of control.

"You really should set things straight with him," he says.

"I will."

"Because if he told his wife—"

"I know," I say. "I'll tell him the truth."

He nods, takes a sip from his coffee. "I should also tell you that I know about that blog you've been keeping."

I blink, at first not understanding. He says he saw it on my computer. I look around my room and don't see it anywhere. It's still out on the coffee table. Did he get up in the night? No, he explains. It was a couple years ago. He's known about it for years.

"I know how driven you've always been toward confession," he says. "And it seemed a harmless way for you to satisfy that need. I used to check it every once in a while, just to make sure you weren't using my name, but truthfully, I'd forgotten about it until recently. I should have told you to take it down when that nonsense started back in December with the harassment complaint."

I shake my head. "I can't believe you knew and never said anything."

He mistakes my disbelief for an apology. "It's all right," he says. "I'm not angry." But he wants me to get rid of it. "I think that's a reasonable request."

When the coffees are gone, I follow him into the living room, feeling out of my body, out of my mind. Bridget's door is still closed; it's early enough that she won't be up for hours. Strane points to the kitten curled up on the sofa. "Where'd that come from?"

"The dumpster in the alley."

"Ah." He zips his coat, shoves his hands in his pockets. "You know, to be fair, you probably touched a nerve you weren't intending to with that professor. I imagine, on some level, his reaction was about his own marriage. Some unresolved issues there."

"What do you mean?"

"Penelope was his student. College, not high school, but still. She's only a few years older than you and he's—what, pushing forty? I think she said they got together when she was nineteen. If I'd been more on my toes, I would have pointed out the hypocrisy. It probably would've shut him up."

Maybe if he hadn't just told me that he'd known about the blog for years, or if I didn't feel so sickened and bruised from the night before, hearing this would shock me. But now, I'm so exhausted, I lean against the wall and laugh. I laugh so hard, it's hard to breathe. Of course she was his student. Of course.

Strane watches me with his eyebrows cocked. "Is that funny?"

I shake my head. Through my laughs, I say, "No, it's not funny at all."

I follow him down the stairwell to the building door and, before he steps outside, ask if he's still mad at me—for calling him a rapist, for running my mouth. I expect a gentle tongue click, a kiss on the forehead. *Of course I'm not.* Instead he thinks for a moment and then says, "More sad than angry."

"Why sad?"

"Well," he says, "because you've changed."

I put my palm against the door. "I haven't changed."

"Sure you have. You've outgrown me."

"That's not true."

"Vanessa." He takes my face in his hands. "We've got to end this. At least for a while. Ok? This isn't good for either of us."

I'm so stunned, I just stand there, let him hold my face.

"You need to create a life for yourself," he says. "One that isn't so focused on me."

"You said you weren't mad."

"I'm not mad. Look at me, I'm not." It's true—he doesn't look at all angry, his eyes calm behind the wireless frames.

For two weeks, I stay in my apartment, camped out in front of the TV with Minou curled against me. I work through the DVD set of *Twin Peaks*, then go back and rewatch certain episodes again and again. Sometimes Bridget watches with me, but when I start rewinding the scenes of violence and screams, the ones in which the good man character is overtaken by a sadist spirit that drives him to rape and murder teenage girls, she goes into her bedroom and shuts the door.

During those weeks in the news, a fourteen-year-old girl named Katrina disappears out in Oregon. Pretty, white, and photogenic, her face is everywhere, the headlines blurring into the TV series. "Who Took Katrina?" "Who Killed Laura Palmer?" Both were last seen running for their lives, disappearing into a grove of Douglas firs. The obvious culprit for Katrina's disappearance is her estranged father, who has a history of mental illness and hasn't been heard from in weeks. Compared with the dozen pictures they have of Katrina, the news uses only one photo of her father, a disheveled mugshot from a DUI. Eventually, the two are found in North Carolina, living in a cabin without electricity or running water. When the father is arrested, he is quoted as saying, "I'm just glad this is finally over." Later, more details emerge—how frail Katrina became while on the lam, that while living in the cabin, she resorted to eating wildflowers to survive. Alone in the living room lit blue by the TV, I mumble things too terrible for anyone else to hear, that I bet a part of her loved it and never wanted to be caught.

Bridget ventures out of her bedroom and finds me stoned on the couch, coughing up tears. She feeds the cat, picks up my empty bottles, leaves the electric bill on the coffee table, along with her half and a stamped, addressed envelope. She knows something bad happened that night Strane came over but gives me room to deal with it on my own. She doesn't ask, doesn't want to know.

❧

To: vanessa.wye@atlantica.edu
From: henry.plough@atlantica.edu
Subject: Seminar absence

Vanessa, are you ok? Missed you in class today. Henry

To: vanessa.wye@atlantica.edu
From: henry.plough@atlantica.edu
Subject: Worried

I'm starting to get concerned over here. What's going on? You can call if that would be easier than writing. Or we could meet off campus. I'm worried about you. Henry

To: vanessa.wye@atlantica.edu
From: henry.plough@atlantica.edu
Subject: Serious concern

Vanessa, another absence and I'm going to have to give you either an F or an incomplete. I'm happy to give you an incomplete and we can figure out how you can make up the work, but you need to come by and fill out a form.

Can you come in tomorrow? I'm not angry, just very concerned. Please let me know. Henry

When I appear in his doorway, Henry breaks out in a smile. "There you are. I've been so worried. What happened to you?"

Leaning against the doorframe, I stare him down. I'd expected a wave of apologies as soon as he saw me. It's unfathomable that he hasn't already made the connection. The night at Browick was three weeks ago, not long enough to forget.

I hold up a course withdrawal form. "Will you sign this?"

His head jerks back, surprised. "We should probably talk about it first."

"You said I'm going to fail."

"You haven't been coming to class," he says. "I had to get your attention somehow."

"So you manipulated me? Awesome. That's so great."

"Vanessa, come on." He laughs like I'm being ridiculous. "What's going on?"

"Why did you do it?"

"Why did I do what?" He sways back and forth in his desk chair, watching me with put-on obliviousness. He looks like a child caught in a lie.

"You attacked him."

He stops swaying.

"You waited outside a bathroom and grabbed him—"

At that, he jumps up and pulls the office door closed so hard it slams. He holds out his hands as though trying to calm me down. "Look," he says, "I'm sorry. Obviously, I shouldn't have done what I did. There's no excuse for it. But I hardly attacked him."

"He said you shoved him against the wall."

"How could I even manage that? That man is enormous."

"He said—"

"Vanessa, I barely touched him."

At that, a lump forms in my throat. *I barely touched him. I touched her, that's all.* Both boil down to me overreacting, determined to portray these men as villains.

To Henry, I ask, "Why didn't you ever tell me about your wife? You must have known I'd figure out eventually that it was her who worked there."

He blinks, thrown by the pivot. "I'm a private person. I don't like to divulge my personal life to students."

But that's not true. I know plenty of personal things about him, details he's offered up himself—where he grew up, that his parents never married, that his sister was hurt by someone older the same way Strane hurt me. I know his favorite bands from high school and his favorite bands now, that he was a burnout in college, one semester skipping twelve credits' worth of classes. I know how long it takes him to drive from his house to campus and that when he grades papers, he sets mine aside for when his mind is exhausted and needs a break. It's only his wife that I know nothing about.

"You know," I say, "marrying one of your students is pretty fucked up."

He hangs his head, takes a breath. He knew this was coming. "The circumstances were totally different."

"You were her teacher."

"I was a professor."

"Big difference."

"It is different," he says. "You know it is."

I want to tell him the same thing I said to Strane: that I don't know what I know. Months ago, I wrote about how different it was with Henry, that I wouldn't be taken advantage of this time. That difference now feels too subtle to locate. I need someone to show me the line that's supposed to separate twenty-seven years older from thirteen years, teacher from professor, criminal from socially acceptable. Or maybe I'm supposed to encompass the difference here. Years past my eighteenth birthday, I'm fair game now, a consenting adult.

"I should report you for what you did to him," I say. "The college should know about the type of people they have working here."

That touches a nerve, his face flushed as he practically yells, "Report *me*?" and for a moment, I see the anger he must have let loose on Strane. But then, conscious of the voices passing by the closed office door, he lowers himself to whisper, "Vanessa, you knew what that man did to this other girl and you made me feel like an idiot when I mentioned it to you. Then you come in here, telling me that he's harassing you, hurting you. What did you expect?"

"He didn't *do* anything to that girl," I say. "He touched her knee, big fucking deal."

Henry's eyes travel over my face and his anger fades. Gently, like he's speaking to a child, he says he heard something else, that Strane did a lot more than touch her knee. He doesn't explain further and I don't ask. What's the use? All of this is impossible to talk about, and trying to talk about it only makes you sound like a lunatic, one minute calling it rape and the next clarifying, *Well, it wasn't* rape *rape,* as though that does anything but muddy the waters.

"I'm leaving," I say, and Henry reaches for me but stops short of touching. He's suddenly anxious—worried, maybe, that I might actually tell on him. Do I really want him to sign that course withdrawal form? I should just come to class. It's only a couple more weeks. We'll forget about the absences.

"I just want you to feel ok," he says.

But I'm not ok. For days afterward, I walk around dazed, unable to shake the feeling of having been violated. During a meeting with my advisor, she asks how I'm doing, expecting my usual aloof response. Instead, I launch into a version of what happened. I try to be vague because I don't want to implicate Strane, so the story comes out patchy and incoherent, makes me sound crazy.

"This is Henry we're talking about?" my advisor asks, her voice barely above a whisper; the office walls are thin. "Henry *Plough*?" He hasn't even been there a year and already he has a reputation for being a man of integrity.

Clasping her hands, my advisor labors over her words as she says, "Vanessa, over the years I've gathered from your writing that something happened to you in high school. Do you think that might be what you're really upset about here?"

She waits, her eyebrows jumping as though prompting me to agree. This, I think, is the cost of telling, even in the guise of fiction—once you do, it's the only thing about you anyone will ever care about. It defines you whether you want it to or not.

My advisor smiles, reaches forward and pats my knee. "Hang in there."

On my way out of her office, I ask, "Did you know he married one of his students?"

At first, I think I've dropped a bomb on her. Then she nods. Yes, she knows. She lifts her hands, a gesture of helplessness. "It happens sometimes," she says.

I tell Henry I forgive him even though he doesn't ever offer a real apology. For the rest of the semester, he wants it to be the same. He tries to rely on me in class like he did before, but I have nothing to say, and in his office I'm fidgety and evasive as he tests out different ways to pull me back. He tells me I'm the best student he's ever had (*Better than your wife?* I wonder), that he did what he did to Strane only because of how much he cares about me. He shows me the letter of recommendation he's already written for my grad school applications, two and a half pages single-spaced about how special I am. Then, on the last week of classes, he asks me to come to his office. Once we're inside, he closes the door and says he needs to admit something: he used to read my blog. He read it for months before I shut it down.

"I worried when it disappeared all of a sudden and you stopped coming to class," he says. "I didn't know what to think. I guess I still don't."

I ask him how he even found it and he says he can't remember. Maybe he searched my email address, or some key words, he's not sure. I imagine him hunched over his laptop at home late at night, his wife asleep in the other room while he typed my name into the search bar, digging until he found me. It's the kind of thing I fantasized about all year, confirmation of my having invaded his life. Now faced with it being true, my stomach turns; I feel sick.

He says he read it to check in on me. He worried about me. "And because you seemed to have formed such a strong attachment," he says, "I wanted to keep an eye on that, too."

"Attachment to what?"

Henry cocks an eyebrow, as though to say, *You know what I mean.* When I only stare back at him, he says, "Attachment to me."

I say nothing and he turns defensive.

"Was that wrong of me to assume?" he asks. "You came on so strongly. It overwhelmed me."

I gape at him, at first baffled—hadn't he singled me out as much as I had him?—but it dissipates into embarrassment because that probably is what I did. I've done it before.

"So that's how you handle students who you think have crushes on you?" I ask. "You stalk them online?"

"I hardly stalked you. The blog was public."

"What did you think I was going to do, run in here and force myself on you?"

"I really didn't know," he says. "After you told me about you and that teacher, I started to wonder about your intentions."

"You don't have to call him 'that teacher,'" I say. "Clearly you know his name."

Henry presses his lips together, spins in his chair so he faces the window. He stays like that for so long, staring out at the courtyard below, that I think he's finished, but when I go for the door, he says, "I didn't tell you this to embarrass you."

I stop, my hand on the doorknob.

"I thought telling you might create an opening for us to be honest with each other. Because I think there are things you may want to tell me." He spins back toward me. "And you should know I would hear anything you wanted to say."

I shake my head. "I don't know what you mean."

"Based on what I read," he says, "I think you might want to tell me something."

I think of the entries I wrote about him, my descriptions of craving him so badly my whole body ached from it, the comments that would show up sometimes in the middle of the night—from him? I swallow hard, my legs shaking, my hands. Even my brain shakes.

"If you already read it," I ask, "why do you need me to say it?"

He doesn't answer, but I know why. Because he needs to know I'm willing. Like Strane insisting I vocalize what I want to shift the burden of culpability. *Talking this out, Vanessa, is the only way I can live with myself. I never would have done it if you weren't so willing.*

"You're an enigma," Henry says. "Impossible to understand."

Again, I get the feeling I could touch him and he'd let me. If I put my hands on him, he'd spring forth as though released from a cage. *Finally,* he'd say. *Vanessa, I've wanted this since I first met you.* I see ahead to the next year, to me working as his assistant, the two of us shut in this office, the inevitable drawn-out affair. I still haven't had sex with anyone other than Strane, but I can easily imagine what Henry would be like. His heavy body, labored breaths, and slack jaw.

And then the fog burns off, my view clears, and he's repulsive, sitting there trying to pry a confession out of me. *You have a wife,* I want to say. *What the hell is wrong with you?*

I tell him I won't be in Atlantica next year after all. "You should give that assistant job to someone else."

Blinking in surprise, he asks, "What about grad school? Are you still going to apply?"

Looking ahead, I can see that, too—another classroom, another man at the head of the seminar table reading my name off the roster, his eyes drinking me in. The thought makes me so tired all I can think is *I'd rather be dead than go through this again.*

The day before graduation, Henry takes me out to lunch to say goodbye, gives me a Brontë novel, a reference to some inside joke we had, with an inscription he signs with *H.* After I move out of Atlantica, his name shows up in my email inbox every six months or so, my stomach lurching each time. Eventually, we add each other on Facebook and I get glimpses into the life I spent so long imagining: photos of Penelope and their daughter, of Henry's graying hair and aging face, each passing year making him look more like Strane. Meanwhile time turns me cynical, suspicious. I strip myself of the fantasy, tell myself that when we met, Henry was bored and losing his youth; I was young and adored him. An older man using a girl to feel better about himself—how easily the story becomes a cliché if you look at it without the soft focus of romance.

One year he writes to me on my birthday, an email sent at two in the morning. I remember you as one of my best students, he writes, and I always will. I start to reply, Henry, what does that even mean? but I stop myself, delete his email, set up a filter so future ones go straight to the trash.

One of my best students. It's a strange compliment coming from a man who once turned a student into a wife.

❧

After graduation from Atlantica, Bridget moves back to Rhode Island and takes the cat. I apply to every secretary/receptionist/assistant job in Portland, and the State of Maine is the only one to call back. It's a filing clerk job in child protective services, ten bucks an hour but really more like nine after union dues. During the interview, a woman asks how I'll handle reading descriptions of child abuse all day every day.

"I'll be fine," I say. "I don't have any experience with it."

I find an efficiency apartment on the peninsula. When I lie in bed, I can watch oil tankers and cruise ships pass through the bay. The job is mind-numbing, and I can afford to eat only once a day if I want to make rent, but I tell myself it's only for a year, maybe two, until I get my shit together.

At work, I sort through files with headphones on, and it's like being back in the hospital archives, the same metal cases and the color-coded stickers, my hair stirred by the air-conditioning. These files, though, contain horror stories worse than cancer, worse even than death. Descriptions of kids found sleeping in beds caked with shit, of infants covered in lesions from being bathed in bleach. I try not to linger on the files; no one specifically tells me not to look, but gorging on the details feels invasive in a way that reading about men and their limp dicks never could. Some kids' files are multiple manila folders filled with endless documents—court hearings, caseworker narratives, written evidence of abuse.

I come across one girl whose case comprises ten overstuffed files held together with rubber bands. Pieces of faded purple construction paper and coloring book pages stick out of one of the files, kid stuff. One drawing appears to be a family chart done in a child's hand; another piece of construction paper reads like a description of what the girl wants in a family. *Wanted: a mother and a father, a dog, and a baby brother.* At the bottom of the paper, written in huge letters: *NO HIPPOCRITCAL PEOPLE PLEASE.*

There's a handwritten letter on plain white paper tucked behind that, the handwriting small, feminine, and adult. I can't stop myself from looking. It's from the girl's mother, three pages front and back of apologies. Names of different men are listed, explaining who is still in her life and who isn't, and from where I read the file—standing at the cabinet, prying it open, not wanting anyone to catch me looking so closely—I can see only half the pages.

If I had known you were being abused, the mother writes, *especially sexually abused, I never would have*— The rest of the sentence is hidden from my view. On the last page of the letter, the mother signs, *With oceans of love, Mom.* Underneath *oceans of love,* there's a drawing of a girl's crying face, her tears pooling into a body of water, a pointing arrow, *ocean.*

❧

Strane visits me in Portland only once. He's coming down anyway for some development workshop, and I'm too nervous to ask if he plans on staying the night. When he arrives, I give him a tour of my tiny apartment, aching for him to comment on how clean I've kept it, the dishes all done and put away, the vacuumed floor. He calls it cozy, says he likes the clawfoot tub. In the living room/bedroom, I make some stupid, thinly veiled comment about the bed. "Doesn't it look inviting?" I haven't had sex for almost a year, need to be touched, looked at. Under my dress, I'm bare, soft and smooth, no tights. That's a sign he is supposed to pick up on. I spent days imagining the sound that would escape his throat when he realized I wasn't wearing underwear.

He says we have to get going. He's made a reservation at a seafood restaurant in the Old Port, where he orders us fisherman's stew, lobster tail over linguine, a bottle of white wine. It's the biggest meal I've eaten since I last went home to see my parents. While I shovel food in my mouth, Strane watches with a furrowed brow.

"How's the job?" he asks.

"Shitty," I say. "But it's temporary."

"What's your long-term plan?"

My jaw clenches at the question. "Grad school," I say impatiently. "I've told you that."

"Did you submit applications for the fall?" he asks. "They should be sending out acceptances around now."

I shake my head, wave my hand. "I'm doing it next fall. I still need to get some stuff together and save money for all the fees."

He frowns, takes a drink of wine. He knows I'm full of shit, that I have no plan. "You should be doing more than this," he says. I sense his guilt. He's worried that he's to blame for my potential being wasted, which is probably true, but if he feels guilty, he won't want to have sex with me.

"You know how I am. I move at my own pace." I flash him my best spunky-kid smile, meant to reassure him it's my problem, not his.

After dinner, he drives me home, but when I invite him in, he says he can't. It cuts me straight down the middle, my guts spilling all over the passenger seat. All I can think about is how in a month I'll be twenty-three and then someday thirty-three, and forty-three, and being that age is as unfathomable as being dead.

"Am I too old for you now?" I ask.

At first he shoots me a glare, sensing a trap. Then he sees my wide-open face.

"I'm serious," I say. It's the first time he's really looked at me all night, maybe the first time since that night in my Atlantica apartment, when he confronted me about Henry confronting him, when he might've raped me, I'm still not sure.

"Nessa, I'm trying to be good here," he says.

"But you don't need to be good. Not with me."

"I know I don't," he says. "That's the problem."

This, I realize, is where it was always going to end up. I gave him permission to do the unspeakable things he always craved, offered up my body as the site of the crimes, and he indulged for a while, but in his heart, he's not a villain. He's a man who wants to be good, and I know as well as anyone that the easiest way to do that is to cut out the thing that makes you bad.

With my hand on the door handle, I ask if I'll see him soon, and he says yes so gently I know he's letting me down easy. His eyes dart away like I'm evidence of something he wants to forget.

Years pass without him. My dad has his first heart attack; Mom finally earns her degree. On a summer afternoon when I'm home visiting, Babe has an aneurysm while running across the yard; she drops as though she's been shot, and Dad and I try to save her as though she were human, pumping on her chest and breathing into her snout, but she's gone, her body cold and paws still wet from the lake. I leave CPS and go from one administrative assistant job to another, loathing the work, the sterile offices, the paper clips and Post-its and Berber carpets. When I find myself googling "what should you do if being at work makes you suicidal," I snap out of it, realize this way of keeping myself alive could end up killing me, and get a front desk position at an upscale hotel. It's low pay but an escape from the fluorescent-lit breakdown brewing within me.

There are men who never turn into boyfriends, who peer behind the curtain and see the mess of me—literal and figurative: the apartment with a narrow path through the clothes and trash leading from bed to bathroom; the drinking, endless drinking; the blackout sex and nightmares. "You're kind of screwed up," they say, at first with a laugh in their voice, an attitude of *maybe this will be fun for a while*, but as soon as I slur out the story—teacher, sex, fifteen, but I liked it, I miss it—they're done. "You've got serious issues," they say on their way out the door.

I learn that it's easier to keep my mouth shut, to be a vessel they empty themselves into. On a dating app, I meet a man in his late twenties. He wears cardigans and corduroys, has a receding hairline and thick chest hair that peeks over the neckline of his shirt, a look-alike of Strane. Through our first date, I pulse my feet, shred my napkin. With our drinks only half drunk, I ask, "Can we cut the bullshit and go have sex?" He chokes on his beer, looks at me like I'm nuts, but says sure, of course, if that's what you want.

On our second date, we see a movie with a plotline about pedophile priests. Through the two hours, he doesn't notice my clammy hands, the little whimpers that escape my throat. Usually I'm good about researching movies beforehand in case there's something that might send me reeling, but with this one I wasn't prepared. Afterward, as we walk down Congress Street toward my apartment, the man says, "Men like that know how to pick the right ones, you know? They're real predators. They know how to scan a herd and select the weak."

As he says that, I see a scene of me, fifteen and wild-eyed, separated from my parents, running in a panicked gait across a tundra landscape while Strane sprints after me, gathering me in his arms without breaking stride. An ocean roars in my ears, blocking out the rest of the man's thoughts on the film, and I think, *Maybe that's all it was.* I was an obvious target. He chose me not because I was special, but because he was hungry and I was easy. Back at my apartment, while the man and I have sex, I leave myself in a way I haven't in years. He and my body are in the bedroom as my mind wanders the apartment, curls up on the couch, and stares at the blank TV.

I stop replying to his texts, never see him again. I tell myself he was wrong. At fifteen, I wasn't weak. I was smart. I was strong.

I'm twenty-five when it happens. Walking to work, wearing my black suit and black flats, I cross Congress Street and there he is, standing with a dozen kids in front of the art museum, teenagers, students, mostly girls. I watch from a distance, clutching my purse to my side. He leads the students into the museum—it must be a field trip, maybe to see the Wyeth exhibit—and he holds the door as they file in, one girl after another.

Just before he disappears inside, he glances over his shoulder and notices me in my dowdy work clothes, faded and old. For years I wanted nothing more than his eyes on me, but now I'm too ashamed of my own face, its fine lines and signs of age, to take a step closer.

He lets the museum door close behind him and I go to work, sit at the concierge desk and imagine him moving through the rooms, trailing the bright-haired girls. In my mind, I follow along behind, don't let him out of my sight. This, I think, is probably what I'll do for the rest of my life: chase after him and what he gave me. It's my own fault. I was supposed to have grown out of it by now. He never promised to love me forever.

The next night, he calls. It's late, on my walk home from work, when the only lit-up windows downtown are the bars and pizza-by-the-slice places. The sight of his name on the screen makes my knees give out. I have to lean against a building when I answer.

The sound of him grabs me by the throat. "Did I see you?" he asks. "Or was it a ghost?"

He starts calling weekly, always late at night. We talk a little about who I am now—the hotel job, the never-ending parade of boys, my mom's pursed-lip disappointment in me, my dad's diabetes and bad heart—but mostly we talk about who I used to be. Together we remember the scenes in the little office behind the classroom, at his house, in the station wagon parked on the side of an old logging road, the rolling blueberry barren where I climbed on top of him, the chickadee call and apiary drone drifting in through the open car window. Our details pool together. He and I re-create it vividly, too vividly.

"There's a reason I haven't allowed myself to remember all this," he says. "I can't let myself lose control again."

I see him in the classroom, sitting behind his desk. His eyes move across the girls seated around the seminar table. One girl looks up, catches him staring, and smiles.

"We can stop," I say.

"No," he says, "that's the problem. I don't think I can stop."

When he moves away from remembering me and begins to talk about the girls in his classes, I follow him. He describes the pale underbellies of their arms when they raise their hands, the tendrils that escape their ponytails, the flush that travels down their necks when he tells them they're precious and rare. He says it's unbearable, the way they drip with beauty. He tells me he calls them up to his desk, his hand on their knees. "I pretend they're you," he says, and my mouth waters as though a bell's been rung, signaling a long-buried craving. I roll onto my stomach, shove a pillow between my legs. Keep going, don't stop.

2017

The week before Thanksgiving, Janine's article is published, but it isn't about Strane. One contextual paragraph toward the beginning mentions Taylor and the online harassment she suffered. The rest is about a teacher at a boarding school in New Hampshire who abused girl students throughout his forty-year career. Eight victims are profiled in the article, their real names used. There are photos of them now and back when they were students, scans of their teenage diary entries, the teacher's love letters. Through the years, he used the same lines on all the girls, the same pet names. *You're the only one who understands me, little one.* The headline of the article cites the boarding school's name—recognizable, prestigious, and guaranteed to generate clicks. It's hard not to be cynical, to assume that's what it all came down to.

Browick publishes the results of their internal investigation into the allegations against Strane, using the sort of impenetrable language that seems intended to mask truth: "We conclude that while misconduct of a sexual nature may have occurred, the investigation found no credible evidence of sexual abuse." They put out an official statement reiterating the school's commitment to fostering an academically strenuous yet safe and nurturing environment. They will be voluntarily updating the faculty sexual harassment training. Here's a phone number for any concerned parents. Feel free to call with any questions.

As I read, I imagine Strane in sexual harassment training, irritated he had to sit through it at all—none of it would have touched him—along with the other teachers who saw me, the one who called me Strane's classroom pet, Ms. Thompson and Mrs. Antonova, who recognized the clues but didn't protest when those clues were used as evidence of an emotionally troubled girl. I imagine them sitting through the training, nodding in agreement, saying yes, this is so important; we need to be these children's advocates. But what have they done when faced with situations in which they could actually make a difference? When they heard of the camping trips the history teacher took each year with his students, when faculty advisors brought students into their homes? All of this feels like performance, because I've seen how it plays out, how quickly people lift their hands and say, *It happens sometimes,* or *Even if he did do something, it couldn't have really been that bad,* or *What could I have done to stop it?* The excuses we make for them are outrageous, but they're nothing compared with the ones we make for ourselves.

I tell Ruby I feel like I've moved from grieving Strane to grieving myself. My own death.

"Part of you died along with him," she says. "That seems normal."

"No, not part," I say. "All of me. Everything about me leads back to him. If I cut out the poison, nothing will be left."

She says she can't let me say that about myself when it's so obviously untrue. "I'll bet if I met you when you were five years old," she says, "you would have been a complex person even then. Do you remember yourself at five?" I shake my head. "What about eight?" she asks. "Ten?"

"I don't think I remember anything about myself that happened before him." I let out a laugh, rub my face with both hands. "That's so depressing."

"It is," Ruby agrees. "But those years aren't lost. They've just been neglected for a while. You can recover yourself."

"Like find my inner child? Oh god. Kill me."

"Roll your eyes if you need to, but it's worth doing. What's the alternative?"

I shrug. "Continue to stumble through life feeling like an empty husk of a person, drink myself into oblivion, give up."

"Sure," she says. "You could do that, but I don't think that's where this is going to end for you."

I go home for Thanksgiving and Mom's hair is cut short, ending above her ears. "I know it's ugly," she says. "But who am I trying to impress?" She touches her fingers to the nape of her neck, where the hair was shorn with a buzzer.

"It's not ugly," I say. "You look great, truly."

She scoffs, waves her hand at me. She's not wearing makeup and the bare skin makes her wrinkles seem like part of her face rather than something she's trying to hide. There's a shadow of an unwaxed mustache on her upper lip and this suits her, too. She seems relaxed in a way I've never seen before. Everything she says preceded by a long pause. The only thing that worries me is her thinness. Hugging her, she feels outright frail.

"Are you eating enough?" I ask.

She seems not to hear me, staring over my shoulder, her hand still resting on the back of her neck. After a moment, she opens the freezer, takes out the blue box of fried chicken.

We eat the chicken and thick slices of grocery store pie, and drink coffee brandy mixed with milk in front of the TV. No holiday movies, nothing heartwarming. We stick to nature documentaries and that British cooking show that she texted me about. While we lie on the couch, I let her wedge her feet under me, and I don't kick her awake when she starts to snore.

Inside and outside, the house has gone to hell. Mom knows but has stopped apologizing for it. Dust bunnies line the baseboards and laundry spills out from the bathroom, blocking the door. The lawn is dead and brown now, but I know she's stopped mowing in the summer. She calls it "gone to pasture." She says it's good for the bees.

The morning I'm set to drive back down to Portland, we stand in the kitchen, drinking coffee and eating bites of blueberry pie straight out of the tin. She peers out the window, through the snow that's started to fall. An inch has already piled up on the cars.

"You can stay another night," she says. "Call out of work, tell them the roads are too bad."

"I have snow tires. I'll be ok."

"When was the last time you took your car in for an oil change?"

"The car's fine."

"You need to stay on top of that."

"Mom."

She holds up her hands. *Ok, ok.* I break a piece of crust off the pie and break that into crumbs.

"I think I'm going to get a dog."

"You don't have a yard."

"I'll take walks."

"Your apartment's so small."

"A dog doesn't need its own bedroom."

She takes a bite, pulls the fork between her lips. "You're like your dad," she says. "Never happy unless he was covered in dog hair."

We stare out at the snow.

"I've been thinking a lot," she says.

I don't move my eyes from the window. "About what?"

"Oh, you know." She heaves a sigh. "Regrets."

I let the word hang there. I set my fork in the sink, wipe my mouth. "I should pack my stuff."

"I've been paying attention to the stories," she says. "About that man."

My body starts to shake, but for once my brain stays in place. I hear Ruby telling me to count and breathe—long inhales, longer exhales.

"I know you don't like to talk about it," she says.

"You've never been that eager, either," I say.

She sinks her fork into the uneven wedge of pie left in the

pan. "I know," she says quietly. "I know I could've been better. I should've made you feel like you could talk to me."

"We don't have to do this," I say. "Really, it's ok."

"Just let me say this." She closes her eyes, collects her thoughts. She takes a breath. "I hope he suffered."

"Mom."

"I hope he's rotting in hell for what he did to you."

"He hurt other girls, too."

Her eyes flash open. "Well, I don't care about other girls," she says. "I only care about you. What he did to you."

I hang my head, suck in my cheeks. What does that mean to her, what he did to me? There's so much she can't know: how long it went on, the extent of my lies, the ways I enabled him. But the small part she does understand—that she sat in the Browick headmaster's office and listened to him call me damaged and troubled and then watched photographic evidence of him and me fall to the floor—is enough for a lifetime of guilt. Our roles reversed, for the first time in my life, I want to tell her to let it go.

"Dad and I used to talk sometimes about what that school did to you," she continues. "I don't think either of us regretted anything more than how we let them treat you."

"You didn't let them," I say. "You weren't in control of it."

"I didn't want to put you through some horror show. Once I got you back home, I thought, ok, whatever happened is over. I didn't know—"

"Mom, please."

"I should've sent that man to prison where he belonged."

"But I didn't want that."

"Sometimes I think I was looking out for you. Police, lawyers, a trial. I didn't want them to tear you apart. Other times I think I was just scared." Her voice cracks; she holds a hand to her mouth.

I watch her wipe her cheeks even though they aren't wet, even though she's not really crying because she won't let herself. Have I ever seen her truly cry?

"I hope you forgive me," she says.

Part of me wants to laugh, pull her in for a hug. *Forgive what? It's fine, Mom. Look at me—it's over. It's fine.* Hearing my mother implicate herself makes me think of Ruby and the frustration she must feel sitting there, listening as I cloak myself in blame. After a while, she gives up repeating the same lines, knowing there comes a point when they no longer matter, that what I need isn't absolution but to hold myself accountable before a witness. So when my mother asks me to forgive her, I say, "Of course I do." I don't tell her again she couldn't have stopped it, that it wasn't her fault and that she didn't deserve it. I swallow those words instead. Maybe somewhere deep in my belly, they'll take root and grow.

It keeps snowing. I do my best to dig out my car, drive the gravel road, but when I gun the engine to get up the hill and onto the highway, the tires just spin. I turn the car around and spend another night. While we watch TV, commercials for the Winter Olympics play, the spray of snow from a freestyle skier, a gleaming bobsled careening down an icy track, a figure skater launching her body into the air, arms crossed tight and eyes squeezed shut.

"Remember when you used to skate?" Mom asks.

I try to think: fuzzy memories of cracked white leather, the ache in my ankles after an hour of balancing on the blades.

"For a while, it was all you wanted to do," she says. "We couldn't get you to come inside, but I didn't want you on the lake without me watching. I was too scared of you falling through. Dad went out with the hose and flooded the front yard. Do you remember that?"

Vaguely, I do—skating after dark, maneuvering around the

tree roots that jutted through the rough ice, trying to work up the courage to attempt a jump.

"You weren't scared of anything," Mom says. "Everyone thinks that about their kid, but you really weren't."

We watch the skater glide across the rink. She turns on the tips of her blades, suddenly backward, arms outstretched, ponytail whipping across her face. Another change of direction and she's on one leg, launching off into a tight spin, her arms stretched above her head now, her body seeming to grow longer the faster she spins.

In the morning, the sky is blue and the snow so bright it hurts our eyes. We sprinkle kitty litter and rock salt on the road and the tires are able to grab. At the top of the hill, I stop and watch Mom walk slowly home, pulling behind her a sled stacked with bags of litter and salt.

❧

The air is sharp with ammonia as I walk through rows of kennels, the concrete floor painted gray and hospital green. One dog starts barking, setting off the rest of them, a range of voices echoing against cinder block. When I was a kid, Dad and I used to joke that when dogs bark all they're saying is *I'm a dog! I'm a dog! I'm a dog!* But these barks are desperate and scared. They sound more like *please please please.*

I stop at a kennel holding a mutt with a blocky head and ghost-gray fur. The sign hanging on the kennel lists the breed as *Pit bull, Weimaraner, ???* The dog's rose ears pitch forward as I press my hand against the cage. She gives my palm a sniff, two licks. A cautious tail wag.

I name her Jolene after she tips back her head and howls along to Dolly Parton on her first night home. In the mornings, I take her out before I even brush my teeth, and we walk from one end of the peninsula to the other, ocean to ocean. When we wait at crosswalks, she leans into my legs and mouths my hand out of pure joy, her panting breaths clouding in the cold air.

We're walking on Commercial Street, past the city pier, when I see Taylor emerge from a bakery doorway, coffee and wax paper bag in hand. It takes a moment for me to believe it's truly her and not my brain's wishful thinking.

She sees Jo first; her face lights up as Jo's tail thumps against my legs. Then a double take when she notices me, as though to make sure her own mind isn't playing tricks.

"Vanessa," she says. "I didn't know you had a dog." She drops to her knees and holds her coffee above her head as Jo launches forward and licks her face.

"I just got her," I say. "She comes on a little strong."

"Oh, that's ok." Taylor laughs. "I can be intense, too." In a singsongy voice she repeats, "That's ok, that's ok." It makes Jo's back arch, her entire body wriggle. Taylor smiles up at me, flashing small straight teeth. Her canines are pointy, like little fangs, same as mine.

"I know I failed you," I say.

It's the chance meeting that makes me say it, having her in front of me when I didn't expect it, didn't prepare. Taylor frowns but doesn't look up at me. She keeps her eyes fixed on Jo, scratching behind her ears. For a moment, I wonder if she'll ignore me, pretend I never said it.

"No," she says, "you didn't fail me. Or, if you did, then I did, too. I knew he'd hurt other girls and it still took me years to do anything about it." She looks up at me then, her eyes two blue pools. "What could we have done? We were just girls."

I know what she means—not that we were helpless by choice, but that the world forced us to be. Who would have believed us, who would have cared?

"I saw the article," I say. "It was . . ."

"Disappointing?" Taylor rights herself, adjusts her purse. "Though maybe not for you."

"I know you invested a lot in it."

"Yeah, well. I thought it would bring me closure, but now I'm angrier than before." She scrunches her nose, fiddles with the lid of her coffee cup. "Honestly, she was kind of sleazy. I should've known better."

"That journalist?"

Taylor nods. "I don't think she actually cared. She just wanted to ride the wave, get a good byline. Which I knew going into it, but I still thought it would make me feel empowered or whatever. Instead I feel taken advantage of all over again." She smirks, scratches Jo behind the ears. "Been thinking about starting therapy. I tried it before and it didn't really do much, but I need to do something."

"It's helping me," I say. "But it didn't fix everything—hence the dog."

Taylor smiles down at Jo. "Maybe I should try that, too."

She seems fragile in a way I wasn't able to see before, not when she and I were in the coffee shop or in any of the stuff she posts online. I see now what should have been obvious, that she was lost and looking for a way to understand it all—him, herself, what he did, and why it still means so much despite it being so seemingly small. I can hear Strane asking, impatient and impenitent, the question that must still ring through her head: *When are you going to get over this? All I did was touch your leg.*

Taylor looks to me. "At least we're trying, right?"

It feels like this is the moment when I'm supposed to open my arms and embrace her, to start thinking of her as a kind of sister. Maybe that could happen if our stories were closer, if I were nicer—though it seems absurd to expect two women to love each other just because they were groped by the same man. There must be a point where you're allowed to be defined by something other than what he did to you.

Before she leaves, Taylor gives Jo another scratch behind the ears and me an embarrassed little wave.

I watch her walk away, not a rumor but a real person, a woman who used to be a girl. I'm real, too. Have I ever thought that about myself so plainly before? It's such a small revelation. Jo tugs on the leash and, for the first time, I can imagine how it might feel not to be his, not to be him. To feel that maybe I could be good.

With the sun on my face and a dog at my side, I have so much capacity for good.

There's nothing else to do but start from here, with the gentle pressure of the leash in my hand, the clink of metal and click of toenails on brick. Ruby says it will take a while to feel truly changed, that I need to give myself the chance to see more of the world without him behind my eyes. I'm already starting to feel the difference. There's a clearness, a lightness.

Jo and I arrive at the beach, empty in the off-season, and she lowers her nose to the sand.

"Have you been in the ocean before?" I ask, and she looks up at me, ears pricked.

I unhook the leash. At first she doesn't realize, doesn't understand, but when I pat her back and say, "Go on," she takes off across the sand, down to the water, barks at the waves lapping her paws. She ignores me when I call, doesn't yet know her name, but when she sees me sit on the ground, she bounds over, tongue out and eyes wild. She flops down at my feet, panting happy little whines.

We walk home under the pale winter sky, and back in my apartment, she checks all the rooms, inspects every corner. She's still getting used to it, the freedom and space. I lie on the couch and she eyes the empty spot alongside my legs. "You're allowed," I say, and she jumps up, curls into a tight circle, and sighs.

"He'll never meet you," I say. It's a hard truth, carrying within it grief and joy. Jo opens her eyes, doesn't lift her head as she watches me. She's constantly taking in my face and tone, noticing everything about me. When I start to drift away, her tail thumps against the couch cushion, like a drumbeat, a heartbeat, a rhythm of grounding. *You're here,* she says. *You're here. You're here.*

Acknowledgments

First and foremost, I have to thank my agent, Hillary Jacobson, and my editor, Jessica Williams, two brilliant women whose advocacy and love for this novel continue to astound me.

Thank you to those who worked to bring this novel into the world, to everyone at William Morrow/HarperCollins, to Anna Kelly and everyone at 4th Estate/HarperCollins UK, and to Karolina Sutton, Sophie Baker, and Jodi Fabbri at Curtis Brown UK.

Thank you to Stephen King, for the early support and for saying yes when my dad asked, "Hey, Steve, would you read my daughter's novel?"

Thank you to Laura Moriarty, who read draft after draft and whose generosity and encouragement helped transform this sprawling, nebulous story of mine into a novel.

Thank you to the creative writing programs at the University of Maine at Farmington, Indiana University, and the University of Kansas for giving me the opportunity to study and write. I'm deeply grateful to the friends I made in those programs who read and loved early versions of Vanessa: Chad Anderson, Katie (Baum) O'Donnell, Harmony Hanson, Chris Johnson, and Ashley Rutter. A special thank-you to my undergraduate advisor, Patricia O'Donnell, who in 2003 commented in the margins of a short story I wrote about a girl and her teacher: *Kate, this made me feel like I was reading* real *fiction*. It was the first time I'd ever been taken seriously as a writer, and that feedback was life-changing.

Thank you to my parents for never telling me to give up and get a real job, for my dad whose immediate response to hearing my book sold was "I never doubted you for a second," for my mum who filled our house with books so I grew up surrounded by words.

Thank you to Tallulah, who grounded me and saved my life.

Thank you to Austin. And here I'm stumped because what is

there to say to a partner so relentlessly supportive and good? "For everything" is the best I can do.

Thank you to my internet pals who have always been my first readers, who supported and encouraged me over the eighteen years I worked on *My Dark Vanessa*. Some are still in my life and some have drifted out of it, but I'm grateful to all for the years of giddiness, vulnerability, and tough love. You are my best, dearest friends.

A special thank-you to the brilliant poet, chosen sister, and best writer I know, Eva Della Lana, who has been a constant source of inspiration and reassurance throughout our friendship. That we met as two teenage girls traveling our own dark landscapes and both made it out alive with our voices, genius, and hearts intact—can you believe how remarkable that is, Eva, how profoundly rare?

And finally, thank you to the self-proclaimed nymphets, the Los I've met over the years who carry within them similar histories of abuse that looked like love, who see themselves in Dolores Haze. This book was written for no one but you.

Kate Elizabeth Russell is originally from eastern Maine. She holds a PhD in creative writing from the University of Kansas and an MFA from Indiana University. This is her first novel.